THE MARKED SON

KEEPERS OF LIFE
BOOK ONE

SHEA BERKLEY

Entangled Publishing, LLC
2614 South Timberline Road
Suite 109
Fort Collins, CO 80525
Visit our website at www.entangledpublishing.com.

Edited by Heather Howland
Cover design by Heather Howland
Cover images by Andrejs Pidjass and wyldraven

Print ISBN   978-1-62061-229-3
Ebook ISBN   978-1-62061-230-9

First Edition July 2012

Manufactured in the United States of America

To my five fallen angels who keep me laughing and crying and then laughing again.

THE BEGINNING

If I never dream again,
I'll fade away
Until I'm only a breath of memories
That can't stay.

DREAMING

I was eight the first time I saw the girl.

Mom freaked when I told her, said I was letting a girl terrorize my dreams, but I didn't get it. They were *dreams*, not nightmares. I don't remember ever waking up afraid. Not back then. So when the dreams kept coming, year after year, each one more vivid than the last, I held onto them like a skydiver clutching his ripcord. No way would I let Mom take them away from me.

It's been years since she's asked me about the girl, but lately Mom's been curious. I tell her I haven't had a dream in awhile. She eyes me like I'm lying.

So what if I am? I may not remember everything about my dreams when I wake up, but I do know when I'm about to have one. My scalp tingles, like tiny bugs zap, zap, zapping along my skin. The darkness behind my lids turns smoky. I've tried to pull away at that point but it's no use. I don't fight it now. Instead I sink into the thick air and come out the other side into a world that is nothing like the one I know...

Yet, it's familiar.

Tonight, the smoke fades, and the girl appears in a thin, white gown. I'm lying in a meadow surrounded by deep woods, one hand tucked behind my head—shirtless and shoeless and wearing a pair of old, ratty jeans. I can hear the TV I left on fading in the distance until only the sound of the meadow fills the air.

She's suddenly beside me, beautiful beyond words, her long, dark hair spilling over her shoulder as she bends to touch my hand. Her cool fingers rest more like mist than flesh in my palm. The rough corset she's wearing cinches the fabric snug to her hips. She's got a definite Victorian vibe going, but it suits her. I'd be lying if I said I didn't like it.

Her violet eyes darken, revealing the silent plea that carries a hint of desperation, and she tugs, urging me to get to my feet. She wants me to run, to escape. In the last two weeks, we've tried, running so long and so hard that we're sure we'll never find our way home again. We'll be lost together forever. It's what she wants. It's what I need. But it always fails. We eventually wind up back at the meadow.

Tonight, I'm content to pull her down beside me, lie in the soft grass, and stare at the sky. Our fingers intertwine, our shoulders touch. We've both gotten older since the first time we met. There were years when we rarely saw each other, but lately, our time together has intensified. There's a feeling of impending doom that wasn't there when we were younger, as if this perfect place of dreams is about to shatter, and we'll never see each other again.

There's so much I want to know. Why do I only dream about her when I need her most? Am I insane? I don't ask. I'm afraid to. I want her to be real. Just a few months more, maybe a year, then I'll grow up and cut this strange, imaginary cord. I can't lose her smile, not yet, or her lips against my cheek—one of her butterfly kisses that's gone before it's begun.

Her silence has never bothered me before. Tonight, all I want is one word.

My name.

I touch her hair, her cheek. I know the tilt of her head and the tip of her lips. I know when she's sad and when joy fills her to overflowing. I've tried painting her in art class, but I've never been able to capture her perfection, because when I wake, her face dissolves with the dream. If she'd just talk to me, I'd remember everything about her. I would.

As we lie there, night and day flash by. One minute the sun warms my skin, the next the stars color it silvery bright. Flowers open and close. Birds sing. An owl hoots. The girl turns and lays her head on my chest. I wrap a protective arm around her and pull her closer, yet it's never close enough. She's my one comfort in life, but being with her is like holding onto sand that keeps slipping through my fingers. Time is running out, and I can't figure out why.

Suddenly, the darkness lowers and the dream grows cold, the woods sinister. She jerks upright. I follow. I ask her what's wrong. Her face shows her terror. Her mouth opens in an attempt to speak. No words follow.

The next moment, she's across the clearing. I call for her to come back. She doesn't. She can't. All I know is that she needs me. Now.

I slam back into consciousness, panting against the thudding of my heart. I peel off the scratchy covers and slip out of bed. The hotel room is dingy, but the night is laced with a full moon's light. I stand at the window and let the hopelessness overcome me as the dream fades away.

Heaving a sigh, I grip the windowsill and roll my forehead along the cool glass.

It's just a dream. Just a stupid, childish dream.

But how I wish it weren't.

PART ⊕NE

What is seen is.
What is heard may be.
Alas, what quickens my soul can never be.

Again

I close my eyes, hoping to break free of this nightmare. Yet, when I open them, the hot breath of the southern summer is truly gone, replaced by a weakened sun and the cool breezes of the northwest. The car windows are open, and in the distance, the wooded foothills along the southern portion of the Cascade Mountains rise and fall like ripples in the earth. It's June. It should be sweat-rolling-down-my-spine hot. Instead, there's a damp chill outside. Not totally unpleasant, but not familiar. I slouch deeper into my seat and glare at Mom.

Her mouth pinches, her skin flushes, and she snubs out her cigarette in a tray overflowing with more than three days worth of ash and spent stubs. "Don't, Dylan. Just keep it to yourself."

She says I'm a petulant teenage boy. I am, but who wouldn't be in this situation? I'm disillusioned. Frustrated. Disgusted by life. I'm seventeen, on the brink of my senior year, and once again, I've been forced to leave everything familiar to me in order to appease another of her emotional breakdowns. Mom thrives on drama. She always has, and I've always played along.

Not anymore. I'm sick of playing the good son.

"All I'm saying is, we didn't have to leave."

"We did."

Same answer. Always the same.

"He left," I remind her for the hundredth time.

She shakes her head, and the few dark curls that have managed to stay bound in her messy ponytail suddenly bounce free to lash wildly in the wind. "His family lives there. You know how people are. Hateful gossips."

"So?"

Her jaw sets at a rigid angle. "I don't want to talk about it. Not to them, and not to you."

"So my life means nothing to y—"

"Shut it!" She blinks rapidly, still staring at the torn-up road. "I mean it. Not another word."

The tears are back. I look away, disgust searing my insides. The cool wind whips through my hair, pounding at my eardrums, drowning out her staccato gasps for breath. "I get it. Nothing's ever going to change."

She ignores me. I'm fine with that—at least, that's what I always tell myself—and soon she's lighting up again. She bought the ten-pack carton at the first gas station we saw on our way out of town. For eight months she didn't take a single drag. Not one. I'd been begging her to quit for years. Did she listen to me? No. But she listened to Jared, her latest ex-boyfriend. *Anything* for Jared. It's the one thing the walking dick did right, but now look at her.

Why did I think she would change? We're drifters, stumbling from small town to small town, staying a year or two until the man-pool dwindles, leaving the next. Mom changes men like some girls change their nail color. When she finally settles on one "special" guy, it's only a matter of time before he leaves, by way of the back door, with an armful of our stuff he can hock at the local pawn shop and a pocket full of what little money he finds in Mom's purse.

I've learned to lock my bedroom door.

The small evidence of our existence on this earth is behind us, rattling around in a rented trailer as it bounces in and out of deep ruts, shaking our rusty, old Plymouth Road Runner until I'm sure the rivets have come loose.

Mom curses as the car whines up another hill. She pumps the slab of steel with the ball of her foot like the hick she is, until the engine revs, re-engages, and spits us forward.

"You coulda at least slept your way into a better car," I mutter, pulling up the hood of my gray sweatshirt. Not likely. Mom's always been better at giveaways than bartering.

She doesn't hear, and it's probably for the best. A fresh round of tears would've been her answer. They're the answer for everything these days.

To the east, the hills climb into the mountain range. I stare out over the forested landscape, seeing but not seeing. My mind is on the girl in my dreams. Pale face. Dark hair. White gown. Eerie woods. Chills sweep my arms. It's just an impression, there and gone before I can capture it, but a strange, deep longing rises in my chest. I've dreamed about her every night for two weeks, and each dream is more intense than the last. Lately, I'm feeling desperate in a way I've never felt before, like I've been ripped out of the ground one too many times, and the next time will kill me.

My thoughts return to the present, and I see the road split. To the left, pavement riddled with water-filled potholes. To the right, dirt riddled with muddy potholes. We turn right.

I slap my hand on the outside of the door. "Seriously? A dirt road?" Trees quickly surround the car, and an unfamiliar thickness invades the air. Our soon-to-be-new home is fast losing its appeal.

"It's a sheep ranch, Dylan. Where do you expect it to be? In the middle of downtown Portland?"

"Not in the wilds of Oregon!"

The car shakes and rattles as we slowly make our way down the torn-up strip of dirt. Mom does all she can to avoid trouble spots.

"This is hardly—" She huffs when the car slams into an especially deep hole and mud splatters in a shower of gloppy brown. The undercarriage smacks the road hard, and she growls her frustration. "—out in the wilds," she finishes, but I can see even she's struggling to believe her own propaganda.

"Yeah, right. There's not even a damn Walmart out here, and Walmart is *everywhere*."

"Don't cuss," she says. "My mother hates cussing."

Good to know. Rattle off the seven unspeakable cuss words the first chance I get, and family or not, if she has any brains, her mom will send us packing.

Trees crowd the road, sucking the air out of the car. I'd forgotten how much I detest the great outdoors. I'd spent my whole life traveling toward the city, longing for a place where I belong, and now Mom slaps me back to square one.

Every so often, another dirt road forks off the main one, but try as I might, I can't see any signs of human life. The road looks like it leads to a campground. What is she thinking? She hates country life even more than I do.

"So, your mom… What am I supposed to call her?"

Her laugh is a short, bitter sound. "How about Granny? That'll rip her up."

"Using me to dig at your mom isn't very mature."

She pushes the dancing, brown curl out of her eyes. "Oh, shut up. You know I'm kidding. Anyway, what do you care?"

"I don't." I haven't cared about anything in a long time, but still. Someone has to be an adult, and it sure won't be her.

And she *isn't* kidding, regardless of what she says. It's good to know I'm not the only one who causes that particular look of resentment to flash in her eyes.

As we trundle over the hard-packed mud, a scruffy, tri-colored dog with a bobbed tail and spindle-legs shoots out of the trees and runs alongside the car, all barks and growls like it's never seen a rusted box on wheels before.

"Beat it, Fido." I swat at it, but it nearly bites off my hand. "Hey!"

"What?"

"The dog almost bit me!"

Mom looks at me like I'm the problem. "What are you, two? Don't touch a strange dog."

Yep. I'm the problem. I slouch back onto my seat. She would side with a mangy animal over her own flesh and blood. I guess that's what happens when you're the unwanted son of a teenage runaway.

The dog breaks away when we round a bend cluttered with trees. Mom mutters a few more cuss words. I close my eyes and sigh. That's Mom. Do as I say, not as I do.

The car veers to the left, and I crack my eyes open. The wall of trees separates to reveal a half-dozen strange, brightly-painted metal sculptures that belong in one of those modern museums only rich people go to. There's something disturbing about the way they rise up, twisting and stretching in a macabre, colorful dance.

Behind them, a huge, red barn overlooks a clapboard-sided house. When we bottom out near the top of the drive, a small woman, pail in hand, turns and watches us from her place on the front porch. I push my hood off to get a better look. "Yee-haw. There's Granny. So where's Uncle Jed, cousin Jethro, and Elly May?"

"Knock it off."

I can feel a headache coming on. "Let me get this straight. You can say whatever you want, but I've gotta behave?"

"Exactly. Nobody likes a smart ass."

"That would explain your lack of popularity."

She blows out the last of the smoke that's rotting her lungs. "For God sakes, would it kill you to be nice?"

The Road Runner rolls to a stop. Mom hops out with a big, yet wary, smile plastered across her face. I'm not at all eager to meet my maternal kin. Honestly, how great can they be? Mom left when she was barely sixteen. My life sucks and I'm still with *my* parental unit. What does that say about hers?

The woman drops the bucket, and when it lands on the porch's wooden planks, the expected clatter is swallowed by the surrounding forest. Her face pales. I recognize disbelief when I see it. Her hands shake as she rubs them down the sides of her worn-out jeans. Granny isn't exactly old. In fact, she's downright young-looking. A little weather-beaten, but still kind of attractive. An older version of Mom.

Mom hesitates. "Hey, Mama. Bet you didn't expect to see me."

I groan. I shouldn't be surprised that she's dragged us all the way up here without telling anyone, but I am. Mom's never been one to bother with practical matters like informing family we're coming to live with them indefinitely.

"Dylan," Mom yells, and motions me forward. "Get out of the car."

Grandma's attention shifts to where I'm still sitting in the passenger seat. Her eyes are big and pale blue, almost see-through. They're kinda creepy, actually.

"Who's that?" she asks. "Your boyfriend?"

I'm a big guy. Not, oh-my-God-look-at-that-giant-fat-boy big, but tall and muscular. I've been known to walk into a bar or two and not get carded.

"Beautiful," I mutter. Gritting my teeth, I get out of the car, one hand on the roof, the other on the door and glare at Mom. "She doesn't know who I am, does she?"

Mom's eyes widen. She looks like she's going to cry again, and burning anger starts to rise inside of me. I try to tamp it down, but I can't. It bubbles over, leaping into my eyes, my mouth, and my heart.

Without another word, I snatch an old army duffel stuffed

with my things from the back seat and slam the door. I don't look back as I retrace my way toward the main road.

"Dylan!"

I ignore Mom's call.

"Dylan, stop."

I do, but it's got nothing to do with her. The crazy dog skids into my path. Its ears are down, and its teeth are showing. Long, mean teeth.

Mom's fingers clamp onto my shoulder, startling me. The dog leaps toward her, and I kick dirt at it and yell for it to go. Amazingly it does. I pull out of Mom's grasp, ignoring the pleading in her eyes. She latches on again. "You can't go. Please, don't do this."

Where does she get off, acting this way? "What do you care whether I'm here or not?"

"You have to stay! If you don't, it's going to get worse."

It *sounds* like she cares, but I'm not easily fooled. I turn away. "She doesn't know who I am. You never told her about me."

"Of course not. I haven't talked to her since I left."

I snap around and confront her. "Why are we even here?"

"There's no other place to go."

"Bullsh—"

"Don't cuss." She glances back and sees Grandma inching her way toward us. "We have to be smart about this. You promised me you'd behave."

The muscle in my cheek twitches. "People make promises all the time they don't intend to keep." Just like she'd promised to quit smoking and drinking and hooking up with men. Promises run cheap in our dysfunctional family.

I will *not* be like her. I will make something out of my life, even if it kills me.

Panic flushes her face. "Please, Dylan."

She's desperate. I can taste it in the air. I should relent, but an unquenchable need to hurt her like she constantly hurts me threatens to hijack my control.

The crunch of gravel stops me from saying something that would push her over the edge. Grandma's within hearing range, a look of suspicion on her face. "What's going on, Addison?"

"Addy," Mom says on a sigh as she turns to face Grandma. "My name is *Addy*. And nothing is going on. This is my son. Dylan."

"Your son?" The news is definitely a shocker for her. "But he's… How old is he?"

"Seventeen," I say.

Grandma appears dazed and more than confused.

"Yeah," Mom blurts out. "Do the math. Sixteen and pregnant. Daddy would've freaked—*I* freaked—so I left."

"What? Your father—"

Mom throws her head back and sways side-to-side like a nervous hen that's been pegged for Sunday dinner. "You know I'm right," she hollers at the sky.

Shadows flit into Grandma's eyes. "He would've been angry, yes, but that was no reason to leave like you did."

Mom's chin trembles, but she regains control. She looks toward the house and into the woods beyond, like she's searching for something. "Well, we can't change the past."

"No. We can't." Grandma glances at me. I can tell she wants to move closer for an inspection, but manners—and most likely shock—keep her back. "It's a pleasure to meet you, Dylan," she says.

Her gaze lances through me. I get this feeling like I should apologize, but I can't think what I've done wrong, exactly. I don't especially like the feeling. So instead, I thrust out my hand and throw her a smile laced with sarcasm. "Hey there, *Granny*."

There's a sudden void of sound, like the whole world stops for a millisecond, shocked by my rudeness. It whispers on the wind, "She's your grandmother. Have a little respect."

She blinks, and then her mouth cracks open into a wide smile, followed by a sharp laugh. She grabs my hand and squeezes. "You're your mother's child, all right."

I stiffen. She has no idea how deeply she's insulted me. Or maybe she does, because the sunlight suddenly splinters in her eyes, and her fingers squeeze mine.

Mom's fixated on the car, and she's as jittery as a crack addict. "Can we unpack, now?" she whines, and lights up a cigarette, sucking so hard the tip burns quickly into squiggly ash.

Grandma lets go of my hand to cup my face. There's an analytical slant to her stare—a "who's your daddy" look. I can see her mentally click through the slim White Pages of her acquaintances, searching for the culprit. A shadow of suspicion flickers before she gives my cheek a gentle pat. "You're a handsome boy, Dylan. I bet your girlfriend is still crying over you leaving."

Girls have been giggling and sighing over me since I hit the sixth grade. I won't lie. I like girls, and I like the attention they pour on me. A lot. But as soon as I get attached to one, we leave. Over the years, I've learned to adapt. To play the field. Life is less complicated that way.

I shrug and look at Mom. "I'm not strictly a one-woman guy, right, Mom?"

She blows out a thick stream of smoke before pitching the spent butt on the ground and grinding it out. "No, you're not."

Grandma's eyes twinkle. "A Romeo, huh?" When I start to pull away, her fingers intertwine with mine, and she leads me back up the dirt road toward the house. "Trust me. A time will come when one special person is all you'll want."

Mom snorts and lights another cigarette.

God, I hope not. The last thing I want is to become like Mom; chasing *the one* and always slinking away with the taste of burnt ash in my mouth.

FORCED BEHAVIOR

In Kera's opinion, there was nothing worse than being forced into a corset and yards of expensive fabric. She looked like a fragile china doll. No one understood her desire to be free, to walk where she wished, to dress as she chose, yet, the traditional mindset of her people made change nearly impossible. *You risk too much*, her father always said, but he didn't stop her from scampering off to Faldon's home, where she learned about the ways of the world outside her staid, dried-up sphere.

Faldon, her tutor, taught her everything from alchemy to self-defense. He talked of places so secret, even her father would gasp at his daring. The old sage treated her as if she had a purpose far greater than being the perfect daughter of a nobleman.

It was because of Faldon that she knew the extent of the violence sweeping her land. Teag was struggling, steeped in a hidden battle for control. And the prize for the victor? A magic so powerful, few had dared to grab it in all the years it had lain in wait for its next host. Now, the warlord Navar, the boldest of those seeking that power, silently crept along the land, spouting the virtues of tradition. Of isolation. Of elitism. Dredging up the Lost King's dreams of a perfect society.

For her people, Navar's offering was as seductive as the most beautiful woman. With each stop on his campaign, the man successfully secured a false sense of well-being. Of being special. And his campaign, his every step, every signed decree, was killing those Kera loved.

At the sound of company, Kera glanced up from the piano's keyboard and out the manor's parlor window to see Navar's well-appointed carriage. It slashed through the rain and up their graveled drive, his black horse tied behind it. It was just like him to arrive unannounced.

Kera rose from the bench so abruptly, their dog, who had been lying peacefully by the fireplace, jerked awake. She heard the butler order a room prepared and saw the housekeeper fly by the open door toward the kitchens to make sure their evening meal would surpass even Navar's jaded tastes.

Why had he come? Lately, something about him had changed. She couldn't put her finger on what it could be, and she wasn't sure she wanted to know. At least he still talked, which he often did, without expecting her to offer an opinion, which she never did.

She couldn't stay and listen to him carry on his one-sided conversation. The far door offered an escape, and she kicked the multi-layers of skirts out of the way. If she were quick enough, she could leave without him knowing she'd ever been in the room.

She'd barely taken a step when her father snapped his fingers, stopping her, and pointed to the piano bench.

She reluctantly sat. "What is *he* doing here? And why must I stay? It's gloomy enough outside without having to entertain the likes of him."

"I would guess he comes for my counsel, and you must stay because you're this home's mistress." Her father stood, presenting himself in fine clothes to match his dignified bearing. He was a scholar, brilliant even by their people's standards. He folded his spectacles and tucked them into the breast pocket of his jacket.

That simple action said it all. No need to invite the appearance of weakness in front of their future king. Kera concentrated on flattening the pleats in her skirts. "I would rather be this home's master and bar the doors."

"Kera…"

She let out a long, venting sigh. "I'll behave."

Her father didn't understand her reaction to Navar. Most thought him handsome, with his dark good looks and perfect soldier bearing, but the more Kera learned about him, the less attractive he became. Her father believed his guidance would cure Navar of his self-centered ways.

Kera didn't share his optimism.

As soon as Navar strutted into the parlor, his clothes painstakingly pressed and shoes polished, the cheerful mood in the parlor evaporated like water in the desert. His dark eyes found hers and wouldn't let go. Not a drop of rainwater had dared to fall on him, yet he moved to their empty fireplace, waved his hand, and wood appeared, along with a crackling fire. The air turned unpleasantly hot. Her day dress smothered her skin, and the tight stays pinched her torso. No amount of comfort could be had in the man's presence.

She produced the required nod to his crisp bow and returned to her music, her fingers searching out the keys to a well-known song. Sadly, there wasn't a lively enough tune to block out the deep, aggressive staccato of Navar's voice. Out of the corner of her eye, she saw him sit in a nearby chair, put ankle to knee, and rub a non-existent spot of mud from his shoe before settling in.

Kera let loose a weighty sigh and turned the page of sheet music. She'd die of boredom if she were made to stay put much longer. Her father's quiet voice became lost in the drone of Navar's egocentric comments, which were accompanied by the slap of his riding gloves against his knee, an annoying punctuation mark to his words. To those who looked, he was a lord in waiting. A king in the making. A conqueror in the flesh. Only she saw him for what he truly was.

A danger to all.

The thought sent a chill through Kera. She abandoned the piano and paced the edges of the room. Still, Navar's eyes followed her. She lifted a book from a table and hid behind its pages. Navar's gaze never wavered.

Irritated, she returned to the piano, clutched her necklace and muttered a tiny spell. A rank odor engulfed Navar, sending him out of his chair. He glared at the aging dog lying oblivious by the fireplace, before moving away.

Much better. She resumed playing.

He paced, then stopped and faced her. "Is everything well with you, Kera?"

Kera's fingers froze on the ivory keys. To anyone listening, Navar's inflection held just the right dash of interest without any real concern. She didn't want to answer him. Didn't want to encourage a new custom of verbal intercourse. A quick glance at her father told her she had no choice.

Staring sightlessly at her sheet music, she said, "I'm fine, my lord."

She was always fine. It lent an air of banality that had kept him at a distance, so far.

The clock on the mantle chimed. Quarter past five. Dinner was *hours* away. Would this day never end? Navar's appearance had already ruined her afternoon plans. After a lesson about the aspects of using the earth's energy to perform magical feats, Faldon had planned to let Kera practice archery.

She sighed. If only they could refuse Navar their hospitality.

An idea formed. A deliciously evil idea that had Kera smiling despite herself. She rose, sweeping the bulk of her heavy skirts behind her, and crossed the room to a clear ball the size of a dinner plate. She stroked it and brought forth the image of their housekeeper.

"Agnes," she whispered, "add another layer of cotton to Lord Navar's mattress. You know the kind. We wouldn't want him to suffer unduly tonight."

Agnes grinned. "I'll stuff it nice and tight, my lady."

"Thank you." She lifted her hand and the image disappeared.

Installing him on the lumpiest mattress should see him off soon. She turned and encountered her father's questioning gaze and smiled. "Lord Navar's accommodations are progressing nicely."

Her act didn't fool her father, but before he could corner her and beg her to be civil, Granel stormed into the parlor, his eyes bright with triumph. "My lords."

Though Granel tried to appear commanding, his clothes always leaned toward dishevelment, which pointed more toward a common man than a courtly one. The stocky lieutenant-at-arms shoved his hat beneath his arm and bowed, displaying a tiny patch of baldness on top his head. Kera waited for him to acknowledge her, but he purposefully ignored her. Nothing new there, and highly desirable as far as she was concerned. The more invisible she became, the sooner they'd leave.

Navar scowled. "Well?"

"You were right." Granel offered up a too-wide smile, more disturbing than any frown. "In the woods, not four leagues from where we stand."

Navar slapped his gloves on his thigh again and stood. "Excellent."

Kera's father rose, a wary expression on his face. "What brings on such good humor?"

"We've found one of the tainted." Navar peered at her father. "In *your* woods."

Her father's face reddened at the suggestion. "I thought you said the last of that plague was eradicated months ago."

Kera moved to join them, but her father caught her eye. She could see the warning behind his calm gaze, could almost hear it. *Stay put.*

Navar pulled on his gloves. "Some will always fight their fate."

"Are you sure it's one of them?" Her father's probe was a risk. If he pushed too hard, Navar could easily become suspicious. It was his nature.

Navar tossed Granel a questioning look.

The little toad croaked on cue. "She's been tested."

Her father leaned out the door and called to their butler, "Barton, my horse, and bring me—"

Navar cut him off. "There's no need, Hadrain. We shall attend to this and be back before dinner is announced."

Navar strode to Kera, grabbed her hand, and lifted it to his mouth. The wetness of his lips repulsed her; it was all she could do not to pull her hand away. His dark eyes, so beautiful yet so hate-filled, peered into hers, completely unaware of her disgust. "Make sure your dinner setting is placed next to mine, Kera."

Her stomach soured. She hadn't missed the threat of impending intimacy. Without waiting for a reply, he dropped her hand and left, cutting a grand figure that would have many women swooning at his feet. Not her. *Never* her.

Kera gripped her father's arm, her fingers wrinkling his sleeve. "What should we do? Tell me it's not too late."

His face had grown haggard, as if the weight of the moment would tear him apart. He cupped her cheek and sighed. "There's nothing we can do now."

"How can you say that? They are our friends. They're counting on us to protect them."

"I know the extent of this problem better than you. I'll go to Faldon. If anyone can help, he can."

Kera followed her father to the door, her fingers crushing the fabric of her skirts. "My tutor? He is a seer who conjures nothing more than tricks to delight a child."

"There is more to him than he lets you see, Kera." With his hand on the door, he turned and leveled a serious gaze on her. "Be at peace. There's nothing you can do."

He leaned forward, kissed her forehead, and left.

She stood, mouth agape, and watched him go. *Be at peace? That was his fine counsel?*

There was no time to change out of her restrictive clothes, not even to step out of the cumbersome bustle strapped around her waist. Kera took to the outdoors, not to follow her father on his empty quest, but to find Navar.

She would stop this madness herself.

Though what could be done once he was found, she didn't know. Kera only knew she couldn't stand by and let him harm a woman whose only fault was to be born of mixed blood.

Unanswered Questions

"And this can be your room, Dylan."

Grandma opens an old paneled door and ushers me into a tidy bedroom situated at the back of the house near the kitchen. Mom's upstairs, collapsed on her old bed, her eyes swollen and red as she relives the pain of being dumped. Again. I'd go anywhere to get away from her right now. A pile of rags scattered in the attic above the garage would've worked.

The walls of the room glow a soft green in the strangely filtered northwest sunlight. Green's not my favorite color—it makes me nervous. In fact, this whole place makes me nervous. We can't stay here.

I toss my duffel on the bed and watch it spring up and down. Seriously. We can't.

Grandma purses her lips. "The bed's a little old, but still comfortable. And the room has lots of natural light," she says, pointing to the open window. A slight breeze ruffles the curtains while Grandma gives the room a critical once over. "It's the only room without a girly theme. I'd put you next to your mother upstairs, but we never bothered changing the girls' rooms."

I freeze. "Mom has sisters?"

A frown tightens her face, and her hands slip down the sides of her pants. It's her nervous habit I'm beginning to notice. "Two. Did she never tell you?"

"Mom's not the sentimental type. There's always been a detour around memory lane."

"I see."

Grandma doesn't, and frankly, neither do I. I plop onto the bed and get swallowed two inches deep into a feather mattress. I struggle to sit up, and when I manage to find my balance, I glance back at her. "It's…um…nice."

I shake my head, surprised I even bothered to reassure her. It's got to be the look on her face. The obvious attempt to please me. The woman deserves some kindness. Mom certainly won't be dispensing any.

"It's always been for guests, though we don't get many here. You have your own bathroom right there." She points to a door on the far wall.

We stay that way for a moment, both staring at the bathroom door, until she turns toward me. "She really never mentioned us? Any of us?"

"Don't feel bad. She barely remembers me half the time."

Grandma gasps. "I'm sure that's not true."

She says that, but I can tell she doesn't believe it. I can tell she knows Mom hasn't changed. Her gaze slides around the room until it lands back on me. I can read the indecision that's torturing her, so I shrug. "I don't know."

"Excuse me?"

"I don't know who knocked her up. She never said."

When I was younger, I made the mistake of asking Mom about him, wanting to tell my friends I had a dad, too. She blew up, slapped me around, and smashed things to bits. When the violence was over, she went into a deep funk. The lesson was painful and potent. Don't ask. Ever.

Grandma's cheeks redden. "Oh no. I wasn't — "

"It's okay. I'm not the sentimental type, either." Mom cured me of that.

Gentle understanding softens her face. "Few in life really are."

Why do I get the feeling Grandma is one of those few?

She makes her way out of the room and pauses when she reaches the door. "Your mother didn't say. How long are you here for?"

No surprise Mom hasn't dropped that bomb yet. I pull my duffel onto my lap, a protective gesture. "I'm not sure."

Even Grandma will be able to see through that lie. If she doesn't, she'll definitely know something's up when I register for high school.

She nods, and nibbles at her lower lip. "Well, then. I guess I'll leave you to unpack. Come on out when you're done. Dinner won't be long."

As the door closes, she eyes me with those strange, pale eyes of hers. I shiver. How weird to be creeped out by your own grandmother.

I'd lay bets on Mom stalling the inevitable "talk" for a whole week, locked in the time capsule of her childhood bedroom, wailing about Jared, and ignoring me and everyone else.

I'm not waiting for her to get all the drama out before I start my new life.

I quickly fill the first two drawers of the old, knotty wood dresser, with its crystal knobs and chipped mirror, before making a quick exploration of my space. The wood smells like lemons, the bathroom like vanilla, and the bed sheets like flowers. I've never smelled so many different scents in one place before. Mom never dusts, uses cheap laundry soap, and tosses me a book of matches, telling me not to set myself on fire while I get rid of the stench.

Nothing says "home" like sulfur and burnt sticks. I'm beginning to see how different Mom is from Grandma.

Maybe it's a generational thing? But when I think about it, Grandma isn't *that* old. Mid-fifties, tops. She has old-lady taste, though. I run a finger along the bristle of an antique hairbrush sitting on the dresser. Beside it are a silver-handled mirror and a tintype photograph of a man and a woman wearing Wild West-type clothing, standing in front of this house. Neither is smiling.

Something hard smacks the window, and I jump. Looking out, I don't see anything. Only tiny, flittering bugs. Still…I glance around the room and shiver. I feel like I'm being watched.

Okay, time to leave.

When I step into the hall and close the bedroom door, the smell of roasting meat makes my mouth water. Mom's a vegetarian—no way will she be eating. She's been fasting for a few days, anyway. In her mind, it adds to the drama of the moment. Too bad, because eating meat in front of her while she tries to win me over to the "animals have feelings, too" philosophy is the only time she looks at me.

As I make my way down the hall, I hear a deep, unfamiliar voice. "Are we supposed to be okay with this?"

I soften my steps, moving slowly, and listen.

"Of course we are," Grandma says. "She's our daughter."

A chair scrapes the floor, and the man grunts as he sits. "It's been seventeen years. Are you telling me she couldn't find a phone?" There's a moment of silence before I hear fingers snap. His voice drops to a hush, highlighting its rough, sandpaper quality. "Who was that boy, the one with the stringy hair…Chris something or another?"

"Mandling?"

"That's it. Chris Mandling. It's got to be him. I never liked that boy."

"No," Grandma hisses back. "They shipped him off to military school almost a year before Addison left."

"Lucy Jones' boy?"

"Be serious. He had buck teeth and a lisp."

"He got braces and a speech therapist. He's fine now."

The sounds of Grandma pulling the dinner together grow louder, and I stop before reaching the threshold to the kitchen. Mom would have a fit if she heard this.

"Think shallow teenage girl," Grandma says.

"Raymond Tiller."

Grandma sighs her frustration. "He's black."

"He was around," he whispers in his defense.

Plates and flatware clatter when she sets them on the table. "I know, but Dylan is as white as they come."

"Mark Taylor, then. He's the whitest boy I know."

"With red hair and freckles. I don't know…"

"You used to like red hair."

"I still do, but we're talking about Addison."

"I know, I know, but I'm doin' this off the top of my head. Most of those boys left the second she did."

There's a moment of silence. Within that time, I realize Mom must've been the high school slut if they can come up with this many possibilities, plus other guys whose names they can't remember. Why am I not surprised?

"Hey!" the man says louder than he should, and then quickly lowers his voice again. "How about Kenny Jacks or his friend, Donny Raynor?"

Grandma lets out a thoughtful *hmm*. "Kenny was a handsome boy, if I recall."

"And always throwing rocks at her window. I nearly shot him that one night, remember?" Excitement ripples through his voice.

"I do."

Kenny Jacks. I thrust my hands in my jean pockets and jiggle my fingers within. I could be Dylan Jacks instead of Dylan Kennedy.

I stand there, trying the name out and hating it, when Grandma comes around the corner and bumps into me. "Dylan!" she yelps, her hand to her chest. "I'm so sorry. I was coming to get you."

"I'm here."

Guilt rings her eyes. "Yes. So I see. Well…"

She takes my hand and pulls me into the kitchen. "Look who I nearly knocked over," she says to the weather-beaten man sitting at the table. "Dylan, this is your grandfather."

He's a solid guy with only a few gray hairs. Where's the jolly smile? The arthritic hands? There's no doubt this guy has tough skin and even tougher muscles. He could lay me out with one well-placed slap. Our eyes meet. I nod. He nods back, and his intense stare tells me he's comparing.

When Grandma sidles closer, balancing three glasses filled with ice, he mutters, "Now that I think about it, the last one isn't it."

I grab the seat across the table from him and sit. Showing disinterest, I fill my plate and say, "Then how about that Donny guy?"

Grandma and Grandpa's eyes lock before Grandma sits. She spreads her napkin in her lap, flattening it over and over again with her palms. "You heard?"

"Yeah. Sounds like Mom got around."

Pain slices through Grandma's eyes before she covers it up. "She was…a challenge."

By what I just heard, that's the understatement of the year. "Did you ever think about using a chastity belt?"

"I thought of hog-tying her in the attic," Grandpa says, "but I was told that's illegal."

Grandma gives him a *be quiet* glare. *What?* he mouths.

She turns to me. "Dylan, you weren't meant to hear what we said. I'm sorry. We should have — "

"Mom's mom. I learned that a long time ago. I can't name you all the *uncles* she's introduced to me. I've got a very warped sense of family now, and more than my share of abandonment issues."

Grandma sighs, and Grandpa places his hand over hers. I don't know why I said anything. It was cruel.

"Well," Grandma whispers, "let's eat."

Before I can react, they each grab my hand. When I'm about to pull away, they bow their heads, and Grandpa prays. I don't know what to do. I glance from one to the other, and quickly look away when they say "amen." My hands are freed, and I feel the need to wipe them clean. No one, not even Mom, touches me without my permission.

"So, Dylan," Grandpa's voice booms, "you like sheep?"

I nearly choke on my pot roast. I've heard all the jokes about sheep herders and ewes. I toss him a horrified look. "No. I like girls."

Obviously he's heard the jokes, too, because he lets loose a big laugh. "That's a huge weight off my mind."

"George," Grandma says in a firm voice. She doesn't look at me, but directs her words my way. "What your grandpa means is that he would like you to go out with him and the sheep."

The devil in me flares to life. "Really, Grandma. I only go out with girls."

Grandpa coughs on his milk, and I find it hard not to laugh, too.

"Honestly," Grandma snaps. "The both of you should be ashamed of yourselves."

I force down my disrespectful nature, and Grandpa clears his throat. "Tell you what, Dylan, tomorrow you can come out with me and see what it's like to run a sheep ranch."

"Sounds…fun." I ask Grandma flatly, "Do I have a choice?"

"No. I need to talk to your mother. Besides, it's a perfect time for you and your grandfather to get to know each other better."

"You're talking male bonding, aren't you?" I shake my head. "Is there beer involved?"

The pair slant worried glances at each other.

Oops. I sit back and give them the smile that always gets me out of trouble. Always. "I'm kidding."

Grandpa stares bullets at me. "Sounds like there's a bit of a wicked streak in you, Dylan."

My smile cracks just a hair. The old guy isn't falling for it. Grandma isn't that impressed, either. Maybe there's a genetic flaw that blocks the full potential of my smile with these two? I clear my throat. "Uh, no, sir. I'm wicked-free."

He grunts, stares a little longer than what makes me comfortable, and then returns to eating his food.

"What are your interests, Dylan?" Grandma asks, fishing for who I am.

How can I tell her when I'm not even sure? Rarely do people ask, and even more rarely do I offer insight. "Long-boarding. Music. You know, the usual stuff."

Grandpa pauses, his fork poised near his mouth. "Sports?"

"Sure." Virtual over actual, but no sense in putting the "today's lazy youth" card on the table. Besides, it feels more natural to steer the conversation toward them and the ranch. "So this is a sheep ranch, huh?"

I'm bored before Grandma takes her next breath. I pretend to pay attention, and instead, wonder how I'm going to survive this encounter. As I plan what classes I'll need in order to graduate, I hear the words "rare," "ancient breed," and "soy."

A guy blanks out for half a second, and suddenly, we're talking about soy? They're not the kind of people who drink soy milk and eat tofu, I hope. Is this my last real meal before they bring out the granola?

I shake myself back to the present. "What did you say?"

"I know. It's hard to imagine, but it's possible our sheep have been around since the ice age."

Images of snaggle-toothed, monster sheep flash through my head. I quickly readjust my thinking when she brings me a picture they use to promote their business. Along the top are the words: *Pine Grove Soay Sheep Farm*, and under it are a half dozen cute, little sheep. And I do mean little. Apparently Soay sheep are the midgets of the sheep world.

"Their meat is all the rage," Grandma gushes as she gazes at the photo. "Your aunt Susie is our top customer. She runs a gourmet five-star restaurant in Seattle."

"Interesting." I give back the picture and quickly stuff another bite of roast beef into my mouth so I've got an excuse to stay quiet, because now I'm fuming.

I've got an aunt who lives in Seattle. Mom could've taken us there, but no. I get quality time with the sheep ranch branch of the family in the Middle of Nowhere, Oregon, instead. Lucky me. Again.

By the end of dinner, they don't know what to think of me, and I'm at a loss about what to think of them. Upstairs, a toilet flushes, then a door bangs closed.

Mom.

Even though Grandma's smiling, stress pulls at her lips. It probably never occurred to Mom what our coming here would do to her parents. Then again, Mom lives for drama. She eats and breathes the stuff. I've learned to ignore it all—well, most of the time—but Grandma might find that hard to do.

Grandpa pushes his plate away and frowns in the direction of the back stairs. He mutters something under his breath, unfolds from his chair, and stalks off toward the den. Grandma sighs when the TV pops on. I get the feeling Grandpa isn't too thrilled with Mom's reappearance, but will suffer anything to make Grandma happy.

Poor Grandma. Does she really think having Mom back is a good thing? She stands, gives me a quick smile, and starts clearing away the dishes. "Pie?" she asks in an overly cheery voice.

I haven't eaten so well in…well… I can't remember. I nod and clear away my place. After she slips the last dinner plate into the soapy dishwater, she cuts me a massive slice of chocolate turtle pie, and then cuts another, smaller one, and hands it to me. "Take this one to your mom."

I'd rather not. My face must show my hesitance, because she purses her lips and pushes me out. "Go on. She loves pie."

Why do I get the feeling I'm carrying a peace offering? It's a waste of good pie, but I do it, anyway.

I navigate the stairs with a plate and fork in each hand. At the top, four doors welcome me. I could play eeny-meeny-miney-moe, but instead, I go to the first door and knock softly. Nothing. The next is empty too. At the third, Mom's sad voice warbles from behind the door. She's talking to someone on her cell phone. I can't make out what she's saying, but it doesn't sound good. I could either give her the pie, or tell Grandma she's busy and leave it to her to interrupt the ongoing melodrama. Before I can step away, I hear the hard click of her cell phone closing, and a bang as it hits the door.

She better not've broken it. That phone is my only link back to my friends.

What am I talking about? What few friends I had have already forgotten about me. When I called Mike the fourth day after we left, it had taken him a whole minute to figure out who I was. Granted, he's not the brightest bulb, but we'd hung out every day at the skate park after school. It's almost as if when I'm there, people love me, but when I'm not, they don't even remember I exist. Mom's the only exception. She remembers me, only she wishes she didn't.

I knock on the door.

"Go away."

"I've got pie."

The door flies open, and Mom stares at me with a tear-stained face. "Did she spit in it?"

I thrust the pie at her. "You're sick, you know that?"

With a shrug, she takes the plate and begins to eat. "What're they saying? Wait. Let me guess. Who do they think it is?"

I don't get it. Mom's pretty. She's smarter than most. And when she's not going ballistic about a guy, she's actually fun to be with. So, why can't she see beyond herself? Doesn't it even occur to her how much pain she puts people through? Puts *me* through?

"Some guy named Kenny," I say flatly.

"Kenny Jacks?" She snorts. "I would be so lucky. Dad chased him off before I got a chance."

I don't want to do this. I don't want to think of her as the town slut. I want a normal mother, one who cooks and cleans and cares for me.

She stuffs the last of the pie in her mouth. I know my disgust is showing. I can't help it.

She swallows and lifts her chin higher. "Don't look at me like that."

"Like what?"

"Like I'm…"

I dare her to say it.

She doesn't, and quickly thrusts the plate back at me and begins to shut the door. I wedge my foot between the door and the jam, determined this time to get an answer. "I don't look like you.

I don't look like them. I've got to look like someone. I've got to *be* like someone. So, who is it?"

Her face sinks into an unattractive pinch. "No one they know."

I spot her bags, still packed, on the bed. She follows my gaze and whispers, "Don't push me, Dylan. You'll know soon enough."

Her response catches me so off guard, she's able to force the door closed. The lock clicks into place, shutting me out for good.

I think I actually hate her.

The plates rattle with my pent-up rage. I want to hurl them to the ground. Shake the walls with an anger so fierce, it would send her into a terrified fit, but I don't. I search for control. I breathe deep. And when my anger calms, I go downstairs.

I don't eat my pie. I can't.

"I'm not feeling so good," I say to Grandma, and push the empty plate into her soapy hands. When I set my untouched pie on the counter, she grabs a dishtowel and sneaks a quick glance up the stairs. She doesn't say anything, but her lips thin.

"I think I'll go to bed," I say.

She nods and wraps my pie in plastic wrap. "Grandpa will knock on your door when he's ready to go."

That's right. I'm playing with the sheep tomorrow. Man, my life sucks.

I peer out the kitchen window. Dark, heavy clouds rush in from the south, and a bunch of fireflies buzz around like they can't wait for the light show to begin. Weird how they're so bright even though it isn't dark out yet. Maybe it's a good sign. Maybe it'll storm hard, and Grandpa will decide not to go.

A guy can hope, can't he?

Before I leave, Grandma asks me to put away an old iron skillet, the kind that weighs a ton and looks like it should be used over an open camp fire. As soon as I take it, pain jolts through my skin. My head swims and my whole body grows weak, like it's deflating.

I drop the skillet and grab my hand. Red welts, pocked with blisters, streak the skin where my fingers touched the pan. I've been burned before, but this one is worse than any I've ever had.

Grandma's face wrinkles with worry. "Are you all right?"

"Yeah, sorry," I say automatically.

As I watch, the blisters begin to fade. The red welts fade to pink. The pain eases. What the—

I ball my hand into a tight fist and eye the skillet. "Old baseball injury."

Grandpa, having heard the ruckus, pokes his head into the kitchen. "Baseball? Catcher?"

"Yeah, sure." I'm not paying attention. I'm freaking out. How can a cold skillet burn me? Stranger still, how can such a severe burn begin to heal so quickly?

He smiles. "Win any games?"

"None I'd want to brag about."

"Tough luck." Grandpa stoops, picks up the skillet, and slips it on top of the cabinets without a problem. "Senior year is coming up," he says. "That's the one that counts."

"Yeah." I take a few steps back, my mind grappling with what *should* be happening and what *is*. The skillet couldn't have burned me. Grandma and Grandpa both touched it. "I'm going to go to my room, okay?"

Grandma gives Grandpa a kiss of thanks before nodding my way. "That's fine, dear. Go relax. You've had a long day."

A Good Day to Die

Navar's trail wasn't difficult for Kera to find. He was a bull, thrashing his way through the forest, indifferent to what he trampled. He would *not* make a good king. His tactics were brutal and fostered loyalty based on fear.

Yet, ever since their king had disappeared, Navar had shown himself the strongest and most able to rule Teag's feuding subjects. And to show he was capable, he had carried on the Lost King's campaign—ridding Teag of all those unworthy to live, so her people would rise to a more perfect and pure state of being.

The neigh of horses and the rattling of soldiers sounded up ahead. Kera stopped running and listened. There were so many men, and in their midst…

Lani.

Kera gasped when she saw her best friend. What was she doing, roaming the forest so close to the forbidden barrier? She knew better. Why would she put herself in such danger?

There could be only one reason. She had sacrificed her own safety for someone else.

Though Lani's blue dress was ripped along the collar, revealing the lace edge of her corset, she stood straight, defiant. The men gripping her wrists wore hard expressions and had even harder eyes. All their hate was pointed at the small woman they held captive.

Kera circled the group. Listening. Watching. Worrying. She had to do something, but what? She stopped at a point where the barrier rose behind her and a wisp of mist hung low to the ground.

Navar said something Kera couldn't hear, but Lani's voice rang loud and clear in the clearing. "It's a good day to die."

Kera's heart froze. Why would she say such a thing? Before an answer could be had, the men forced her to bow. In a long, graceful flex of his arm, Navar pulled out his sword, and without hesitating, brought the blade down in a perfect, deadly arc, separating Lani's head from her shoulders.

Kera's hands flew to her mouth, muffling her sharp cry. She staggered back, eyes wide with horror. The men holding Lani's body let go, as if she were nothing but a piece of garbage better left untouched.

"No." The word stumbled dryly from Kera's lips. She lurched back, though her eyes were still glued to the gruesome scene. "No, no, no." Her horror turned into a physical pain she couldn't control. She clutched her stomach and shook her head, repeating the word more and more loudly.

Her gaze landed on Navar, her anger so hot and so heavy, she felt she would burst if she didn't release the scream rising in her throat. "Murderer!"

The accusation echoed through the forest. War-hardened horses pranced nervously. The soldiers began to search the area, their swords raised, ready to battle the unseen.

Navar pushed his men into action, hatred contorting his handsome features. "Go! Bring out the hounds. Do whatever it takes to find the others."

She had to get away. Had to hide. If she didn't, they'd find her and kill her just like they had Lani.

Something solid halted her retreat. The barrier.

A heavy mist swirled forward, entwining about her like angry vines. It hung thick, swallowing her skin, invading her lungs. She couldn't breathe. Her head grew light. She closed her eyes and thought of her friend, and when next she opened her eyes, she was standing on the wrong side of the shimmering wall that divided the human realm from hers. She continued to back away from the site of Lani's death, her stomach roiling, her mind screaming an alarm. How had she crossed through? It couldn't be done—shouldn't be done. Everyone knew that.

Her nerves stretched taut. Any minute, one of Navar's men would rush through and grab her. She turned and ran, tears of sorrow, regret, and helplessness pouring down her cheeks. When the trees grew thinner, she staggered to a stop. The pine needles beneath her feet were brittle, not soft. The air smelled musty, not tinged with the hint of burning coal.

She pushed through the wild undergrowth, cognizant of the differences, yet seeing the familiarity that joined this realm to her own. What kind of danger lurked here? It couldn't be worse than what was happening in her world.

Kera closed her eyes, shying away from the pain of Lani's death. Her father had tried to protect her from the dangers that had infiltrated her home, but the horror of what she'd seen etched itself into her mind, blinding her path with misery and the knowledge that even her father was helpless to stop the madness that had invaded their land.

From the expression of absolute hatred on Navar's face, the madness would continue.

For Lani's sake, Kera wouldn't allow herself to succumb to grief. She had to get back to her realm, had to protect those who were at risk of falling into Navar's hands. God only knew what kind of evil he was planning.

The person she feared for the most was her father. Even now, Navar could be questioning him, ferreting out his involvement with the outcasts, and demanding to see her. Though her father's blood flowed true, he walked a fine line. If Navar knew he lent resources to those he called the "tainted," the warlord would have no qualms sentencing her father to death.

She couldn't stay in this realm.

Rubbing at the gooseflesh covering her arms, Kera surveyed the area. She had no idea how far she'd run or where she'd find the wall. A better view was needed, but she couldn't move in her clothing. With deft fingers, she unlaced her shoes and struggled out of her dress. The bustle, a contraption of wire, horsehair, and cloth that surrounded her hips, came loose with one tug of the buckle. Lastly, she rolled down her stockings.

When she was done, she stood amid a clutter of garments in her underskirts, shift, and corset. She gathered them, then placed her belongings under a pile of leaves at the base of a tree. Free to move, she was up the tree in no time and moving from branch to branch.

In this realm, her balance was off. Her legs leaden, her movements slower. Her breathing grew heavier. The bond between her and her father was stretched too thin. She floated to the ground and steadied herself.

And then she felt it. A ripple of power. She stopped and turned. Beyond the trees, spread out on a tract of cleared land, was a farmhouse, and within…

Dylan?

SEEING THE IMPOSSIBLE

Once in my bedroom, I shut the door and unclench my fist. The blisters are almost gone. I know I didn't imagine the burn. I can still see the lingering redness, feel the tightness along my skin.

I kick off my shoes and head toward the bathroom. The area is stark; a sink, a shower and a toilet. Nothing fancy adorns the tiny room other than white paneling along the lower half of the wall, yellow paint to the ceiling, and an old hand towel with pink roses along the bottom. The pipes groan as I soak my hand, and before my eyes, the skin loses the last bit of pink. Maybe the burn wasn't as bad as I'd thought.

When the throbbing stops, I wash my face and brush my teeth. Even though it's not close to dark outside, I'm exhausted. Mom has a way of doing that to me.

I go over every possible way I can change the path my life has settled into. It would be so easy to drop out of school and leave.

Too easy. Too appealing.

I'm stuck in a rut, but at least I'm going forward, even if it's only an inch or two. If I bail and head into the world now, I'll become another statistic, just like my mother.

My fingers grip the sink, and I stare into the mirror. The

toothbrush handle pokes out of my mouth, but I ignore it to stare hard into my eyes. *You gotta make it. Hang in there.*

But what happens after I graduate? That's the question I've avoided asking myself. Is not having a tangible vision regarding the future a bad sign? Even Mom, a woman no sane person would want to emulate, has basic expectations. For me, there's just a huge void I can't seem to fill with a purpose.

Mom says I'm different. I *know* I am. I've had a sense of not belonging my whole life. Flickers of unexpected sight...motion slowing...speeding up. Of feeling disconnected. Out of place. Out of time. It's gotten even worse the last few days. The look on my face is grim, and it's suddenly really hard to swallow. I'm ready to crack. Calling on the last of my determination, I force the tension from my body and finish brushing my teeth. The well water tastes heavy, like there's a ton of metal in it, and my stomach gives a little twist. I give one last swish and spit before flicking off the bathroom light.

The whip of a coming storm rattles the house and spreads clouds like fingers across the sky, turning the approaching clouds a muddy orange-red. The fading light shines through the open window. I check to make sure no suicidal fireflies have sneaked past the screen as I slowly shimmy the window closed. The air immediately grows stagnant. I stand with my hands on the curtains, ready to close them. Maybe I should keep the window open? It's not like I'm afraid of a little rain.

As I debate the idea, the hairs on my arms rise, and my skin tingles along the back of my neck. The forest hovers beyond the back fence like a giant waiting for its supper. The wind quickens the leaves and rustles the undergrowth. Shadows of the coming night have already found their favorite haunts. It's not a familiar sight, but nothing seems odd.

And then a flicker catches my eye.

I lean forward, my eyes focusing on the spot.

Another movement. The swish of light colored fabric, an unnaturally white arm, and a heart-shaped face. A girl among the high branches of the massive trees, *leaping* from branch to branch. I gasp, holding my breath as the figure sails through the air and floats slowly—too slowly—to the ground. She stops, her body a wisp of pale flesh amid the tower of trees. She turns, and her gaze slams into mine.

I stumble back, inadvertently yanking the curtains across the rod, and plunging my room into various tones of cheerless gray. My body warms like someone's poured scalding coffee down my throat and I can't swallow.

I didn't see what I just saw. I couldn't have.

My hands. They're shaking.

What am I, bent? I place my finger along the nubby fabric near the curtain's edge. I lick my dry lips. The vein in my neck throbs sharply. Slowly, I ease the curtain to the side and peek out.

The bare yard is lit by the brilliance of the setting sun as it slides beneath the dark clouds. Beyond the fenced-in yard, trees block the bulk of the sunlight from filtering through. Soon, the approaching storm will block out all the light. I scan the area, and just when I'm about to give up and breathe easier, far within the trees there's another pale flicker of movement.

Someone—or some*thing*—is definitely in the woods.

IN THE BLINK OF AN EYE

I back away from the window even as I tell myself to sit tight, but I can't. I'm suddenly possessed with the need to know who—or what— it is, and this need is a pull I've got to obey.

I dive for my shoes, slip them on, and dash out the door and into the unknown. My heart thuds wildly. It's a girl, and I've got a feeling she's the one from my dreams. I don't understand how this is possible, but it doesn't matter. I've lost all ability to stop. I ricochet around the kitchen corner and catch Grandpa's eye before I speed out the back door.

"Dylan?" he shouts. "A storm's coming."

I don't answer, just race into the backyard, fall over the strawberry pot with its pathetic amount of fruit, run past the greenhouse, and punch through the back gate. I don't slow down until I burst into the woods and trip over the uneven ground. I catch myself on a nearby tree and stop. A strange lightness seizes me. The whole forest seems to take a breath, its shadows hiding what I'm searching for, but I keep moving forward.

The air is electric, like I've stumbled into a force field. The feeling of being different, of sensing things that aren't there, prickles my skin. I usually turn back when I get this feeling.

Not this time.

I push off the tree and step forward. The hairs on my arms rise again. I rub them down, but they won't stay. With each step, I press farther into the forest and further into a feeling of unease.

When I was little, I had a reoccurring dream where jagged, bare limbs bent down and attacked me. I would fight them off, but eventually, they'd twist their spindly branches around me and lift me high into their boughs. I'd scream, thrash, break off twigs... then fall. Before I hit the ground, I'd wake and see Mom standing in the doorway of my room, staring, her arms wrapped around her torso. She wouldn't say a word, even as I whimpered for her. She'd just stare, then leave.

Despite those memories crashing in on my thoughts, whatever this urge is that's infusing me pushes me past my tree aversion and keeps my feet moving.

The leaves shiver in the wind, their sound like little whispers, condemning, plotting. Blood rushes through me, flooding my skin, until I'm so hot I feel light-headed. My hands grab for support, clutching one tree and then the next as I pull myself forward.

Behind me the trees crowd in, blocking my view of the house. I usually have a good sense of direction, but time feels suspended. The wind whips my hair into my eyes. I bump into another tree, feel that strange breath, like everything has shifted, and I hug the trunk tighter to keep from falling. I push my hair out of my eyes, and when I do, I see the girl weaving noiselessly between the trees, her gown a glaring white flag against the darkened forest. Goosebumps pebble my arms.

I follow. I can't seem to stop myself. As I stumble into another tree, she stops. I hide, peeking between a gap in the twisted branches. Her gown flutters up, revealing a quick flash of pale leg. It's only then that I realize she's glowing. Her skin radiates a strange, murky light.

A ghostly light.

Wait, the girl in my dreams is a ghost?

"Wake up," I rasp, and pinch the skin above my elbow. Pain ripples up my arm. Nothing changes. The girl in white continues her journey. Her thick cord of dark hair dances along her back as she moves.

I must be dreaming, and yet the cold, wet wind bites at my skin, and my cheek stings from pressing it against the rough tree bark. You don't feel pain in dreams. I know from experience.

She reaches a small clearing. If she gets too far ahead, I'll lose her. The impulse to follow, to connect with her, is overpowering.

I push away from my hiding place and draw in a breath to call out to her. As I do, sweat trickles down my neck. A strange ache stabs through my bones. I watch as the air in the clearing thickens in front of the girl. A sudden mist ripples forth, stretching out its glittering fingers as if to grab her. I put my hand on the tree to steady myself, unable to look away.

"Hey!" I finally manage to shout.

She spins around. Surprise registers on her face, and in the blink of an eye, she disappears.

I force my eyes closed and then open. Only a small wisp of the strange mist remains.

My hand finds my head of its own free will, a reflex, as if my mind will explode if I don't hold it in. I've been dreaming about a ghost, and now it's here. In my grandparents' backyard.

And it saw me.

It actually *heard* me and looked straight at me.

A shiver snakes down my spine. Every horror flick I've ever seen flies in a chaotic jumble through my brain, and one irrefutable fact stands out. Something everyone agrees on.

Once one of "them" sees you, it's never good.

The time between light and dark accelerates and night

soon rules. The wind gains strength as if to warn me of my own stupidity. From this spot in the woods, I can't see the lights to my grandparents' house. I'm alone. In a strange place. A flash of lightning rips across the sky. A loud clap of thunder shakes the ground. The air around me crackles. The feeling of being watched returns, but I can't see anything.

Panic settles in, and I plow back the way I came, not paying attention to my steps, which have grown wilder since I chased the girl.

She saw me.

No. I made her up when I was a little boy. She was never real, ghost or otherwise.

She saw me. She saw me. She saw me.

I stumble, catch myself, and forge forward. I've been dreaming about a ghost. My genetics being what they are, I could be crazy. Mom certainly is.

A drop of rain lands on my forehead. I brush it away. A useless gesture. Within minutes, the rain streaks between the trees as if searching just for me. I finally break through, glad to be out of the woods. With rain pelting down, I run along a dirt path that's grown muddy and slick, and I nearly slide past the back gate in my rush to safety. When I dash through the back gate, I find Grandma standing on the porch, her hands on her hips and a frown on her face. "Where in the world did you tear off to?"

I vault up the stairs, out of the rain, and into the bright halo cast by the porch lights. My heart is beating in my throat, and my side aches from running. I may be taller, but when I look down at Grandma, something about her makes me feel very small. "I thought…well…the woods and…"

I try to catch my breath and focus my thoughts, but it's like a fever has set in, making my tongue thick and dumb. No way am I telling her the truth: that I saw a ghost, a female ghost dressed in white, one whom I've been dreaming about my whole life. It's so cliché, it can't be true. To save myself from embarrassment, I search for a logical answer that won't reveal itself. No doubt I look and sound like a complete idiot.

"Look at you," she finally huffs. "You're filthy. Those pants have a good four-inch layer of mud on them. And I suppose those are your only decent pair of sneakers?"

They are. I throw her a pained expression.

She sighs. "Wait here."

The back screen door squeaks open and slaps shut as she goes inside. I'm shivering now. The wind is cool, and my clothes are wet, and I feel every inch of the weather. Thankfully, Grandma returns in no time with a towel. "Take off your clothes and wrap yourself up in this."

I stare at her, embarrassed. "Y-you want me to st-strip out here?"

"Well you're not getting into my house with those clothes on. Don't worry. There's no one around for miles. You could strip naked and do yard work, and no one would be the wiser."

I can feel the forest and all its secrets looming close by. Apparently Grandma doesn't know about the ghost.

She hangs the towel on the railing. "When you're done, put your dirty clothes on the chair," she says, pointing to an old rocker moving back and forth in the wind. At least I hope it's the wind. My imagination is caught, and I can't seem to look away.

"Dylan!" Grandma calls, snapping my attention from the rocker back to her. She looks me up and down and shakes her head. "What's wrong with you?"

"N-nothing. I'm just c-cold."

She rolls her eyes and holds out her hand. "I'll take your sneakers and clean them now, but I suggest you hurry up and develop better common sense, because this is the one and only time I'll help you this late."

I nod, kick off my shoes, and hand them to her. She grimaces at the muck stuck on the soles and dripping from the laces, and goes inside.

I turn around and peer into the darkness beyond the glow of the back porch lights. It's kind of weird a ghost would show up before it was completely dark out. Then again, I'm no expert on the subject. Maybe ghosts can appear whenever and wherever they want.

With that in mind, I quickly strip to my boxers, wrap the towel around my waist, and place my wet clothes over the rocker before going inside. I wish I could forget what I've seen, but I can't. My insides are all jittery, and I still can't think straight.

I catch Grandpa's eye as I make my way to my bedroom, and his gruff voice follows me. "Bet you won't do that again anytime soon."

The crazy dog is sitting at his feet, and the light from the television washes Grandpa's face in a strange, pale light. I'm reminded of the girl, and wonder how long she's been haunting the woods. What if she was part of our family? Cursed to roam the land until someone frees her from this world? Maybe she's been visiting my dreams because I'm the one who's destined to free her.

Maybe I'm not the only one who's seen her.

I step closer. "Hey, Grandpa?"

He grunts, and continues to watch TV. The dog's ears flatten, and he growls at me like he wants to rip out my throat.

My nerves prickle, but I stand firm. It's only a dog. Grandpa wouldn't let it attack me. At least I hope not. He's probably thinking I'm not the brightest kid after the stunt I just pulled, and if I get bit, I deserve it. "Do you have a computer?"

He finally looks at me. "Whadaya want one of them for?"

"I don't know. I was just wondering."

"Your aunt Susie gave me satellite TV and a computer for Christmas. Told me getting on the internet would do wonders for the ranch, but I got all the business I need. If someone wants me, I got a phone."

I shake my head. Old people.

Seeing my disbelief, he snuffles and turns back to the TV. "Anyway, when they installed the satellite, they set me up for internet service, but I haven't dug the computer out of the box yet. Why bother? Hackers'll just mess it up."

Everything is set up and the computer is still in the box? He had to be kidding. I clutch the towel tighter. "If I show you a few tricks and install a crap load of protection to keep hackers out of your hair, can I use it?"

He stares at me for more than a few seconds, like he's digging through my brain for information. "This isn't about any of those porn sites, is it? That stuff will rot you to the bone."

My throat tightens, and a flash of heat burns my face. Talk about uncomfortable. "No, sir."

I don't usually use formal address, but I'm hunting for some good luck.

It doesn't look like I'm going to find any, until he shrugs. "I guess so, but I'll be watching you."

I exhale and turn away. A little research will do me good.

After a quick shower and dry boxers, it's late and everyone else is in bed. You'd think with all the times I've been forced to move, a new room and strange noises wouldn't be a big deal. With everything that's happened, I can't settle down. I can't stop thinking about the girl in white. It takes me a second to find my cheap-as-dirt MP3 player that I picked up at a pawn shop in Texas three years ago. I flop onto the bed, plug in my ear buds, and zone out to the sound of heavy drums, wailing guitars, and the lead singer's gravelly voice.

Staring at the ceiling, I begin to memorize its subtle pattern. I've got dozens of ceiling dips and shadows in my head to compare this one to. That eerie "new room" sensation slowly dissolves and my body grows heavy. I finally unplug myself and slip into a restless sleep.

Flip and turn. Jerk and sweat. Against my will, the smoky shadows envelop me, and when I'm spit out onto the other side of my subconscious, the girl is there. I can see every slope and curve of her. She doesn't look like a mental creation of the perfect girl, yet she's perfect. In every way. We stand, toe to toe. She cups my cheek, the feel feather light, and my skin tingles. Her breath slips across my skin as she whispers in my ear, "Who are you?"

I jolt awake, shaking. Sweat clings to my skin. I'm at a loss as to where I am, and then I hear voices. Arguing.

The clock reads ten after midnight. I pull my hand down my face and sigh, listening to the shrill tone leaking through my door. I know that voice. I roll out of bed, and ease my door open, only then hearing the other voice calmly striving for reason. I soundlessly make my way to the kitchen, but stop short of the room at a point where the shadows hide me.

Grandma sits at the table wearing a bright pink, girlie nightgown. It's nothing like I expect a grandma to wear. She holds a cup of coffee in her hands and a shocked expression on her face. Mom, still in jeans and a t-shirt, is leaning against the counter, tapping an unlit cigarette. Her face is stiff, her eyes haunted. She wants to light up, but she's smart enough not to do it in her mother's house.

Grandma shakes her head. "You can't leave him."

"He belongs here."

No guesses needed to know who *he* is.

"What does that mean?" The confusion in Grandma's voice matches what I feel.

"I can't deal with him anymore, okay?"

"He's your son, Addison."

Mom taps the cigarette so hard, the end splits and tobacco spills out. She cusses and gives Grandma a hard look. "You're wrong there. I've tried to ignore the signs, but they're getting stronger. He's his father's son through and through. Love 'em and leave 'em Dylan. But that's not all. Far from it."

Grandma only sputters. "I-I don't see how—"

Mom leans forward. "He's obsessive. Whatever he wants, he gets. He doesn't back down until he does. Just watch. You'll see. It's *unnatural.*"

"And you blame Dylan's father? I thought he didn't know his father."

"With his DNA? Dylan doesn't have to know him."

"Honey, it sounds like you're punishing a boy for his father's sins."

A bitter bark of laughter escapes Mom. "Dylan hasn't been a boy for a long time now. God knows why he's still hanging onto me."

"Addison!" Grandma scolds gently. "Dylan loves you."

Tears flood her eyes. "He pities me."

"Baby," Grandma's voice holds a wealth of sympathy, and she begins to rise. "You've had it so rough for so long..."

"Don't." Mom motions her back down and turns away, gripping the countertop until her knuckles turn white. Her back is to me, but her voice shakes with emotions I've never heard before. "I can't do this anymore. I've given him as much as I can. He's changing too fast, and now..."

Her sudden, tiny gasp for breath is swallowed by a sob. "Nobody understands. It's so hard. Looking at Dylan. Seeing *him.* He's stealing Dylan away, and I can't stop it." Her chest stutters up and down, and when she looks at Grandma, there's a deep-seated dread behind her eyes. "Worse, I don't want to. Dylan doesn't belong. He's never really belonged."

Grandma puts her hand to her temple, as if to cradle her mind, to comfort her distress. Thick silence descends on the kitchen. The truth is finally out. Deep down, I've always known. The scared looks. The nervousness.

The empty hole I've always carried within me grows heavy.

"Honey," Grandma finally says. "I don't know what to say."

A sad vulnerability washes over Mom's face. "You know, I thought I loved him. He was so handsome, and I was so young. I thought we'd be together forever. But he showed me the cruelest fairy tale of all, and I can't pretend anymore."

"Addy." Grandma holds out her hand, begging Mom to take it.

Mom stares at the hand, the pull to take it a visible struggle. Her eyes reflect her tension as they shift to Grandma's blue ones. "You love me, don't you?"

"Since the moment you came into my life."

"You want me to be happy, don't you?"

"That's all I've ever wanted."

"I brought Dylan here to set him free." Mom's lips quiver. She puts her fingertips to them, whether to stop their trembling or stop the words that flow in hurtful waves. "Please," she whispers past her fingers, "make him go. If you don't, I honestly don't think I'll ever be happy again."

With Grandma shaking her head as if she can't believe what she's hearing, Mom whirls about and runs out the back door.

I shiver though I'm not cold. My mind feels like it's encased in ice, and I need to chip away at the frozen bits and pieces to figure out what's going on. None of it makes sense.

Grandma stays seated, her eyes unfocused and confused. "Oh God," she whispers. "This can't be happening. Help her."

I hear the car start. Mom has run to the front of the house.

She's leaving, and I can't seem to feel anything. I stand there in the shadows, a shell of skin and bones, with a battered soul.

Grandma gets to her feet and heads toward the front door without seeing me. I've become a shadow, and I follow quietly behind her.

She pushes the screen door open and steps onto the front porch among the calls of the crickets and frogs. Mom's car speeds away, trailer in tow, spitting mud and water and gravel toward the porch and off into the yard, where bits of rock ping off the ugly metal sculptures. Grandma's hands cover her mouth, and after a moment, her breathing becomes a ragged mess.

Mom's done it again. She's left her family with no excuses, except for a finger pointing squarely at me. The unwanted son. I push at the door and Grandma twirls about, her eyes shadowed by sadness. "Dylan. What are you doing up?"

"She's gone." Something inside me is slowly withering, taking me with it. Nausea creeps over my body.

She stares after the twin spots of red swiftly fading from sight. "She'll be back."

"No, she won't." It's as if Mom's been whispering it in my ear since the day I was born. Everything she's done has led to this moment. It's hard to feel sorry, or mad, or anything. I'm too numb.

We continue to stare at the lights until they're swallowed by the night. "I guess that's why she never said much on the way up here. She never intended to stay."

"She'll be back."

Grandma sounds confident. "Is that what you told Grandpa the first time she left?"

Her arms snake about her waist in a comforting hug. "She came back."

What's wrong with her? Mom ditches her family for a nomadic life and for seventeen years she doesn't contact them—not even to say she's alive? I seriously don't get it. What bizarre hope is Grandma hanging onto?

Out of nowhere, anger, fueled by my sour stomach and a killer headache, wells inside me. "Stop kidding yourself. She didn't come back. She barely slowed down to throw me out of the car." I thrust out my jaw and glare up into the star-spangled night. "God! She just keeps the surprises coming, doesn't she? Too bad they all suck."

"Don't say that." Grandma wraps her warm fingers around my arm. I can feel her shaking. "Your mother is—"

"Yeah," I interrupt, saving her the effort of lying. "I know. You forget, I lived with her longer than you did. I know *exactly* what she is."

I have no energy left. Shaking from the weakness that's suddenly infected my body, I tug the screen door open. "I'll leave in the morning."

"What?" Grandma blocks my way inside. I could pick her up and toss her aside, but she doesn't seem to understand that fact. Her eyes have taken on a strange light. "You aren't going anywhere. You're home now."

Home? I don't know what the word means. She's upset. She doesn't know what she's saying. "You don't owe me anything. Why should you? You don't know me."

"Yes, I do. You're my grandson, and that's all I need to know."

"Even if Mom's right?" I challenge. "I'm no angel."

"No one around here is. We're all a rotten bunch of apples, so you'll fit right in. You're staying, and that's that."

I stare at Grandma. Her pale eyes crackle with undeniable authority. It won't last long, her wanting me. I change friends faster than I do TV channels, and no one has ever kept in touch. I disappear, and they're happy to let me go. Grandma just doesn't know any better yet.

She lets out a breath of pent-up air. "Go to bed. I'm gonna pray that tomorrow is a better day."

"Whatever."

She pushes me inside. "Just wait. It will be."

I head toward my room, my feet dragging. I'm barely holding it together. My insides melt, but there's no warm fuzziness to this feeling. It fans out in wave after dangerous wave. And when I reach my bed, I fall onto the too-soft mattress and stop thinking.

Yet sadly, I live on.

Armed and Dangerous

The hounds were out in force. Navar's nasty creations, more monster than manageable, were scratching the land and sniffing the air when Kera stepped back into her own realm. She hadn't thought they would be so close. With her mind filled with Dylan, she'd burst through the barrier and into a net of trouble. She cautiously moved away, but not fast enough.

The hounds yipped and howled, catching her scent. She sped through the forest, lunging around the brush and vaulting over obstacles until she reached Lani's sister and the caves where society's undesirables hid. She released a sigh of relief only when she crossed the secret entrance, still invisible because of its collective spell that also covered any scent or tracks leading there. For now, she was safe. At least, as safe as she *could* be.

She'd let the shock of finding Dylan alive in the human realm distract her and she'd nearly been caught. Her foolishness surprised her.

To those who stopped to stare, she nodded a harried greeting. How scandalous she must look, all disheveled. Yet the few mothers she spied rocking their children wouldn't condemn her. Their eyes held only curiosity and concern.

The people were a ragged group, and their plight tugged at Kera's heart. Through no fault of their own, they were bound to a dark existence. Their skin had grown pale and thin, and their eyes red-rimmed. Yet, these were the strongest of their kind. Disease had ravaged many, taking the weak and helpless, and now hunger threatened those who remained. Tunnels were being excavated in an effort to secretly bring in supplies, because with Navar and his men so close by, she and her father had been forced to cut back on their weekly visits.

With shaking hands, Kera wiggled into the space allocated for Lani and her sister Signe. She found Signe huddled around an earth heater, a metallic contraption that poked into the ground and gathered the earth's heat, keeping the cave warm and dry. She was humming a sad tune and sewing a button on one of Lani's shirts. Seeing Signe brought to mind kindness and secrets and forever friends.

Signe glanced up, and the hurt in her eyes mirrored Kera's own. Tears sparkled behind her lashes. "She's hanging in the square. Nailed to the post like a criminal. Her head on a spike. What was her crime?"

Shame pinched Kera's chest. While she'd been hiding in the other realm, one of her best friends had been mourning the death of her sister. Alone. She knelt before Signe and hugged her. "She was innocent. The sweetest of us. I followed Navar, thinking I could help her, but there were too many of them. I'm so sorry."

Remembering her inability to rescue her friend had bile rising in her throat, and to think of her hanging in the square for all to see… Silent tears broke free.

Signe hugged her tighter. "She wouldn't have wanted you to risk your life for hers. You know she wouldn't."

"I know, but—"

"No. Don't do that to yourself." Signe gripped the edge of her sleeve and patted away the evidence of their sorrow. It was only then that she noticed Kera's lack of clothing. "What's going on?"

Kera stood. That she'd been able to break through the wall separating the two realms still unsettled her, and seeing Dylan kept her off balance in a way that made everything she did seem unreal. "I…I need to borrow some clothes."

Signe pushed back a lock of curly red hair that defied containing and looked down at the clothes in her hands. "You can have these. I don't know why I'm mending them. She's not coming back, I know that, but I couldn't bear to see them in such disrepair." The freckles splashed across her nose and pale cheeks brightened, as if she were admitting to doing something wrong.

The clothes she held were cut in a boy's style, but were made for Lani. She wore them when she went foraging, more of an excuse to scout out the area for anyone nosing around. It was a job Lani had taken upon herself, and one the group took advantage of.

Signe tied off the thread and stood. "I won't ask you where your clothes are, but are you in trouble?"

Kera's gaze swept the tiny space. Their only privacy from the others who lived in the caves was a rickety screen made of woven branches. The whir of earth heaters, plus the sound of tunnels being dug, rattled the air.

Fearing they could be overheard, Kera kept her voice quiet. "What do you know about the barrier?"

Signe turned Kera around and helped her out of the cumbersome layers of underskirts. "Not much. Only that to go there, to try and cross between the realms, will bring about death."

She turned Kera back around and handed her the trousers.

The well-worn cloth slipped over her skin, whisper soft. It wasn't the first time she'd worn Lani's clothes, but pulling on the dark trousers made her wonder why Lani hadn't worn clothes that blended in with the forest. Why wear a bright blue dress?

"Lani was found close to the barrier." Kera watched Signe's face. "Too close."

Her friend bit her lip in an effort to stop its trembling. "She was foraging. Don't look at me like that. She wouldn't cross over. What would she gain by doing so?"

Now she knew something was wrong. Lani never foraged in anything but the clothes Signe had just mended. She couldn't keep the secret a moment longer. "I found a rip in the wall."

Signe hugged Lani's shirt to her chest. "How? Where?"

"So you know nothing about it? Did Lani?" Kera held out her hand for the dark shirt.

"No." Signe handed over the shirt and shook her head. "She would have told me. You know her—she told us everything. If the wall is weakening, then it has to do with Navar. Everything is falling apart, and it's all because of him. He'll do anything to gain the throne."

Kera finished buttoning her shirt. "You're probably right. Navar's treachery shouldn't surprise me, but it does."

Signe swept Kera's heavy braid aside and helped her into a canvas duster. Buttoned, it fit tightly around Kera's torso, but the fabric had been scored around the legs for ease of movement. When Kera stood still, it hung like a proper lady's coat. Lani had called it practical femininity.

Signe adjusted the sleeves by cuffing them once. "You're lucky you got away. He's cast a net of fear so wide, no one feels safe. Those who used to be our friends are turning on us to save their own skins."

With the collar flipped into place, Signe's hands stilled, chilling Kera's neck. She slowly pulled them away and her voice grew thin. "Did she die quickly?"

The pain of losing her sister filtered through Signe's words. Kera looked straight into her friend's eyes. "Your sister is the bravest woman I've ever known. Her death was quick."

Signe closed her eyes and nodded. "I told her not to go foraging."

"Are you in need of food?" The supplies had been thin lately, but she hadn't thought their stores had gotten dangerously low.

"We're always in need, but she could've waited. I-I think it was a ruse. She was a protector at heart. I believe she wished to make sure everyone was safe before she came home."

"That sounds like her." Lani and Signe weren't just sisters, they were best friends, all three of them were. Losing Lani was like losing part of herself.

Kera turned away, but Signe wouldn't let her go. "You see it, don't you? The stench of decay beneath the perfection Navar is creating? We can't afford to ignore it much longer. If we do, we'll all perish."

Kera saw it. Signe feared it. Lani had died because of it.

Never again.

"I won't let anything happen to you. To any of you." Kera squeezed her friend's hands. "I promise."

"Lani promised me that, too. I'm just afraid—"

Whatever she was going to say, she stopped short and moved away.

Afraid of what? Kera could badger Signe to find out, but she was barely holding herself together. Things were spinning out of control. Kera didn't like the helplessness that had infused Teag. It weakened the people and made them more susceptible to Navar's wishes. She had to find a way to infuse them with hope.

She had to get rid of Navar.

A fine sheen of sweat formed along her temples. She'd contemplated getting rid of Navar before, but never seriously. Her people wore blinders, and ripping them off wouldn't be easy. She'd have to make people see Navar for who he truly was. Once his true nature was revealed, she would somehow force him from power.

Show Navar that he wasn't—

Her mind flashed to Dylan and the power she felt in his presence. If she could tap into that power, she could use it to neutralize Navar's reach for the throne. Except, Dylan lived beyond their world. Why he lived there and not here was a mystery she needed to solve. So deep in thought, she jumped when Signe touched her arm.

"What's wrong?" Signe asked. "You're breathing oddly."

Kera's confidence immediately sank, knowing Signe would most likely disapprove of her plan. "What if I told you I crossed the barrier?"

Her friend gasped, and her pale skin turned even paler.

"I didn't mean to, but when I did, I saw *him*. The boy from my dreams."

"Oh, no…"

The look of disbelief mixed with dread on Signe's face matched the feeling inside Kera. "I know, but when I saw him, I felt a surge of power."

"You think he's a *first*?"

Kera nodded. "Trapped in the human realm. He has to be, right? It would explain our dreams, how intense they always are. How whenever we need each other, one of us appears."

Signe wrung her hands. "You must be careful—"

"The hounds are close!" A child ran by, his warning a harsh whisper. "The hounds!"

The digging machines stopped. The air stilled. Everyone held their breath.

All too quickly, the bay of the hounds echoed within the caves. They were close, but by the sound of it, they were moving fast, and…away from the area. Knowing that didn't stop Kera's skin from crawling. Like all of Navar's creatures, the beasts didn't differentiate between their intended quarry and those unfortunate enough to find themselves in their path. Only one thing could make Navar pull the hounds away from the hunt.

There were other, more deadly hunters in the forest.

Kera glanced at Signe, who had turned to rummage in an old bag.

"I have to go," Kera said.

"Wait. Wait."

"Signe, I have to go." She had to get home, had to warn her father they were making another sweep for the undesirables.

Her friend brought out a small bundle and pressed the package into Kera's hands. "One of the boys…he found it and brought it back. It's Lani's." She took a step back. "Take it. It's useless to me."

Once unwrapped, the shiny blade's edge winked blue in the dim light. Lani's dagger, made of *incordium*, the strongest metal created by the ancients. Kera looked to Signe. "I can't take this."

"Yes, you can. I know it's old, but its properties are useful, especially against magic, and I know you know how to use one. She'd want you to have it. *I* want you to have it."

Signe wasn't like Lani. She had a soul so gentle, she couldn't eat a carrot if she thought a rabbit had eyed it first. The metal felt warm in Kera's hands, and if the legends were true, *incordium* wasn't just strong, it was a conductor. It could absorb and spit back any magic that was aimed at its user. It was Lani's most prized possession.

And now it was hers.

A husky thank you passed Kera's lips as she tucked the dagger under her belt.

"Keep it on you at all times."

Kera nodded mindlessly.

Signe grabbed her friend's arm. "Kera, please do as I ask. You're taking too many risks."

"I'll keep it on me." It was a promise she could easily keep. After a quick hug, she paused by the woven screen. "I'll be back with provisions. Tell everyone to stay put."

Kera slipped out of the cave's entrance and raced over brambles and dodged trees, moving in the opposite direction of the hounds and their handlers. She had neared the edge of the forest when she heard the unmistakable *swoosh-click* of broken wings.

Millispits. Tiny, winged amphibian-type creatures with sharp, serrated fingers, no mouths, and large, glowing eyes. Imperfectly created from magic to do two things: kill anything that moves with their serrated fingers and long, venom-filled tail, then die.

Beads of sweat dotted Kera's skin. They were close. Too close. She pulled out the dagger and scrambled up a tree, the weight of the *incordium* calming her. Crouching on a sturdy limb, her back to the trunk, she waited for the ground swarm to pass.

With quiet precision, she slowed her breathing. Her muscles ached within her confined position, but she didn't dare move.

The swarm stopped. The familiar sounds within the forest were gone, leaving a dead silence more terrifying than the sound of the millispits. Kera's imagination wouldn't still. She didn't want to see what they were doing, but she had to know. Ever so slightly, she shifted her weight.

Crouched in the brush a short distance from her, a mountain lion panted, its attention centered on the swarm gathered on the ground, waiting. The soft huff of its breath filtered through the underbrush, and in the blink of an eye, the swarm attacked, bleeding and stinging the predator from its hiding place. It didn't get far before it was covered with millispits. A few seconds more, and it stopped moving, then died, while dozens upon dozens of millispits twitched their last beside it.

Disgusting creatures. One more reason why she hated Navar. He thought he was so clever restricting their movements to the forest and making sure they couldn't fly by breaking their wings, but they were the epitome of evil. Except for the creature they were killing, only the moon's glow saw them dead.

How could anyone create something so malevolent and call it a necessity? Life had lost its value. Killing was all Navar understood these days.

Out of the corner of her eye, Kera saw a few millispits leap-flying from tree to tree, their broken wings fluttering grotesquely, their thin, springy legs pumping, their large eyes searching. The viscous goop covering their bodies helped them cling wherever they landed.

The flutter and splat of a millispit sounded close by.

Her breathing became a ragged whisper of sound as Kera watched the slimy creature slide into view near her shoulder. The large, red eyes zeroed in on her.

Before it could warn the others with its throaty grunt, Kera flipped her knife into her opposite hand and, in two precise swipes, detached the creature's tail and head from its body. The carcass flopped onto a nearby branch and dangled by a thread of mucus.

Kera suppressed a shudder and looked away only to hear a throaty grunt. Turning back, she found another millispit hovering over the dead one's dismembered body.

It was time to move. Kera leapt to a nearby branch, flying through the air until she landed easily on the next limb, only to leap off that one as quickly as she could.

The millispits below fluttered their wings, many rising off the ground a few feet until they could cling to the trees and begin the climb. Most stayed on the ground, matching her move for move.

All she needed was to get out of the forest. Navar had created the creatures to hunt down the "tainted" hiding in the forest, and Kera had never been so thankful for the magic that kept them bound to the area. Sensing the thinning of the trees, the millispits throaty grunts grew more excited. Kera had no idea what they were saying to each other, but that they had even a minute trace of intelligence was frightening.

With her lungs burning from the effort to stay ahead, Kera leapt to the last tree limb that could hold her weight, then jumped to the ground. The millispits were still too close. She darted forward, the dagger gripped tightly in her hand, and burst from the forest. Whirling about, she held the dagger in front of her and glared back at the creatures swarming toward her.

The majority of millispits stopped, but a few continued forward. Kera's eyes widened. Somehow, the magical boundary didn't exist for them. With a cry of alarm, she staggered back and swung at the first one to reach her, cutting it cleanly in half.

She continued to back up, hacking at one and then another. When they lay at her feet dead, she peered at the mass of millispits. How had these few crossed? It should have been impossible.

The millispits' grunts reverberated within the group. Suddenly, over a dozen leapt forward, crossing the boundary line.

The line that should kill them instantly when crossed, but didn't.

Kera turned and ran.

There was no avoiding the village. Darting down the cobbled streets, Kera scanned for items she could use to protect herself. The first house she came to had a rainwater barrel, its lid halfway off. Kera grabbed the lid by the knobby handle and held it in front of her like a shield.

She faced the millispits just in time. Three of them smacked into the lid and embedded their tail stingers into the swollen wood.

A cry of "millispits" echoed close by. A horse harnessed to a wagon screamed as the creatures clawed their way over it. One came close and she batted it away, but not before its serrated claws cut her cheek. As she made her way deeper into the village, those who weren't out in the fields came to her aid. Bursts of magic careened around Kera, but no amount of magic affected the millispits. Only a direct hit with Kera's *incordium* dagger ended their lives.

In no time, viscous slime covered Kera's blade, dulling its impact. After slicing one of the creatures in two, she paused and swiped her weapon clean on her pants.

Looking around, she saw a little girl standing in the doorway of her house, crying as her mother fought off a millispit with a blast of steam she'd collected in her hands. The ball of hot air struck the slimy creature, stopping it for just a moment before it shuddered back to life.

Kera spotted another millispit creeping forward, its serrated fingers clicking on the cobbles as it eyed the child. Darting over, Kera got between the girl and the creature. Grunts sounded, and before it could move closer, Kera swept the blade through its body, cutting it in two.

"Go inside," she ordered the little girl. "And don't come out until it's safe."

The girl nodded and then screamed, pointing to something over Kera's shoulder. With a hard shove, Kera forced the girl inside, slammed the door shut and turned, dagger at the ready. Five millispits came at her. She cut down the first in mid-flight. The second flapped into the door and hung there, eyeing her. Its tail zipped toward her. Kera sliced off the stinger, then used the butt of the dagger to smash its head. A slap of goo hit her skin, and then a sharp pain pierced her collarbone. Another moist plop landed on the side of her neck followed by a pinch. Another jabbed her thigh.

An involuntary groan rolled from Kera's throat. The dagger slipped from her fingers, and she collapsed to her knees, her hands clawing at the millispits, jerking the nasty things off her body before she fell.

The last thing she saw before she passed out was the tip of a millispit's tail, its stinger still pulsing venom into her leg.

Millispits kill always, Navar's voice echoed in Kera's head. *Wait and see. They will see the end to our half-breed problem.*

CHANGE HAPPENS

Waking in a strange room makes me nervous, but then last night comes flooding back. Mom's gone, and she didn't even say good-bye.

I should be mad as hell. Instead, I'm oddly confused.

The actual words have already faded, but I remember Mom being sad, angry even, and the one thing I can't forget is how afraid she sounded. Of me.

At one point, she loved me. I'm almost sure of it, but it's like remembering a movie I haven't seen in a long time. There are images of warmth, but no real sense of reality.

He's changed too fast.

What did that mean? I recoil from the question, unsure I even want to know.

Someone knocks on my door.

I groan and sink under the covers. I don't want to see anyone. I don't want to do anything but close my eyes and recapture the painlessness of sleep.

The door opens. Light footsteps cross the room. They stop by the bed.

"Dylan?" Grandma calls in a gentle voice reserved for the

mentally fragile. I should know. I've used that tone on Mom more times than I can count.

The down-filled bed pulls me deeper, and I willingly escape into the cocoon of feathers and warmth.

She doesn't try and get me to come out. She places something on the bedside table and leaves, closing the door softly behind her.

Cocooned in the bedding like I am, the heat, which is at first comforting, becomes stifling. Cool air finds me as I struggle free of the covers. With a hard push, I roll to a sitting position and slouch against the raw ache that won't go away. A letter lies on the bedside table with Mom's handwriting on it.

I feel like I'm strangling on a mixture of hope and fear. My fingers shake as I reach for the envelope and rip it open. Mom's sweeping handwriting unfolds across the page.

Dylan,

I can't stay here, and I can't take you with me. You know how guys are. One look at a kid and they freak. Maybe alone, I can find someone to love me. You're going to think that's lame, but I don't care. You don't need me anymore. You haven't for a long time. I'm not going to feel bad about this, so don't try following me and laying on the guilt. I'm over that. I was never a good mother, anyway.

Addy

I reread the letter over and over again. This is her way of letting me down easy? There's so much she doesn't say. My vision blurs, until I can't see the letters or even the paper. I love her, but I don't count. I can't remember a time when I did.

I fall back on the mattress. Nothing enters my mind or leaves it. I'm detached from everything except each breath I take.

In and out.

The letter slips from my fingers. I don't react.

In and out.

Minutes pass, or is it hours?

In and out.

The door opens. Grandma whispers my name. She picks up the letter, gasps, and cradles my cheek in her palm. She speaks. I don't hear.

I'm aware, yet unresponsive—a lump of living flesh. She calls Grandpa. Their voices are muddled. I can hear their concern, but the words don't sink in. Grandpa grabs my hand and hefts me up and over his burly shoulder. He carries me to the bathroom and gently places me in the tub.

Without warning, a shock of cold water slams me back into reality.

Sputtering, I struggle to sit up, blinking against the heavy stream and cussing up a storm.

A far-off voice calls, "Is he okay, George?"

Grandpa turns the water off, his eyes on me.

I'm shivering like a newborn puppy, and I clench my teeth to stop their chattering. "That was messed up!"

He throws a relieved glance over his shoulder. "That fixed him."

"What's going on?" I say.

Grandpa hauls me to my feet. "You needed a little jolt. You know, a kick start. Seen it a million times in Nam."

"S-seen what?"

"Shock." He throws a towel around my shoulders and helps me out of the shower. The bathroom is barely big enough for one person, let alone two big guys. He rubs the towel vigorously along my body, reawakening my nerves and warming my skin. "You shut down, so I restarted you."

He pokes his head out of the bathroom and says, "He needs new skivvies and some jeans."

Grandma hands them over, her face wreathed in concern, then steps back out of sight.

"Strip and put these on," Grandpa says, and hands me the clothes.

He keeps me steady while I do as he says, and after I'm dressed, he leads me out. When I see Grandma, she puts her hand to her chest and sighs. "You scared me to death!"

I slowly lower myself to the bed. "Sorry, I'm not really sure what happened."

An unasked question passes between Grandma and Grandpa, who's standing beside me. He nods, and she shows me the letter. Everything rushes back. I feel sick, and to my horror, I start to cry. I never cry. Grandpa brings my head to his torso. He rubs my hair as Grandma squats before me. She takes my hands as tears slip down her cheeks. "I don't understand the need that's in her, Dylan. It isn't your fault. Do you understand that? She's selfish and weak, and you deserve to be treated better. We all do."

I can feel their pain, the longing they have for a daughter who will never love them back. We all want the same thing, but only I know it will never happen. I've come to accept the absence of Mom's love, while they still cling to hope.

This new understanding soon leaves my eyes dry. I refuse to wallow in self-pity. It's better to feel nothing than hurt like this. I breathe deeply and evenly, and slowly push away.

Grandma rises, her pain still obvious as she wipes at her tears. At least she's able to function like life is worth the effort. "I'm going to cook something up. Something big. What do you want, Dylan?"

I feel empty, but not in a way that food will help. I can't speak yet.

Grandma's question falls to Grandpa. He pats my back and says, "Make us a meal fit for men."

She grins, but it doesn't reach her eyes. "I can do that."

"George," a disembodied voice crackles.

Grandpa fishes for a small walkie-talkie clipped to his belt. He presses a button along the side. "Yeah, Reggie?"

"We got problems over here on five. You need to see this to believe it."

Grandma stands in the doorway, a 'what now?' look on her face.

"What's going on?" Grandpa asks.

"I don't know. It's like..." There's a big pause. "I don't know. You seriously need to come over here."

Grandpa shares a quick glance with Grandma before pressing the button. "Okay. I'm on my way."

"I've never heard Reggie so upset," Grandma says as Grandpa heads through the doorway.

He stops and looks back at me. "Get dressed. You're coming with me."

"Now, George," Grandma warns. "He's been through enough."

"He needs to get on with life," he says, still staring at me. "Come on."

He leaves, expecting me to follow. I don't want to think, let alone move, but I know an order when I'm given one, and like it or not, I find myself moving. He served in Vietnam. Saw combat. He's the type who expects obedience even if you're wounded and can't see through the blood dripping into your eyes.

I pull on a T-shirt, slip on some socks and shoes, and follow Grandma's nod toward the back of the house. Once outside, I follow Grandpa's voice. He and the dog that nearly bit me are waiting in a shed, surrounded by all sorts of machines and some more of those weird sculptures that are in the front yard. The dog hovers near Grandpa in a protective manner. I'm smart enough to keep my distance.

On seeing me, Grandpa points to an ATV. "Ever driven one of these?"

"No."

Grandpa tosses me a set of keys. "Time to learn."

When he says learn, he isn't talking about teaching me first. He expects me to learn on the go. As he pulls away, his dog sprints ahead, and I turn on the hulking machine and follow.

Grandpa shouts instructions army boot camp style, and I do my best, but I'm failing fast. I nearly give myself whiplash, sputtering along the dirt path that runs behind the house. I'm terrible at switching gears and grind them until my ears ring. After a while, we rumble into the forest. Grandpa stops and opens a gate, which is attached to a fence that zigzags between the trees and out of sight.

"I got into the sheep business to keep the forest scrub from taking over," Grandpa says, climbing back onto his ATV. "It cuts down on fire danger, which is always a worry with trees surrounding you."

A few minutes later, we pull into a small glen packed with sheep. Dozens of tiny brown dots of fluff outfitted with curved horns and lamb faces, look our way. Nothing seems out of place, but being new to the sheep business, I wouldn't really know.

A guy around my age sporting long, shaggy black hair, a man in his fifties wearing round glasses, and an old guy who's as weathered as an ancient oak tree stand over a downed sheep. The men are a ladder of years. The younger guy only has to look at the older men to see his future self. Sheep herding is obviously a family business around here—one I'm not so keen to follow.

On seeing us, the middle-aged man comes jogging over, along with five dogs. I barely miss running them over with my ATV before I manage to come to a bone-jarring stop.

Grandpa rumbles up and shoots me a warning look—like I *tried* to run them all down. He greets the men while I get off my ATV and step one foot too close to that crazy dog. It bares its teeth and lets out a mean growl. I've had enough trauma lately, and I'm not about to let a dog bully me. I throw the mangy thing an angry look and snap out a command. "Sit."

The dog immediately sits amid a flutter of ear positions and sad, little whines. More whining joins his, and I notice the other dogs are sitting, too, confusion in their sad eyes. Everyone stares at me just as strangely.

"What?" I ask.

Grandpa calls his dog to him, but the dog only looks at me. He calls again, and finally the dog slinks away, tail between his legs.

"Your grandmother never told me you had experience with dogs."

"I don't." I've never had a pet in my life. "Mom says I'm allergic."

Grandpa's jaw twitches. "I think your mom's full of it."

He's probably right. Knowing Mom, she didn't want to bother with me *and* a pet.

Grandpa quickly sends the dogs out to keep the sheep in a tight knot and away from the downed ewe. "All right, Reggie, what happened?"

"It's Willow," Reggie says in a pained voice. "She's dead."

A series of cuss words fly out of Grandpa's mouth, and he crosses his arms over his chest. "How?"

They go to where the other men are and I follow. It's a strange sight. The ewe is lying on her side like she's asleep, but there are a lot of red speckles in her wool, and when Grandpa digs deeper, he finds tiny marks where blood has seeped out. He sits back on his haunches, his eyes still on the ewe.

Reggie scratches his head. "I don't know anything that does that."

Grandpa examines the poor animal, taking pictures with his camera phone as he does. "There's blood everywhere."

The old man standing next to Reggie does a bunch of quick hand gestures, and I realize he's using sign language. He and his son begin arguing, and I see the old man is lip reading. After a few moments, Reggie shakes his head and turns away, but the old man pulls him back.

"What's he saying, Leo?" Grandpa asks.

The younger guy—who's probably a few years older than me—digs his toe into the earth and mutters, "Something about men from another world." His deep voice is at odds with his young appearance.

"Aliens?"

"Just Pop being Pop."

Grandpa's hand balls into a fist, and he slowly mouths the words so Pop is sure to understand. "I don't need superstition right now. I need answers."

The old man drops his hands. Leo shrugs at Grandpa. "Sorry. He can be crazy."

"Mind your manners," Reggie snaps. He squats next to the dead ewe. "What's your take, boss?"

"I don't know." Grandpa's forehead wrinkles. He probes the tall grass around the ewe. "Where's her baby?"

"Can't find him."

Grandpa stands. The skin around his eyes crinkles against the mid-morning sunlight as he looks around. "Any prints?"

The three men grow nervous. "None."

"Any clues at all?" Tension mounts in Grandpa's voice.

Reggie shakes his head. "Not that we can find."

"Look harder," Grandpa barks, and then eyes Leo. "Get me my kit."

As Reggie and Pop fan out to do another sweep of the area, Leo brings back a small plastic box. It's some sort of medical kit. Grandpa pulls out a needle and a tube and draws some blood from the dead ewe.

I squat down next to him. "What do you think happened?"

"I'm not sure."

"A vampire bat?" Leo suggests.

"Bats around here are insect eaters. You'd have to go pretty far south to get vampire bats."

Leo leans closer and whispers to me. "Pop swears these woods are haunted by people we can't see until they want us to see them. By then, it's too late."

An unexpected prickling attacks my skin. Haunted? I quickly stand and peer into the woods. Did the girl in white do this? I shiver. The thought is beyond creepy.

Grandpa scowls hard and shakes the vial so the blood won't clot, completely unaware of Leo's new theory, and my sudden attention to it.

The trees crowd the meadow, all nearly identical in height and color, except a nearby tree. There's a dark, strangely-shaped spot midway up its trunk. I skirt the dead ewe to get a better look. "What's this?"

Grandpa and Leo join me. The tree is scarred, the design rendered in deep, blackened strokes. From far off it looks like a smudge. Only when I get closer can I make out the design, and it isn't pretty. There's something sinister about the circle and the deep gouges that pass through it.

Grandpa shouts over his shoulder, "Are any of the other trees defaced like this one?"

Reggie and Pop rejoin us, and when Pop sees the symbol, he steps back and spits on the ground.

Reggie touches the scarred bark. "This isn't good."

"Why?" I ask. "It's just a stupid design someone etched into the tree."

"This isn't just some stupid drawing. It's a mark of intent." He pulls his fingers away, and he sniffs at the black residue covering his fingertips. "And it's burned in blood."

Grandpa peers into the woods. I avoid looking at him, taken aback by the sharp edges that abruptly appear on his face. At the base of the tree, something shimmers in the leafy debris. I squat, pick up a stray twig, and poke at it.

"What's that?" Leo asks.

I raise the end of the stick for Grandpa to see. "Blood, I think." I dig deeper and uncover the carcass of the lamb, burned, buried, and hidden by a mess of scattered leaves.

The girl in white. A dead ewe. Blood spilled under an evil-looking symbol. A burned lamb. What kind of crazy, whacked-up place did Mom drop me off in?

Grandpa's face hardens, and he glares at the three men. "Get this flock out of here, boys. Leave twenty of the older ones behind."

The men nod and begin separating the sheep. I look at Grandpa. "This is some kind of cult thing, huh?"

"Something like that," he says, though he's distracted as he stares at the crude altar. "There's an empty black plastic bag in the front compartment of my ATV. Go get it."

I do as he says, even as a deep uneasiness slithers beneath my skin. This is out of control. I can't believe Mom wanted to get rid of me so badly that sticking me in husbandry hell with a satanic cult on the loose really sounded like a reasonable option. God, she must hate me.

When I return, Grandpa's on the phone with his closest

neighbor, grilling him to see if he knows about any strange activity happening in these parts, and to keep his eyes open. He puts the phone away and takes the bag from me.

"Are you going to call the police?" I watch him slip the dead lamb in the bag and stand.

His eyes darken. I can actually see the hardened soldier in him take over. "You're looking at him."

Grandpa is a cop? "You don't look like a cop."

"Most of the time, I don't have to be. We don't get much trouble around here. Never have."

"So, what're you going to do?"

"Dig in and wait."

As he strides away, I get the distinct feeling he's comfortable with shooting first and apologizing later.

LUCKY T⊕ BE ALIVE

Kera awoke stretched out on a bed, swathed in gauzy fabric. Steam hissed and bubbled. Water dripped slowly, pinging and plopping against glass. At the sound of bottles clinking, Kera peered across the room. Faldon, dressed in his ratty, old lab coat, his hair standing out like an eaglet's baby tuff, softly whistled a tune while he quietly puttered with his medicines. Two rows of beds, most empty, faced each other in the long, narrow room. She'd been in the infirmary many times, but mostly to help Faldon practice the art of healing.

"I'm not dead?" The croak of her voice hurt her throat and head.

The old sage drew close and smiled. "Nay, not today, though if you'd been brought to me any later…"

The clothes she'd borrowed from Lani, and the dagger, were lying on the bedside table. She touched the dagger. Signe's gift had saved her life. "If not for this, I would be dead."

"*Incordium.* A priceless gift. It can cut through anything."

All Kera cared about was that it had helped her kill the millispits. She struggled onto her elbows, touched the spot on her neck and winced. "It's hot."

"My magic is still working and may take a few more hours to

draw out all the poison." He pushed her back down, a stern look in his eyes. "It's best you stay in bed."

Normally, the command would irritate her, but all she wanted now was to lie still. "D-did anyone else get hurt?"

"Only you. Navar has felt the sting of your father's displeasure on that count." He leaned closer and whispered, "Your father is secretly pleased by the boldness of your ability, as am I. All those lessons you talked me into giving you… I feel almost safe taking credit for your skills. Almost." He pulled back, picked up a cup on the nearby bedside table and splashed water into it, then added a few drops of medicine. "Be that as it may, Navar is forbidden to use those creatures here. Ever."

It was hard to believe her father would confront Navar. "He won't obey that command."

"He will, at first. The displeasure of the people must be avoided, but then he'll become king and do as he pleases, which is why he needs a soft, feminine hand to guide him." Faldon pressed the cup into Kera's hand. "A draught to help you heal. You'll be set right by this evening."

Kera drank the medicine and handed Faldon the empty cup. "I pity the woman forced to have him."

"Why say forced? She will be queen. A title sure to dazzle any maid."

"A crown is not so alluring if it's attached to a man more murderer than leader." She closed her eyes. Already the medicine made her wish for sleep. She put her hand to her heart. "Lani's dead. Navar killed her himself. I saw it."

"I'm truly sorry."

"She's hanging in the square, her head on a spike." It made her sick to even say it. "As soon as I'm better, I'm getting her."

Faldon squeezed her hand. "She's gone. It seems someone took her body down last night."

A sigh escaped, and with it, the knot of tension she'd been carrying since Lani's death. "Thank you."

"Don't thank me. There are others who loved her as much as you." He placed the cup on the bedside table, his eyes staring at nothing and everything. He saw the future, and she longed to ask what he saw of hers, but that was a subject he refused to broach. No amount of her whining would change his mind. So she chipped away at his knowledge about Teag's future, demanding answers to questions that weighed on her mind.

"Why have we given Navar such power? It's not right." She glared at Faldon, knowing he wasn't the problem, but he wasn't doing anything to solve it, at least not fast enough.

"The majority are behind him. He's been given their allegiance. You know once given it can't be withdrawn, even if they're moved by regret. Pride is a dangerous virtue."

Frustration made her cheeks hot. "There has to be a way."

"Only if someone stronger defeats him, and there's no one stronger than Navar." Faldon turned to her. His eyes grew gentle, and he swept the hair from her face. "Be at peace. There's nothing you can do."

"Nothing I can do," she muttered. It was unlike him to think such a thing, let alone say it.

He left, and as her eyes began to droop, his words pierced like a dagger in her side. He was just like her father. Both couldn't see beyond the moment. There had to be someone stronger than Navar. Stronger and nobler. "Someone…we must find someone…"

One name flitted through her mind over and over as the sedative took effect.

Dylan.

Wired for Trouble

I pull the ATV to a stop in front of the house, near the huge iron sculptures, glad to be back from the Clearing of Death—aka pasture number five. I study the sculptures, trying to see the beauty within the bizarre, and shake my head. I don't get them. They're just a bunch of intertwining metal coils and tall spires, painted bright colors, poking out of the front lawn like aliens guarding the mothership.

Then again, one man's art is another man's lightning rod.

I need to walk through them to get to the house, and when I do, my stomach roils and threatens to empty. My head spins. Before my legs give out, I stumble up the porch steps and lunge for the front door.

Once inside, I slam the door and lean against it. This doesn't feel like a normal headache. I take a few steadying breaths before my stomach settles and my head clears, yet the headache lingers, burning like third-degree sunburn. I slowly push away from the door, still feeling weak.

"Dylan? Is that you?"

"Yeah," I manage to croak.

As I walk toward the back of the house, the migraine fades

enough to keep me from puking, so I head for the unopened computer box Grandpa has stuffed in the corner of his den. I need a distraction. Plus, if there's any info on what's happening floating around, I should be able to find it online.

When Grandma comes in to check on my progress, I plug in the last wire to the satellite modem and sit back. "That should do it."

I rub at my head where it still throbs. I've never been sick a day in my life, but the headaches… At times they're so bad, I can barely think.

"What's wrong?"

"Nothing. Just a headache."

She looks me over, and for a second, I fear she's going to sink into the role of inquisitor. Instead, she says, "I'll get you something."

It's then I realize Grandma doesn't gravitate toward unpleasantness. While Mom wallows in tacky displays of emotion, splattering everything and everyone unfortunate enough to be close by, Grandma still clutches the dream of the ideal family. Poor Grandma. Nothing will ever be right when it comes to Mom.

Or to me. My genetics have been stained by a nameless father and a self-serving mother. No matter what I do, I'll never be clean. Sometimes I wonder why I even keep trying, since I'm predestined to fail at life. But I keep going.

There's nothing else to do.

Grandma's gone and back in no time, with a glass of water and two candy-coated pills. I hold out my palm, thinking if any kind of drug could fix the hole in my soul, I would down the whole bottle. I quickly pop the pills in my mouth and nearly choke on the metallic taste of the well water. Why do I even bother? Nothing helps, but I know it'll make Grandma feel better.

"A-are you doing okay?" she asks.

Not even close. I swallow my heated reply and turn back to

the computer. "Yeah."

And that's it. No prodding. No digging on her part. Just a quick question about Mom's effect on me. She doesn't know I've embraced the void. It's easier than trying to get rid of it.

She stands back when I slip in front of the computer and bring it humming to life. Before I switch on the monitor, I see her face reflecting back at me, clouded with anxiety, a condition she's had since the moment I showed up. It's got to be rough being saddled with a kid you didn't know existed until a day ago.

I click on the monitor, erasing her image. "So…I've got to do a little set-up work still, register this, and get an account going, if that's okay."

"Of course. What do you expect to find?"

"I'm hoping whoever messed with your sheep have some kind of website. A lot of them do." I put my hand to my temple and give it a quick rub before I get started.

Out of nowhere, she asks, "What do you think of the sculptures?"

I look at her. "What?"

"Out front. The sculptures. Do you like them?"

From where I sit, there's a clear view of the front yard and the collection of strangely contorted metal statues. I'm not a huge fan of abstract art, but then it hits me. What if Grandma is the artist? No need to let her know how I really feel. "Yeah, sure."

Her stare lingers. It's one I know very well. I've had it directed at me my whole life. She's trying to figure out what's wrong with me. Good luck. I've got issues nobody would want to poke around in. Her frown deepens. Maybe she knows how messed up I am, but she doesn't want to say anything because she's too nice.

"What?" I ask. "Just say it."

Worry tinges the edges of her clear blue eyes, and then a wobbly smile appears. "Oh, never mind. I'm a silly woman."

It's the stress of Mom, me, and the dead sheep. For reasons I don't want to explore, I reinforce her fantasy that everything is fine, and I lie to her. "It'll be okay. All we need is a lead. Something to point us in the right direction."

She continues to hover over my shoulder as I get everything up and running. I can feel her eyes on me. It's not the first time people have stared, but from her, it's disconcerting. Her gaze is intense. More calculating. Every time I glance at her, she looks away.

Digging into cults and covens is boring work. Some are real, some are weird, and all of them lead me nowhere. Grandma eventually wanders off, saying something about dinner, and I can finally heave a sigh of relief. I click here, move on there. Nothing.

Hours slip by. Grandpa hasn't returned, and it's getting late. I sit back in the chair and plow my fingers through my hair. I've checked out local cults, blood sacrifices, and ancient symbols for evil. Nothing matches. Although I think it's a long shot, I type in a search for the girl in white.

Hundreds of references pop up. Mexican folk lore. Movie and book references. Even girl rappers who dress all in white. I keep narrowing my search, until I find myself on some guy's website and read his post from last night.

> *dudes you will not believe what just happened… i saw a ghost… for real… i was walking in the woods (on my way home from this awesome party over at Hank's house) and a heavy fog rolls in… okay that's not so weird for around here but the next second this girl appears out of nowhere… she's seriously pale… I mean glow in the dark white… creepy, dudes! get this… she's hot! who knew dead chicks could look so good? i totally freaked… nearly pissed my pants! but when I looked again she was gone.*

I click on his profile. All the basic info is there.

I'm straight and single and looking for action. Live in the rainy Northwest, so you know I'm a serious drinker and will smoke anything that can be rolled. Junior at Northcreek High.

I do a quick search on Northcreek and find it's the nearest high school to where I now live. A rush fills me. Bingo!

I click on his email address and type out a quick message.

hey. i'm dylan and am new to the area. i think i saw your ghost... want to swap stories?

I call out to Grandma, "What's the phone number here?"

She tells me, and I type it out and tell the guy to call me. I'm not holding my breath that he will, but it's worth a try. I write down as much as I can about him, visit his photo area, and study his face. He's a big kid, one of those guys that'll jump out of a moving car onto a skateboard because someone dares him. I know this because there are pictures of him doing it. The last one shows the waist of his pants hanging near his knees along with his boxers, and he's screaming at the top of his lungs with a "holy crap!" look on his face. It's not a pretty sight. I'm surprised the board didn't snap in two.

I shut the computer off and hunger gnaws at my gut. When's the last time I ate? The sun is going down, and I find Grandma in the kitchen, hulling a huge bowl of strawberries and staring out the window toward the woods.

She smiles when I come in. "Look at this, will you? I swear, overnight, those strawberries in that pot took off. I've never seen them this good."

I look in the back yard toward the strawberry pot I'd nearly overturned last night and the plants are full and heavy with fruit. Weird.

"Find anything on the computer?" she asks.

"Not really. Where's Grandpa?"

She nods toward the woods. "Out there still."

"He says he's digging in."

"I wouldn't be surprised." She continues to snip the tops off strawberries and drop them in a bowl, as if nothing were out of the ordinary.

How can she act so cool? My nerves stretch into thin, taut ropes. I wait for them to snap. A latent protective streak emerges, shocking the hell out of me. No way can I stay still and wait for whomever—whatever—to show up and do some more damage. "Do you think he needs company?"

"I'm sure he'd like that. Why don't I fix a snack, and you can take it to him? Do you remember the way?"

"Yeah." I never get lost. I'd like to think that's one of the reason's Mom never got worked up when I was out late. She knew I could find my way home no matter where I was. In reality, she probably just never cared if I ever showed up or not.

Unwanted memories begin to swirl through my mind; I push them away and say the very last thing I want to. "Let me help."

In no time, I'm out the door with an old rucksack slung over my shoulder, carrying a "snack" that weighs ten pounds. Grandma offers me the ATV again, but I refuse. I've been walking my whole life. No point in changing now. I stick to the trail that runs behind the back fence for as long as I can, keeping a wary eye on the woods.

I don't remember why I developed an aversion to nature. All I know is that something happened to me when I was younger, a memory I can't recall that makes the event all the scarier, especially since it scared not only me, but Mom. I've buried the memory so deep, it's impossible to bring it forth. Only the recollection of rough bark and strange whispers hovers near the edge of my thoughts.

I'd refuse to go to the park with Mom because there were so many trees. I'd beg her to move us to the city instead of the next hick town on her list so I could avoid trees altogether, but she would always stare out the window and shake her head. "You can't go to the city."

When I hit my teens and asked again, and once again she said, "You can't go to the city," I heard what she was really saying.

I didn't belong in the city.

She thought I was too stupid or too ugly or too something. Whatever it was that made me different, I knew I couldn't control it. It was inbred in me, and Mom liked it less than I did.

I stop where the trail to pasture five starts. The sun is setting, and the wind is rattling the leaves. I don't think about what I'm about to do; I dive in.

Shadows lengthen as my feet carry me deeper and deeper into the woods. Once I pass through the gate, the trees begin to move, swaying in an invisible wind—a wind I can't feel. Cold sweat prickles my skin. I stretch out my stride and break into a run, zipping past the trees so fast, I can't feel anything but the rush of air against my skin, or hear anything but the *whooshing* it makes in my ears.

I break into the small meadow, my vision shattering into a thousand bright lights, and I bend to catch my breath. I've never run that fast. Ever. It felt surreal.

A hand slaps my back, and I nearly fall over.

"Whoa there, Dylan," Grandpa says, catching me so I don't fall. He looks back from where I came, and tension fills his voice. "Is anyone following you? Did you see someone?"

I climb out of my fear and blink back the haze that's surrounding me. "No, everything's okay." Straightening, I shrug out of the backpack and hold out the bag. "Grandma sent me to give you a snack."

He takes the bag. "No time to eat. We've work to do. Ever shot a gun before?"

I snap my gaze to his. What he's saying crashes in on me. "No. Isn't that illegal without a permit, or something?"

"My property, my rules." He gestures toward a tight cluster of trees. "I've dug the foxhole over there. Prime spot."

Foxhole? Why do I get the feeling it's not connected to a furry little guy's den?

"Come on." He grabs my arm, leaving me no choice but to follow.

"I'm thinking with these trees at our back, we're good." As he jumps down, I can only stare at the massive hole he's dug. His dog is checking the place out and on seeing me, his ears prick up, and he scooches into the corner, whining. The last thing I want is to deal with a crazy Grandpa *and* a crazy dog. I wish he'd leave.

As if he can read my mind, the dog jumps out of the hole and trots away.

"Scooter!" Grandpa yells. "Where're you going, boy?"

The dog stops, looks back, and then heads into the small cluster of older sheep.

Grandpa eyes me. "I don't think my dog likes you."

"That's okay. I'm not a dog person."

"I'm setting up the supplies. Got a flashlight and extra batteries and this," Grandpa says, grabbing a huge, weird-looking shotgun made of heavy plastic and metal. "Now *this* is what I'm talking about. She's pretty, isn't she?" He rubs the barrel as if it were a living thing.

Grandpa's snapped. He's out to kill something I suspect is

already dead. I shake my head. "I can't shoot anyone. What if I accidentally kill somebody?"

He laughs, and the sound isn't pleasant. "Boy, you need a lesson in guns. This," he says, holding out the gun, "is a 40mm riot gun. It shoots out these, along with other things."

He tosses me a small, heavy square. I catch it in my hands and test its weight.

He smiles. "Bean bags will give a guy one heck of a kick in the pants."

"Where'd you get it?"

"Got a friend who's into non-lethal force. I use these to scare away wild dogs, wolves, and the occasional black bear."

I jump into the hole and give the bean bag back. He hands me the launcher. The plastic grip feels cool beneath my fingers, yet there's a heaviness to this weapon that doesn't feel right. I try to concentrate as Grandpa shows me how to load the bag and explains the mechanics of shooting.

I shake my head as I study the big gun. The unsettling feeling that's crept over me won't go away. "I don't know. It still looks like it can do some serious damage."

He claps me on the shoulder. "Let me tell you something. This great country of ours was founded on our right to bear arms. To defend our families and homes. To provide food. A gun is a tool. It's not evil. Only the intent of the one holding it has that distinction."

I understand what he's saying, but it's something else that's bothering me. The launcher still feels threatening. The forest tilts and spins as I stare at it. I quickly lean the gun against the side of the foxhole. As soon as I do, the world rights itself.

I've gotten into a few fights, but they were all fist fights. Guns seem a bit extreme. I look over at Grandpa, unsure how to deal with this.

He vaults out of the hole and heads to his ATV. He brings back a small case and hands it to me. "Put this in the corner."

I take it and read the box. US Army MREs. I put them where he tells me, and no sooner than I do, he hands me something else. Bottled water. I put the big bottles beside the MREs. When I turn back, he's holding out some binoculars.

"Go easy with these, boy. They're expensive."

I put them to my eyes and fiddle with the knobs. They aren't binoculars—they're night vision goggles.

"A man needs to take care of his tools as carefully as himself," he says, while scrounging near the ATV. "Remember that."

"Yes, sir."

Night has found the woods. Pretty soon it'll be pitch black. Grandpa's face is shadowed, as if he applied a coating of combat grease to every hollow. I put the goggles with the rest of the supplies, and when I turn around, he's there again, handing me not one, but two rifles.

The cold iron blisters my fingers, and I hiss at the pain. These have nothing to do with non-lethal force. A wave of nausea passes over me, and I dump the guns near the rest of his supplies and try to ignore the throbbing in my hands. I've got bigger things to worry about right now.

This is not the simple wait and see Grandpa had led me to believe.

He's back at the ATV shoving boxes of ammo in his pockets. After hiding the ATV in a cluster of bushes, he grabs a blanket and trots back. As nimble as a twenty-five-year-old, he jumps in the foxhole and begins spreading out what I now see is actually a camouflaged tarp.

Excitement rolls off him. The old guy is really getting into this—maybe flashing on some war memories. I hope not. When it comes to people, I like them whole and bullet-free.

I slide my tongue over my suddenly dry lips. "Grandpa," I say against a tight throat. "What're we doing here?"

He stills. There's tension in his features I've never seen before. An unflinching disquiet shines in his eyes. "Waiting for trouble."

His stare lingers, and the warning is clear. Get on board or get out.

I nod, and he turns away to finish his preparations. Restlessness invades the foxhole, and it makes the hairs on my arms rise.

Oh yeah. He's definitely flashing.

Like a Knife Through Butter

Hours later, the moon was high and Kera lay in the infirmary wide awake, refreshed by Faldon's magic. She only felt a slight twinge when she touched the sting sights. Never one to stay put, even with her father barking orders to do just that, she found herself more restless than ever.

And she knew exactly what she needed to do.

Throwing off the covers, she strapped the dagger around her waist and treaded softly to the door. The back alley abutted a wall, though it was no normal wall. The builder had tried to disguise what it hid. Kera saw the barrier clearly now. It was as if, once she'd crossed it, she'd become sensitive to its presence. She pulled her fingers along the bricks and watched the energy sparkle and snap.

She pushed at the wall. It held firm. She pressed her shoulder against it, then her back. Nothing. It felt impenetrable. How had she pushed through before?

She backed away, staring at the wall, and put her hands on her hips. Her fingers brushed the dagger.

The dagger. The wall.

What had Faldon said? That *incordium* could cut through anything?

"Lani. You didn't."

She pulled the dagger free and placed the tip against the bricks. A tiny push. A sudden pop and sizzle. The *incordium* blade slid neatly into the barrier and a new opening appeared. She quickly sheathed the dagger and gripped the cold edges of the wall. The wet mist clutched her fingertips, already urging her forward. With a pull, the opening grew, and the thick mist burst free like a wild thing, wrapping her in a tight embrace. The air grew thin. Her head spun, and she gave in to the pull.

This time, even Faldon wouldn't approve of her boldness. This time, she'd have to make sure he didn't find out what she planned until the deed was done.

Fireflies

I want to leave, but I can't. If I do, Grandpa might do something stupid. Like kill someone. It's not like I really care—my feelings are compressed into a hard, tight knot nothing can break apart. I just don't want any more trouble. I'm tired of *that* demon following me.

The tarp keeps us dry in the foxhole. He lounges at one end and I sit at the other, cracking my knuckles. After fifteen minutes of watching him scan the area, I consider grabbing his cell phone and calling Grandma, but I don't. Mom's beaten her up enough. Grandma deserves a break.

The more I think about it, the more I believe Grandpa's going through a rough patch. I can handle rough patches. Mom's given me loads of experience in that area. All I need to do is keep him calm. "So, what's the plan?"

"We wait." He pulls out a bundle of zip ties. "Which do you want to do? Shoot or zip?"

Instinct tells me to zip, but I'm afraid Grandpa will shoot first, restrain later. "Shoot," I blurt out, then groan inwardly. How did I get myself into this?

"Okay." He sounds proud, as if my wanting to shoot another

human being is some rite of passage into manhood. Maybe for the Vietnam era guys it was, but not for me.

He picks up the bean bag gun and launches into another round of safety lectures. He doesn't sound crazy. So why do I have that weird feeling something is about to happen? I try and concentrate on what he's saying.

"… so you see, it's really easy."

"Yeah, well…um," I sputter. "What if I can't shoot anyone? What if I freeze up?" I've seen enough war movies to know it happens.

Grandpa purses his lips and after a moment, snaps his fingers and points at me. "Have you ever played with those paintball guns?"

"Yeah." Last year, we had a junior class trip to a Civil War living history museum, and on the way home, we stopped off at a huge complex that had laser tag and paintball yards.

"Did anyone get hurt?"

That day had been a blast, but it hadn't been pain free. "Most of us came away with a couple of bruises."

Grandpa pats the bean bag launcher. "That's what this does. Sure, the bruises are a little more intense than what a paintball can deliver, but it won't kill if you don't aim for the head. It's been my experience that once they see us and our guns, they'll lie down and beg us to zip them."

He sounds pretty sure, and as the night swallows the last rays of the sun, I hold onto that hope.

As soon as the darkness descends, the soft chill of night takes hold and things gather close. It's brisk enough to keep me awake, but not throw me into a teeth chattering call to the nearest woodpecker. Grandpa and I speak in whispers. What is it with the coming of darkness? It's almost like there's a rule that makes everyone talk in a hushed voice.

I shut my eyes, searching for the strange sensation that hovers close by. I inhale the wet, loamy earth with its sweet-smelling layer of rotting debris. The trees feel too near. I imagine I can feel the limbs grow. The roots dive deeper. The sap ooze beneath the bark.

The flutter of bird wings echoes in my ears. The scampering of a fox. The snuffle of a mole. The ground gives a quick shudder and my eyes pop open. "Did you feel that?"

Grandpa frowns. "Feel what?"

"The ground. It shook."

"Boy, you need to calm down. You're imagining things."

Am I? I try to relax, but my senses have taken over. The woods have come alive and I can't quiet the feeling. Ever since coming here, nothing feels right—I feel different, but I'm not sure why. It's unnerving.

I turn my attention on Grandpa, needing the distraction of his voice. "How long were you in Vietnam?"

He leans his head back and sighs. "Too damn long."

I can tell by the tone of his voice he isn't interested in pursuing the subject, but I can't stop. "Do you still get nightmares?"

The night is full, but I can see him, the look on his face, the sharp angles of horror. "Nightmares come and go. Nobody truly forgets the kind of shit I went through."

There's a light buzzing sound in the air. Bees? A twig snaps and Grandpa is instantly alert, reaching for his night vision goggles. His voice is whisper soft and filled with tension. "Grab your gun."

I follow the sound and see something small and furry nuzzling at a patch of mushrooms. "It's a raccoon."

"Don't be so sure."

"No, it is. I can see it. Right over there." I point to the little guy.

"Over where? I can't see past my nose without these, and you're telling me you can see a raccoon at twenty paces?"

Grandpa must be half blind. I pick up the flashlight, click it on, and point it directly at the raccoon. It freezes for a split second, then scurries away.

A strange look crosses Grandpa's face, and he shakes his head. "Give me that." I give him the flashlight, and he flicks a switch to change the color filter to red before clicking it off. "Why do I suddenly feel old as dirt?"

The buzzing is louder, and I glance at Grandpa. "Do you hear that?"

I can see him strain at the night, listening to the flock. "Is it one of the sheep?"

"Sounds like bees."

"Can't be. Bees return to the hive at night." He leans forward. "What the…"

A collection of sparkling little lights hovers along the branches of the far trees. "What is that?" The lights slip over the meadow and pause above the sheep. The flashing pulses are no bigger than bugs. "Are those fireflies?"

Grandpa stares out over the meadow. "Can't be. We don't have those bright fireflies around here."

I slump back into the foxhole. "What else could they be?" I ask, but in all honesty, I've already lost interest.

"I'm a sheep rancher, not an entomologist." He sits beside me with a heavy sigh. "Full moon."

"What?"

"Whenever there's something odd going on, it usually has to do with a full moon." He clicks on the flashlight, coloring the immediate area in soft red, and scrounges among the food Grandma packed. "I guess the MREs from the Army surplus shop were a bit over the top. I should've guessed your grandma wouldn't let me stay out here without something good to eat." He pulls out two ham and cheese sandwiches and holds them out. "Want one?"

"Sure." I take one, and after he plops a wide-mouthed bottle full of vitamin-enhanced water in front of each of us, he clicks off the light. I bite off a chunk of sandwich, lean my head back, and stare up at the night sky.

One of the fireflies has made its way over to where we are. The buzz of its wings is louder than I expect. Grandpa chugs his water, and with a quickness I find hard to believe, snags the bug in the bottle.

I hear a faint squeal and turn my head, listening for the sound again, but the night is quiet except for the buzzing. I turn back to Grandpa and his glowing bottle. "Won't it die in there?"

Grandpa sits back, and the light slowly fades. He gently shakes the bottle until it glows again. It's bright enough to light Grandpa's face. "I'll let it go before then. My brother and I used to catch all sorts of bugs when we were young. If they had wings, he used to tear them off so they couldn't fly away. Kept them prisoner in a terrarium."

"I thought you said you weren't into bugs?"

"What boy isn't? I'm just not familiar with every species that inhabits these woods." Grandpa pulls the bottle close to his face and peers inside. "I've never seen anything glow with this kind of wattage. What kind of bug are you?"

The buzz grows even louder, the light in the bottle brighter. I shift and look out over the meadow. The tiny fireflies frantically dart about.

And then all the sheep slump to the ground.

"Grandpa?" I whisper roughly and turn to him. When I do, his arm relaxes and the bottle rolls out of his fingers and across the ground toward me. His eyes are closed and his mouth is hanging open and a deep breath rattles softly in his throat.

He's asleep. Dead asleep.

I give Grandpa a harsh nudge. Nothing.

"Grandpa!" I yell and shake him vigorously. "Wake up!"

A firefly darts free of the trees and hovers over me. Something very strange is going on. As the firefly continues to hover, a smattering of shimmering dust floats down and lands on my head.

With a quick shake, the stuff flies off, and I scowl up at the bug. That is definitely *not* normal. I make a grab for it, but it darts away, and in no time, the firefly returns with a friend. More of the strange dust falls directly onto my face. I sneeze and shake the dust off again.

The fireflies gasp. I glare up at them. A collective squeal sounds and they dart away.

Fireflies do not gasp *or* squeal.

Grandpa lets out a loud snort and slides along the wall of the foxhole until he's lying on his side. An ominous quiet descends. Within that tense silence rises a strange noise. The bottle resting near my thigh quivers. The firefly—or whatever it is—buzzes brightly, slamming itself against the cap in a bid for freedom. On the next zip and push, the cap shoots off and the firefly darts away.

All of a sudden, half a dozen of the strange bugs hover over me. Dust falls like snow, covering every inch of my head and clothes. I sneeze and sneeze and when I'm done, I'm ready to rip some wings off. A savage growl rumbles from my throat and I pounce.

The bright lights splinter and collide as I chase them around the clearing until they all disappear and I'm left standing in the middle of a flock of snoring, geriatric sheep.

My chest heaves and my mind glazes over with anger. I haven't squashed one of them.

"Come back here, you…"

I don't have a clue what they are. All I know is Grandpa's asleep. The sheep are asleep. Even the bad-tempered dog is asleep. I'm the only wakeful being in sight.

Goose bumps spring up along my arms. I'm not alone. I twirl around, my senses on high alert. Near the cluster of trees, I see her.

The girl in white. She's barely three feet from the foxhole, crouching as she stares down at Grandpa. Tucked into her waistband is a wicked-looking knife.

"Hey!" I shout.

She startles, and in a blink, she's gone. Such an impossibly quick disappearance unnerves me, but the sensation I'm still being watched gnaws at my skin. I stare into the woods, and just past a heavy clump of brush, I see her staring back at me. Without thinking, I take off after her.

I'm not a runner. Something about participating in aimless exertions of energy has never appealed to me, but as I stretch out my stride, I feel a ripple of power just like earlier, only stronger. It feels good. My reflexes are quick, my breathing strong. As the chase wears on, I wonder at the game she's playing. She's fast, far faster than last time, but so am I.

I hurdle the fence. Dart around trees. Scare creatures from their nests. In no time, I encounter a strange heaviness in the air. The same eerie, glimmering mist. I stagger to my knees and fight off a lightheaded feeling, sucking in air and calming my racing heart.

I know she's gone, yet the scent of summer lingers. Like before, the woods have swallowed her whole, leaving only a trace of mist in her wake.

I know her, but I don't. It's frustrating.

"I'll help you," I say to the empty space yawning before me. It's a guess, but I've got to believe she needs my help. Why else would she continue to haunt my dreams and Grandpa's sheep?

I wait.

Nothing. She really is gone.

Retracing my steps is easy, and before long, I enter the clearing where Grandpa sleeps, undisturbed. I try waking him again, but he only snuffles and snorts. At least he's smiling. That's more than I can say for myself. Not with what I just witnessed.

I go to the sheep and count. One is missing.

"Not again!"

I search the perimeter of the clearing. No new symbols are etched into the trees. I can only hope I've disturbed whatever that girl and those flying lights came to do. There's still a chance I can find the ewe, but how can I leave Grandpa for more than a few minutes? Even though I chased the girl off, the tiny lights are still around. I can't leave Grandpa at their mercy.

I vault into the foxhole, unclip the walkie-talkie from Grandpa's belt, and press the button. "Umm...hey. Anybody there?"

The line is silent. I try again.

"Anybody? Come on. I need some help here."

"Who is this?" comes a sleepy, deep-timbered voice.

"Dylan. Who's this?"

"Leo. You're that kid the boss brought today?"

"Yeah. I'm his grandson."

"Good for you. So what can I do for you at one *as-early-as-hell* o'clock in the morning?"

"We need you to get out here to number five. Another ewe is missing."

He cusses. "Not good, bro."

"Yeah, but it gets even weirder. I'll explain when you get out here."

"On my way."

I wrap a blanket around Grandpa, jump out of the foxhole, and pace. They're going to blame me. I know it. If I were them, I would.

For some reason, the guns make it all seem worse. I jump back into the foxhole, wrap the tarp around the weapons and extra ammo, and tuck them near grandpa's hidden ATV.

I'm still restless. Round and round I go, scanning the area

while I keep an eye on Grandpa and the sheep. Twenty minutes later, the rumble of a couple of ATVs pierces the silence. I rush to the head of the path where the headlights shoot jagged beams through the trees. The first vehicle comes to a stop, and Leo hops off as his dad rolls up next to him. They've pointed their headlights at precise angles that flood the meadow with light.

Leo's normally low voice rises in alarm. "What'd you do to my sheep?"

While Leo goes to check on the flock, Reggie steps in front of me, blocking my way to the ATVs like I'm some kind of criminal, ready to bolt. "Where's your grandfather, boy?"

I point to the foxhole. "He's out cold. I can't wake him up."

Reggie goes to Grandpa and shakes him, but he sleeps on. "What happened?"

I pace, plowing my hands through my hair until it's a tangled mess. I want to tell him, but who in their right mind would believe me? Instead, I say the only thing I can. "I don't know. We were talking and eating and the next thing I know, he's sawing logs so loud I can't hear myself think. I tried waking him, but he won't wake up. And then the flock passed out, too, and the next thing I know, one of them is missing."

Leo nudges one sheep after another. "What did you do? Crush sleeping pills in their drinking water?"

"I swear," my voice cracks. "I don't know what's going on."

Reggie motions me into the foxhole. "Help me get your grandfather to my ATV."

We struggle under the weight of Grandpa, and I wince. The blisters on my hands are still tender, though once again, they're healing faster than what's normal.

"What happened?" Reggie asks, nodding toward my hands.

"Allergies," I mutter. It's the only explanation that comes to mind, though I'm pretty sure he doesn't believe me.

Eventually we manage to get Grandpa straddled onto the wide seat. Reggie sits behind him, securing Grandpa in a tight hold before starting the engine.

I can't let him leave thinking I had something to do with this. "I know you don't know me, but I didn't do anything to him. I wouldn't."

Reggie's gray eyes are a shock against his leathery skin. If a person had the ability to see into someone's soul, this man did. Though it's difficult, I hold his gaze. There's a hint of doubt in his eyes. I can't blame him.

He revs the motor as if he's about to leave. I remind him, "One of the ewes is missing." I stare into his eyes and feel the weight of what I need to do. "I'll look for her."

His steely gaze searches my character for any defect. I'm riddled with ugly, but I've learned to hide it well. He revs the motor again. I could really do with a bit more encouragement. I'm freaked out. Does anyone care?

Indecision flashes on Reggie's face. "Find the ewe," he says to his son. His gaze flickers between us. "Take the kid with you. I'll be back after I get the boss home."

With that, he eases the ATV around and heads out at a bumpy, bone-jarring crawl.

Leo and I stare at one another. I don't blame them for being suspicious, but what can I do? Tell the truth?

"So, let me see if I follow you. Everything goes straight for sleepy-bye—everything but you."

"Yeah." The truth sounds like a lie, but there's nothing I can do about it.

"Yeah. Like that's a believable…"

His voice trails off. The lights of the remaining ATV splash across the clearing illuminating everything. Illuminating me.

"What the…" Leo frowns and leans close.

I look down. I'm still covered in that strange dust.

"Is that glitter?"

He reaches out a hand, and I jerk back. "Don't touch me." The last thing I need is for Reggie to return and find his son passed out on the ground. No one would believe I'm innocent then.

With one pass over my shirt, a small amount of the strange dust collects on my fingertips. It feels like silk and smells like summer rain. I blow it off my fingers and it disappears before it hits the ground. Weird. "Did you just see that?"

His face doesn't crack. "Give it up, bro."

I swipe at the dust that made Grandpa into Rip van Winkle, and watch it plume off me then dissolve into nothing again.

"Don't play me," Leo says, his anger beginning to show. "What *is* that?"

I ignore him and give my shirt another swipe. A crackling laugh escapes me, and I quickly bite my cheek.

Keep it in. Don't let the stress show.

Leo storms away, and then switches back, stopping a few feet from me. "Listen, you gotta tell me what happened."

"You wouldn't believe me." Even *I'm* having a hard time believing it.

"Try me."

He wants me to trust him? "Seriously? I get the distinct impression you guys want me gone."

"I'm not gonna lie. You give off an odd vibe. So yeah, I don't trust easily. My dad, Pop—they don't either. But your grandpa is like family to us. Something's going on. Pop says these woods have always been a little iffy and now you're—" He waves his hand up and down to draw attention to what we both know is there. "Look at you. Unless you keep a bottle of glitter on hand because you want to feel pretty?"

I rub my head, trying to clear it. "I must be getting a serious buzz off the pine. None of this can be real."

"No trippin' going on here. Just tell me what you know, and we'll go from there."

The deep timbre of his voice has a strange, lulling effect. Maybe I've fallen into an intense dream and all I need is an equally intense jolt to wake me up? I let loose a vigorous shake of my head and give my cheeks a few quick slaps.

Fantastic. Now I'm covered in glitter *and* my ears are ringing.

The ache of keeping everything in presses down on me. Sympathy shadows Leo's face, urging me to unburden myself. My throat tightens, trying to suppress what I'm about to say. The first step toward relief is hard, but I push past the knot. "Do you believe in the supernatural?"

"Ghosts?" The shadows of sympathy on Leo's face are suddenly unreadable. "Bro... Pop is so wired for that stuff, I can't *not* believe in it." He gets really still, and his voice lowers to a soft rumble. "What happened?"

"I thought they were fireflies, but they're nothing like anything I've ever seen. This stuff... I think it made everything fall asleep." I brush at the glitter, and a sliver of unrest pushes deeper under my skin.

"Not everything." Leo's eyes show his doubt. "You're still awake."

I yank off my shirt and snap it clean, cussing as I do. What if Grandpa sleeps forever? What if I get arrested? Go to jail? My future is as good as done.

I shake the shirt again and again. Why didn't the dust work on me?

Leo steps closer, grabs my shirt. "It's gone."

Gone? All of it? I inspect my shirt, my arms, my pants. He's right. There isn't one speck of glittering dust on me or the ground around me. It's like it never existed.

He lets his end of the shirt fall. "So, what happened?"

I glance at the sleeping flock. "I don't know. I swear. When they left, the girl came. Actually, I don't know if they left because she came, or she showed after they left. It's not really clear. I'm still freaked."

A shiver rattles my bones. I've done something I've never done before. I've left myself open to ridicule. Leo's gone completely unreadable. I struggle back into my shirt. "I know how this sounds, but I swear, I chased her and then she disappeared."

"Are we talking about a ghost?"

I'm not about to tell him I've been dreaming about her. "Yeah. I mean, she looks like one and acts like one, so…she's a ghost, right?"

"Bro…"

"I know. See? Who's going to believe that? Any of this?" I plunge my fingers through my hair, straining to keep from screaming, and finally rasp, "What if my grandpa doesn't wake up?"

"Then you inherit the farm."

I gape at him in horror. "I-I don't want the farm. I don't even like sheep or any of this crap."

"I'm kidding. Get a grip. He's asleep, not dead." He scans the meadow. "Shelley's my best breeder. I shouldn't have left her, but she didn't take this time around. She's the first lamb the boss gave me to bond with. She's sweet and smart and…" He clears his throat. "We gotta find her. Any suggestions? And crazy's no problem."

It seems 'crazy' is all that's happening around here between Grandpa's sudden case of narcolepsy and Leo's disturbing relationship with his ewe. The guy seems a little too attached to his farm animals. "Okay, if all this is all real, and those little glowing monsters took the ewe, they must have lifted her off the ground to do it. They can fly."

I check Leo for his reaction. He's trying to cover up his alarm, but it screams from his eyes. "Huh?"

Why look at me like that? He said he'd welcome crazy. "I thought they were fireflies, remember? It explains why we never found any footprints around the dead ewe. When I first saw the lights, they were high in those branches." I point to where we'd seen them enter the meadow.

"Magical flying lights and a ghost. It's been a busy night for you."

"You have no idea."

Leo sighs, then slowly begins to nod until his head is bobbing with hope. He claps his hands, the echo of the sound fading into the trees, and grins. "Why not? Okay! Let's do this."

We decide to leave the ATVs behind and go on foot. I'm glad for that. With the flashlight from the foxhole clicked on, we enter the trees where Grandpa and I first saw the lights. A feeling we're being watched creeps along my subconscious.

Get the sheep and get out. Get the sheep and get out.

"I can't see a damn thing," Leo complains after tripping over the dark undergrowth for the third time.

"Take this," I say and hand him the flashlight. As always, my eyes quickly adjust to the darkness.

We make a wide circle of the area and come up empty. A good chunk of the night is already behind us, but there isn't even a hint of light to be seen.

"This is hopeless," Leo says.

I almost agree, but...

Something tells me to head back to the part of the woods where I last saw the girl in white. "Follow me."

As we move deeper into the trees, the leaves whisper in the wind. Leo seems unconcerned by the noise. My gut tenses, but I press on.

Eyes glitter in the dark. A fox. More raccoons. Rabbits. An owl stares at me from the high branches. It's like all the creatures of the forest have come out of their burrows to take a peek at the intruders.

Go away, I say in my head.

The animals slowly retreat. I shake off the bizarre impression of power and push ahead of Leo.

Three quarters of the way to where the girl disappeared, a cluster of bright lights dance amid the leaves. I grab Leo by the arm.

He instantly clicks off the flashlight when I point toward the lights.

He cranes his neck. "Where?"

His low voice booms over the muted sounds of the forest. I hiss at him to be quiet, but when I look again, the cluster of pinprick lights is gone. I shake my head. "Over there," I whisper. "I saw something."

"Let's check it out." When we get to the spot, Leo shines the light up the tree. "I can't tell, but I think something's up there."

With one flick of his thumb, the light whitens and shines on the twitching, dangling hooves of the ewe stuffed halfway up the tree.

"Bro," Leo says in a voice rattling with awe. "Sheep fly. No one's going to believe this."

"*I* don't believe it," I mutter. "We can't tell anyone. They'll think we're nuts."

Staring up at the ewe's lolling head and twitching legs, I shake my head. We'll have to climb halfway up the tree to get it, and seeing as how Leo's still gawking at the ewe, I'm the climber. I place my hand on the tree and the bark quivers beneath my fingers. I jerk away and look at my hand. I flex each finger into a rolling grip, then spring them open again. What's wrong with me?

The flashlight is shoved into my hand, and the cold feel of plastic erases the tingling from the bark. Leo pushes me to the side.

"Hang on, little mama." He grabs hold of the nearest limb and starts to climb. "Daddy's coming to get you."

"Seriously, dude," I mutter under my breath, "you need to get a girl."

⟨∞⟩

Shelley, who'd been content to lie quietly in Leo's arms, begins kicking when we reach the meadow. She lets out a weak bleating noise, and the flock stirs. Reggie and Pop are there, urging the sheep awake and onto their feet for an inspection. Only a few still struggle to rise. I can only hope this means Grandpa will be fine.

"You found her!" Reggie shouts as he lets an ewe go and readjusts his glasses. "The boss will be glad to hear it."

"See?" Leo says with a big grin. "Your grandpa's fine. Everything is as sweet as candy. Cool as ice. No worries at all."

Pop frowns, signs something to Leo, but Leo waves him off. "Pop wants us to stop goofing off and get to work."

Pop's shaggy gray hair and bushy brows surround a face that looks concerned—especially when he looks at me. He does another sign and spits before turning away. Somehow, I get the feeling Leo's interpretation isn't exact.

We finish checking the sheep to make sure they're all okay, and when that's done, Reggie tells us to go. He and Pop will do the rest. Thank God. I'm dead tired. My brain's fried, and my arms and legs don't feel attached to my body. I blink, but my eyes stay closed longer than I want. Leo's having the same problem. As we stumble along the woodland path, the sky grows lighter. The cool dip of night wanes. It'll be warmer today, though not hot. More like springtime in the south.

When we pass the point where the bulk of the flocks are penned, Leo turns down a dirt path and manages a weak, "Later, bro."

I barely have the energy to nod. Ten minutes later, I push into the backyard via the old gate and squint up the porch stairs.

While I'm standing there, debating on whether or not to fall flat on my face right here, right now, or attempt the impossible, the back door opens and out steps Grandpa, a coffee cup in his hand. Cool. Grandpa's not dead.

"Find the ewe?" he asks.

I nod.

"Good. Coming inside?"

I nod, but my feet won't move.

"Today?"

No explanation about his sudden narcolepsy. No questions as to what I know. If ignoring the obvious is what he wants, I'm all for it. I force one foot forward, and then another. Once I get the momentum, I forge up the steps and brush past Grandpa, who holds the door open for me.

Grandma clucks her tongue. "You look like you've had a long night. Hungry?"

I grunt and crash around the corner and into the hallway. I don't stop until I reach my room. I forget about brushing my teeth or stripping off my dirty clothes or even pulling back the pristine white comforter. I fall onto the bed, arms splayed, head to the side and hanging slightly over the edge.

I'm asleep before I take my next breath.

BLESSING ⊕R CURSE

Kera sighted the target down the shaft of her arrow, pulled back, and let it fly. Immediately, she notched another arrow and let it go before the first arrow found its mark. The thud of each impact was clean and crackled with enough energy to stop a man in his tracks.

Faldon grunted. "You would've made a fine soldier."

"Not dressed like this." Kera shook the bell sleeves of her crisp, blue morning dress. The flounce of lace, yards of fabric, and starched ribbon that encased her were hardly conducive to the sport.

"Your father wasn't happy, hearing you were running around in boys' clothes." Faldon had returned his attention to his books, pacing back and forth behind her.

"Why is an adventurous nature cheered on in men, but stifled in women by yards of fabric?"

Faldon chuckled, but didn't lift his head from his reading. "No man wants to marry a woman more manly than he."

She picked up another arrow from the dozen she'd stuck in the ground near her feet and studied the pointed end. "The male ego. I'll never understand it."

"Not something I'm surprised to find out."

His cavalier attitude was wearing thin. She needed him to pull his nose from his studies and do something. "What if there could be found someone more powerful than Navar?"

The thought of the power surge she'd felt when she saw Dylan wouldn't leave her. She'd never experienced that kind of energy from anyone. It could've been a fluke, an anomaly in his world she wasn't aware of, but she didn't think so. In fact, she was sure it came from him. To top it off, the pux had no effect on him. All these years she'd believed he was a fantasy, a childish whim. Gooseflesh rose on her arms when she conjured his face in her mind's eye.

Behind her, Faldon had set up a makeshift lab. He avowed natural sunlight far exceeded any light he could conjure to see the subject he so intently explored. With her question hanging in the air, the sage lifted a quizzical brow while he busily inspected the remains of one of the millispits that had entered the village. "More powerful than Navar? Tell me, would that be a blessing or a curse?"

Good question. Kera notched the arrow and pulled back on the string. "Is there a test for a pure heart?"

"There is no such thing. Besides, the heart is deceitful above all things. You, more than anyone, should know that."

"But what if—"

"Kera." Faldon sighed. "There is nothing any of us can do. It's set. Navar has gained the loyalty of our people. The die has been cast. He will be king."

Anger exploded in the twang of the bowstring as she let the arrow fly. It joined the cluster of arrows already in the target. She snapped her head toward Faldon and gifted him with a heated glare. "I can't live with that, and neither should you."

He jerked his nose out of his curiosity and hissed, "You have no idea how hard it is for me to admit, but the time for fighting is over. It's our duty to see Navar on a path of devotion. He displays promise. He needs direction. Focus."

She strode over to him, letting all her distrust and disappointment flow from her body. It pulsed like a living entity, grabbing his full attention.

Faldon leveled a warning eye on her. "Control yourself, Kera. Never let your emotions show. We've talked about the consequences time and again. Do you not care?"

"Oh, I care. But tell me this, am I the *only* one who cares that *Navar the Great* will destroy Teag? He doesn't care about his people. Look at what he deems a reasonable weapon," she said pointing at the dead millispit. "What manner of man creates something so wholly evil? I swear to you, he will never be happy until everyone is quaking in fear of his every move."

"There are ways to mollify a man if one knows them." Faldon turned back to his specimen and clicked his tongue after he slit the creature's abdomen wide open, then scribbled in his notebook.

How typical of him. Say something that highlights her ignorance and leave it at that. Not today. She would have an answer. "And you know those ways?"

He let out a sharp bark of laughter. "Though to your young eyes I'm nothing more than a grumpy old sage, I'm a man, and I know how a man thinks."

"Tell me."

"Not yet. Oh, do not give me that look. Everything has it's time."

Kera snorted. "Between you and Father, I will never know a thing."

"You know more than most women. Trust me. All too soon, you'll wish for ignorance."

"Ignorance leads to foolishness, and I'm not much interested in being labeled a fool."

The old man mumbled unintelligibly to himself, completely

ignoring her argument. It was like talking to a hunk of stone. He was more interested in poking into the disgusting creature than the future of Teag.

"Look, Kera." His face paled as he held out the dissected millispit.

Though she cared little to see the inner workings of a millispit, Kera looked where the tip of his knife pointed—a collection of gooey bubbles. "What's that?"

"Eggs."

She took a closer look. "They're reproducing? But that's impossible."

"Why? I'm sure Navar never gave it a thought. This explains why some were able to cross over the boundaries of Navar's magic. Born free, they were never bound by that magic."

"He's polluted our woods? With those things?"

"I can't even guess at the gestation period." There was real fear in Faldon's voice. He created a cup from the dirt at his feet, plopped the egg-laden millispit into it and snapped his fingers. Fire erupted in the bowl and burned it to ash. His eyes sought Kera's. "We have to burn them all. Now."

He turned and strode away.

Kera stared at the cup. The blue-black fire sputtered once, twice, then died. Navar's hatred was bad enough, but now it had made him dangerous in the most thoughtless way possible. Without boundaries, his creations would destroy anything and everything in their path.

Without boundaries. She'd helped him there. She and Lani. It was highly possible that the wall's failure had to do with using the *incordium* to slice into it. *Incordium* nullified magic, and just like Lani, she had thoughtlessly used the blade to break through the barrier.

There was no doubt now about what she must do. Dylan had

kept pace with her in the woods. He exuded a power he shouldn't have. He had to be one of them.

Tonight, she'd sneak out.

It was up to her to convince Dylan he was needed here. She ignored the skip of pleasure at the prospect of seeing him again. It was the promise of finding a solution that caused her excitement, nothing more.

Saving her world took precedence over everything. She was of noble birth. She knew her place even if her father and Faldon had forgotten theirs. She could only hope Dylan would understand his.

Somehow, she would make him understand his duty. If not, she'd very likely end up dead. If there was one thing she knew for certain about her future king, Navar did not tolerate dissension.

Ever.

She brought her heel down onto the cup and ground it into the dirt. "All hail our wise king. He'll be the death of us all."

NOTHING TO DO

A knock sounds on my door, and I sputter awake. It's two in the afternoon, or so the clock says. My neck's stiff, and I rub the back of it, feeling the knobs of my spine as they crack back into place.

"Dylan?" comes Grandma's soft voice as she hesitantly opens the door. "You have a phone call."

Who'd be calling me? I don't know anyone here. Then a thought pierces my brain. I push up on my elbows. "Is it Mom?"

I can hear the hope in my voice, and I hate myself for it. I'm not supposed to care, but I do.

Grandma bites her lip and shakes her head. "No. It's someone named Jason."

Jason? Who the—

The image of a big kid on a skateboard flashes through my mind. I bolt upright and hold out my hand for the call. "It's the internet guy," I whisper.

She gives me the phone.

"Hey," I say, as I watch Grandma inspect the chaos that was once her guest room.

"So, you want to swap stories?" Jason asks, his doubt heavy in my ear.

"Yeah. Can we meet?"

"I think I'm a little old for you."

"What?"

"Don't you guys usually pick on eight-year-olds?"

I watch Grandma enter my bathroom. She gasps at the mess and begins to clean.

I move to the opposite side of the room for more privacy. "That's disgusting. I'm not like that."

"Don't they all say that right before they get you?"

"Listen, I just wanna compare notes, not become best buds."

"Relax! I'm funning with you, new guy. Do you honestly think I'd call if I didn't know this number? You're grandpa is the *man* in these parts. Everybody knows his long-lost daughter showed up, dumped her bastard, and then ran. Again."

"Great." At least I wouldn't have to introduce myself to everyone at school. "So, are you interested?"

"Lucky for you, I'm bored. Give me an hour." He hesitates. "Is, uh, Officer Newman there?"

I blink back my surprise. "I, um…" This was the first time I'd heard my grandparents' last name—and it didn't match mine. "My grandpa's here."

"Cool. My dad wants me to explain the *incident* before Mr. Tucker does. I don't know why he went off on me. His sheep really know how to rock a mohawk. I'm posting the pictures as we speak—you should check 'em out. Anyway, I've gotta pretend I'm sorry and hopefully get my hand slapped instead of a fine."

One thing I know about Grandpa is that he's a black and white kind of guy. Screw up, and you pay up. "Good luck with that."

"Yeah," he says on a laugh. "Kissing old butt blows, but you gotta do what you gotta do. Later, dude."

"Yeah."

I hang up and slouch back on the bed. I'm not so sure I like

Jason. It sounds like he's one of those rebels without a cause. Bored, with nothing to do. Claiming he's seen a ghost could be his way of gaining attention. It could be a coincidence that he described her as a girl in white. Didn't all movies show the women floating about in white gowns?

"Well, now," Grandma says on a sigh, pulling me out of my reverie. "That's better."

She stands, clutching all the objects she'd had on the dresser to her chest, and has a pleased expression on her face.

"What are you doing?"

"You don't want to stare at this old junk. I'm taking it out of here. We'll have to see what we can do to make this room yours. Posters. Paint. Whatever you want."

What's she talking about? "You can't do that. This is the guest room."

Her eyes twinkle above a soft smile. "I'd rather have you here than any guest."

She cups my cheek with her free hand, her touch gentle and kind, and kisses my forehead as if she loves me. My tongue is glued to the top of my mouth. I stare as she leaves, unable to speak. To think.

I place my elbows on my knees and slip my fingers through my hair, feeling completely unworthy of her affection. She doesn't know me. She'll change her mind. Everyone does, eventually.

A layer of grit crumbles beneath my fingertips. I need a shower. I drag myself into the bathroom and plunge beneath the metallic slap of well water. My eyes close, and a vision of the girl in white flashes behind my lids. The intense urge to find her grows, just like the intense need to follow her in my dreams. But to find her, I've got to go where she is. Into the woods. My stomach twists as if I've eaten something rotten.

There's something seriously unnatural going on in those

woods. I've got to get over the fear that seizes me every time I'm surrounded by trees. I'm not five anymore. Because of the girl in white, I'll be in the woods more often than not, trying to catch her. I've got no idea how I'll do it, but I'm good at thinking on my feet.

When I come out of the bathroom, I feel a lot better and am confident I can out-maneuver Jason if he becomes a problem. Right now, he's one more prick in a pile of idiots.

Bastard.

I yank on a clean t-shirt and jeans. He called me a bastard. It's just a word, but it feels worse than that.

As I slip on my shoes, the doorbell rings. I go to the living room and come face to face with a massive lump of meat. At about five-foot-nine, Jason is as compact as they come. I'm not a lightweight, but this guy's neck and head are the same size. I knew he'd be big from seeing his online photos, but I didn't think he'd be a physical anomaly. He has muscles in places I didn't even know had muscles. I hope the added meat hasn't compacted his brain to the size of a pea.

"Hey," I say.

He nods, then gives Grandma a shy smile that enhances the thickness of his neck. "No, thank you, Mrs. Newman. I'm fine."

"How about you, Dylan? Hungry?"

I am, but I'm far more interested in what Jason has to say. "I'll get something later. Jason and me...we have stuff to do."

Grandma's mouth forms a small "o," and she smiles sweetly. Too sweetly. "I'm all for friendship, so long as it's not destructive. How about you, Jason?"

Subtlety isn't her forté.

Jason lifts an eyebrow, even his forehead has more muscles than mine, and I groan my embarrassment. "I promise we'll be good little boys. Come on, Jason."

I lead him out the front door. We round the front corner of the house, past the laundry flapping on the line, and traipse along the back fence. Jason's on my heels like a mastiff after a criminal, until we come to a secluded part in the dirt road that winds along the area behind the house. If we go straight back into the woods, we'll run into the spot I last saw the girl in white.

"Were you high?" It's a fair question. He'd said he'd been at a party, and his blog is plastered with photos of a kid too stupid to say no.

"Had a beer buzz, but that's it. I don't do drugs."

I look him over. Who's he kidding? He's a walking steroid advertisement. "Seriously."

He actually blushes. "Hey. The supplements my dad gives me will help me get into a top college and then straight onto the pros. It's guaranteed."

Talk about trust. What his dad is doing to him is messed up. "Aren't you a little short for football?"

"Wrestling," he says, and takes a threatening step forward. His jaw could be made of granite and his eyes of tempered steel. This guy's definitely got the intimidation act down.

I stand my ground. Good thing I'm taller, and considering the weight of that muscle he's carrying, I'm probably quicker. That he believes his Hulk impersonation is due to natural supplements means I'm definitely smarter, so I'm still feeling confident.

"So, you say you saw a ghost," I challenge.

"You calling me a liar?"

"Did you see her?"

The muscle in his jaw bulges, and he sizes me up. After a few seconds, he forces himself to relax. I guess he doesn't think I'm worth the effort. "I saw something."

He looks away, like he's uncomfortable. Something's wrong here.

"Where'd you see her?"

"I don't know. In there," he says waving his hand toward the woods.

Too vague. I let him see my doubt, and the muscle in his jaw pops out. "Look, I know I saw something, but to say it was definitely a ghost...that's pushing it."

"You didn't have a problem saying it online for the world to see."

His lips grow thin and colorless and the whites of his eyes are showing. He's nervous. Now that I think on it, he sounds like he's trying to convince himself nothing happened—that he dreamed it.

Maybe he did.

I hope not. I've got a plan, one where I need a true believer, someone who takes chances. Leo would do in a crunch, but his mellow attitude is a problem. Jason, however, is perfect. A daredevil waiting for the next thrill.

I take a chance and say, "I chased her the two times I saw her."

His face pales. "You saw her two times?"

"Yeah."

"You really expect me to believe you saw *my* ghost *twice*?" Suddenly, he doesn't sound so unsure, but then he grins and shakes his head. "Oh, no, you don't." He makes a circle around me, whipping his head from side to side, trying to spot anyone else hanging around. "Okay, is Nugget in on this? Rigley?"

"I'm not kidding. I saw her. Twice. I chased her, and she disappeared." At his continued insistence this is some sort of prank, I search for something better. Something that he can't deny. My mind flashes to the moment the girl turned with a look of surprise on her face. "Do you remember how you felt? Like someone sucked all the oxygen out of you? There was this heavy mist and then feeling lightheaded and wanting to puke. The air sort of shimmered and then she disappeared."

He stops, and his eyes widen. "I remember the mist." He

shivers, and his voice gets tight. "But I forgot all about being lightheaded."

"That's what happened, wasn't it?"

He doesn't look pleased to admit it, but I can see the truth in his eyes. Finally, he nods. "Yeah. That's how it happened."

He walks down the lane a few paces and then whirls about. Excitement infuses his features. "I was beginning to think it didn't happen. When you sent me that email, I thought someone was punking me."

"I'm not. Trust me, I'd rather not think about it, but I can't. She's in my head." More like she's crawled into my brain and won't let me go. I'm thinking about her all the time now. What if I'm not the only one? Jason did call her *his* ghost. The thought of Jason obsessing over the girl in white irritates me. So much so that I find myself asking, "Do you dream about her, too?"

"If I'm going to dream about a girl, it's going to be my girlfriend, Lindsey Crandal, the hottest sophomore *ever*. She should be a senior, but she flunked the eighth grade, twice." A lecherous look floats across his face. "Seriously, with a body and face like hers, she's doesn't need brains."

One would think a guy with Jason's genetics would look to sharpen the intelligence factor in the girlfriend department. Then again, who says opposites attract?

His smile turns wicked. "So, how long you been dreaming about dead girls?"

Well, lookie there. He's got more wit than I thought underneath all that muscle. "Not girls. *A* girl." I cast him a wary glance. This could all go wrong from this point, but I've got to take the chance. "I want to catch her."

Jason's heavy brows lower. "How do you catch a ghost?"

"I don't know. But I need to try. We've got dead sheep, and she's somehow linked to it all."

"My dad told me about that. They say it's some kind of cult thing."

I shake my head, feeling the weight of what I need to do grow. "It's a dead girl thing. I'm almost sure of it."

Jason pops his knuckles and looks around for any lurkers. "You sure this isn't someone playing a mind trip on us?"

I've been tripping since the moment Mom and I stepped foot in this place. It's as if I knew something would happen before it did. Maybe I should take comfort in knowing I've got a good internal alarm system.

"I've been here two days. I don't know anyone who'd do this, do you?"

"No one smart enough to get it together this quick."

My muscles bunch and roll, and I try to relax, but I can't. "We both saw her. I've seen her more than once. If anyone's being punked, it's me." I look at the forest and so does he. Maybe he doesn't believe, but I do. "This is real. *She's* real. I can feel it."

As I stare at the forest, the wind blows a soft whisper, challenging me to find her. Before I can change my mind, I say, "I'm going in tonight. You wanna come along?"

He stares into the woods, his face reflecting the absurdity of the invitation. "Ghost hunting, huh? That's dedicated insanity, even for me. We might be talking possessions and poltergeists and demons. Don't you read Stephen King? Bad things happen to people who go after that stuff. It's stupid."

"Yeah, I know." But ignoring what's going on could be far worse. "So, you in?"

"Dude." His voice fills with excitement. "I'm *so* there."

Jason blows off his talk with Grandpa, and before heading home, promises to meet me later tonight. I go inside, head for the refrigerator, and pour myself a glass of milk. When I close the door, Grandma's standing there, holding onto a basket of wet laundry, mostly mine. Her unexpected appearance makes me jump, and I spill a little milk over the top of my hand. "Geez, Grandma!" I lick the milk running down my thumb.

She looks past me and into the back yard. "Where's Jason?"

"He went home."

I hear Grandpa talking to a man in the living room, and a sudden string of cuss words courses down the hall and into the kitchen. All of them have to do with Jason.

Grandma winces and shakes her head. "Why does that boy love trouble? Mr. Tanner is furious, and for good reason." She hefts the laundry basket higher on her hip and rolls her eyes when the man's voice cracks under his anger. "I'd stay out of sight until the fuss is over. I'll be doing laundry out back if you need me."

After the back screen door bangs shut, I head for the front room, drawn to a commotion that, for once, doesn't involve me. I can hear the strain in Grandpa's voice as he tries to calm the man down.

"I agree. I'd be mad, too, Ed."

Leaning my shoulder against the doorjamb, I watch the drama unfold, and leisurely sip my milk.

"Ruined three ewes before I stopped his shenanigans," the man standing in front of Grandpa yells. His face is red all the way to his receding hairline, but it's his eyes that have me staring. They bulge under a vein that splits his forehead in two. "He's not just my problem, he's behind your trouble, too. I'm lucky he didn't kill any of mine."

"Now, we can't jump to conclusions—"

"We can. That boy's a nuisance. How many complaints do you have on him already?"

" There's a wild streak in Jason, no doubt about it, but what teenage boy doesn't have one?"

"I'm telling you, he's one step away from real trouble. You know what they say about people who abuse animals. Damn psychopaths. Kill us all in our sleep." He thrusts his hands in his pockets. "Trespassing and destruction of property. I want that in my complaint."

"I've got that down, but I'd rather you take this up with the boy's dad."

"Carl's an idiot."

Grandpa sighs and leads the man toward the front door, where they stop. "Ed, you know I'm not a man to make excuses, but that boy's wild because Carl's hard on him."

Ed purses his lips. "I hear you, but a man's got to be held accountable for what he does."

"Agreed. Tell you what—I'll talk to Carl. We'll ask for reimbursement regarding any damages and have Jason come over and do some chores for you—mucking and combing wool, or doing odd jobs. You can have him one week for each sheep he clipped. How's that?"

"Free?"

"You bet. Since it's doubtful we can drive the demon out, we can at least work it into exhaustion. Show him what his life will be like if he continues to cause trouble."

"You're sure he's harmless?"

Grandpa laughs and pounds Ed on the back, but there's a false sound to his laughter. Ed doesn't look convinced. "Hell, Ed. No one, given the right circumstances, is harmless. Including you."

Ed grunts. "All right, then. I'll be expecting him sometime this week."

"You're a good man."

The screen door squeaks open and then bangs shut. The house

descends into quiet.

I make my way back to the kitchen, draining the milk from my glass as I go. So, Jason is a delinquent. I figured that out by reading his website. Am I wrong to trust him?

Grandma comes in with a load of dry laundry, mostly sheets and towels. "Is something the matter?"

"No." At least I hope not.

She takes a few steps, and I stop her. "Grandpa won't mind if I hang out with Jason tonight, will he?"

She arches an eyebrow, and her voice drips with sarcasm. "You mean the Jason that was over here this afternoon? The one Mr. Tanner is spitting mad over? That Jason?"

When she puts it like that, the idea doesn't sound so smart, but I don't think she understands. I'm not actually asking permission. I'm giving her more of a heads up, something I never bothered doing with Mom.

She heaves a heavy sigh. "I'd hoped he'd settled down a little, but it doesn't look like that's going to happen. He needs a firm hand before he gets himself into some real trouble."

"He's not so bad. Really."

I think she's about to tell me I've got no business hanging out with Jason, but instead she gives me a nod. "Maybe all Jason needs is a steadying influence—an older boy to look up to. You could do a good deed with him, Dylan."

My jaw hangs open. She thinks I'm a positive role model? If I weren't so shocked, I'd laugh. No one's ever handed me that job before. And if she knew what we were about to do, she'd know I'm not someone to trust.

"Be back by a reasonable hour," she says, as she walks away.

I smile. "I will."

Luckily for me, I've yet to find an unreasonable hour.

INTO THE WOODS

Jason's late.

I hitch my backpack higher and pace back and forth along the dirt path.

The air sparkles with change as the sun begins to sink toward the horizon. It'll be another hour before it sets and a bit longer than that before true darkness settles in. I look at the woods and then down the dirt road. I thought Jason was really into the idea. Guess not.

I shift the flashlight into my other hand. Click it on, then off. It works. I glance around and sigh. On my own again. Nothing new there.

"You look nervous. What's going on?"

I spin around and run head-on into Leo. "Hey," I say, nearly dropping the flashlight. "Give a guy some warning."

He smiles. While I store the flashlight in the backpack, he thrusts his hands into the pockets of his khaki shorts. "Don't be jealous of the skills. What're you doing?"

I mimic his stance, pushing my hands deep into the pockets of my well-worn, baggy jeans. "Nothing." It isn't a lie. I'm standing alone in the middle of a dirt strip. That is the definition of nothing if ever I heard one. "What're *you* doing?"

"Nothing." Leo shakes his head in that laid back, too-sleepy-to-care attitude he has. "That's kinda pathetic. It's a Friday night, and neither of us has a chick. 'Course, you don't know any, so I guess that makes me the bigger loser."

He focuses somewhere behind me. "Jason," he calls.

I turn and see Jason barreling down the dirt path like a bull running the narrow streets of Pamplona. He comes to a stop beside us, not even panting hard, and looks from me to Leo, a question in his eyes.

"Haven't seen you in a while. What're you doing, bro?" Leo asks.

Jason shrugs his shoulders. "Nothing. What about you?"

"Same old nothing, as usual."

I glance between the two of them. "You guys know each other?"

Leo smiles. "Living out here, you make friends where you can, with any idiot that's around."

"I'm an idiot? You're the one who sounds like a SoCal pothead." Jason playfully pops Leo in the stomach. A quick tussle follows. It breaks up quickly, and when the dust settles, we all look at each other.

"So…" I'm not sure what to do next.

"Yeah," Jason says, directing a questioning glance my way.

Leo rolls his eyes. "You guys are doing something, huh?"

This is stupid. Each of these guys knows portions of the craziness that's been going on that the other doesn't. If I were smart, I'd get Leo to come along. Whether or not he wants to is something else. I take a chance and blurt out, "We're going into the woods to find the ghost."

I couldn't have shocked him more. "You're joking, right?" He looks from me to Jason, who's got a huge grin on his face, and then back to me.

I shake my head and find a similar grin is on my face. "You wanna come?"

"Bro…" He draws the word out. "I'm standing in the middle of nowhere, with no girl in sight and a long night ahead of me. Got nothing better brewing."

"All right, then." It feels odd hanging with these guys. I'm not much into group activities, and that I think three makes up a group is telling. My friend status hangs near zero.

Jason thumps me on the back. "Where to?"

I know exactly where. I dig out the flashlight and hand it to Leo. "Come on."

We enter the forest, armed with the knowledge not all is as it seems. Even though it's still light, I know the girl in white could already be here. Stalking us. Is she the reason my skin crawls with each step I take?

The trees in this area are well spaced, and the three of us trudge along, side by side, but I'm leading. As they talk about what's to come, I hear things that can't be, like little whispers and grumblings. My jaw aches from the tension I'm carrying. I do my best to ignore the odd noises and keep walking.

"How do you know about all this?" Jason asks Leo.

"One of my sheep flew into the trees."

Jason laughs. Thinks Leo is joking. Then he sees our unsmiling faces and sobers up fast. "How?"

Leo shoots me a silent question asking why I hadn't told Jason about the ewe. I don't know why. Maybe it's the one-too-many theory. Like one too many cookies makes you sick, or one too many yawns makes you tired. For me, maybe one too many crazy stories makes you crazy.

I'd rather not sound crazy, so I say, "Go ahead and tell him."

Leo jumps at the chance. "Little flying lights lifted her up and carried her into the trees."

"What?" Jason exclaims. "You're kidding me, right?"

"Bro," Leo says in his deep, smooth voice that implies trustworthiness. "It's insane, but it's real. I saw it with my own eyes."

The trees grow thicker, our way more erratic, and I glance at Jason.

Skepticism lurks in his eyes. "Is this some kind of alien experiment thing?"

"We don't know," Leo says at the same time I say, "No."

I'm probably asking to get teased, but I decide it's time to share what's been rumbling around in my head. "I've got a theory."

Sort of.

"Let's hear it." Jason moves around a thin pole of a tree, his expression eager. Eager to mock or eager to learn? "Come on," he presses, when I don't immediately speak up.

"It's gonna sound stupid," I say, as I avoid touching the trees. It's getting harder to do, but I'm determined. The air is getting heavier. My mind is growing sharper, seeing things that can't possibly be happening. The earth is moving. Grass springs from the earth, and tiny vines shoot up to cling to whatever they can find as I pass. The trees quiver, not from the wind, but from within. I shake my head to clear it of the impossible. When I reopen my eyes, everything is still.

Jason whips himself in front of me, forcing me to stop. "I'm used to stupid."

"Me too," Leo says. "You should hear Pop go off. Ghosts. Aliens. Headless chickens that won't die…"

The pair lean in. My audience of two hangs by the thread of my imagination. But this isn't something I've made up. I know what I saw was real, and I've only found one plausible explanation. "The lights are a kind of plasma."

Disbelief shadows their faces. It's a hard sell, but I think I'm on to something, so I go further. "A ghost can materialize in several forms. They can manipulate plasma. Jason and I saw the girl form. Grandpa and I saw the glowing lights. None of us have seen both at the same time."

"Plasma," says Leo, digesting the theory.

Jason snorts and shakes his head. "Where'd you learn that? Comic books?"

"You can go back if you don't want to be here," I say.

Jason grins. "Lighten up, new guy. I'm on your side. I saw her, too, but come on, this is pretty weird shit you're shoveling at me."

"Look, it's a theory. I don't know what they are, but I know they're real."

"And you think the girl and those things are connected?" he asks.

"That's my guess. Anybody have a better theory, speak up."

Leo jabs his toe into the dirt. "She could be from another dimension."

Jason and I give him blank looks.

"You know. Einstein? His theory of eleven dimensions? Which is cute, because I've personally calculated twenty-six."

He looks expectantly at us. I glance at Jason, see his confusion—not that it comforts me much, because Jason's not exactly an honor roll student—but at least I'm not the only one lost here.

Leo sighs. "Hello. String theory? You know, how electrons are like vibrating guitar strings? If you manipulate the energy, like plucking a guitar string, you can split time, move through dimensions. The scary part about string theory is that it's connected to dark matter, which is like a black hole on steroids. Use it, and you can get sucked into nothing, which, you know, would be a wicked ride to instant death."

"Uh-huh," I say, my brain still grasping at what he's saying.

"Yeah, but then she glows, so I'm also thinking there's some sort of bioluminescence happening. Mix oxygen with Luciferin, and bam! She could've been trying to communicate with you. Did she pulse, like Morse Code? Or she could've been luring you away to eat you."

Jason turns to me. "Plasma, huh?"

"I like the ghost theory, too." Leo's jumps in. "You know, plasma's an ionized gas, the fourth state of matter. Its free electrons are charged, which makes it magnetic."

We stare at him like he's grown two heads.

Jason looks him up and down. "Who *are* you?"

"What? I like science."

"You really need to find a girl," I say.

Jason nods. "Definitely."

"It's common knowledge you can see the stuff when it heats up," Leo says in his defense. "Stars are made out of plasma."

"Okay." I seriously need to start paying attention in science class. "But ghosts make everything cold." I know that from watching the Syfy channel.

Leo shrugs. "Maybe it sucks the heat out of the air and everything around it in order to materialize?"

"Makes sense," I say, "in a soul-sucking way."

Jason stares at Leo and holds up his hand as if he's at school. "So, how do we get rid of it?"

Whoa, what's Jason talking about? "Guys, we're not here to get rid of her. I just want to catch her. Talk to her."

"That's right," Jason smirks. "She's your dream girl."

"She's not—"

He turns to Leo, cutting me off. "So, how do we catch her?"

Leo looks from him to me, and lifts his eyebrows. "Don't look at me. I don't know."

"Great," Jason grumbles. "We're tracking an entity that comes to life by sucking all the heat out of the air, and all we have is a flash light and Dylan's backpack. What's in there anyway? Better be a ghost de-materializer."

"Scared?" Leo asks, and rubs Jason's hair like a father would his son. "You want to go home, little man—"

Leo stops. His hand moves along Jason's skull. Their eyes lock. "When'd that happen?"

Jason shoves Leo's hand away. "None of your damn business."

I don't have a clue what's going on, but I know it's not good. "Guys?"

Leo won't stop. He wrestles with Jason, though having fifty pounds on Leo gives Jason all the advantage, and they fall to the ground. Pinning Jason isn't Leo's objective. It's the guy's shirt. With one swipe, he's got Jason's shirt over his head, his back bare to our eyes. Bruises and welts criss-cross his back like a three-dimensional chess board. Just looking at them makes my back hurt.

Leo hops up. "Look what he did to you! Why do you put up with it?"

Jason struggles to his feet, pulling his shirt down and throwing Leo an angry glare. "What am I supposed to do? He's my dad."

"But he beats you," I say.

Jason gets in my face, his lips as thin and bloodless as the whisper he lets out, "I hit back. So can we drop the 'poor Jason' bit?"

"Sure." What else can I say?

Silence fills the air until Leo breaks it. "We should have brought sweaters. Technically, when we find her, we could go hypothermic."

Jason turns and pushes his way into the trees, trampling bushes and grumbling to himself about amateurs. Unsurprisingly, our lack of preparation doesn't alter our plans. Leo follows Jason, and I bring up the rear. I want it that way. Jason's leading us in the general direction of where I've seen the girl.

The gray tones of evening find the forest quicker than the open fields. The shadows thicken and blur the edges of my vision as we make our way further into the trees. Without trying, I'm aware of the life that infuses the forest. I can sense where an owl has made her nest, how she and her mate take great care to guard it from predators. I know what creatures lurk beneath our feet, scratching and digging as they rummage for food. Eyes of differing sizes blink red against the deepening night, watching me pass. The trees huddle closer, like their branches are reaching out to pluck me from the ground.

The forest exhales as if, in one breath, it wishes to tell me something. I shut out the noise.

Move faster. Got to move faster.

The ground behind me suddenly rises, sweeping me along on a wave of dirt until I bump into Leo.

He glances back at me. "Bro, what's your hurry?"

I search the woods. Nothing is there, yet something hovers close by. It's coming for me. Closer and closer.

I push Leo. "Go, go, go!"

The tremor in my voice urges him on. He slams into Jason and the three of us race ahead. Tree limbs slap at our faces, tug at our clothes. We trip, yet we don't fall. Leo's breathing roughens. Jason rips apart anything in his path, daring the woods to stop him as he bowls forward. In no time, we stumble into the clearing where the girl disappeared the first time, and I turn around, conscious of the weight of eyes on me. I don't see anything. My hands find my knees and I suck in air that still feels too thick. Too strange. Too heavy.

Jason plants himself in front of me and scowls. "What the hell was that all about? Look at my arms."

Scratches line his forearms, his face. I gulp in more air and force myself upright. "Sorry. I…"

A light buzz sounds, and I whirl around to face the forest. Jason does the same. "What?"

Leo bumps into us, and we three stand back to back, our eyes searching the forest beyond. The buzzing grows. My gaze ricochets from tree to tree. "Do you hear that?"

"What?" Leo asks, his voice higher than usual. The beam from the flashlight he's carrying whips around. "What do you hear?"

"Buzzing."

As soon as I say the word, tiny lights fly into the clearing and head straight for us. Leo ducks and weaves, but they expertly separate him from us. I whip off my backpack and swing. It catches nothing but air. One light rushes close and knocks me off my feet.

I can't believe I'm flat on my back on the loamy ground staring up through the tree limbs. I need to get up. The limbs suddenly bow. They're coming for me. I flip over and bounce to my feet, darting away, searching the clearing for Leo and Jason.

Leo is gone. I hear his faint screams for help, and shout for him to come back.

Jason nearly tramples me as he bats and cusses at the darting lights. His movements are slow, his voice a warble of disbelief. He rakes his fingers through the air like he's trawling for shrimp, yet nothing is caught.

The lights fly off, and Jason staggers toward me, his breathing deep and ragged. I catch him. His face shines pale, his muscles tighten, as he stares up at me. "What the hell is going on?"

"I don't know." Grandpa and I hadn't been attacked. Not like this.

The shadows darken. I hadn't thought this through. It's just like Jason said. Bad things happen to guys like us. I should've read more Stephen King.

Jason holds up his left arm, and the hair on it stands straight. His eyes lock with mine. The vein in his neck throbs. "I know this feeling. It's her."

The sensation of all the oxygen being sucked out of me descends. I nearly sink under Jason's weight. "We've got to get out of here. Can you walk?"

What am I saying? I can barely move.

"I don't know." He clutches at my shoulders and blinks heavily. "I'm dizzy. So sleepy."

I take a good look at him. He's covered in glittering dust.

He sags further into my arms. "I don't feel so good," he says, his words elongated and distorted. I spy a fat bush and struggle with his bulk toward it. Before I drag him two feet, mist spews out of thin air. My nerves tingle, as if I can feel every molecule shift and grow. It's not a comfortable feeling.

"Dylan!" Jason's weak warning slips between his flaccid lips.

His eyes flutter shut, and he's out.

Shit!

I look to the right. To the left. I've got no idea where Leo is. The mist swirls and dips, stretching and contracting. The hairs on the back of my neck spike. The area is deathly quiet, and one thing is definitely clear.

The ghost is rising, and I'm the only one left standing.

Stepping Through Air

Mist ripples in front of me, threading through the air. If I stretch out my hand, I can touch it.

I don't.

Instead, I ease backwards, dragging Jason with me, keeping my eyes glued to the strange, misty fingers. When we reach the shelter of the trees, intense friction skids across my skin, and the girl in white appears amid the shimmer. Her halo of dark hair whips about violently as the filmy gown slaps against her legs. She takes a step forward. Her bare feet wriggle in the spongy soil of the forest, crackling the dry leaves beneath them.

Ghosts have feet?

The mist evaporates and the forest is quiet and still once again.

My gaze skims from her feet, over the belted nightgown that clings to her body, up to her violet eyes. She's beautiful, but how can she be real?

She stares back at me, unselfconscious, her body glowing softly from some inner light.

My grasp weakens, and Jason slips free. His head thuds onto the mossy ground, but I don't react. All I see is the girl in white. Smell the scent of summer wafting off of her.

She moves slowly forward, and my retreat mirrors her steps. For the life of me, I can't turn and run, though leaving is the smart thing to do. My feet won't obey common sense. It's the questions that keep me near; they won't shut up. Who is she? Where did she come from? What does she want?

She stops and holds out her hand. "Don't go, please."

Her voice cascades around me like soft rain, dripping with an elegance I've never heard before. I'm speechless. Completely transfixed. Her graceful movements against the too-thick air are like the dance of a snake charmer, hypnotizing its foe. I explore every detail of her face, searching for the flaw that will prove this is a hallucination, albeit a really intense one.

Everything looks and feels normal. At least as normal as a guy in the forest meeting a girl wearing an old-fashioned nightgown while his buddy lies passed out nearby can feel normal. I'm sure situations like this have happened to tons of people…on drugs.

I close my eyes. I'm going crazy. This can't be real. *Wake up, wake up, wake up.*

I open my eyes and see her tilt her head to the right. She takes another step forward, and this time I don't move. Her big, luminous, violet eyes contain a hint of pleading. I drop my gaze to her mouth and wonder what it would be like to kiss her.

She steps even closer, unafraid of me. "Is your friend all right?"

The sound of her smooth voice invades the quiet of the night. I could listen to her talk for hours and never grow bored, yet I've suddenly lost the ability to speak. My voice has grown sticky, like I'm talking with a mouth full of peanut butter. "Um... I… He's…"

I blink and she's at Jason's side, cupping his face. "The *pux* didn't hurt him, did they?"

How did I not see her move? "The what?"

She looks at me, and I lose all ability to think straight. "The *pux*. Tiny winged creatures that glow." She touches Jason's arm, and a tense frown settles on her face. "I'm ashamed. I knew the wall had been weakened, yet I've kept silent. A disastrous mistake on my part."

She isn't a ghost. No way. But she isn't normal. She stepped through air, appearing out of nowhere. No one can do that. "Who are you?"

She closes her eyes for a moment, and the long, thick lashes framing her eyes lay against her cheeks. "You know me, Dylan. I'm Kera. Kera of Teag. I shouldn't be here, but we've shared our dreams for so long, I feel as if I already know you."

"You really are the girl from my dreams?"

"Yes. I don't understand why you're here in this realm. It makes no sense."

"Hold on, are you telling me you're from another dimension?"

"Yes."

Holy crap! My balance fails, and my back slams against a nearby tree trunk. I stare at her as if I've never seen a girl before. Leo was right?

No way.

This is too sci-fi for me. It's too Hollywood-gone-special-effects.

She stands and takes a few steps toward me. "When I felt you, I had to see you, to prove to myself your existence, and when I pushed through the barrier, the *pux* must have followed." A flush tints her cheeks pale pink. "Everything's a mess, now. My father will be angry when he finds out what I've done. I'm not supposed to be here, but I couldn't stay away. Once I saw you, I knew."

I push away from the tree and wave her silent. "Wait. You didn't know I was real? You thought *I* was a—"

"Childish hallucination. I've always had a good imagination, something my father constantly scolds me about."

Emotion I don't understand shimmers in her eyes. I can't look away. I know getting close isn't wise—

But she's so pretty, my inner voice whines. And if she's the girl from my dreams, I've known her forever.

And then I see the knife tucked into her belt, glinting in the moonlight, and remember what Leo said. Is she just trying to lure me away to make me a midnight snack? "What's with the knife?"

"It's for protection."

Normally I'd let it go, but she's touching it in a way that makes me want to take a big step back. "Protection against…?"

"Evil," she says, as if I'm a little slow on the uptake. "Dylan, you have no idea how long I've waited to meet you." She glances up at me through her thick, dark lashes. "When I realized who you must be, I couldn't stop thinking about you."

If any normal guy heard a knife-wielding, beautiful girl say she couldn't stop thinking about him, he'd run. So why am I still standing here? I shake my head. "This is crazy. If you're the girl from my dreams—"

Nope. Stop, stop, stop.

"—but, you're not. You can't be real. She's not real. I made her up."

"I'm real." She holds out her hand. "Touch me."

My chest tightens, and my heart thuds wildly. She's hit my weak spot. Man, oh man, I'd like nothing better than to touch her. My resistance wanes. My body leans forward. And then, at the last minute, I snap straight.

No touching. I've got a horrible feeling if I do, I'll never be able to think clearly again.

At my sudden withdrawal, her eyes well with tears, and though she tries her best to stop them, they slip down her cheeks.

Wow. That looks real. I watch a single teardrop fall to the ground and splatter onto a dead leaf.

Really real.

Unlike Mom's, Kera's tears affect me. A strong need to help her attacks my hesitance. I should be protecting her, not hurting her.

I turn away, confused by my reaction. What's wrong with me? She appears out of nowhere, searching for me, because she felt me? This has all the earmarks of a slasher movie. Boy takes a walk in the woods with his friends. Suddenly his friends are gone. Out of nowhere, the beautiful, otherworldly stalker from his dreams appears, only to change into a hideous beast that devours him whole. Yeah, that does *not* sound cool. I should be concerned. So why aren't I?

"Let me get this straight. You expect me to believe there's another world connected to this one?" I rub my forehead as if I can erase the idea, but it won't go away. "Alternate universe. Parallel realm. This is totally mind blowing."

"Dylan. Can you feel it? Try. You don't belong here. Something must have always told you that." Her words sound desperate.

Seeing the uncertainty that must show on my face, her tears spill more freely. No blubbering mess. No ranting. No demands. The raw emotion playing on her features surprises me. She really, really, *really* wants me to believe her, like it's a life and death thing.

Weird.

Weirder still, her quiet tears pluck to life some residual feelings I had abandoned for dead. That flicker of hope scares me more than I'd thought possible. "You don't know what you're saying. This has got to be a mistake."

"No mistake. You're the one I've been waiting for."

A groan escapes me. Great. She's like Mom, searching for the perfect guy. I've got news for her. I'm not perfect. Far from it. I don't need another psycho female in my life. Not now.

I turn away, and force myself to take a step.

My chest pinches.

Stay.

I take another step and some strange connection we share races through me, forcing me to turn around. I slowly pivot, and when our eyes meet, I can't look away.

The strange energy that pulses off her pulls me forward, gives me strength, cracks open the part of my heart I thought I'd closed up for good. She's daring me to trust again.

The glimmer in Kera's eyes urges me closer. There's an aura of magic around her, and I can't lie. It excites me. With each step, senses I've only half used burst open. The forest shudders, willing me to see all that it is, and unlike the times before, I don't freak out as the soft vibrations of life bloom under my feet.

This time, it feels completely natural.

I stop only inches away from her, and we stare at each other. My heart pounds and swells along with hers. A lone tear drop clings tentatively to her bottom lashes. Instinctively, I raise my hand to wipe it away, but I stop short. My throat grows tight. "Don't cry."

She wipes at her wet cheeks with her palm. "I rarely do. It's because there's so much at risk. I can't lose you, but I'm at a loss as to what I should do. My instincts tell me we should quit this place. Now. But I can't leave the *pux* here. They're too vicious."

I can feel the dilemma tearing at her. I don't understand everything she's saying, but at this moment, I'd do anything to ease her mind. I hold out my hand. It feels natural, like it's something I've done a million times before. "We'll make it right. We'll find your *pux* and send them home."

She stares at my hand, then tentatively slides hers into mine. A shock surges through my fingertips and up my arm. My heart slams to a halt, and when it starts again, it beats in perfect time with hers.

"You can't tell me you feel nothing now." Her grip tightens as if her hand wants to meld with mine. "From the moment I first saw you, I trusted you, Dylan. Now I know I was right to find you."

"What do you want from me?"

"I don't know. I just know you're the one that'll made everything right again."

I don't have a clue what she's talking about, but a strange warmth grows in my chest, one I'm not sure I want. "You shouldn't trust me. I'll just disappoint you."

She grazes her fingertips along my temple, so gentle. So familiar. "I know your heart."

She's insane, I tell myself, but I know it's not true. I'm scared to believe someone is willing to accept me for me. Something very odd is happening. I'm on a precipice of knowledge. If I yank away, I'll tumble back into my old life, where feelings of helplessness reign, but if I lean forward, I'll shatter the glass that separates me from what I should've known all my life.

Something that would've given me comfort and strength.

Something Mom denied me because it scared her.

I've smothered the strange feelings since I was a boy. I let Mom control me. But no more. I'm my own man now.

My breath grows still, and I force out a ragged whisper, "Seriously. Who are you?"

"Who banished you here, Dylan? Who forced you from our world?"

At my blank look, her hand in mine begins to glow. The warmth of her palm spirals through me. Images of paradise careen through my brain, fighting with the reality of my painful past, showing me that my life until this moment has been a terrible lie.

She unlocks the lost and faded parts of my dreams. The meadow fills my mind. We're small, laughing at things young kids laugh at. I spill my secrets, share my sorrows. Over the years, our time together lengthens and wanes, but when we're together I hold her, touch her, kiss her. She touches me and all my worries disappear. I revel in the peace only Kera gives me.

She's my friend, the *only* one who's been there for me.

And I love her. I have since…forever.

I can't breathe. Worse, I can't accept what she wants to give me. I've been burned too many times.

I shake my head, and pull away. "Stop."

She frowns, not letting me go. "You are one of the *firsts*. I know it with my whole being. We are Keepers of Life. Living here has kept your powers dormant."

"I don't think so." I take a step back. "I'm a regular guy, and not a very interesting one at that."

"Who lied to you?"

Her sharp demand causes me pause. "No one. It's the truth."

A strange light enters her eyes. She pulls me down, and we fall to our knees on the loamy ground. She twists my hand, palm down. As I try to pull away, I feel her body crackle with tension. She holds tight.

"Call to the earth."

I don't understand, but worse, her quicksilver mood reminds me of Mom. I don't like mood swings. I've learned not to trust people who flicker from one emotion to another. If she were Mom, I'd simply walk away, but this fragile-looking girl is strong. Insistent.

"Do it!"

I stare at her, reading her as I would Mom, seeing the quick rise and fall of her chest, the wild look in her eyes, the tightness around her mouth. The strong sent of burnt almonds, bitter and unpleasant, overshadows her summer scent. And then it hits me.

She's scared.

The violet of her eyes grows hot. Instinct guides me. I slide my fingers along her cheek and ease my thumb back and forth along her cheekbone, willing her to calm down as I stare into her eyes.

Slowly, her tension eases.

"Let go," I rasp.

Her pink lips part and the tip of her tongue darts out to wet them. "You don't understand. I've risked so much to come here." She pulls away and wraps her arms around herself, as if she wishes nothing more than to disappear. "You have to believe me. You belong in Teag. I know it's true."

It's one thing to accept that somehow we've been sharing our dreams. It's a whole other leap to believe I've got magical powers.

Like a fledgling bird spreading its wings, she uncoils her arms and stretches out a hand. In mere seconds, the earth rises beneath the shimmer of her palm. Her fingers contract into a tight fist and the earth settles, as unremarkable as it was before. "It's our gift. To refuse it is unthinkable."

What she's offering would explain a lot—dreams spent riding on the wind, the feeling of being watched whenever I've entered the forest, of knowing things I shouldn't know, of the unstoppable desire to move quickly, of feeling the ground rise under my feet tonight as we hurried to the clearing. It's a crazy thought, but…

I raise an eyebrow. "Call to the earth, huh?"

She nods, and a spark of anticipation flickers behind her eyes.

I hold out my hand, close to where she put hers, and wish for the earth to rise. My palm glows warm and under it, the dirt mounds higher and higher. As it rises, Kera straightens, excitement building within her.

I rear back, shake my hand as if I can blow out the light, but it's too late. The glow that infuses my palm creeps up my arm. I bolt to my feet, yelping and shaking, willing the progression to stop. In less time than it takes me to flick on a light switch, my skin shines with a soft, earth-friendly wattage all its own. The hum of magic rushes in my veins. I can feel the power slowly build, then decrease, then build even higher.

"There," she says, her smile not at all reassuring. "Is it proof enough? You're in the wrong place with the wrong people."

"This isn't funny. Make it stop." I hold my arms out as if I'm diseased.

"You've tapped into the power. Once done, it can never be undone."

"You mean I'm going to be like this forever?" I don't recognize the tense pitch in my voice. My life is over. Not that it was fantastic before, but now it'll be positively depressing, because who wants to be friends with light bulb boy? I don't.

"Power always has its drawbacks." She touches my arm and the glow quickly fades. "There are ways to control it."

Seeing it fade allows me to relax, almost. "I'd rather stay off the grid, if you don't mind."

Excitement flashes in her eyes. She grabs my arm and tugs me forward. "We must catch the *pux*, erase any imprint we have made here, and return to Teag."

She wants me to go with her? I pull away. Too much is happening too fast. "Slow down. Let me think."

She crinkles her nose, annoyed with me already. "What is there to think about?"

A lot. If I disappear, what will my grandparents think? Not to mention everyone who knows I'm here.

They'll think I'm my mother's son. A complete waste. Doomed to fail.

The thought sours my stomach.

Kera steps close and cups both sides of my face, immediately regaining my attention. She's so close, I can smell the promise of never-ending summer rising off her skin. I should step away, but I don't. It feels natural to be near her. To touch her like I have a million times in my dreams.

Waves of compassion roll off her. "You have been in so much

pain, knowing you were different but not knowing why."

I focus on her lips. They're perfectly shaped. Perfect for kissing. I sway forward, itching to touch her. My head bends, and my hands reach for her. She closes her eyes. The lure to let go hovers so near...

Jason's deep sigh worms into my ear. The events of the night leading up to this moment come crashing in. If it weren't for my impulse to find Kera, Jason wouldn't be lying helpless on a pile of rotting leaves in a dead sleep.

Action without thought is a life guided by impulses. The saying describes Mom perfectly. I'll be damned if it will me.

My hands stop. I feel the heat radiating off her skin, hear the pounding of her heart. I don't know how it's possible to be so close, yet still not touch. It'd take only a slight nudge to end this torment. Not too long ago, I would've given in. Not now. I drop my hands and pull away. The control it's taking to not give into my desire is going to kill me.

Her eyes flutter open. Confusion plays on her face. "What's wrong?"

"Nothing. Everything." My throat is thick. I hear Jason sigh in his sleep. "I can't go."

"Your heart is torn?" She looks from me to Jason and then back again, as if she's taken aback by the possibility.

The way she says that...

"No! No. Seriously, me and him, we're just friends, and not even good ones."

One of her perfectly arched eyebrows lifts, and she backs away. Is she leaving?

"Wait," I cry, and make to follow. When her skin slowly brightens and the trees begin to sway and whisper among themselves, I hesitate.

The earth quakes, and I jump back as tree roots bubble up like worms after a heavy rain. I stumble onto firmer ground as they grasp Jason.

A sinking feeling hits my stomach. "What's going on?"

The roots twist and roll over Jason, pulling him close to the base of a huge tree, where several spindly limbs lower, wrap around his limp form, and drag him into a protective hug, high in its crowning boughs.

My mouth hangs open. "I should probably be concerned about this, huh?"

Kera takes my hand in hers. "You worry too much. Up there, he'll be safe until we return."

When I continue to stare at Jason resting high in the branches, she forces me to look at her with a touch of her finger on my chin. "Trust me, Dylan."

When I look at her, everything makes sense. But it shouldn't make sense.

I swallow and the knight in shining armor I didn't know existed within me rises to the challenge. "All right. I'll help you find the *pux*, but I can't go back with you. This is all too…I don't know—"

She gently lays her fingers on my mouth, stifling my words. "Don't worry. Tomorrow will answer itself."

Her answer is said with confidence, but if I listen closely enough, sadness lingers close to the edges of her words. I wonder at its cause. I itch to know everything about her.

She felt me. What the hell does *that* mean? This strange, gorgeous girl entered my world because of me. I feel the pulse of our heartbeats within our clasped hands, how they've merged as one, and God help me, I don't ever want her to let go.

THE TROUBLE WITH PUX

Our fingers entwine as we step from the small clearing into the forest. I can't deny her, or the feelings I have for her, but they scare me.

"We haven't much time," she explains. "The *pux* have been here too long already."

I give a start as branches and brambles skitter out of our way. I look back and see them crowd together as if to better spy on us as we go. Crazy.

When I continue to follow, I can feel her pleasure. It's tinged with a feeling of desperation that still alarms me, but I've fallen for her bait. What guy wouldn't?

"We need a trap."

"There's a net in the shed." I don't want to risk getting it, though. Whatever magic fills these woods, it's coiled tightly around us. I want this moment to last forever. I want *her* for forever.

A knowing light enters her eyes. "We needn't go so far."

She lets go of my hand and the separation is like a sharp bite. I want her back. She sinks to her knees, muddying her gown, and sifts her fingers through the forest debris until she's collected a handful of twigs.

She tosses the twigs in the air. They quiver, split, twist, and bend, then fall into her glowing hands. With a shy smile, she hands me the perfectly woven, ball-shaped trap. "Come on, let's go."

She tugs on my arm as I stare dumbfounded at what she's done. "So the *firsts* have the ability to control nature?" It's the only explanation, though I really don't get the whole nature moving on its own thing. Twigs that are on the ground are the bits trees shed—like dead skin. No life in them.

A frown mars her face. "Not exactly. Through magic, we learned to harness the power of the earth. We're bound by law to work in harmony with nature."

She stops and touches a tree. It shivers and lowers a branch where a vine has grown. With one touch, a small, pink bud appears and blooms. She picks the flower and hands it to me. "We strive to maintain perfect balance, in nature and in life."

It's a real flower, soft and fragrant like the soap in my bathroom. "Can everyone from Teag do this?"

She nods. "Through an amalgam of magic and science, but some of us are more powerful than others."

"You must be one of the powerful ones."

Startled, she asks, "Why do you say that?"

"I don't know. You're here, aren't you?"

Those violet eyes slip away. "I'm not so very powerful, Dylan."

Who is she kidding? "From where I'm standing, you are."

She shakes her head vigorously. "You have more power than anyone I've ever known."

I let out a disbelieving laugh. I'm a reject. It's the only life *I've* ever known. "You're saying I can do what you do?"

"Yes. Call on the power. For real, this time. Believe it."

The earth did rise for me. Just a little bit, but I panicked…

I glance at the vine.

Believe. Just believe.

I touch it, and instead of one, a profusion of flowers springs forth, like yellow popcorn kernels popping white along the vine. I yank my hand away.

Kera gasps as the spectacle continues up the branch.

"Um...sorry about that." This whole magic thing is more complicated than I thought. I need to relax. I roll my head, and then I touch it again. The flowers curl back into buds and recede into the vine. I grimace. I just want a few to sprout. I touch it again, and the perfect number spring forth this time. I stare at my finger, at its tiny glowing tip. I barely had to think, and I'd done that?

Awe fills Kera's eyes. "Dylan, I've never seen anyone do that. Ever. No wonder I felt you."

And we're back to the 'I can feel you' thing. There's no denying we have an odd connection, but some part of me resists the thought that I'm a magical creature. It's all just too surreal.

I play a solo game of catch with the soccer-ball-sized trap and avoid the subject of me having magical power. I'm like a computer that's been fed too much information. I need to shut down that particular file or crash.

I spin the trap in my hands, impressed with its construction. "So, these *pux*. They're small, but I get the impression they're not good?"

Kera's eyes cloud. "They're creatures of chaos. In my world their powers are contained. Because of that, their temper falls on each other, and they war non-stop in a bid to eliminate the competition for their master's affection."

"Who's their master?"

"The Lost King. He was banished to the underworld when he tried to claim himself a god. Now we're leaderless and suffering under a man who's grasping for power."

I toss and catch the trap again. "A magical guy with a god complex. Nice. Sounds like you guys have as many problems in your world as we do in mine."

"No place is perfect, no matter how much you wish it were."

I couldn't agree more. "So, how do we catch your *pux*?"

"That's been my problem. It's like they have a sixth sense when I'm near."

"Then we need bait. What're they attracted to?"

"Humans. In times past, they took great pleasure in tormenting them."

That doesn't sound good. At least Jason and Leo are safe. "Oh, no—Leo. I forgot about Leo!"

The terror etched on his face when he ran past me flares in my memory, and I know exactly where the *pux* are. Leo is too good of an opportunity for them to pass up.

I toss Kera the trap, grab her hand, and pull her back toward the clearing, fighting back the brambles and tree limbs. Why don't they move for me like they do for her? As soon as I think it, they start moving out of our way.

"Where are we going?" she asks as she runs to keep pace.

"To get Leo. The *pux* were chasing him before you appeared."

We come to the clearing, and I dive into the forest at the point where Leo darted into the trees, flailing and shouting. The *pux* have had free reign over Leo for more minutes than I want to count. What if they're torturing him, bleeding him dry like they did the ewe? My fingers clamp Kera's more tightly as I pull her along.

A flash of tiny lights appear ahead of us.

"Quiet. The *pux* are very skittish," she says.

Her skin pulses bright, and the ground beneath us rises. It's like riding a skateboard. I flex my knees as it carries us along on a silent wave of forest debris.

As we move further down the random path Leo left behind, I hear a muffled groan. Kera squeezes my hand. The rolling mound fades beneath our feet, and her glow quickly dims. She points toward a clump of trees framed by tall grasses, thickly-leafed deer ferns, and wildflowers.

We creep along, hunched over, until we're squatting behind the natural screen. I separate a few fronds and spot Leo laid out flat on his back. His shaggy black hair is tied in knots, his clothes are torn, and he's bound with thin rope made of finely-woven grass blades. Varying sizes of mushrooms have sprouted around him in a tight circle.

"What're they doing to him?" I whisper.

Kera's eyes grow round. "They're preparing him for his new life as their slave."

"You're kidding. He's a hundred times bigger than they are. How can they enslave him?"

Her whisper is tense. "I told you. Their powers are far stronger here. If we can't rescue him, they'll enslave him in their underground world, and he'll be only the first of many. That's why it's imperative we catch them and take them home." She nips nervously at her bottom lip. "We have to break the circle before they realize our intent. Otherwise, we may lose him."

Great. Tiny beings with supernatural power that have taken an odd liking to Leo. Pop, with his superstitious mind and evil glares, will kill me if I don't rescue his grandson. I take stock of what we have. Kera's quickness and strange powers, me and some iffy powers, and a trap made of twigs. Surprise is the only thing we have that's of any real use.

"Is there a special way we need to break the circle?"

"Crush it. If we're not quick enough, it won't go well for your friend. He'll disappear into their underground labyrinth, where we may never find him."

Her words startle me. "You're serious?"

She nods. "They may be small, but they're nasty creatures when riled."

Lucky for me, so am I. A hasty plan forms. "I'll rush in and destroy the circle. Hopefully that'll keep them busy, so you can start rounding them up."

She puts a heavy branch in my hands and I look at her blankly. "To hit them," she says, and moves into position.

I'm no hunter, and I'm definitely not a guy who's willingly swung any kind of club before. I'm out of my element. Rescuing someone is for Boy Scout types. Doubt slams into me, and I hesitate.

Kera catches my eye and smiles. Her faith in me has a calming effect. Okay, so I may not be a Boy Scout, but how hard can smashing a few mushrooms and catching some crazy lightning bugs be?

After I'm sure Kera's in position, I leap forward, hold the heavy branch over my head, and scream, naked warrior style, as I head straight for the circle.

The bulk of the tightly knit *pux* squeal and burst apart like an exploding firework, their trails of light streaming up, out, and away. Both of Leo's legs have begun to sink into the ground. I dive for the mushrooms and slam headfirst into an especially stubborn *pux* who yanks at my hair, as if to steer me away from my target. I don't slow down, and crash through the circle. Coming to a stop beside Leo, I roll on my back and shake off a couple of *pux* clinging to my branch.

I pop to my feet and start swinging. With one swipe, mushroom caps explode and stems crumble. Yet more appear as the *pux* scamper to re-knit the circle. The *pux* on my head tries to wrangle me away from the mushrooms and the destruction I'm determined to complete, but I ignore his painful urgings and obliterate one of his comrades with a swing that would make my old high school PE teacher proud. I quickly backhand another one, sending it flying. Kera pops out of hiding and chases down the *pux*, snapping her trap like a greedy turtle.

A slew of *pux* dive at me, and I get a taste of their true nature. Their little knives dig into my skin, slashing and poking like fire ants on a rampage. When one gets a little too close to my eye, I take no prisoners. The branch leaves nothing but splats of smooshed *pux* in its wake. With an especially vicious yank, the one in my hair sounds an alarm, and he and the remaining *pux* I haven't killed go careening into the woods, where Kera gives chase.

I stand, both hands gripping the branch in front of me, panting like I just broke the Olympic record for Whack-A-Mole. I feel every nick and scrape, yet I'm happy. I'm the one left standing over Leo. I grin at the dead tree limb. Maybe I should have taken up baseball.

Leo moans, and I chuck the branch into the bushes. He's restless, fighting to get up as he sleeps, but the grassy ropes and the ground over his legs keep him down. In no time, I free him. He doesn't appear to have any serious injuries, just a few rips in his clothes, a daisy-chain necklace, and one crazy hairstyle.

"Leo?" I grip his chin, his lower face puckering in my hand. "Leo!"

He struggles free of my grip and lashes out, nearly punching me in the face. His words are muddled and his reflexes slow as he lurches to his feet. He stands, swaying for a moment, before stumbling around and falling to his knees. "Bro," he says clearly before falling flat on his face.

Kera reappears, and I turn to her. "We've got a sleepwalker."

She frowns. I follow her gaze and find Leo lazily chewing on a clump of grass. With a slap and a yell, I get him to spit it out. I wipe the green spittle off his mouth with the edge of his shirt. "We've got to do something."

Kera moves to my side. "There's nothing we can do but wait for him to wake up." She holds out her trap. "Take heart. I caught one!"

Behind the twisted twigs, a light flutters. It glows brightly for a moment as it struggles to be free, but soon, it dims and grows still.

"One?" I'm feeling defeated. At this rate we'll never get them all.

"Don't fret. We'll find the rest."

"I can't leave Leo here. Not like this. What if he gets hold of some poisonous plants, or walks off and falls into a ditch and breaks his leg?"

She shakes her head. "You worry so often, I'm surprised you're not covered in warts. Worry is a human trait."

What does she expect? I live in a human world. She'd worry, too, if she'd never had a solid sense of identity or a real home. Until Grandma and Grandpa, if I'd disappeared, no one would've noticed I'd gone, or cared if I'd ever lived at all.

"Let me ease your mind," she says. That strange glowing-hand-thing begins, and in moments, the sound of something big and dangerous fills the night. Out of the forest leaps a massive gray wolf. I jump back as it swings its head back and forth, lifting his nose to sniff the air. Kera goes to him and scratches his ears, whispering strange words. When she backs away, the wolf circles Leo, and like a dog chasing its tail, he twirls about before sinking to the ground beside my friend.

"There," Kera says. "Safe 'til morning."

"I know this fairy tale," I say, not even trying to keep the worry from my voice. "The wolf eats the little girl in the red cape."

"Leo isn't a girl."

She obviously wasn't raised with Grimm's stories whispered in the dark, the more gruesome the better.

"Never mind. Are you sure it won't, you know, maul him, bite him, eat his intestines for breakfast? The usual wolf thing?"

The wolf lifts its head and growls. I cringe and take a big step back. Leo struggles to sit up, and the wolf forces him back down by laying its big head across his torso. "Why do I get the feeling Leo's not going to thank me if he wakes up before we get back?"

The trees creak and sigh, and from out of the darkness, Jason appears, passed from tree to tree, until he's suspended high in the branches over Leo, still asleep.

Kera pats the tree and smiles at the wolf. "That's better. Take care of them until we return." She motions me forward. "Under their care, your friends will be safe until all the *pux* are caught."

A sharp bark of disbelief escapes me as I reluctantly follow her. "Sure, 'cause this is all totally normal."

She must be serious about these *pux*, because before I can say another word, she's way ahead of me. I catch up to her and say, "They're gone, and we've only managed to catch one. Not good odds. How are we going to find them, now?"

She holds up the trap. "We have someone who can find them for us."

I step close to examine our prisoner. Since it's no longer glowing bright enough to burn my retinas, I can clearly see it's a female, perfectly proportioned, with long, tousled blond hair and black eyes. Translucent wings snap back and forth like a bee as she saws uselessly at the trap with a jagged, crystal blade.

Her clothes are wispy and light and full of color, and I can't help but think of *The Borrowers* or *The Indian in the Cupboard*, books I used to read when I was younger.

"She's like a tiny person." Her looking so human is something I didn't expect. "Gross. I just smooshed a bunch of tiny people."

"Not exactly. She's a form of sídhe," Kera says in a matter-of-fact voice, "and much too unruly to trust."

That's what people always thought about me. I suddenly feel an affinity to the tiny girl. "Poor little thing."

I raise my hand to touch the trap, and when I do, she bares her teeth, lifts her tiny blade, and glows so bright, I'm shocked I don't go blind.

I snatch my hand away. "She doesn't look like she'll help us."

Kera holds the trap in front of her. "*Pux* can't stand being separated from the group. Come on," she says, jiggling the cage and frowning at her prisoner. "Find your friends."

The little *pux* stiffens and leans forward, sniffing the air. Her attention immediately sharpens toward the south, and she glows brighter.

A wide grin spreads across Kera's face. "We go that way."

"Huh. She's like a bloodhound, only not."

We let our captive guide us, and it doesn't take me long to realize where we're headed. A barn rises past the line of trees, and a few yards behind it is Leo's house. Muffled shouts come from inside.

As Kera hangs the trap on a nearby branch, I race toward the house.

Pop barrels out of the front door, his eyes wide with horror as a cluster of lights swirl around him, pulling at his hair and nipping at his skin like nasty bugs. His fear-filled gaze lands on me, and then his eyes roll back, just before he crashes like a dead man onto the porch.

"Pop!"

Kera appears behind me, and on seeing her, the *pux* dart away. She drops to her knees and checks Pop's pulse. "He's asleep."

Relieved, I step around a collection of fishing poles and a few fishing nets left out on the porch, and open the front door. When I enter, a hiss of anger rolls through the *pux*. A book immediately zips past my head and slams into the wall, followed by a dog collar and a tea kettle. I duck into the melee, dodge the *pux* as they bounce off the walls, open cabinets, knock over dishes, scatter paper, and torment the old dog huddled in the corner. I pick up a rolled newspaper and smack my palm with it. The sound makes the *pux* draw back.

"That's right. Big bad guy wants to play some more baseball." I'm not about to give them time to form an attack plan. I step forward and start swinging. "Kera!"

The screen door bangs behind Kera when she enters the house. The *pux* sound a collective gasp and fly down the hall. Their loud buzzing grows as I race after them. They dart into the last room and I follow, but stop short when I see a group of *pux* yanking out strands of Reggie's hair. Kera comes up behind me and whispers, "They need the hair for one of their spells, one that will have him doing all sorts of tasks for them."

That didn't sound good.

The *pux* spot us and fly in a hissing mass through the open window. Sticking my head out after them, I search for the little glowing lights, but all I find is Pop, gently snoring on the porch. I pull back into the room and survey the damage. Clothes hang out of dresser drawers and sag off hangers. A bottle of spilled cologne scents the air with its heavy, musky fragrance.

Kera rights the bottle and points out tiny foot prints. "They bathed in it. If they're not rolling in the dirt, they're rubbing themselves with flower petals."

I shake Reggie's blankets clean and resettle him in bed while Kera searches the house for any remaining *pux*. An eerie quiet permeates the house. Kera meets me in the doorway of another room.

"Are they gone?" I ask.

"Not far, I'm sure."

Cautiously, we make our way to the front of the house, my rolled newspaper at the ready. The windows are open, and there's no sign of the *pux*. What we do find is chaos. Not one surface is saved from destruction.

I pause at the kitchen. The refrigerator door hangs open, as well as every cabinet. Broken pottery, jam jars busted and oozing sticky, mushy fruit, and upended milk cartons lie on the floor. I kick the fridge closed, slap each cabinet door shut, and take a dishtowel to the spilled milk. When I'm done, I find Kera in the living area, wading through papers and displaced cushions as she murmurs softly to the dog.

"It's okay." She stoops and runs her hands along the dog's head and quivering back. "It's all over now. Don't worry. No one blames you."

He looks up at her with trusting eyes, and I see him shudder with relief.

"What should we do about Pop and Reggie?"

Kera straightens. "They shouldn't remember a thing."

I survey the mess all around us. "I think they're going to notice something happened."

Kera nods toward the dog. "He'll do what he can."

"You expect me to believe the dog's going to clean up?" Even as I say it, the dog rises and begins to nudge fallen books aside and replace the couch cushions. *Just accept it and go on*, I tell myself.

Kera searches the yard while I scoop Pop into my arms, carry him inside, and lay him on the couch.

When I straighten, Kera shouts, "Dylan! Hurry!"

The alarm in her voice has me bounding out the front door. I come to a stop when I see her walking toward me with a cluster of bright lights surrounding the trap she's holding at arms' length.

"They're trying to free her. Hurry and slip something over them."

Glancing about for something to use, I spot the fishing net near the front door. I grab it and race back to Kera. The ball of flickering lights reminds me of how bees cluster around the queen to protect it. They're so intent on rescuing their friend, none of the *pux* react until the net is over them and I'm twisting it closed. Then, their buzzing becomes deafening.

Kera sighs in relief. "Finally," she says, and hangs the *pux* in a nearby tree. We stare up at the ball of light dangling like a Chinese lantern. The light casts a golden glow around us.

"Did we get all of them?" I'm not convinced. From prior experience, catching them all at once seems too easy.

"No *pux* will ignore another's call for help. They'll risk their own lives for each another. It's the one honorable thing they do."

"What're you going to do with them?"

"Take them back where they belong." Her gaze lands on mine, and a sense of sadness seeps from her. "I couldn't have done this alone."

We stand, gazing at each other beside the netted *pux*, our silhouettes outlined by their pulsing light.

I'd promised to help catch the *pux* so she could take them home, but now that it's done, a feeling of impending loneliness creeps over me, snagging painfully against my ribs. "So this is it, then?"

"I can't chance them getting loose."

"No. You can't chance that." With the evidence of one night of their destructive ways behind us, her concern is understandable. I gaze out at the night, judging the time to be close to three in the morning. I'm not tired. I'm hopeful—a condition I'm not used to. "Do you have to go now?"

"I think I must," she says in a voice so soft, I need to lean forward to hear it. She leans closer. "What about you? Will you come with me? Find out why you were abandoned here? We need you, Dylan. *I* need you."

"I want to, but I can't." The reasons are complex, and ones I need to work out before I decide to do anything. The smell of sorrow, like burnt molasses, invades her summer scent. I take her hand, needing to touch her. "I'm sorry."

My heart twists, but in a good way. What's wrong with me? Everything feels different. I feel different. For the first time in my life, I feel free.

It's her.

If I had always known she was real, known she was out there waiting for me, would I have done things differently?

I memorize each dip and rise of her beautiful face as I finger the gentle roll of her dark hair. I palm her cheek — her skin carries a hint of silkiness — and I wonder at the warm contact. The rightness of her. I would have been a better person.

The air hisses with the unspoken. I lean closer. "Kera. I…"

The glow from the *pux* dims and their buzzing fades. Their curious little faces stare out at us.

"Yes?" She leans closer, until we're only a sliver apart.

I don't know how to explain what I feel, how to express the longing, how the air between us is my enemy because I want her in my arms and nowhere else. My hand slips away. "I'm going crazy. I want to believe all this, but — "

Kera throws her arms about my neck and brings her lips to mine. I give in and lift her into my arms, holding her tight. She tastes of sweet clover. Of promises that will never be broken. Of memories we've shared and those to come. The kiss deepens and my senses explode. Her hands clutch at my hair, and I pull her even closer, reveling in the comfort of belonging.

Slowly, she pulls away. Her lips touch my ear, her breath whisper soft. "Believe, Dylan."

"I do," I say, like a lovesick puppy. She pulls away, and I fall into her eyes, into the magic that surrounds her. I want her to stay exactly where she is, to never let her go.

She steadies herself by clutching my arms. "When I felt you, I hoped. When I touched you, I knew. We are meant to be. Forever."

First date declarations are never a good sign. Warning bells usually sound. *Time to break it off with the clingy chick.* The possessiveness shining from her eyes should scare me a mile away from here, but it doesn't.

A laugh bursts from her throat. "Look at what we did, Dylan!"

The ground around us has burst to life. The grass is thick, the wildflowers brilliant. A nearby vine drips heavy, lilac-colored blossoms. It's like we've stepped into a kids' movie. All that's missing are twittering birds, a cute deer or two, and a guy singing some catchy theme song.

She's right. We're meant to be together. There isn't a doubt in my mind.

Her fingers push a strand of hair off my forehead, and I lean into her touch. She smiles knowingly. "This is torture, but I have to go. The *pux*... I need to take them back before they slip free."

She takes a step away, and I grab her hand, stilling her. "Come back. Tomorrow."

I don't care if I sound desperate. I've never felt this way before, and I don't want it to end.

Her smile widens, and in a split second, she's back in my arms, pressing her lips to mine in a hard kiss. She pulls away way sooner than I'd like, as reluctant to leave as I am to let her. "You don't have to ask. Now that I've found you, I'll never let you go."

Awaken to Reality

I lean against the tree where we'd left Leo and Jason, and let out a deep, happy sigh. "She's amazing."

My joy is contagious. The bark skitters beneath my back. The trees above me dance and litter my shoulders with glistening, pale green leaves. A lone bluebird darts in front of me, twirling in a show of acrobatics, while a squirrel scampers from limb to limb and chatters excitedly at me.

Leo and Jason sleep next to me. Long gone are the wolf and Jason's high, branchy bed. Soft, thick moss I called forth cushions their heads. Me. Not Kera. I created the little tufts. I hold my fingers in front of my face.

"Seriously amazing." I'm enamored as much with my newfound power as I am of her.

I stretch out my hand. My palm grows warm, and a soft glow slips over my fingers and up my arm until I'm flush with power. I shut the glow off, then turn it back on. Off and on and off, blinking like a traffic light. I'm in complete control. No more worries about becoming a human glow stick. I call on the power again. The earth bubbles and up pops a vine, which slithers along the ground until it reaches the nearest tree. I watch as it hugs its way up the trunk and huge, trumpeting orange blossoms sprout along its shoot. I close my fist and the vine stills, yet it thrums with life, as does the whole area. The once plain pocket of forest is dotted with flowers and grasses and all sorts of growth that I've coaxed from the ground since Kera left. My skin dims to its ordinary pallor, yet I feel like a master painter perfecting the landscape stretched out before me.

Ordinary painters create illusion. I create stunning reality.

The sun rises, although there is no visual sign of it this deep in the woods, except for the brightening palette of light grays, rich greens, and muddy browns. Rain patters, but we stay dry thanks to the heavy cluster of boughs I've woven over us.

Jason stretches and knocks into Leo, who grunts and pushes him away. Slowly, Jason's eyes open and he sits up, confusion on his face. "What's going on? Did we sleep out here?"

I nod.

"Why?" He yawns and stretches some more. "I hate camping, and don't take this wrong, but I don't know you well enough to want to spend the night getting wasted in the woods with you."

"You don't remember what happened?"

His eyes narrow, and I can almost see his brain clicking back in time. "The ghost. We were going to find the ghost."

Leo pops up, all decked out in flowers and ripped clothing, his hair a mass of knots and finely leafed plants. His glassy-eyed expression sways from Jason to me.

"What the—" Jason scoots back. He turns to me. "What happened last night?"

"Tiny people," Leo says on a rough whisper laced with fear. "Glowing tiny people. Am I right?"

Jason's eyes widen. He jumps up and spins around, his stance defensive and alert. "Where are they?"

Excitement thrums against my bones. I can't keep silent a moment longer. I lean forward, the excitement in my voice catching their attention. "Guys, something amazing happened last night."

"Is it going to explain the way he looks?" Jason asks.

"Watch." I stand. Heat flares. The soil bubbles beneath my feet higher and higher, and then I'm off, surfing around the area, dodging trees and debris, laughing at the shocked looks on their faces.

Jason yanks me off the dirt mound when I pass, slamming me to the ground. The wave of soil that had been beneath my feet immediately flattens and I find myself staring up into his angry face.

"What the hell is going on?" he growls.

I jump up, and Leo, with his goofy hairstyle bobbing as he moves, stands between us. I try to push past him as I yell at Jason. "That was messed up! What's wrong with you?"

Jason's lips thin, strengthening his scowl. "I don't know. It was wrong. Unnatural."

Leo places a hand on each of our chests, becoming a tall, thin partition that barely stops me from thrashing Jason, here and now. "Take it easy. You caught him off guard is all."

"Yeah," Jason says, scratching the stubble sprouting on his chin. "What happened to you? To us?"

"I'm trying to tell you. Those lights? They're the *pux*. They came, and you guys fell asleep, just like my grandpa and the sheep." I glance at Leo. "Kera came, and we stopped them from making you their slave. They completely trashed your house, by the way, but we caught them, and she took them back."

"Who's Kera?" Leo asks as Jason says, "Back where?"

"Kera's the girl! The one we came to catch. She's a…she's a…"

"Ghost?"

"No. She's something else. Something amazing."

Leo's eyebrows rise. He drops his arms and steps beside Jason.

"You like her."

"What?" I ask, my mind full of Kera.

Leo nudges Jason. "He likes her. Look at him."

Jason's body contracts into a hard knot, the tension in him aching to explode. "I don't care. He made the earth move. He rode it like a wave. That's not normal."

"No. It's not." I face them. "*I'm* not normal. I'm a *first*."

Leo and Jason exchange a worried glance.

"Okay, bro. You can be first," Leo says. "And it's your right to be as abnormal as you want, so long as you keep it cool."

There's a definite calm-the-crazy-guy tone to his voice. I'm done being the odd man out. "I'm not crazy. Finding her is the best thing that's ever happened to me. Haven't you guys ever felt like you didn't belong? That something was missing? I know what's missing now. I get it. Watch."

A sudden glow sweeps through my body, and the nearest tree shudders to life. One of its limbs dips and lifts me up. The guys yell and duck, only straightening when they see me jump from branch to branch with abandon. The movement is freeing, knowing the trees won't let me fall. Jason and Leo gape up at me, shocked by what I'm doing. With one last leap, I land in front of them, breathless with excitement.

Confusion, fear, and disbelief intermingle on their faces, but I can't stop. The release of power is pure bliss. Chest heaving, I lift up my hand and a hawk spins through the trees and lands on my arm. I stroke its feathered head.

Jason's eyes are wide with alarm. Leo blinks rapidly, as if his brain can't keep up with everything he's seeing.

The hawk tips his head and screams, a warning to fear him. I can feel the rapid beat of his tiny heart, how he wants to be free and fly. I can't deny him and lift my arm. The hawk takes off. "It's wild. Kera says *firsts* can control nature, can make stuff happen that humans can't. I don't understand it completely, but I'm not going to stop. I can't stop."

Leo peers up at the trees. "Are they alive?"

I feel their restlessness, but little else. "Not in the same way you and I are. All I know is, if I ask, they do whatever I want."

"So they won't attack us?" he presses.

I smile and shake my head. "No."

Leo goes to a tree and puts his hand to it, like he's trying to do a Spock mind meld or something.

Without warning, Jason moves right in front of me, an intensity I've only seen on his web site photo album shining from his eyes. "Can I do what you do?"

"Not by yourself."

"But you can make it happen, right?"

The temptation to try pushes at my thoughts, but my grandparents will be up soon if they aren't already. I need to be smart about this. "I don't know. What if we're seen? It's getting light."

"You worry more than my grandma," Jason says on a groan. "It's raining, Superboy! No one will see us. Come on. You gotta share the moment." He looks to Leo for backup. "Am I right?"

"It'd be cool," Leo says with an ambiguous shrug, but there's a glimmer of hopeful excitement in his eyes.

The haze of heavy rain clings to the forest. Jason's right. No one will see us, and it would be fun to see what I can do.

I let the power race to my hands. On seeing them glow, Jason shouts. Leo smiles.

First things first. I call for clear skies above us. As soon as I ask, the clouds begin to swirl until a hole punches through the clouds, revealing a band of blue sky. Though rain continues to sweep down heavily on the rest of the forest, where we are, the sun shines. I stare at my hands.

Jason lifts his face to the light. "That is totally cool."

Leo smiles even wider. "Bro, you can control the *weather*."

The awe in his voice echoes the awe I feel. Whatever I wish seems to happen without me even trying. This isn't just cool, it's freaking surreal. I can make things happen people only dream about. Excitement jets the power-charged glow along my arms, rocking the ground where we stand. The two of them shout their surprise, and I grin. "I hope you guys are ready for this."

I call on the earth and dirt rises under their feet. Jason's bulkiness totters for a second before he catches his balance. Leo flexes his knees, surprisingly steady on his feet for a lanky guy. Their faces are taut with expectation.

"Here goes." I concentrate and send the pair darting between trees, narrowly missing shrubs and low hanging branches. It doesn't take long before I get the hang of it.

Riding my own dirt wave, I speed them along, direct them through clearings, and rip new trails through the underbrush. We race, pitting ourselves against each other, trying to knock one another off balance.

We plow through the woods, scaring the wildlife as we rush by. We circle around and before too long, we end up back where we started. Leo and Jason laugh, and while they're distracted, I step onto a branch and disappear into the trees.

The dirt under their feet grows flat. "Hey!" Jason shouts.

They search for me, calling my name, but they don't know to look up. I finally yell down a challenge. "Ready for some real fun?"

Without warning, I send tree limbs to pluck them from the ground. A thought fires within me, and Leo is catapulted into the air. He yells, long legs and arms flailing, and I send a branch to catch him. When he hits, a shower of leaves cascade toward the ground.

Jason crouches on his branch, muscles tight with expectation.

"Do it!"

The branch quivers, and he goes flying. I leap along the branches with my friends, growing more confident in my abilities by the minute. With my control, there is no fear of anyone falling. We leap among the trees like crazed squirrels. Pine cones are plucked from their limbs, and a game of dodge the pine cones commences. Jason leaps from a nearby branch and whips a particularly large pine cone at me, which smacks me dead center on my forehead.

For a brief moment, my attention wavers. A mistake. Jason takes that moment to leap to the next tree, yet there is no branch waiting to catch him. He hits the edges of several spindly limbs, vainly grasping for a handhold. Leo yells. I shake off the surprise and concentrate on a tree. Its roots ripple up, shredding a jagged line into the ground as it leans forward and extends a branch. Jason lands in a leafy fist only a few feet from the ground.

My ragged breathing sounds loud in the sudden quiet. Shaking free of the leaves, Jason twists about and glares up at me. "You trying to kill me?"

The limb dips and he slips to the forest floor where Leo and I join him. "Sorry, I…"

I rub my eyes, suddenly more tired than I've been in a long time. The weight of exhaustion presses down on me, pulsing like a living thing, demanding I close my eyes and sleep.

I slump forward and Leo and Jason catch me. Leo slings my arm around his shoulders. "Are you all right?"

The rain I'd been holding back finds us. Jason swears as he slips into place beside me. "You look wasted. You need to lie down."

I raise my droopy eyelids, but my legs feel gummy. My head is spinning. I can't focus. Even my mouth refuses to work properly. I can only grunt.

Their whispers lap against my ears, waves of sound I can barely distinguish as sleep presses down on me.

"Let's take him home," Leo says.

"Dude," Jason huffs, his arm tightening around my waist. "He can barely walk. Adults don't like seeing their kid dragged home semi-conscious. Trust me on this."

"We can't leave him here in the rain."

They argue over what to do with me, but finally, Leo convinces Jason I'd be better off at home.

My eyes flutter open for a brief moment as they haul me across the area where I'd created beauty out of nothing. The ground is torn up, and the trees are ragged and bald in spots. Destruction rears up wherever I look.

My eyelids droop. I feel like I've been hit by a bus. "Too much," I slur over and over again. I can't move, and my feet drag furrows into the forest floor, scarring further the beauty that had once been.

It's no easy task getting me home. The wind picks up, and the rain slithers between the high limbs to plaster our shirts to our skin and mud to our shoes. When we finally get to my house, Grandpa pulls off my shoes, slings my arm around his shoulders, and drags me inside. "Looks like you boys had one hell of a night."

"Too much." The words rumble once again from my throat.

He snorts as he shoulders his way into my room. "I'll say. Boys and liquor do *not* mix."

I'm not drunk, I want to say.

But you are, a little voice inside of me says. *Drunk on magic.*

Unexpected Complications

Holding the netted *pux* up, Kera said a quick spell, binding them to her realm before letting them go. It was the best she could do.

No guilt threatened her resolve as she watched them buzz high into the trees where they'd most likely begin plotting another way to cause havoc.

"Out in the dead of night in your underclothes? Scandalous. I never pegged you as a rebel," said a soft feminine voice drifting out of the darkness.

Kera jerked around, dagger in hand. Reclining on a low branch was Lucinda, another one of Faldon's hopeless causes, and about as unlikely to become a useful member of society as a dragon. Her snow-white mane cascaded over her milky-white shoulders as she flipped beneath the branch, dangling for a moment before dropping to the next, her eerie, pale-green eyes studying Kera.

"You do know it's forbidden to use that particular spell on living creatures," she said.

Kera's stomach knotted.

"Don't get me wrong. I agree. The *pux* should be contained." Lucinda leapt from her branch, and in midair, gobbled a *pux* before she landed, catlike, onto another branch. "They're far too tasty to let roam at will."

Lucinda's gaze latched onto the knife in Kera's hand. The playful tilt to her lips disappeared, and a dangerous look entered her eyes.

Kera slowly returned the dagger to her waistband. She'd do anything to calm her unexpected visitor and get her to leave. "I had no choice. They've been—"

"I'm sure your reasons are sound." Lucinda interrupted, her intense look morphing into a conspirator's grin. "I certainly won't tell anyone."

It was just like the manipulative creature to dangle a promise in the air, only to snatch it away without warning. Kera had to obtain a true vow, one Lucinda wouldn't break. "Promise me you won't tell anyone what I've done."

"About binding the *pux* or consorting with humans?"

Kera clutched her necklace. "I never—"

"Who am I to judge? I'm not one to use a proper door either, especially one guarded by three warriors who have orders to kill anyone crossing between worlds." Lucinda dropped gracefully from the tree and sauntered over, her hips swaying in her clingy, silk dress. She stopped only a few feet from Kera and leaned in. "Messy business, being killed. I don't recommend it."

Kera tried to ignore the quiver that unexpectedly raced up her spine. Had Lucinda seen? Could she sense her fear? Wild things always knew when a person was afraid, and right now, Kera had never been so terrified.

A knowing expression crossed Lucinda's face. "You're shivering. Chilly?" A plain dress and dark blue coat appeared in Lucinda's hand as if she'd pulled them from the air. "You'll need these."

Kera took them. If Lucinda thought she'd need them, she'd gladly take them, but it didn't waylay her fears. "Why are you being kind?"

"Now I *am* hurt." Lucinda moved close—too close—and peered at Kera's lips as if she could see the kiss that lingered there. "A woman in love is hard to resist."

Kera's fingertips covered her mouth. "I'm not in love." The hateful creature couldn't know about Dylan. Not yet.

Lucinda's bared her startling white teeth in a smile that was anything but comforting. "Be at rest, little liar. I won't tell your secrets."

Kera's fingers crushed the woolen dress. "I don't lie. We of the *first* can't lie."

Lucinda let loose a throaty laugh and moved silently into the darkened forest. "You owe me, Kera, daughter of life…and death. You owe me."

Magic whooshed from the direction Lucinda disappeared, and Kera caught sight of a fluffy white tail before it melted into the darkness.

"Lucinda, wait." Kera called, but the evil creature stayed away.

The forest grew still, subdued by the hunter in its midst. Gooseflesh rolled along Kera's arms, and she buffed them away. Whenever possible, it was best to avoid a *lutine*. They were ferocious and too cunning to trust. Having one know your secrets was a danger that made Kera more than uncomfortable.

She eyed the barrier. If you didn't know about the opening, you wouldn't see it, but she knew it was there. Now, so did Lucinda. If the ability to break through the barrier didn't worry her before, it definitely did now. She'd have to tell Faldon. He'd know what to do.

Kera put on the dress, wrapped the coat around her body, and returned home, her thoughts full of Dylan and the shock of finding him.

She'd made it through the marbled front hall and halfway up

the grand, curving staircase when her father's loud call stopped her in her tracks.

"Kera! Where have you been?"

She whirled about, forcing her eyes to widen with innocence. "I was out walking, enjoying the night air. I couldn't sleep."

"We have company."

Navar came into view. His entitled demeanor demanded attention as much as his heavily adorned military attire. The goblet full of wine appeared especially fragile in his hand. He raised the glass to her and smiled—a beautiful smile that held so much hate. She heard the murmur of others. A celebration was underway. What horrible deed had Navar done now that warranted cheer?

Kera bobbed a quick curtsey. "My lord."

Her father stood at the bottom of the stairs, resplendent in a suit of superfine black wool paired with a cream colored vest shot with gold thread. His expression was unreadable, stiff. Something was terribly wrong. "We only awaited your return to—"

"Look at her," Navar interrupted. His dark eyes reminded her of two drops of rancid oil; whatever they touched came away with a greasy stain. "She's given us a good chase, but I warn you, Hadrain, a spoilt daughter makes for a spoilt queen. You assured me she was neither."

Kera's breath stilled. "Queen? Me?"

Guilt traced the contours of her father's face. "Kera." Her name on his lips sounded lost. Disconnected. "I meant to tell you, but the timing was never ripe and…"

Navar stepped forward and held out his hand. "Now the time has come, and your presence is required."

Kera didn't acknowledge Navar. Her eyes were only for her father. "When?"

"You marry in three days' time."

Pain ripped into her and threatened to erase every last speck of joy. The thought of Dylan, knowing he waited for her...that she couldn't wait to see him again…

Navar moved closer, his hand held out confidently, his smile certain of her reception of the news. "Come. Join us as we celebrate our union."

She couldn't move. Her gaze flickered from Navar to her father and back to Navar's hand. He had killed her friend with that hand. No amount of washing could cleanse the blood from his fingers. She took a step back, reviled by the thought of him touching her.

"Kera," her father warned softly.

She didn't listen. She backed up the stairs as if she'd stumbled into a den of murdering thieves.

"That's right, my dear." Faldon's voice filled the awkward silence as he swept forward out of the shadows. "You must change. The occasion is too important for such simple attire."

Kera didn't gracefully exit their presence. She turned and darted up the stairs as if her life depended on it.

Once in her room, she slammed the door. How could her father give her away like she was some forgotten trinket, recently found and unwanted? She paced her room and tugged at a loose string along the sleeve until it began to unravel. Her maid entered, carrying a dress Kera had never seen.

"Where did you get that?"

At the sharp question, the young girl faltered in her duties. "It is part of your trousseau, my lady."

"You made this? In secret?"

"Not just me. Your betrothed ordered it. A whole wardrobe awaits your inspection."

Kera's chest tightened, and she said on a strangled voice, "Where's the gown?"

The maid glanced from the gown in her arms to Kera. She'd been with Kera for years, knew her every wish before Kera spoke it, but now the girl seemed at a lost as to what she should do. "My lady?"

"The wedding gown! Where is it?" Her voice sounded harsh. Accusing. Her own maid had conspired against her, and Kera hadn't seen it coming. How had she been so blind?

Hesitance showed on the maid's face. "The seamstress isn't finished. It should be ready in time. I promise." The maid stepped forward, a little smile tugging at her lips, presenting the dress in her arms for Kera's inspection. "This one is my favorite. I know how you love the color blue."

Kera and Lani both loved the color. Had her maid seen Lani hanging in the square? Did she know that headless body was Kera's best friend?

"I would rather rip it to shreds than put it on."

The maid's smile fell. "You don't like it?"

Kera had to gain control of her emotions. She took a deep breath and managed a brittle smile. "No, it's just…I only wish I'd been informed. I would've loved to have an opinion in the matter."

"I warned your father, but he insisted you adored surprises."

A feeble laugh escaped. "He was wrong."

"I'm sorry." The maid held up the dress. "But it's lovely. Truly. All of them are."

It *was* beautiful. Kera fingered the silk. She'd have to put it on. Nothing could be done but make an appearance, mollify the crowd, and then escape.

The party was torture, the good wishes endless. By the time the sun rose, Kera was allowed to retire to her room. She tried to sleep, but thoughts of her father's betrayal flooded her mind. When her father tapped on her door, she lay abed, refusing to open her eyes. She was like the living dead—breathing, yet empty.

By late afternoon, she got up. Another dress she'd never seen had been laid out for her, the fabric luxuriant, the construction perfect. She hated it on sight. Even so, she put it on.

Navar had sent a few of his men to watch her. Luckily, she knew more ways to escape her home than they did, and slipped out through a secret door at the side of the house. Since her father had betrayed her, her only ally was Faldon. They had a lot to discuss. Too many disasters were converging to give her peace of mind. Navar couldn't find out about Dylan. Nothing mattered except keeping him safe. She and Faldon had to figure out a way to repair the barrier.

When Kera approached the sage's home, she saw a gathering of young men—servants of the council members—milling around outside. Uncertainty made her slow. So far, none of them had noticed her, but if she lingered any longer, that wouldn't be the case. One of the men stood and turned in her direction. At the same time, a milk-white hand darted out and pulled Kera into the late afternoon shadows.

Lucinda's eyes danced mischievously as she put a finger to her grinning lips. "If you want to know, come with me."

Trusting Lucinda was like playing with a fireball—hold on too long and she *would* get burned. Kera bit her bottom lip for an indecisive second, then nodded. In the blink of an eye, they became a translucent vapor. If her captor let go, Kera felt as if she'd descend into a puddle at her feet. Not the most comforting image.

Lucinda guided Kera past the men, and together they slipped inside Faldon's house.

With Lucinda's hand in Kera's, they walked among the councilmen whose murmured distress melted into an unsettling chant. Among them stood her father. Kera wasn't surprised. Whenever the council met, her father was in attendance. This was his land, and any problem would ultimately fall in his lap.

"Are you sure?" her father asked, his face wreathed in displeasure.

The councilman he questioned straightened to his full height. "I have it on good authority there's a young man in the human realm, one who supposedly has power beyond his circumstances."

Kera's grip tightened, but Lucinda only shrugged as if to say she had no idea how they'd found out about Dylan.

"But to suggest it's one of us. So close." Faldon's gray hair fluttered as he gave his head a strong shake. "It seems unlikely. How could the council not know for all these years?"

"That is for you to find out," the councilman said.

Faldon bowed deeply. His job prohibited him from refusing; even if they wished him to hunt down his best friend, he'd do it. It was his duty as their sage.

Kera's father and the rest of the men filed out, but the lead councilman fell back, an air of seriousness infecting even his slow blinking. "You must be quick. The longer we delay, the more risk we incur. If he's one of us, we must act quickly."

"I'll find out what I can," Faldon said, though he didn't sound pleased.

When he finally closed the door on his guests, his face revealed an unexplained sadness. He went to a trap door situated in the middle of the floor and tossed it open. As he descended the steep stairs, he called out, "Bodog! Bring me the scrying stone."

The fingers gripping Kera's hand loosened, so her body materialized. The council knew about Dylan. Kera touched her forehead in an effort to suppress her rising alarm. It rose, anyway.

Lucinda cheerfully hopped onto the table, crossed her long, lily-white legs, and combed her hair with her fingers. "Troubles come, troubles go, that's all us love struck, miserable souls need know. You've been a naughty girl, haven't you?" Her smile broadened. "How delicious."

Kera frowned. "Must you sound so pleased? Don't you have *pux* to eat, or bunnies to terrorize?"

"If they catch him, they will give him the mark. And that will be that." The *lutine* wrapped a lengthy strand of stark-white hair around her fist and leaned forward, eagerness transforming her face. "I live to see how you extract yourself from this mess. Will you continue your rebelliousness, or heed your duty? The fate of the kingdom lies on your shoulders."

Kera's cheeks burned, and she ground out, "Look elsewhere for entertainment."

With a final glare at Lucinda, Kera left Faldon's house.

All she needed was one last moment. One last touch. One last memory of happiness before her life became a never-ending series of misery and loneliness. Though she wished differently, the answer wasn't as difficult as Lucinda would like to believe.

She was a daughter of Teag, a daughter of life. She only had one real choice.

ᛗARKED

When next I open my eyes, a face stares back at me from outside my window. Startled, I roll off my bed, scraping my bare knee along the mattress frame. Cold, hardwood floor meets my bare chest. I notice a tiny rip in my Lucky Duck boxers along the waistband.

I really like these boxers.

A groan escapes as I pick myself up and look out the window again. The darkness is broken by the glow of Kera's face. Her pale beauty is frightening—in an unbelievably perfect way.

I grab the pants I'd worn the other day, all rumpled and stiff from air drying on the floor, and pull them on as I stumble to the window. With a quick shove, it opens. Outside, it's stopped raining. The air, thick with the scent of mud, pushes into my room. I pop the screen out, and hold out my hand to help Kera climb in. Once she's inside, she presses her lips to mine.

Nothing feels better than touching Kera. I hold her close, feeling her heart beat behind her ribs. The heat of her hands on my chest is impossible to ignore as I kiss her, teasing her lips, and ultimately torturing myself until my control is almost gone. I pull away, putting my forehead to hers, and silently count to ten. Counting to a hundred wouldn't help. Holding her intensifies my feelings of recklessness.

I can't let go.

I pick her up. You'd think her dress with its yards of material would be a problem, but it isn't. Not for her. She wraps her legs around my waist and rakes her hands through my hair. I place my head on her chest and close my eyes. The rapid beat of her heart matches my own. The scent of her is as heady as the feel of her in my arms.

"You smell like summer and—" The scent pulsing under her skin teases me with every breath and touch, building until I recognize the burnt sugar taste of how she feels. "—sadness."

She captures my lips with hers and slowly slides down my body until her feet touch the floor. Our kiss deepens, her embrace turns desperate. Her kiss fills with misery. The room turns too hot, too claustrophobic. I can't think. I try pushing her away, but she clings to me. Her breathing quickens, and she shivers within my arms. I sense real fear in her. Though she protests, I finally manage to step free. One, two, three steps back, separate but still connected. I can't stop staring at her, wanting her. She's like…

A drug.

What's happening to me? I've suddenly become one of those obsessive creeper guys that end up following a girl around school, just staring at her like I've never seen a beautiful girl before.

But I haven't. Not like her. Not in the flesh.

I slide my hand down my face and swallow hard. If I allow myself to get attached…

I can't. She'll leave me. Everyone does, and I really, really, really don't want her to leave me. My cheeks flush. I'm heading for disaster. I should pull over and stop this right now, but I can't, and that twists my gut into a billion knots. I take another step back.

She makes to follow me, and I hold her off by thrusting out my palm. I can't afford to lose control. Not with the fear that's inside me, and the crazy vibe radiating off of her. "What's wrong?"

She stops. A yearning so strong whips through her and into me. "I had to see you once more before their plans come to pass. It's my fault, Dylan. I tried to come to you sooner, but my father—" Tears flood her eyes. "My father and then Navar put his men to watching me."

"What're you talking about?" The clock flashes 12:08 a.m. I've been asleep for more than fifteen hours.

"When everyone went to sleep, I slipped out. They *know*," she wails. "My father. The council. They know about you."

I take another step back, needing the space to keep a clear head. The fear on her face sends a flash of apprehension through me.

"They should want you to join us, only they don't. It makes no sense."

A bitter laugh escapes me, and the tension that had been building suddenly dies. She's not saying anything new. No one wants me. No one ever has. Even my grandparents will turn against me. It's only a matter of time. "That's the story of my life."

It's like she doesn't hear me. Her brow crumples. "When you were ignorant about being a *first*, it was fine. They had no knowledge of you, and you didn't understand the power at your fingertips. Not until I showed you. And now that you know and they know—" Her voice grows tight and her gaze snaps to mine. "They must feel threatened."

"Threatened? By me?" I shake my head. "That's stupid. I'm not dangerous. What do they think I'm going to do? Take over their world?"

I laugh, but Kera doesn't join me. Her gaze widens with horrified clarity. "That is exactly what they think."

My smile instantly fades. "That's not funny."

"I agree."

This can't be happening. She has to be wrong. "So, how'd they find out about me?"

"I can only guess. Maybe they sensed the power in you that your world doesn't possess."

"Who exactly are *they*?"

"The council. Somehow, they know you can do things few can do. And—"

"That's ridiculous," I say. "I did exactly what you did."

"—once they are afraid, they will stop at nothing to neutralize that threat."

"I'm telling you, I didn't do anything."

"You must have," she insists.

"Like what? All I did was act like an idiot. We all did."

"We?" Her voice clouds with fear. "Who was with you?"

"Jason and Leo."

"The humans? You showed humans what you are?"

What is she going on about? She'd seen them, and not once did she say to keep the new me a secret. "They won't tell anyone. They're not like that." But even as I say it, a small flicker of doubt emerges.

"What did you show them?"

"Stupid stuff. We jumped in the trees and surfed on the ground—you know, like you showed me. Once I figured out how to control everything, it was no big deal." Not until I'd suddenly run out of energy. My body still doesn't feel a hundred percent.

I debate telling her that, when a knock sounds at my door. Grandma's hushed voice calls from the other side. "Dylan? Are you awake?"

The door begins to open. My heart pounding, I rush over and wedge my foot against it, hiding the bulk of my body so that only a sliver of my face shows. "Easy there, Grandma. You don't want to see what's on the other side of this door."

Behind me, Kera's climbing through the window. When her gown catches on a nail, she panics and begins tugging on the fabric, with no success. No way will Grandma understand why there's a girl straddling my windowsill after midnight, dressed like a character out of a Dickens novel.

I peer into the darkened hallway and see Grandma wrapped in her robe. A blush heats her voice. "Oh. I was in the kitchen. I couldn't sleep and I heard you…" She turns to go, but then quickly spins around. Her pale blue eyes pierce right through me. "How are you feeling? Any side effects?"

"No," I say too quickly, and then calmer, "I'm good. Thanks."

"Do you need anything? You haven't eaten all day. You must be hungry."

I've just found out not only am I not popular in this world, I'm even less popular in Kera's. Food is not a priority right now, and that's saying a lot. I'm always hungry. "No, that's okay. I'm good 'til morning."

A moment of silence between us grows as Grandma tries to hide her distress. I look back at Kera and see a woodpecker fly in and begin to peck at the nail. The moment feels surreal, like Kera should start singing or some crazy guy will grab her from behind and take her back to his shadowy kingdom. I turn back to Grandma, who frowns.

"What's that noise?"

"I think it's a woodpecker." I cock my head, pretending to listen, but the only thing I hear is my impending doom. I've got to get rid of Grandma, but I can't think how.

"It sounds like it's coming from your room."

"Yeah, it does. Um, so…"

I stretch out the word as long as I can, and her hands clutch the lapels of her robe, bringing the terry cloth together in a tight grip. Our eyes meet. I get the feeling she wants to say something and she's building up her nerve.

"Yesterday," she begins hesitantly, "you getting drunk. It wasn't about your mother, was it? She loves you, Dylan. She may be confused right now, but I know she loves you."

It would be so easy to blame everything on Mom, but I can't. "It wasn't about Mom. Really. I wasn't thinking. It won't happen again. I promise."

"All right." She eyes me through the tiny crack, and I can see the doubt and worry that shadow her face. "But if you need to talk, family is best. Those boys and what they have to offer, well, you'll find no answers there. Only more problems."

Great. My grandparents think I'm on the fast track to rehab. I nod and pour as much repentance into my voice as I can. "I know. Thanks."

She leaves, though not before she gives me another sad, disappointed look. I hate that look. When I close the door, I hear a ripping sound, and turn to see Kera tumble out the window. The bird follows, voicing a strange squawk. I rush over and stick my head into the cool night air. Kera lies on the ground. Her deathly pale face stares up at me.

I snag a clean shirt and tug on my shoes—without socks— before vaulting over the window sill. I land next to her and help her up. "Are you all right?"

She pushes me away and scrambles to her feet. Her eyes are huge and fill with horror. "Your mother's human?"

I step closer and cup her cheek. She feels feverish. "Kera, what's wrong?"

"Our realms have been separate for so long, I didn't even consider it. Your power. Its strength. But it can't be." She grabs my hand and pulls me close until our faces are only an inch apart. "Lie to me, Dylan."

"What are you talking about? Why would I—"

She squeezes my fingers, her grip desperate. "Tell me a lie. Any lie."

She's acting odd. Okay, odder than usual. My grip tightens, and I stare into her eyes. "I want you to go, and I don't ever want to see you again."

When I press my lips to her forehead, she bursts into tears. Pulling her closer, I feel her shake. Her hand slips along my chest and my muscles jump beneath her fingers. I pull away. She doesn't need to look far to see how she affects me. "It's a lie, Kera. I'd die if I never saw you again."

"I know. *Firsts* can't lie. Don't you see? You're a half-blood. An abomination."

The weight of her words sinks in and squeezes my heart. "What're you saying? What's really going on?"

Wiping at her tears, she hesitates for a moment before saying, "I've been such a fool. The *pux*. They were following *you*, drawn to your power even before you knew you had any. I told you they're sly creatures.

"After I released them, they must've told the council, and now they know you're a powerful half-blood, more powerful than you should be. Worse, you can deceive at will. The council has spent years upon years making sure our blood is pure. The extent they'll go to in order to keep it pure is frightening."

My jaw tightens, but I force it to move. "How frightening?"

"It's what I've been trying to tell you. They've marked you for death, and now I understand why."

"Death?" The word reverberates through my head.

A hoot from the woods makes Kera jump, and she searches the darkness. "Make no mistake. They're coming for you, Dylan. We can't stay here. Come with me."

She pulls on my arm, dragging me toward the woods. I follow, but seriously… she's got to be kidding. "Slow down. Can we please go back to that whole death thing?" I say, as she forces me into the woods. I can't hide my doubtful smile. "Come on, Kera. You're being a little over-dramatic, don't you think?"

Secure within the protection of the trees, she spins around and glares at me. "This isn't a joke, Dylan. We're running out of time."

This can't be happening. How can she want me to go? Just because she thinks I'm in danger—that someone wants me dead—she wants me to disappear? It's ridiculous. "You're overreacting. I'm nobody. They're going to figure that out, and then it'll be fine."

"I wish I were overreacting." Her eyes sparkle like sharply cut gems, edging out the misery that clings to her. "The one thing I'm completely sure of is that you must leave here and never come back. Promise me, Dylan. Only when I know you're safe can I be at peace."

I shake my head, denial flooding my brain. "You can't be serious. I can't leave like that." The thought of disappointing Grandpa, of abandoning Grandma so soon after Mom's "Long time no see, by the way, here's my son...gotta go," churns my stomach. The pain Mom put them through was unbearable, and I won't add to it. I've fought too hard to not go Mom's route.

I shake my head again and step back. "I'm not leaving."

She grabs my hand, and warm compassion touches the brittleness of her gaze. "Every day, their memory of you will fade just a little bit, until it will be as if you never were. You mustn't think on it. You *must* save yourself."

It feels like a vise is crushing the life from my chest. "No. You're wrong."

Misery returns to her eyes, and her voice turns insistent. "Humans don't have the ability to remember us for long. We become unreal. Part of their dreams. Fantasies."

"I'm not a fantasy," I growl and shake off her grip. "I'm *real*."

My world pitches, and everything suddenly becomes crystal

clear. All my life, I've easily faded in and out of peoples' lives. Not because I didn't matter enough to remember, but because I'm really more fantasy than flesh and blood. I can't accept that.

"Someone will remember me," I insist.

"For a time…"

"It'll break my grandma's heart if I leave."

"Even if it means saving her?"

"From what?"

"From those who are hunting you. Your father must have left your mother to save her. Don't you get it? War tore into our land. Rules were made. Humans abandoned. Those with mingled blood were terminated."

She has no idea what she's saying. "My father's disappearing act didn't save my mother. If you knew her, you'd know that." I search for a way to explain the impossibility of what she's asking me to do. "I get that you're scared, but I can't go with you. Not yet."

Silence falls. Kera curls her fingers into the fabric of her gown and glances away. She's pale. Her teeth nip at her bottom lip. "How can I make you understand? There is no more time. You can't stay here, Dylan…and you can't come with me either."

My heart stops for a split second, and a hot flash of warning burns along my skin. "If we go our separate ways, it won't save me, either."

"Don't say that. You have to leave. Forever. This isn't a game. It's real."

Whatever's going on, she believes it wholeheartedly. I graze my knuckles down her cheek. "I'm not going anywhere without you."

Frustrated, she pounds her fist on my chest. I can feel the heartache and need clashing within her. "I refuse to let anything happen to you."

"Something already has." I bury my hand in her hair and gently still her struggles. When her eyes find mine, I tell her the truth. "I love you. I have for a long time. When I'm with you, everything feels right. Everything *is* right. If you make me go, I'll be miserable for the rest of my life."

A groan rattles from her throat. "I was wrong to find you. I've destroyed the one person I would love forever."

"Then you love me?"

"You must listen. Believe me. I can *never* see you again."

I shake my head. This can't be happening. She doesn't mean it. The scent of burnt molasses coming off her is overwhelming. She thinks she's trying to save me, but it won't work. "Answer me, Kera. Do you love me?"

"To our kind, love is a curse as much as a blessing. To be loved and then abandoned is a torture that will never fade. For the humans who truly love us, it's even worse." Misery colors her face. "You must leave. It's the only way you'll be safe."

Pulling her to my chest, I kiss the top of her head. "Kera, do you love me?"

Tears stain her cheeks. "I won't see you die."

"I won't die. I'll find a way for us to be together. I swear it." I close my eyes and hold her tight.

Kera moans like she's in pain. "How can I say goodbye when my heart begs me to stay?"

I tilt her face up to mine. "Then stay with me."

Her expressive eyes soften. She rises on her toes; our lips coming closer, inch by slow inch. She believes. I've won. No more talk of leaving.

My expectation is met with a passion-filled kiss. Pleasure ripples through me. I feel strong, like there's nothing I can't do.

Without warning, she breaks free and backs up, killing my short-lived joy. Grief lines her face, and her eyes fill with sorrow. "Whatever you plan, it won't work. You're a half-blood. If I don't love you, then we're safe, and we'll both forget. You'll find another."

"I don't want anyone else." Why is she being so stubborn? I step forward, my hand outstretched. "Come on, Kera. Don't give up. Not yet."

She moves further away and places her hand on a nearby tree to steady her footing. Her body quivers with each breath she takes. "I won't risk your death."

On a sob, she turns and dashes into the woods.

I race forward, only to have the tree's branch suddenly block my way. Angry, I wish the tree gone, and no sooner do I think it than the tree uproots and crashes to the ground, splintering into a billion pieces. I plow after Kera, leaving a path of destruction in my wake. When I finally catch up, the mist's glittering fingers are closing around her.

"Kera!"

She looks back at me. The unearthly vortex whips her hair and clothes into wild collision.

"It's too late. You love me," I say.

Sadness clouds her eyes, and her lips part on a whisper. "I always have."

Before I can reach her, the air swallows her whole, and nothing remains but the soft echo of her words.

I place my hand where she disappeared, and the heat of her warms my fingertips. I splay my fingers and concentrate. The heat of her begins to move away. I follow it to the right, and as I do, the air ripples. For the first time, I can see the barrier that separates our two worlds—a mirage of energy that has become my enemy. Slowly, I drag my fingers along its invisible force, following the heat of Kera's body as she moves along its length on the other side. She pauses and so do I.

My hand hovers over the pulsing hot spot. "Can you hear me?" I whisper. "I won't leave you."

A handprint shimmers in the air before me, and I press my palm to it. I could push through the barrier, grab her, pull her through. It wouldn't take much.

And then it's too late. She's gone.

I stand there, jaw clenched, as the pain of her leaving slices through me. It's so deep and so profound, I nearly pass out. I can't live the rest of my life without her. This is no schoolboy crush. It's real, it's raw, and it's ripping me apart.

This is what my mother felt after my dad left. Only now do I understand.

PART TWO

Misplace the mind,
wait and see,
The wonders of what cans't,
can be.

FALLING ⊕VER THE EDGE

I try to force my hand through the barrier, but the wall fades into nothing, like it doesn't exist.

I quickly retrace my steps. My fingers slip along the rapidly dissolving energy field until I come to a point where it feels cool, and slightly moist. This is it. This is where she broke through to her world.

I concentrate on the spot, and for a second, the air splits, and I can see a small opening slowly knitting itself together. I grasp the edges. They're hard as ice, and their cold bite stings my hands. It doesn't stop me from pressing forward and pulling it apart. Thick mist rushes around me, its fingers splintering the darkness. The familiarity of the forest shatters as a whooshing sensation pulls at my limbs, drawing my body into a whirling vortex. For a second, I'm blind to everything but the white heaviness that clings to the air…and then the damaged barrier spits me out. The mist slithers away as my feet touch solid ground. Cobblestones, to be exact.

I'm shaken, my head's spinning, and I'm sucking down air. I drop my head between my knees and fight the blackout that threatens to overwhelm me. It takes a moment for the world to settle. Unsteadily, I turn to see where I've come from and find a real wall, bricks and mortar running in a staggered line until it meets with the buildings on each side. I'm standing in a dead-end alleyway. I run my hands over the bricks until my fingers clasp the edge of the capstone and then jump, hoisting my stomach onto the top of the wall. It's solid. Real. The wall runs for yards and yards in either direction. It's part of a bigger structure. A walled town. Beyond the town is a stand of trees that widen into a forest. I jump back down and push on the wall. It appears solid. I move my hand to the left and the rip appears.

I pull away and whip around, my eyes taking in my surroundings.

I expected trees, a mirrored image of my world, but what I see is far from that. More like a living museum of the past, complete with sounds and smells of a time on the brink of modernization. I can even smell the oil burning in the streetlamps. It doesn't take long for me to begin to panic.

"Kera," I whisper harshly. "Kera!"

I take a step forward. There's no sign saying *Welcome to Teag*. What if there's a trick to entering her world? Like maybe I was supposed to think about my destination, and since I didn't, I'm lost in another realm?

Apprehension, like tiny bullets, riddles my thoughts. The night lies thick and heavy, broken only by the odd sounds of animals. Horses, I think. A few dogs bark. Then, from my right, footsteps. The thought of standing here, waiting for whomever it is to find me, attacks the vulnerability I've tried for years to hide.

I'm weaponless other than my ability to manipulate nature. Stuck in a lifeless alleyway. Any form of nature is over the wall and far away. Kera said the power comes from the earth. It's time to find out if I can tap into it wherever I am. I reach out and power rushes into me. I'm stunned by the feeling—it's like I can feel all the way down to the core of the earth. My hands light up like I've dipped them in radioactive goo. Even my vision has turned night into day.

Kera breaks through the night, her gown swirling around her ankles as she comes to a stop at the mouth of the alleyway. Her face pales with shock. "Dylan! Y-you can't be here."

My vision instantly dims. The nightlight effect fades, and I go to her, wanting to hold her, even as I fight the frustration her defection has caused.

Desperation flares from my core. If I blow this, I might as well stop breathing. "How can you think you're doing the right thing? You love me. This is ridiculous. You're trying to get me to leave so I can live, but you don't get it. Life without you isn't worth living."

A loud clang of a clock sounds. She puts a hand to my mouth and shakes her head. "You have no idea what kind of danger you're in."

She grips my arm and pulls me forward, muttering under her breath about hiding me until she can send me back. We exit the alleyway, skimming the edge of the street like shadows. I hiss her name to get her to stop, but she won't.

Why is she being so stubborn? With a firm tug, I pull her to a stop. Her mouth rounds with surprise. I peel off her fingers and kiss her palm, feeling her hand curl against my cheek. Her skin is hot and smooth, and with each breath I grow stronger and more convinced I'm exactly where I should be.

With her.

I stare into her eyes, forcing her to see the truth. "It's too late. You can't hide me, and I'm not going back, not without you."

Her eyes widen, and she tries to pull away. "It's impossible."

It's not quantum physics. Okay, traveling through to another dimension is, but what *we* have is simple.

She bites her lips a bright red, making me uneasy. She's not telling me something.

"What's really going on? Tell me, Kera."

"I can't." She yanks free and rakes her fingers through her hair. Her gaze roams the area. Mine follows. This place could be a Hollywood sound stage of an old New England town. There's an apothecary, a boot maker, and a photography shop showing the tintype process of capturing one's image. The roads are narrow, built more for horses and carts than cars, and there's a lingering odor of burning oil and coal and soiled hay.

I can't stop to think about where we are. I don't really care. I'm with Kera, and from what I can tell, the street's deserted, but something's making her jumpy. When she turns to face me, her lips are pinched of color.

She looks lost and so alone. Uncertainty rolls off her. I step closer, shielding her with my body. I bend close and whisper gently into her ear. "It'll be okay. I won't let anything happen to you. Let me help."

I kiss her temple, willing her to trust. She shivers, and I can feel the war waging within her. Those violet eyes turn pleading, begging me to stop her from saying anything more. But I can't. I need to know. I urge her confession free. "What aren't you telling me?"

Her voice is pale and hard to hear. "I…" She wraps her arms about herself. "I-I'm like you. Exactly like you. I'm a half-blood, tainted by a human mother."

I couldn't have been more shocked if she'd spontaneously combusted into a pile of ash. "But you said they kill half-bloods here."

"Only if they know."

I shake my head, disgusted by the risk she's taking. "What's wrong with your dad? He should've sent you to your mother."

"She died soon after my birth."

Her confession chokes all the anger out of me. "There has to be someone—"

"He had no other option. After my birth, war broke out. It decimated whole families. Before he knew it, the gateways were locked, separating our worlds forever."

"Until now."

"The gateways are still locked and guarded. I've done a terrible thing. I've turned the barrier's magic against itself. That's how I entered your realm. And each time I have, I've met with trouble." She nervously scans the street as if she's expecting someone to jump out and grab her. "My father's risked so much to protect me, and look what I've done." Her violet eyes widen. "Trouble falls in threes. Did you know that?"

"I'm not superstitious."

Hopelessness drowns out her scent of summer, covering it with the frost of winter ice. Even her hands are freezing. "You being here is a disaster."

I'm a disaster. Yep, that sounds familiar. I'm losing her. She's melting into a pile of emotional goo. "Kera, it's not as bad as you think."

"It is!" The vein along her neck jumps heavily with each heartbeat as her gaze skitters from window to door and beyond. "You're marked for death, and if they find out I'm not who they think I am, they'll kill me, too. The council's right. Nothing good comes when our worlds intermingle."

"We're not going to die."

Her glare sharpens. "Oh, really? I've seen what they do to people like us. I've seen the lengths they'll go to, to purify our land. Death will be a blessing, Dylan, and there's nothing we can do about it. Nothing."

"You're giving up too easily."

"You have no idea what's happening." The smell of a stoked fire finds us. Her muscles tighten as she searches the rooftops. "We can't stay here."

She tries to push away, but I won't let her go. I run my hands up and down her arms. "Look at me."

It takes her a moment, but she finally does. I dig deep for whatever power this land holds, call it to me, and when it appears, it surges through me and into her, and she gasps. Our eyes lock, and I rasp, "I'm not afraid."

It's a crazy thing, this confidence I have. I don't know where it's coming from, but I have no problem embracing it. "This feels right. I was born to be here, to be with you, and no one has the right to tell us differently. I'll protect you. Do you trust me?"

Her eyes search my face, and her voice grows thick with emotion. "I want to be who I really am. I'm just afraid."

We really are two of a kind. I slip a stray curl of her hair behind her ear. "We'll find a way to make this work, Kera. I swear it."

A bird swoops down and chirps in her ear. "Someone's coming," Kera says.

She grabs my hand, but it's too late. A man lopes into view, sees us, and shouts for us to stand still. Yeah, right. We take off down the street, turn the first corner, and stumble into a series of crates. Kera mumbles something under her breath, and they snap into stairs like Lincoln Logs. We run up them, and as soon as our feet leave the first tread, it disintegrates. Before I can even process the feat, we vault over the wall and run for the trees. The guard isn't far behind us, blowing his whistle and shouting for his partner.

The trees slow us down. We need cover, some way to blind him. As soon as I think it, dirt swirls around the man and he staggers back, rubbing at his eyes. I throw Kera to the ground and roll, commanding the leaves and debris to surround us. When we finally settle, we're completely camouflaged, tucked beneath a patch of brambles.

The wind stops. Another man joins the first. "What's going

on?"

"A couple. I gave chase, but the wind blew dirt in my eyes, and now…" Confusion twists his face.

The second man comes within feet of us. "I don't see anyone."

"I told you. They're gone now."

"Come on." The second man moves off, his footsteps rustling in the scattered debris, and the first man grumbles a bit before joining his friend.

Silence sharpens until the same bird wriggles his head between the sticks and warbles a sharp song.

"They're gone," Kera says.

I command the debris clinging to us to fly off, and when it does, I slant a disbelieving look at Kera. "You can talk to birds, too?"

She rolls away and sits up. Her eyes grow dark violet as she stares back at me. "What did you do?"

"What, this?" I stand and shake off the dirt clinging to my clothes. "We needed to hide, so I thought if we could somehow get covered with leaves, they wouldn't see us. The next thing I know, we're covered. Pretty cool, I'd say."

"I've never seen anything like that."

I pause in plucking twigs from my clothes. "It's kinda new to me, too."

She looks me up and down as if seeing me for the first time. "Maybe we *can* find a way to make this work."

I help her up. "So you believe me now?"

She examines my hands. "I don't understand what's happened to you, but they're right. You keep doing things you shouldn't be able to do."

"Ever since I entered your world, my power has grown. I belong here."

"What about your grandparents?"

"I'll explain it to them. They'll have to understand, just like your father will have to understand."

She slips her fingers between mine. "My father isn't the problem."

Euphoria conquers all my doubts. I'm with Kera, and that's all that matters to me. "Everyone will understand. You'll see."

Hands clasped, we quickly move through the woods and away from the men. The trees sigh and rumble as we pass, while tiny lights flitter thorough the branches like floating diamonds. "Are those what I think they are?"

She doesn't bother looking. "*Pux*. They wouldn't dare harm us here."

"Why do I have a hard time believing that?" I throw out an image of me plucking off their wings and feeding them to hungry rats if they continue to spy on us, and they dart away. It seems whatever I want is granted. Power surges through me, bolstering my confidence. "We need a plan. A way to be together without freaking everyone out."

She pulls me along, and I notice she's concentrating on getting somewhere and not on what I'm saying.

"Where are we going?" I ask.

"To Faldon. He's our sage, my father's advisor."

It doesn't seem wise to involve someone else. I wrap my fingers more securely around hers and pull her to a stop. "Does he know you're a half-blood? Does he know about me? About us?"

"He knows more about me than anyone. And what he doesn't know, he'll soon figure out." She glances around. "We can't stop here. Please, trust me."

I don't have any choice, and we quickly slip back toward town. When we break through the trees, we come to a field with tightly-bound, straw targets set out for practice shooting. In the far corner, a large barrel reeks of ash. Kera pulls me along until we're at a gate inserted into the wall. Its door is wide, but thick, its lock a heavy thing made of brass. She taps the lock with her finger and mutters a word I've never heard, then pushes on the gate. It's doesn't budge.

"Damn the man. He's changed the spell."

As she works on the lock, I see a massive house in the distance that's ten times bigger than any I've ever seen. Its gates are imposing and solid. I point and ask, "Who lives there?"

She barely gives it a look before turning back to the lock. "I do." She rattles the gate and curses again. "My father is lord here."

"You're kidding me." I shouldn't be surprised—Kera is the epitome of a young lady of wealth—but I am. "You're like nobility?"

She nods, turns, and slides down the door until she's sitting in the grass, her head in her hands.

"This isn't the best hiding place." I whisper near her ear. At her scathing look, I straighten and shrug. "Just saying."

"I'm thinking."

While she thinks, I peer through a hole in the door. Candlclight flickers in one of the windows. I hear a cow low and chickens cluck. There's something about the place that's more than quaint. It's archaic.

I pull back and notice the sky is changing from black to blue. The sun is rising, but there's no sound of a morning TV show or buzz of a clock radio. All I hear is the sound of the earth slowly waking. It's a calm that calls to me. A serenity which is in complete contrast to the chaos of my mother's life.

Manic, I understand. This deep, sweet peace feels foreign. I prop my back against the door, and slide down to settle beside Kera. As she rests with her hands cupping her ears and her foot tapping impatiently, I let go of my fear of silence and let it sweep me into a moment of relief.

I really, really like it here. Life has never felt so… right.

Without warning, Kera leaps to her feet, mutters another

unrecognizable word and taps the lock. It clicks, and she pushes the door open. The door I'm leaning on. I promptly fall back into the yard and catch myself on my elbows.

She throws me a wide smile. "He's clever, but not clever enough. Stop lolling about, Dylan. We have to find you a place to hide before everyone is up and about."

A quick assessment of myself makes me wonder how I appear to her. I never thought my vanilla taste in clothes would mark me as a stand out, but if the men dress as differently as the women do here, I must look strange.

"Faldon's home." She points to the light coming from a window. It's a large home, set apart from its neighbor by a spacious yard. We pass a carriage house, a small barn, a shed, and a vegetable garden encased by a stacked, rock wall. The place is pixel perfect. Not a crumble of mortar or a misplaced bucket can be seen.

It's a quick dash to the back of the house where Kera raps on the back door and gives me a worried glance.

"What?" I ask.

The door flies open. "Kera!" The sound of her name booms across the yard. "By God, you've given me a fright. Your father is beside himself. He demands to know where you are, and in all honesty, I couldn't give him an answer."

"I'm sorry. I had to leave, but I'm back, safe and sound. And not alone." She turns and waves me closer.

I step into Faldon's view, and we both blink our surprise. From the sound of his forceful, deep voice, I expected him to be big and barrel-chested, but this man has thin arms, stick legs, a bony chest, and an abundance of long, gray hair that's spiked at odd angles. I've got a fairly decent imagination, but "old crazy science guy," dressed in dirty brown pants and a white shirt, stained and riddled with burn holes under a flowing lab coat, isn't what I expected a trusted nobleman's advisor to look like.

The color drains from his face. "Baun?" he says, and clasps his hand to my arm.

What's up with this old guy? Kera seems just as confused. Faldon's grip tightens. His eyes fixate on me, which raise the hairs on the back of my neck. The light from the rising sun accentuates the sharp planes of his face, yet reveals a glimmer gathering in his eyes.

His trance lasts for more than an awkward moment. When he realizes he's staring, his eyes harden, and he looks me up and down, and not in an I'd-like-to-be-your-friend kind of way.

Though he's thin, he's strong. And quick. He yanks me and Kera inside and slams the door. I stumble into the cool darkness of his home, catching myself on the scarred top of an old, wooden table littered with all kinds of glass apothecary jars. In the middle of the table, strung out like an octopus at a science fair, a bulbous vial with coiled pipes jutting from it sits atop a flame. Amber liquid bubbles through the pipes, which drip into small flasks.

It smells like death.

Kera gasps and waves the air in front of her nose. "Where's Percy? She'll have your head for messing up her kitchen."

"She took that silly maid home. Said she was allergic to cats. Families shouldn't lend out children if said children have leaky eyes, hiccups, and cry for their mother nonstop."

We're in a *kitchen?* Behind the chemistry-set-gone-wild are pots and pans, hanging like hats on the wall. Floor to ceiling cabinets line another. A massive stone basin fills a far corner, looking more like a bathtub than a sink, and next to that, an ancient stone oven spreads its bulky legs and pot belly into the room like a sleeping giant.

Underneath the herbs hanging near the fireplace, a belligerent clatter rises. Instead of a bird clinging to a stand, I see the impossible—a tiny, red and gold tipped dragon. Its barbed tail

snakes around the post, and its beady eyes lock onto me. With a
hop, it swings free, darting to a lower perch where it stretches into
a display of scrawny, scaly arms and paper thin, iridescent wings.
Its claws rake the air as its scaly back curves into a high arch, and
it lets out a steamy hiss.

This is a dragon? It's so…puny. Who'd be scared of this little
thing?

While Kera explains her absence to the old guy, I round the
table and reach out to touch the dragonette. A tiny arc of flame
spews from its mouth, and I rear back as the smell of burnt hair
rises from my forearm. "Hey!"

Small plumes of smoke curl from its nostrils, and it sucks in
more air, readying itself for another hair-singeing spark. "Be silent,
Blaze," Faldon says, waving the dragon quiet.

I turn to the old man. The azure blue of his eyes darkens. His
chest puffs out regally, and he says in that deep, proud voice, "*Who
is this?*"

Kera moves to stand next to me and places a hand on my arm.
"This is Dylan. He's—"

"The one you've been seeing?" Faldon interrupts. "The one
who has the council in an uproar?"

Kera shoots a quick, apologetic glance at me before nodding.
"Yes."

The old man's shoulders droop, and he shakes his head. "And
you brought him here? Oh, child. What have you done now?"

I don't like this guy. Can't he see Kera's hands shaking and
the fear shining in her eyes? I pull her close, and as soon as she's
tucked under my arm, she relaxes and closes her eyes. I glare at
Faldon in his dirty pants, burnt shirt, and boots that are covered
in a rank-smelling substance. "If you want to help us, great. If not,
then we're gone."

Kera jerks back. "Dylan!"

"I'm telling you, we don't need him."

"Silence!" Faldon's eyebrows arch, and he looks from me to Kera. "Love? Is this the reason?"

She nods. "I didn't search for it. It came to me. You've always said it would come when least expected. You were right."

"But a half-breed?"

My jaw hardens. "How do you know what I am?"

His nostrils flare as if *I'm* the one who stinks. "I would not be much use as a sage if I didn't use my gift."

Kera nods. "He's like me, Faldon."

"Like you." The old man turns his gaze on me, and a thoughtful expression enters his eyes. "That would make sense, but he's nothing like you, Kera. You're special."

She breaks free, and latches onto Faldon's wiry arm. "They already search for him."

"You should not have brought him here."

"She didn't," I say. "I followed her."

"Promise me you won't reveal Dylan to those who are looking for him." She turns to me and says, "When *firsts* make a vow, they are honor bound to keep it."

The man's cheek spasms a few times before he asks, "Will you tell him all our secrets?"

"All of them, unless you promise me you'll keep him safe."

He cups her cheek with a speckled hand. "Is this your final choice? Think clearly. Once made, it can never be broken, for when our kind fall in love, it's forever."

Her violet eyes soften, and her cheeks pinken and glow with confidence. "Yes."

In that one word, the power of her love is like a living caress.

Faldon sighs. It's a heavy thing, weighed by grief, as if she's just signed her death warrant. "Then I give you my word."

She relaxes. "There's much to discuss."

"Not now. Your father's on the hunt. Go to him, though I don't know what you'll say to explain your absence."

"Don't worry. I'll figure out something."

He cocks an eyebrow. "A lie?"

"A more palatable truth."

When he opens his mouth to argue, she shakes her head, and he sighs. "You're a stubborn girl. Be careful it doesn't lead you wrong." His meaning is as clear as if he'd shouted, "*Save yourself and dump the guy.*"

She comes and stands in front of me, her eyes sparkling with a determination that sets me on edge. Her dad may not have had options before when the *firsts* turned against half-bloods, but that isn't the case now. I take her hands in mine. "You don't have to do this, you know. We can leave."

Faldon snorts from where he rummages in a corner of the room. "There's no hiding from those who search for you."

My jaw flexes. I'm about to tell him off when Kera's fingers caress my cheek, bringing my attention back to her. "Stay here. I'll come back as soon as possible. In the meantime, do as Faldon tells you." When I frown, she smoothes the lines away and pleads, "For me."

How can I say no to that? I pull her into my arms. "I'll do whatever you want, for now. Do what you've got to do, but when you get back, you're going to have to start trusting me."

I pull her close, our lips touch, and she melts against me. The kiss is one I have a hard time ending.

Faldon clears his throat, which finally pulls us apart. Kera gives him a quick hug. "Take care of him. I'll be back soon."

With that, she's gone. I want to go after her, but I don't.

Why do I get the feeling letting her go will be the biggest mistake I've ever made?

The Truth Hurts

Taking the horse and cart into the woods was a gamble Kera had convinced her father they needed to make. She needed to see Signe. She needed to know the people in the caves were properly stocked. Though if one of Navar's men saw them, they'd be hard pressed to explain why it was laden with so much food.

They reached the caves without incident, but it didn't ease her father's mind. He sent a few of the men to watch for intruders as he called others to help unload. A boy in pants with deep cuffs because they were too long, and shoes with the toes cut out because they were too small, ran through the cave. He had the role of calling people to the store house, an area carved out of the rock near the entrance. Kera smiled, hearing his excited, high-pitched voice echo within the cave.

While the supplies were doled out, Kera took Signe's portion and went in search of her friend. As she moved among the people, she noticed a difference in how they were treating her. Like she was someone special. She couldn't figure it out, until one woman bravely stepped forward and congratulated her on her betrothal. "With you by his side, he'll listen and stop this madness."

The woman sounded so hopeful. Kera's heart twisted. Those

surrounding them spoke up. Everyone felt so sure she was exactly what was needed to bring their misery to an end. She had no idea how she broke free, but the rest of her journey to find Signe was done with her head down, avoiding anyone else who thought to "congratulate" her.

She found Signe in a back area where they'd set up a makeshift market. The people of the caves had created a miniature town, a way of life that imitated, as best they could, what they'd had when they were free—before Navar, before the Lost King. So many of the younger people didn't know any other way of life. They rarely went out, and when they did, it was mostly at night.

The marketplace was emptying fast by the time Kera entered the area. Signe's business of selling reworked clothes was a favorite, so it didn't surprise her when she saw her friend bartering with a customer and the customer's eight-year-old daughter. Signe saw Kera and waved her over.

When she came closer, she heard her friend say, "Yes, it's used, but what isn't? I've taken only the best thread from the least worn garments and covered any flaws the dress had."

The woman clucked her tongue, and pressed her daughter forward, saying they had to collect their food, but her little girl wouldn't be budged. She only had eyes for the dress. The mother saw the stubborn set of her daughter's chin and quickly came to a price, a half tin of coffee for the exchange.

The mother and daughter hurried off toward the front of the caves like everyone else, and Kera handed over the bags packed with essential food and a few luxury items, and gave her friend a disapproving smile. "I've brought you coffee and tea. Whatever you need, just ask me," she said, and then remembered, this would most likely be her last visit. That realization had her biting her bottom lip.

Signe stored the supplies Kera gave her out of the way and

tucked the tin into a threadbare carpet bag. "I know, but a full tin of fresh coffee is worth three times as much, and I can barter it for something I really need."

They both fell silent.

"I know you know," Kera said. The whole cave was buzzing with the news.

Signe clutched Kera's hand. "It's horrible. How could your father do this to you?"

"I don't know." Kera gently pulled her hand free. "I don't want to think about it."

She fingered the garments her friend had made, the work intricate and worth ten times what she was selling them for.

"You must hate me," Kera said, looking back at her friend. "We're exactly the same, yet I'm free to come and go while you must stay in here."

The old Signe would have let loose a playful quip, but the new Signe was sullen. Hopeless. "I don't have room to hate anyone but Navar."

Kera nodded to a woman who hurried past, feeling the same as Signe, but Dylan had given her hope. Hope for a life far away from Navar's madness. She stepped around the display, her nerves on edge. "Will you feel the same after I tell you what I've come to say?"

Signe locked her fingers with Kera's and pulled her down onto the rock beside her. She searched for eavesdroppers, but most of the people had left, so she turned back to Kera. "You've not done anything stupid, have you?"

"No." Had she acted that unstable of late? "Not in my opinion."

A thoughtful expression crossed her friend's face. "But in your father's opinion?"

"Well," Kera hesitated. "He won't be happy. Not at first. But once he knows…"

She brought their joined hands to cover her face and let out a soft moan. When she peeked out from behind their hands, she couldn't stop the smile from popping to her lips.

Her friend's attention heightened, and she squeezed Kera's hands, pulling them away from her face. "It's about the boy, isn't it?"

Kera nodded. "Dylan."

"You saw him again?"

"He's here, at Faldon's." Just saying it made her smile grow wider, and her heart beat faster. "We're running away together. Somewhere safe."

The smile that had matched Kera's suddenly disappeared. Hands that had clutched hers in excitement now dropped away. "Oh, Kera. There's no such place."

"You're wrong. Wherever we go, he'll make it safe. He's amazing. It feels like he has unlimited power. I don't know where he gets it, but I've seen it, and I just know he'll do anything for me. For us."

"And that sounds normal?"

The bitterness in her friend's voice was unmistakable, and it cut into Kera's euphoric mood. "What do you mean?"

"Navar has the same trait."

A deep frown cut into Kera's forehead. "No, Navar thinks only of himself. Dylan is nothing like him."

"Only that he'll do anything he can to get what he wants, and he wants you."

Kera's back grew rigid. "That's not what's happening at all. Why are you acting this way?"

Signe's face softened. "I'm seeing what's happening with clear eyes."

"No, you're seeing it through a haze of mourning. I know you miss Lani. I do too, and I don't want to leave, but I can't marry Navar. I can't. I have a chance at happiness, Signe, and I'm going to take it. Nothing you say will stop me."

She stood, and her friend's shoulders caved. Kera paused. She couldn't add to Signe's sorrow. "Just so you know, I never intended to leave you permanently. We'll come back and get you. I promise. I'd never leave you to live the rest of your life like this."

Signe's raised her head, her eyes drawn with sadness. "What about the others?"

With that simple sentence, Kera's world crashed.

There was no way Dylan could save everyone. It was an impossible task. Yet she finally saw what she didn't want to see, the hopelessness behind these people's routine of living. They'd scratched out a life as best they could amid the worst conditions possible, and Kera's willingness to turn her back on them made her gasp for breath. She was being selfish. A true *first*.

Shame heated her cheeks. Shame for considering leaving her people and shame because she couldn't do what she feared she must. Panic rose within her chest. "Don't ask me to give him up. Please don't."

Her friend stood and gathered Kera in her arms. "Never. If he's as strong as you say, he'll find a way to be with you *and* help save us all."

Kera clutched her friend close. "I want that, but it seems impossible."

"Not every good thing comes easily. In truth, very little does."

Neither of their lives could be classified as easy. They both lived in constant fear of being caught. Kera stepped back and dabbed at tears that threatened to fall. She'd made her share of mistakes, and she'd almost made the biggest of all. "He's good, Signe. He really is."

Her friend cupped her cheeks and smiled that sweet smile Kera thought she'd never see again. "Then he'll do what's right."

Omission of Truth

She's gone. It feels like my heart's been ripped out, and I don't like the feeling. I turn and stare at Faldon, who's staring back.

"Did the *pux* tell you about me?"

"I told you, I need nothing so archaic. My gift is that of a seer. I've known about you since the moment you took your first breath. I imagine the *pux* were the ones who informed the council."

"Don't you know for sure?"

The wrinkles on his face deepen. "I know the council is aware the wall has been breached, but they don't know how. I assume Kera has found another way though?"

I ignore his question, and I ask one of my own. "You see the future? Tell me about mine and Kera's."

"I'm allowed glimpses, but the whole story is never revealed."

How convenient, and said like every fortune-telling con-artist he'd ever encountered on the street. I wait to hear more, but he's done sharing.

Finally, Faldon looks away and moves to the stone sink. He returns to the table and plops a bowl down between us. Inside, tiny fish slip and slide along their scaly bellies. The stink rolls through the kitchen. That's where the death smell is coming from—not whatever he's brewing. It smells ten times worse than canned cat food.

He fetches the bird stand, and the tiny dragon flaps its wings as Faldon places it and the perch near the table. Grasping a tiny fish by the tail, he holds it out to his Mushu-sized dragon. He flicks the fish in the air and watches the dragon gulp it down.

Faldon pinches another one in his fingers. "Love is our curse."

It's going to be like that, huh? "So I've heard."

"This is not an easy thing you've taken on."

"That's funny, 'cause for me, it's easy to love Kera."

"Love can kill as easily as it can create."

Yep. This guy's a winner. Why did I think I could find a place to belong here? The human side of me doesn't fit in. I take in the open floor plan. Steep stairs line the wall opposite the fireplace. The place is cozy. Nothing like the man in front of me.

It must be an act, this cool indifference of Faldon's. I can play the same game. If I pretend like I don't care, he won't know how much I do. "You always so morbid? Let me guess. You never found your soul mate and now you're bitter because of it."

"She died in the war. A victim of hate because she loved so many."

I grow still as his pain rips into me. He's concentrating a little too hard on feeding his pet. I'm not such a jerk that I can't admit when I've crossed the line. "Sorry. I shouldn't have said that."

"You're young. Death shouldn't be on your mind." His gaze slams into mine, and I can't break away from its intensity. "But the path you've chosen will surely put it there. You can't have Kera."

"Why not?" Was I created only to stir up disgust? Why was my search for a moment of happiness a bad thing? "What's so wrong with me?"

I try to hold back my anger, but it floods my system, itching under my skin. My whole life I've been clawing my way toward one moment of happiness, and every time I get a glimpse of it, someone tries to jerk it away from me. I've had it with being abused. I shove a chair across the room, startling the tiny dragon into another hiss and fire spit. I ignore it and storm toward Faldon, stopping inches away. "Why can't we be happy? Who says we can't?"

I'm being an ass, but I can't help myself. I stand, chest heaving, basically doing my best to intimidate him, but my little fit doesn't faze the old guy. He continues to feed his creepy little pet. "Not I, if that's where your mind wanders. Others who fear change and who love power above all else are the ones to blame. Make no mistake. They're ferocious in their desires and will stop at nothing to secure their claims. Murder is *not* beneath them."

"I'm not scared."

"Only fools rush into a fight and sacrifice others without thought."

"Do you see me rushing?"

He picks up the bowl and looks at me. "Then you know all there is to know?"

About Kera? Yes. We're two halves of a whole.

"I know she's half human. I know we share something different. Special. I also know this is one messed-up place that kills innocent people. You've managed to keep her secret safe so far, but it's getting harder, and I seem to be the only one who's willing to do something before your little deception explodes. What else do I need to know?"

"Then she's told you why she ran to you? Why she had to see you. *One last time*?"

"Because I'm marked for death? Yeah. Let me tell you something, I'm not exactly wanted in my world, either."

"Sit," he says.

I stand while he puts the bowl of fish in a cabinet, then gives a large, old-fashioned hand pump a few good yanks, so he can wash his hands in the stone sink.

When he returns, he pulls out a chair. "Sit. There's more to her visit than she let on."

I don't like the sound of that. The vibe coming off him tells me he's conflicted. He cares deeply for Kera—that's clear—but I get the feeling his goal is to try and talk me out of doing what I've come to do.

I grab the chair and sit, crossing my arms over my chest. "Okay," I say in a rough voice. "Give it a shot. Convince me we're wrong."

The dragon sidles closer to Faldon, and a rumble starts in its throat. Faldon touches the pointed horns, letting his finger bump down the scaly back. He gets to the base of the tail and looks up. "You misunderstand my intent. I only wish to open your eyes."

"Then open them."

"Kera is betrothed."

Whatever I thought he was going to say didn't even come close to this. I know what he's saying, I've heard the word before, but it can't be real. I sit forward. "You're lying."

"I can't lie. They marry in two days."

I slouch back into the chair. "Two days?" How could she tell me she loved me when she's going to marry another guy? It doesn't make sense. What we feel for each other is real. It's once in a lifetime. I'm sure of it. "She's being forced, isn't she?"

Faldon's expression tightens. "He's a famed warmonger. A prince, of sorts. He can give Kera everything her heart desires."

He's not answering my question. "But she doesn't love him, does she?"

"He can give her every comfort she wants. Keep her safe. What of you? What can you give her?"

"Love."

"A love laced with fear?" he scoffs. "Scared every moment

they'll find you and end your lives? That kind of love?"

The shock of her omission is wearing off, and this guy is really beginning to annoy me. I sit up straight and stare him down. "Love that protects. That allows her to be who she is. *That* kind of love."

"The kind of love you've always longed for but never found until now." His voice drips with sarcasm, and he smiles, sensing he's gotten under my skin. He flicks his hand in the air as if to shoo away a pest. "Pretty, yet empty, words, and spoken by one who isn't even fully a *first*."

"Is that's what's got you all woman scared?" I'm good and ticked off now. My mind churns, twisting my emotions into an ugly mess I can't control. I've never felt like this. It's not me, but like a train barreling toward a dead end, I can't stop. I stand, kick back my chair, and close my eyes. Power floods into me, and when I open my eyes, everything has a sharp edge. Colors are hot. The air electrified.

Faldon steps back. Panic flares in his eyes before he covers it up. "What are you doing?"

I smile, not letting on what's straining to get out. The house begins to rumble. Floorboards shudder. Rafters groan. Dishes shake and fall to the floor. The little dragon squawks as his stand sways violently. Somewhere in the house, a cat howls.

Faldon frowns. The control he has is impressive, but I can hear his heart beating fast. He's uncomfortable—maybe even scared—but not convinced.

It's time to convince him.

The front door flies open, then bangs shut. The pump floods the sink with water. The flame under the vial shoots higher. The window panes shatter one by one. Faldon flinches with each explosion.

Near the stairs, a trap door is flung open and a withered, dust-covered little man scrambles out.

"What goes on here?" he shouts at Faldon.

The sage grabs the table for support, his eyes showing his distress, and the little man's frown deepens. The dwarf's projecting ears twitch, swinging their fleshy lobes, while his eyes lock onto me.

I hear neighbors run from their homes, yelling for their loved ones. The stand shakes harder, begins to topple. The dragon leaps into the air and darts around the room, spitting fire and zipping past us. The dwarf's hair catches on fire and he yelps and pats the flames out, then points an oversized, gnarled hand at me. "Stop. Stop. Bodog says stop!"

I close my eyes and take a deep breath, and when I open them, the sharpness fades and the colors dull, and Faldon and Bodog are staring heatedly at me. I throw a superior smile at Faldon. "I told you. I'm not scared."

"Destruction and chaos!" cries the dwarf, his attention split between the pair of us. His disproportionately large hands flail and his massive feet stomp. "Have you no sense?"

Faldon manages to catch the dragon and cuddle it to his chest.

"Well?" My question is clear. Is he friend or foe?

Footsteps rush toward the front door. A hard knock and shout follow. "Faldon. Is all well?"

Faldon glares at me. "*Fool.* Your stubbornness and obsession with Kera will be the end of you both." He pushes me toward the withered, little man. "Take him. And make sure no harm befalls him."

Though he reaches barely taller than my knees, the dwarf wraps his meaty paw around my hand, and with a vise-like grip, drags me into the hole and down the stairs leading beneath the house. The trap door squeaks on its hinges, and bangs shut.

Darkness encases us in a slick and musty smelling tomb.

"Quietly now," the dwarf says in a harsh, breathy voice as he tugs me deeper into the pit. "No room for mistakes."

He isn't kidding. The space crowds my shoulders, and I bend forward so I don't hit my head on the sloped ceiling. Voices chase us deep into the dark until we finally level out. In the cool, damp air, Bodog sparks a wick coiled within a lantern. Light flares, and he swings the lantern in front of him. The first things I see are twisted, brown tree roots poking through the earthen walls like fingers through mud. Mushrooms, aglow with an eerie light, cling to every opening.

Huffing and puffing, he heads down the tunnel, taking the only light source with him.

"Wait!" I shout. "Won't we be going back up soon?"

I try several more times to get his attention, but nothing I say stops the little man. The light slowly fades, and I'm forced to follow him to the entrance of an open space. In the middle of the room sits a tiny wooden table surrounded by a clutter of axes and shovels, wheelbarrows, and strange, sled-like carts. A ratty bed sits in the corner, and one change of clothes hangs on a peg beside it. A layer of dirt covers everything. I stand at the entrance and watch the pale little man shuffle from disheveled pile to disheveled pile, rattling whatever lies beneath and creating a storm of dust.

"How will we know when Faldon's guests leave?" I ask.

"Talk, talk, talk," he grumbles, then adds, "Silence broadens the mind."

Seriously. Is this guy some sort of philosopher? And then I hear it—the soft echo of Faldon's voice along with his guests. There has to be some kind of ventilation system that he's using to listen in on Faldon's conversations. Clever little dwarf.

I slowly make my way to the table that's on the scale of a Little Tykes picnic set. It's not only dusty, it's filthy with remnants of last night's—and probably all last week's—food glued to the surface. The benches tucked underneath aren't much better. I wonder if it'll hold my weight.

"I'm going out on a limb here, but I'm guessing you don't own a scrub brush."

"Don't touch anything." His gravelly voice matches his wrinkled form. "This is all Bodog's. Not yours, halfling."

I can't say I'm fond of my new host's attitude. "How do you know what I am?"

He grunts like it's obvious. Then I remember he can hear what goes on above ground, and I feel stupid. "Did no one tell you eavesdropping's rude?"

Turning away he mutters, "Destruction and chaos."

It's not like I wanted to shake the house off its foundation. I was pushed into it. Besides, this place doesn't look like it's ever been cleaned. I sit, finding my knees nearly level with my ears. Uncomfortable doesn't even begin to explain my position. I scoot my legs out, dig my elbows into my thighs, and rub my hands through my hair, scrubbing away the tension that fills me. All I want is to be with Kera. Why is that so difficult?

My host, who's busily tending to his piles, is ignoring me, but I need to talk. "I'm in love with Kera."

He grunts and pushes his way deeper into a pile of junk.

"She's in love with me."

He grunts again and pulls out an old shirt so disgustingly dirty, a small cloud of odor billows from it when he drops it to the ground.

I wave the smell out of my face. "Lived here long?"

"Faldon rescued me. Brought me here, and here I stay."

"Rescued you from what?"

He stops for a moment as if lost in memory. "The king's court." He disappears into the pile.

That answers my first question. Obviously, the *firsts* are in charge. All other species, including dwarves and dragons, are beneath them. And in Bodog's case, literally. This guy might be able to answer more questions than I first thought. He pops back into view holding a cockroach, and tosses it, hissing and squirming, into his mouth. Crunching away, he returns to his scrounging, or maybe *foraging* is more accurate? I can only hope he doesn't want me to join him.

"What do you know about Kera's betrothed?"

"Bad man. Very bad."

My senses sharpen. That's at odds with what Faldon told me. "What do you mean?"

"Navar has one goal. To be king of the *firsts*."

Ambition isn't one of my strong qualities. Presently, I aspire to graduate high school. Being king is beyond my scope, and frankly, I don't care. "Yeah, but he loves Kera, right?"

The dwarf's ears twitch. He pulls a big rock from a nearby pile, and without warning, flings it onto the table. It shakes the boards and rolls to a stop in front of me. Usually, when kids start picking up rocks and looking around for a target, I hightail it out of there, but since Bodog is such a little guy and I'm not, and he isn't reaching for another rock, I take it he wants me to look at it. I pick it up. Cold, hard, and dull, it lays heavy in my hand. I wait expectantly for its meaning.

The dwarf frowns at the rock. "Granite. Navar's heart is hard and dense. No light can penetrate. No love."

My grip tightens on the rock. "But Faldon thinks if Navar finds out about Kera being a halfling, he'll protect her."

A deep rumble crawls from Bodog's throat. He charges forward and grabs a pickax. I hurl the rock, lose my balance, and tumble off my seat. His big paw of a hand bats away the rock; his wiry muscles swing back the ax. I duck, my hands protecting my head. But instead of attacking, he heaves the weapon at the wall behind me. With a loud ping of metal hitting stone, a tumble of rocks cascade to the floor. Dust fills the air.

I straighten, chest heaving and coughing. "Are you insane? What was that all about?"

When the dust settles, Bodog goes to the new pile of rubble and pushes aside the rocks. He motions me to him. I hesitate. This little guy isn't as harmless as I originally thought. He motions again, and though I'm probably stupid for doing so, I get up and peer down to where he points. There, beneath the rocks, he reveals what remains of a cluster of mushrooms. Pulverized into mush.

His large eyes hold a hint of sadness. "Rocks crush."

I swallow hard and stare at what he's done. The imagery of Kera crushed by Navar is frightening. Who should I believe? Faldon or Bodog? I glance back at the dwarf, whose eyes haven't left me, as if he's trying to relay whatever it is he can't put into words, and an epiphany strikes. Faldon is a good man, but Bodog, with his keen sight and ever twitching ears? Nothing gets by him. "Faldon really is living in a fantasy world, thinking everything's going to turn out fine, isn't he?"

Bodog nods. "He sees good in all things. Has made choices he should not."

Obviously. The guy's got a living fire starter for a pet, and allows a dwarf to undermine the foundation of his home.

"Not you." I look at his papery dry face, and into his clear eyes. "You see what's really there, don't you? You listen to the stories, but hear the truth."

Bodog nods again. "Navar cuts down that which does not bend."

Kera and I are about to defy a man who doesn't like the word no. My heart drops. This changes everything. Navar has got to go. I'm not sure how to make that happen, but I know I'll need back up. "Do you have paper and a something to write with?"

I can hardly wait as he finds me what I need. With a shaking hand, I scribble a quick note to Kera.

I've got to go, but I'll be back soon. I promise.
Love you.
Dylan

I fold it, then hold it out to Bodog. "I need to get this to Kera. I don't want her to worry."

His thick fingers take the note, and he places it in his tunic.

"Is there another way out of here?"

Within seconds, Bodog plops a heavy clump of paper onto the table and unfolds it, revealing a rough schematic of his underground home. Tunnels stretch in all directions like a hungry spider stretching toward its kill, but the leg of tunnels I'm interested in is the one headed in the direction of the barrier and home.

I point to the tunnel. "Is this one good? Does it have an opening?"

"Small." He gives me a quick measure. "You won't fit."

"Let me worry about that."

Poisoned by Greed

The bright sunlight broke through the windows and scattered the darkness within the manor house. Her father had returned long before. If she hurried, she could find him and relate what she knew about the wall and Navar and Dylan.

After the power Dylan had shown her, she knew without a doubt he was the answer to their problem. He was special. Even Faldon sensed it, although grudgingly. She would make her father see there was another option for her. For Teag.

Kera rounded the corner off of the kitchen hallway and came face to face with Navar. His eyes cut into her. "Returning from another walk? Alone?"

Should she lie? There was no need, at least, there didn't seem to be one. "Yes."

"How is it you slip away so easily?"

"What do you mean?" Let him think she had no idea his men were ordered to follow her.

His hand touched her arm, and it was all she could do not to pull away. "I searched for you," he said gently. "Where do you go?"

"Wherever my feet lead."

"Into the forest?"

Kera nodded and stepped back, searching for an acceptable excuse to move on.

"I'm concerned for your welfare. There are creatures in the forest that are far from friendly. Murderous, even."

"I am aware of that." And Navar was one of the deadliest she'd seen. She couldn't reveal her true thoughts, so she tilted her head and glanced up at him. "But thanks to you, we live in a peaceful time, and I can enjoy my walks."

"Flattery from you? It's my lucky day." His touch suddenly grew rough. His hands fell onto her, searching. When he pulled away, he had the *incordium* dagger. "You're full of unexpected surprises."

She made a grab for the dagger. "You have no right to take that."

His grip tightened painfully. "I have every right. Faldon is a fool instilling a false sense of security in you. From now on, you will stay close to the manor."

She struggled to free herself from his hand, but failed. "I'm not yet your wife."

The sound of her father's and Faldon's voices echoed in the hall. Navar smiled and let her go as quickly as he had grabbed her. She rushed to the stairs.

"I have business to attend to," Navar called after her, "but never fear, I'll be back well before the festivities begin. Tonight's a new beginning for the both of us."

She stopped, but didn't look back. "Yes. A new beginning." The thought made her stomach clench.

Outside her room, two men stood guard. She stared, daring them to look at her. Neither did. Her father approached, his face a stern mask of reproof. Must she listen to him lecture her about Navar? He opened the door for her, and as soon as he closed the door, she snapped.

"Your choice of husband is such a gift. What woman does not pine to be a prisoner in her own home?"

"I thought him the best solution. Have you a better one?"

She wanted to say, "Yes, far better than the monster we're about to collude with," but the less he knew, the better. "Have you not wondered what he'll do once he discovers my secret? You can't share your powers with me forever."

"He'll know your value by then."

Navar was a man who saw no value in anyone but himself. She had always known that. Surely her father had noticed by now.

At her icy silence, he sighed. "I'm sorry." Her father cupped the back of his neck as if the weight of the world rested there. "Navar listens to no one. When I returned and he learned you had slipped away, he flew into a rage the likes I've never seen. He no longer hides his true nature."

"He never did. You chose to ignore what was before you."

"I knew about his faults, but not his true heart. He's filled with a greed he can't quench."

Her demeanor grew wary. "What do you mean?"

"At your wedding, he will demand a tribute from every lord."

"A gift isn't uncom—"

"This is no gift. It's a demand for money or a life. If the tribute can't be paid, and trust me, there are few who can pay Navar's demand, the nobles will be forced to hand over someone from their own families."

"Noble slaves? It doesn't make sense."

"It does, Kera. He'll demand an unbreakable oath. It's his way of binding the nobles to him."

Her breath froze in her lungs. "He can't do that. The council won't allow it."

Her father moved to the window, and the tension in his body heated his cheeks. He looked feverish, completely unlike the man who was always in control. "There's something you need to know. When the council petitioned Navar to be king, he agreed, but on one condition."

"What condition?"

"A tribute. He demanded more money than any of the council could afford. He knew it. Now he has their oath. There's a way a man can gain power without expending much energy."

"Control the council, control the people."

"Yes. He convinced them he's the only one keeping our people from civil war, and he may be right."

Kera grabbed her father's hand. "This wedding can't take place. You have to see that now. You have to get me out of here."

Misery tinged his voice, pinched his lips. "You know I can't. I promised him your hand."

Her father, in his desperation to keep her safe, had foolishly bound her to the man who was the cause of all their problems. She took a deep, calming breath. "I didn't make any promise. And even if I did, I can break my vow."

Her father shook his head. "You don't know what you're suggesting."

"It's not a suggestion." She squeezed his hand. "It's for the best. You know it. Just promise me you won't stop me from leaving."

"Kera..." His voice cracked on her name. "I can't. I told you, he went into a rage when he couldn't find you. He came to me and vowed he would burn our village to the ground and kill everyone if I didn't control you. I love you, but I can't let that happen." Defeat entered her father's eyes. "You will marry him. I'm sorry, but there's no other choice."

Ashes in the Wind

The weight of the sword Bodog had given me before we'd left his earthen room slaps between my shoulder blades. The dwarf had assured me a sword is a needed commodity in his world. That he actually believes I'll know how to use it is flattering, but his confidence in my abilities is misplaced.

The light from Bodog's lantern slips silently along the passage, highlighting the underworld in an eerie light. Sound is stolen. Dead air presses inward. Outside the tiny circle of light, the world ceases to exist. Nothingness is only an arm's reach away, and that threat of eternal darkness makes my legs feel unsteady.

I hurry after Bodog, eager to leave this oppressive, wriggling cluster of earthen legs that seep tear drops of water as if mourning the roots that dig into its skin. Before long, we come to an incline. The tunnel narrows. Bodog sets down the lantern, drops to his knees, and scuttles forward, wiggling and squirming into a tiny hole. I follow him, squeezing my shoulders together while I struggle upward on my belly. The hilt of my sword snags on a root, and I wiggle myself free. Dirt from Bodog's efforts to make the hole above us a little bigger rains down on me, until finally, he pushes a clump of grass back and he's out.

A pinhole of light shines down. The stale air grows sweeter where the tree roots amass, entangling each other in a way that could easily imprison me underground, forever. Halfway up, I get stuck, my shoulders squeezed so tightly, my ribs ache. I close my eyes and feel the power fill me. The earth shudders, and in one motion, it takes a breath, expanding the hole. Twisted tree roots move, scraping away the earth. Slowly, I forge my way to the surface, pushing aside dirt and debris until I'm out of the hole.

While I shake off the clinging dirt, Bodog eyes what used to be the small opening to his tunnel, his ears twitching, his face crumpled with irritation. He holds out the flap of grass that shielded the opening, but it's far too small. From his grumbles and mutterings, I catch only one word: "Ruined."

For such a messy little guy, he's finicky about his tunnels. I guess he isn't fond of visitors who may fall in. "Stand back," I say.

I urge the roots back to their original positions, feeling the ground rumble, bow, and pull at the displaced earth until the tunnel is half its size. "How's that?"

He sticks his head in the hole and snuffles and wriggles before popping back out. "Good enough."

It's exactly how it was before, but I refuse to get sucked into an argument. Instead, I'm itching to take off. I need to get back to my world, find Grandpa, and ask what I should do. As soon as I think it, the air shifts and a curved ribbon of energy floats toward the east.

"Do you see that?" I ask Bodog. The ever-helpful guy grunts. It's his affirmative grunt. The negative one has more of a snap to it. That I've already figured this out is a little surprising.

When I face him for a final farewell, a bright lash of midday sunlight slips through the tree branches, burning the brown bark as well as Bodog's skin. Before my eyes, his color deepens from chalky white to cinnamon brown. Bodog, with his too-big feet, twitchy ears, and big eyes squinting against the sun, has taken on the appearance of a feral night creature caught in the light.

I take a step toward him, troubled by his appearance. "Are you all right?"

The light abruptly vanishes, and a heavy darkness descends. He sniffs at the air and hunkers close to the cover of the trees. "Isn't safe here. The trees are aflutter."

I know what he means. They shift and sigh and act like they'll pull up roots and walk off. It's creepy. At every sound, Bodog's muscles spasm, and his weight shifts from foot to foot. "They'll know now. They'll feel it. Too risky."

I don't know what he's talking about, but the poor guy's a nervous wreck. I never expected him to come with me, and I don't want to bring him any trouble. "It's okay, Bodog. I can take it from here. You can go."

He willingly nods, and to my surprise, as soon as he's close to the entrance to the tunnel, his skin whitens again, matching the pale mushrooms he cultivates deep underground. Before he slips away, he glances back. "There is a darkness in Navar that only death can appease."

"Okay, *what?*"

My question goes unanswered as Bodog disappears into the tunnel. "Bodog," I grit out in a harsh whisper, but the grass is now securely in place. He's gone.

I let out an irritated sigh. It's suddenly dead quiet, like the forest is taking a nap. At midday? There should be a riot of sound and movement.

They. Bodog said something about *they.*

Warnings tingle along my nerves. I back away from the now-camouflaged hole, my ears attuned to the slightest sound, my gaze searching. A sudden dark wind rises, and the trees huddle closer.

I make my way from the small clearing and follow the streak

of energy. The ribbon behind me disappears as soon as I pass. I've got to get to the wall. I need to tell my grandparents what I'm about to do. Get their support. Make them believe that this place is my world, that I belong with Kera. They'll be disappointed. Probably confused. I won't tell Grandma about the danger I'm in. Grandpa will understand. He'll agree. Danger is unavoidable no matter what I do or where I am. Marked is marked. I'd rather fight them in this world, where my powers are strongest, than in my world, where they're sketchy and sap the strength out of me.

Shadows grow and clouds gather overhead. Yet, within those shadows hover specks of light. Glittering, twinkling light.

Pux.

I trust them as much as I trust my mother to be reasonable.

The lights skitter across the ribbon of energy like kids on a playground, their buzz a soft drone in my ears. I abandon the ribbon, but not fast enough. The buzz grows, and their pursuit is on. At first, the trees are obstacles I'm forced to dodge, until I remember my powers. Suddenly the trunks bend and twist out of my way, leaving behind a subtle shimmer of leaves that float to the ground.

Soon, the lights are far behind me, and the wall looms ahead. To my left, a wet heaviness fills the air. I follow it until a low blanket of mist appears. Oxygen grows thin. I stumble against a large tree. My fingers scrape along the bark as I sink to my knees. I breathe deeply to catch my breath. I know this feeling, this strange lightheadedness.

The vein in my neck throbs painfully. I peer around the tree trunk.

A door in the wall hangs ajar.

Amid a swirl of glittering mist, a man stands at attention few yards away, gripping a horse by its bridle. He's dressed in a militaristic blue, with a stiff collar, gold epaulets on his shoulders, and medals on his chest. He's obviously waiting, but for who?

The horse moves, stomping its feet and snorting its discomfort, yet it remains by the stoic man. As the mist slips along the ground, a twinkle of *pux* emerge from the gateway, followed by twenty men dressed in strange armor, carrying a variety of weapons. The smudges of black and streaks of red make it clear they've been up to no good.

My stomach knots, and I want to throw up as I watch the men wipe the blood from their swords. Whose blood is it? My nerves fairly jump out of my skin with my need to find out. I force myself to stay put even though my mind races with possibilities. What have they done? Who have they killed because of me?

From the midst of the group, a dark-haired man steps forward, and the one holding the horse bows low. "Happy return, Lord Navar."

My fingers dig into the bark. So this is Navar. Armor shines dully across his broad shoulders, making him look like bear trapped in a cage. His dark hair gleams blue-black in the struggling light of the sun. He tosses a crossbow at the man before slamming his sword into the leather scabbard riding on his hip.

His face is a mask of hard planes, his voice devoid of warmth. "Do I look happy, Granel?"

The servant straightens, his face sober as he catches the pair of blood-stained, leather gloves Navar tosses him. "What disturbs you, my lord?"

"I don't like wasting my time. Your information proved false once again."

"The power surge was felt in that area. We even have witnesses."

"You place too much trust in the *pux*. Your continued reliance on those mindless creatures will be your downfall." Navar swings atop his horse and glares down at the man. "A half-breed with special powers is as much a myth as a unicorn. Until you have more accurate information, do not waste my time."

"There's someone who knows more than she's telling."

Navar's nostrils flare and his face darkens. "Careful whom you drag into this hunt, Granel." He tugs on a new pair of gloves and slips the reins firmly between his fingers.

"Faldon protects her, but I believe it's worth a chance."

Navar stares into the distance. "If she knows, I'll find out. For the sake of caution, post a guard, but keep him hidden. If this myth materializes, let him think he's safe. The sage has revealed the future. I won't be caught unaware."

The man bows, and Navar kicks his horse into motion. As the group follows, he pulls an experienced-looking guard from the formation and orders him to stay behind and out of sight. The guard makes a quick loop of the area, and then climbs a tree to wait.

For me.

Easing back, I press my spine into the prickly bark and rub my hands through my hair. It's obvious they don't know I'm in their world. According to Navar, I'm not even real. Granel is a problem. He believes in my existence and has enough sway over Navar that he's gotten him to at least consider the possibility I'm a threat.

After seeing what I've just seen, I've got to get back home now more than ever.

Before I can move, the guard appears, dangling upside-down from the branch above me with a smile that doesn't reach his eyes. "Hello, mutt."

He cartwheels out of the tree, lands on his feet, and swings his sword at my neck in one fluid motion. I dodge the blade and spring to my feet, calling on the tree branches to capture him. The man is quickly tangled, yet with a heavy blow, his sword slices neatly through the wood. He drops to the ground, unfazed.

Eyes glittering, he stalks me.

I fumble for the sword Bodog gave me. This guy is a hardened soldier. I don't stand a chance.

I dodge his blade time and again, feeling the whistle of cold steel every time it passes. I manage to pull out my sword, and then something unexpected happens. The blade ripples to life with a flash of fire. I thrust the sword in front of me and gape.

The soldier stops and smiles. "Well, well, well. You're full of surprises."

"Just wait. I've got more," I say with confidence I don't exactly feel. Hopefully, my act has him thinking I'm used to a good, flaming sword fight. To back up my false confidence, I find myself lunging forward, my flaming sword slicing toward his head. He spins away, and the battle begins in earnest.

I must be crazy. I've never fought with a sword. He acts like he was born with it in his hand. His blade comes frighteningly close to my head and cuts off a few strands of my hair. Trees are used as vaulting points. Branches as obstacles. Forest debris whirls. We tussle, and my sword flies out of my hand.

Desperate for cover, I duck behind a tree, breathless and sore. I'm at my wit's end. How long can I postpone the inevitable? I duck as his blade swipes at me again. I don't want to die. Not like this. Not here. Not now.

He charges again, and I quickly snap my legs and arms straight; the ground opens up and swallows me at the moment his blade arcs down.

I don't know why I did it. Being buried alive isn't pleasant, but I'm fairly certain it's better than being hacked to death. The earth presses in on me, and it takes all my power to keep the dirt from smothering me. I've barely counted to five when I pop back up a few feet behind the unsuspecting warrior, who is stabbing at the earth where I'd disappeared. I rush him, snare his waist, and ram him into the nearest tree. The bark splits. The core cracks. The guard's sword drops to the ground as the tree snatches him inside. Tree sap pours over him. His face, once so confident, crumples in horror. I stand back and stare at the bark slowly mending itself, sealing the warrior in a living casket.

With a shiver, I stumble back, disgusted by what I've done. "Don't think about it. Not now," I rasp aloud. I did what I had to do. Kill or be killed. Won't Grandpa be proud? The thought doesn't calm my churning insides. I'm sick with adrenalin, but I can't stop now. I've chosen a path that can't be erased.

Turning, I pick up both swords and run to the wall that stretches out in front of me. I'm not sure if I've become sensitive to it, or if the strange power I possess somehow called it into showing itself. It doesn't really matter. With a hard push, I ram through the door. My bones ache. My skin tingles. The sick feeling grows. Mist wraps around me and pulls me forward. When the unpleasant sensations of traveling between the two worlds ends, I'm standing in the woods.

A haze of heated smoke snakes between the trees. Ashes swirl in the wind, and the taste of death is in the air.

Escape into Trouble

I stow the swords nearby and chase the smell of fire, emerging from the woods a few miles from my grandparents' house. Smoke hangs thickly, wrapping around the area like a heated blanket. People are dashing here and there, their confusion clear on their faces. The chaos I'm seeing is hard to believe. As I make my way down the road, I see dead animals lying in a far paddock. Farther along, people scream for water to douse a burning hay bale. A ewe bleats from within a field, eyes rolling with fear as flames lick closer. I see Mr. Tanner, his arms streaked with dirt and soot, standing, dazed.

"What happened?" I yell above the din.

"Don't know," he calls back. "Someone's torched the farms along the road. The Delgatos, Lorrings, mine... Killed sheep. Horses. Dogs..." He sweeps a hand through his gray hair, his eyes reflecting his shock.

"Are you all right?"

"Half my flock is gone. Slaughtered. My barn's burned. Who'd do this? It's daylight. How'd we miss seeing them?"

I know, but I can't say. "Is my family all right?"

"Who?"

"My grandparents. Officer Newman and his wife."

"Their place was hit first." He shakes his head, his voice quivers. "Terrible. Just terrible."

His words echo in my head. I had followed the heat of the fire here, not thinking to go home first. Fear crawls through me, and I back away from Mr. Tanner and run—run until my legs ache, but I don't stop. I don't think about the destruction I pass. If I do, I'll only see what I can't bear to face. That I brought this devastation here.

I punch through the back fence of my grandparents' house, the force adding to the hiss and pop of a dying fire. Only when the charred side of the house comes into view do I stop. That crumbling mass of shattered beams and smoldering debris used to be my bedroom. Now the space is a blackened, damage-riddled hole.

A fair distance away, a handful of volunteer firefighters collect their gear, shouting about another fire that needs their attention. The back door bangs open as Reggie emerges from the house, his face clouded, his body rigid. He storms forward, and I back away.

My heart rate spikes. "What's going on?"

"What did you do?" The muscles in Reggie's face harden. His lips thin, and his eyes narrow. "Where is he?"

I trip around a wheelbarrow. "What are you talking about?"

"Don't play stupid. First your grandfather, a man who deserved better than to be beaten and left for dead in the woods, and now Pop. He's missing. Where is he? What did you do to him?"

My gaze whips to the house. "Where's my grandpa?"

"Pop said from the beginning that death hovered around you. I swear to God, if you've harmed him…"

He's blaming me? The men on the other side of the fence quickly look away. I turn back to Reggie, the confusion about what's happened starting to clear. "You think I tried to kill my grandpa? Where is he? Where's my grandma?"

"Where's my dad?" The shaking in Reggie's arm flows into his whole body. He's lost control and his face contorts into a violent mask. "Start talking, or I swear I'll beat it out of you myself."

When he steps closer, I grab his arms, my hands glow hot against his skin. He fights me as I stare into his eyes. "I'd never harm him...or anyone."

I project the core of who I am, convey my true soul. The jolt of raw feeling pouring into his body startles him. He fights to be free, but I won't let him go. Not yet. Not until he sees I'm not the monster he thinks I am. Lumbering around the yard in our strange embrace, we fall. I brace for impact while still holding onto Reggie. He lands on top of me, and I grunt. His angry face hovers over me. He pulls his free arm back, and balls his hand into a fist.

His knuckles slam into my jaw. Pain explodes in my head. Our eyes lock, and I see the fury that's raging in him. He pulls his arm back again, and it's then I realize this isn't going to end any time soon. I don't want to hurt him, but I don't want to be hurt, either. I know what it's like to kill a man, and I'm not eager for a repeat.

Reggie's eyes grow wide. He hesitates. "You've killed someone?"

I blink. I didn't mean to delve that deeply, to reveal so much.

A snarl ripples across Reggie's face. His fist tightens.

I brace myself.

"Dad!" Leo runs into the yard followed by Jason and Jason's dad, Carl Delgato. Mr. Delgato yanks Reggie off me, and I let him go. Reggie's eyes are wild with alarm. Leo grabs his dad's shoulders and gives him a quick shake. "He didn't do anything. Mr. Delgato says he saw Pop by his place not more than a half hour ago."

Reggie pushes out of Mr. Delgato's restraining hands and stumbles back. "You need to go," he says pointing a finger at me. "Whatever the hell you are, we don't need your kind of trouble here."

Leo frowns and steps toward his dad. "What's wrong with

you? Didn't you hear me?"

Reggie ignores his son, and his eyes fixate on me. "You don't belong. You know it, and now, so do I. When I get back, you'd best be gone."

He storms away with Carl Delgato on his heels, and Leo and Jason turn to me with nothing but questions in their eyes. Nothing is going right. I'm running blind and falling with every step I take.

Leo motions toward his dad. "What's he talking about?"

I pull the pair aside, out of earshot of the men working nearby. "I had to show him who I am."

Jason frowns, and then his eyebrows pop into a high arch. "You don't mean—"

"That I'm part of the *firsts*. He didn't seem too keen on it."

A smirk crosses his face. "It's like telling him you're a Dungeon Keeper, twelfth level, and you need to put his beating heart in a box and give it to your master as proof of your loyalty."

I throw him a disgusted look. How can Jason joke at a time like this? Leo smacks his friend in back of his head.

Jason throws up his hands in surrender. "Okay, okay. But seriously, I'd think you were nuts."

He has a point.

Leo sweeps his fingers through his hair, looking more frazzled than a laid-back guy should. "We've got burned houses, dead livestock, and no one's seen anything. Did my dad tell you that your grandpa's at the hospital?"

"You saw him. Your dad wasn't in the sharing mood," I say.

"Well, don't worry, your grandpa's in the hospital and your grandma's with him. That old man is lucky he's got one tough hide. Someone worked him over good."

My chest grows tight with helplessness. None of this should be happening. Kera and I didn't do anything wrong. All we want is to be left alone. Now the council has declared war on everyone who's had any kind of association with me. My eyes sweep the people milling around—that means everyone within miles are in danger. I need to end this. But how? I'm no soldier. I don't know the first thing about fighting. Hooked up to "Halo" with a bunch of internet geeks, yeah. But the real thing? I'm making this up as I go, and so far, I'm not doing so hot. Grandpa was my only hope.

"My grandpa's going to be okay, right?" I ask Leo.

"Yeah, he won't be walking around for a couple of days, though. And then there's Pop. He got spooked last night and disappeared. That's what my dad's all fired up about. With Pop gone, and your grandpa found all mangled up, and then you were missing, well…"

"I came out the bad guy. Nice."

"Yeah, well, nobody's perfect. I told him you wouldn't do anything like that, but you know parents. They think we're all brain dead or something."

"So," Jason says in a drawn out manner that hints at his curiosity, "where've you been?"

"In Teag," I say distractedly. "The land on the other side of the wall." With my first plan totally screwed, I'm desperate for a back up. Grandpa was the one with all the authority around here. Who did one go to when the authorities were laid up?

A strange look crosses Jason's face. "What wall?"

"Listen, I don't have time to get into it. Stuffs going down on her side that's really messed up. Kera's getting married to some whacked-out, wanna-be king, and I'm pretty sure he's the one who messed up my grandpa, torched the house, and went ballistic on everyone around here."

Jason's head swivels from side to side, his eyes scanning the area. "We've got *your kind* in the neighborhood now?"

"Yeah, and they're pissed. They don't exactly like me."

Leo purses his lips and gives a quick hum. "Sounds like your popularity has taken a serious hit lately."

"Really?" I couldn't help the sarcasm. I'm more like my mom than I want to admit. All I wanted was a better life, but all I got was more trouble. "This is pretty par for *my* life."

"You against the world, huh?"

"Two worlds, actually," Jason adds.

"That's rough," Leo says.

I don't need Leo's compassion. I need a miracle. My frown deepens. "It gets worse. Kera's like me, a half-blood, only they don't know it yet, and when they find out, they'll kill her."

"Wow," Jason mutters. "They're like cannibals." We stare at him blankly, and he shrugs. "You know. They eat their own kind, so to speak."

I drag out a heavy sigh. "Yeah, well, until I do something about them, they're going to get a lot nastier."

"Like…?"

I wave at the house. "Take your pick. Burn up houses. Kill sheep. Kill people. I don't know. But they're not messing around. They do *not* like humans, and they really don't like guys like me."

"Bro," Leo breathes, the sound of fear in his voice unmistakable. "That sounds like a war."

I know where the fault lies. "Look around. It is."

Suppressed energy pours off Jason. He can barely stand still. A dangerous twinkle of excitement flickers in his eyes. "You gonna ask us to help?"

"Are you offering?"

"I'm not bad in a fight."

I believe him.

Leo stares at the ground, tense and quiet.

"You don't have to help," I say. "It's my fight."

His head snaps up. "They're threatening all of us now. I don't like it, but I'm not going to hide. I'll help."

"This could get ugly," I say.

Leo motions to the burned and dying around us. "It's already ugly."

We make for the woods, creating a plan on the fly. Go in, get Kera, bring her back, and have Faldon fix the wall behind us. It's the only way to stop the violence.

"It's too simple," I say, worrying.

Jason shakes his head. "Complicated gets you in trouble. Trust me, I know."

I've seen his daredevil pictures, heard about his juvenile record. I trust him.

We burst into the clearing and bypass the foxhole. With my powers, I'm fairly confident I'll be safe, but Leo and Jason need some form of protection. Grandpa's guns are still hidden within the bushes, tucked neatly under a tarp beside the forgotten ATV. While the guys stuff their pockets with ammo, I hesitate.

Is this really a good idea? Is there another way?

I can't see any. The *firsts* have pushed too hard. They've attacked innocent people.

The guys check over their rifles and count out the ammo, increasing my confidence that they're familiar with guns. Jason slings one over each shoulder and looks at me. "Ready. You sure you don't want one?"

"I've got a pair of swords hidden by the wall."

"Swords. Wow." He doesn't sound impressed. "Suit yourself."

Leo hefts his rifle. "I'm ready."

We start for the wall. The mood between us has grown serious, our steps firm, our bodies tense, as we push through the woods. The path we're following bends around a clump of trees, and on the other side, Pop stands directly in our way, a determined tilt to his body, like he's been fighting all day, and he isn't opposed to getting his rumble on.

"Dude," Jason whispers to Leo. "I don't think your grandpa is having a good day. He looks a little strung out."

Jason isn't kidding. Pop's clothes are a mess and his hair—what's left of it—is spiked on his head and not in a cool way. Scratches cover his face, and his gaze darts around the area like he expects a mountain lion to spring from the bushes and maul him.

"Pop?" Leo says in a gentle voice. "You okay?"

Pop pushes past Leo and grabs my wrist. His eyes burn into mine. I pull back, and he finally lets go and waves his hands, signing.

Leo interprets in that deep, smooth voice of his. "He was afraid they'd gotten you."

My body stiffens. "You saw them?"

His face tenses and his eyes grow large and frightened as he signs.

"Only shadows, but he knew who they were," Leo says.

Pop's eyes remain fixed on me as his hands speak and Leo interprets. "A long time ago, they were common. But then things got bad. A couple of kids disappeared. Taken by the *firsts*. He knew the gateway to their world was on your grandparents' property, but not exactly where. He convinced your grandmother to put those iron sculptures in the woods, thought everything would be fine. Iron steals their power, makes them sick, but after a while, she stopped believing and pulled them all down. Not too long after that, strange things started happening again."

"Like what?" I ask.

"Creepy feelings. Like being watched. That's when your mom started behaving oddly. A boy appeared. She became obsessed. It lasted for a whole summer. And then he left. Your grandpa said he'd never seen anyone cry as much as your mother did."

Leo's interpreting grew slower. "Your grandmother feared the boy would come back for her daughter, so Pop told her to put the iron sculptures around the house to keep the boy away. The day she did was the day your mom left."

Pop looks from Leo to me and drops his hands.

That's it? At least I know why I always feel sick when I get too near those sculptures. I tap Pop on the shoulder to get his attention. "Okay, but what's all this got to do with what happened last night?"

"Ever since you came here, the feeling of being watched has returned. Pop says he knew they were back, and it had to do with you. They won't go away. Not now. Something about you—"

Leo stops and presses his lips together.

"What?" Jason asks.

Leo shakes his head. "Nothing."

Pop's jaw clamps and he stares heatedly at Leo.

"What did he say?" I press.

I can tell Leo doesn't want to say it, but Pop urges his grandson until he finally stutters out, "Something about you has disturbed the natural order of things."

I can't bear the compassion in Leo's eyes, and turn away. There it is again. I'm unnatural. That uneasy feeling in my stomach returns. It's not like I don't know it already, but to hear someone else say it makes it all that more real.

Jason's voice lowers into a movie trailer commentator, rumbling intensely. "A young man struggles to belong in a world not made for him. A mysterious female calls from anoth—"

"Shut up, Jason," Leo snaps. "This is serious."

"Just trying to lighten the mood," Jason says.

Leo ignores him and clamps a hand on my shoulder. "Pop doesn't know what he's saying."

"Yeah. Sure."

"You guys," Jason says. "Pop's hands are moving again."

We turn, and Leo interprets for him. "Whatever is going to happen won't be easy. The breach in the wall must be closed."

Jason glances from me to Leo. "He knows about the wall?"

"H-he helped secure it, along with your grandmother," Leo says in wonder. "He says it'll take time to fix. He's working on it."

My heart freezes. "You can't close it yet. I've got to get back. I need to get Kera out of there."

Leo watches his grandfather's hands closely and then sighs. "He says no. He's got to fix it as soon as possible."

"Screw that. It's only a matter of time until they find out she's like me. They'll kill her. I'm going, and I'm bringing her back. It's the only way to stop all this." I get in the old guy's face and use my height and anger to intimidate him. "Close the opening before then, and I swear I'll do whatever I can to break it down. I've opened it before. I'll do it again."

The truth—that I didn't open the path between the two worlds to begin with, and that I haven't a clue how to do so if he actually succeeds in closing it—isn't important. What he doesn't know won't hurt him and can only help me.

Wouldn't you know? He doesn't scare. The old guy persists in shaking his head and signing out his warning: doom and gloom if the barrier remains damaged. Leo tries persuading him. He doesn't budge. It's hopeless. I can feel my frustration build. We don't have time for this.

And then...

"I'm going with him," Leo yells at his grandfather.

Pop's eyes nearly bug from his head.

"Yeah," Jason steps forward. "So am I. You gonna lock us in that world of fairy tale freaks for good?" He slants a glance at me. "No offense."

I wave Jason back and give Pop my most earnest plea. "All I need is a day. That's it. One day. I know where she is. It'll be clean and easy, I swear. Then we can close all the openings for good."

For all I know there are dozens of them. I don't want to even think fixing it might be impossible.

Pop's eyes nearly explode out of his head when he understands there's more than one hole in the wall. The problem is clearly bigger than he imagined. He looks from one to the other of us, then shakes his head. His finger jabs at his chest, then his hands swipe away from his torso.

Leo groans. "He's coming with us."

Jason rolls his eyes. I nod. "Fine." I take one of the guns from Jason and pitch it at Pop. He easily catches it. The old guy's hovering around ancient, but he's quick and wiry. And let's face it: I'm desperate. At this point, I'd take a hundred-year-old, one-armed, peg-legged, toothless hag if she volunteered.

What Isn't, Is

After I drag the swords from their hiding place and strap mine onto my back, we move to the opening where I first saw Kera disappear. The sun's rays struggle through the thick forest canopy and shatter into tiny stripes of dim light when they hit the tree trunks.

I can feel the barrier's strange energy without trying. I can see it, but Jason and Leo can't. "Concentrate. Look harder."

"Maybe if we squint?" Leo says, and narrows his eyes into tiny slits.

Jason, with his head tilted and his eyes scrunched, slowly bends toward Leo. "You see it yet?"

Leo shakes his head. "I want to see it."

"Maybe it's not really there?" Jason reaches out his hand, but where the wall should be, it isn't. Not for him.

Leo taps Pop's shoulder. When his grandfather looks up, Leo asks, "Do you see the wall?"

The old man nods.

"What's it look like?" Jason asks me.

"Like a wall, but not. It goes on forever."

It's not made of stone or wood. Not anything I've ever seen before, but it's real. I run my hand along the smooth surface.

Sparks of energy tumble beneath my fingers, and Jason's eyebrows shoot up. "Okay. I see that."

Leo rubs his hands together. "Let's do this."

So this is what it's like to have real friends, to have someone to rely on. No one has ever had my back before. I was a flash, a nobody who didn't matter.

Nervous tension flickers inside of me. I've got power my friends don't. Is it wise to pull them into this?

I hold up my hand, stopping them. "Wait, you guys. You don't have to do this. It's not your probl—"

"Like hell it's not," Jason says. "They burned down our barn. Killed our best dog. Don't tell me this isn't my problem. They think they're so bad ass? We'll show them bad ass." Jason pats my cheek with his calloused palm and nudges me to get going. "Let's go bust up their party."

Jason's enthusiasm is disturbing, but expected. He's in this for the rush. He's a wild card, which could be a problem. I'll have to keep an eye on him.

I face Leo and Pop. The younger one shrugs. "I don't say this often, but Jason's right. If we don't stop them, who knows what they'll do? They think we're not worth caring about. We're disposable. And if you're right, your girl won't be alive much longer, either. This isn't about you anymore. Their mistake was going after you through us."

The thought of Kera dying makes me sick. "Okay, then. I know of three openings. One that opens into town, the main door, and this one, which is connected to their forest. The first two are too risky, so we're going in here." I move to where the opening is slowly repairing itself. "This part isn't going to be pleasant."

I pull the barrier apart. Mist rushes forward. Leo staggers into Jason, who's just as unsteady on his feet. Jason groans. Pop grabs Leo, supporting his grandson with one wiry arm, and they step into the mist. I grab Jason, and together we move into the void. Moist air presses in on us. Jason struggles like he's drowning. When we push through to the other side, he collapses to his hands and knees, his rifle swinging forward to dangle beneath his nose. Pop seems okay, but Leo's pea green. He turns and throws up.

I'm worried about stopping here. After the first guard went missing, Navar could have found the weak spot and set a guard here, too. Memories flash in my mind's eye, repeating the scene of the tree swallowing the guard. The horror on his face when the bark closed over him...

I push the thought away. I had to do it, and I'll do it again if forced to defend myself. If forced to defend Kera.

"Stay here. I'll be right back." I quickly check out the area. Though I don't see anything odd, I'm not reassured. Navar probably knows I'm coming, thanks to his seers, and I've got a feeling he's not one to give up the chase. When I return, Jason is on his feet and Leo isn't as sickly-looking.

"We've got to get moving. Ready?"

We take off.

Trust is a crazy thing. I don't have only my life to protect, but four more. It's an awesome responsibility—one I hope I can manage, but I fear I can't. My mind keeps returning to Kera, telling me she's all that matters. Faldon was right—my obsession is out of control. I only see Kera. Only want Kera. If I don't free her from her realm, destroying anyone and anything that gets in my way, I'll go crazy.

I don't even recognize myself.

Our pace is fast, but easy. I'm reminded time and again they can't move as quickly as I can. When we come to Bodog's tunnel, I enlarge it. "There's this—" How do you explain a creature like Bodog? "—guy down there. His name is Bodog. He's different. Don't freak, okay? I'll do all the talking."

Pop nods and slips into the tunnel. Leo follows, but Jason hesitates. "I'm *so* not into dark, tight places."

With a dad like his, I can only imagine what he's done to terrorize Jason, but I don't have time for this. "Sorry. It's the only way to get where we need to be without being seen. It gets bigger, if that helps."

There's a scuffling noise to our right. Someone's near. "Get in," I urge sharply.

Without waiting, I shove Jason into the hole, and as he makes his way down, cussing me out, I stay above ground and tighten the earth until the opening is camouflaged. I call on a nearby tree, and its limbs lift me high. The glow radiating from my body is a dead giveaway to where I am. I soften it and stand still. From this vantage point, I can see the woods stretch out in all directions.

The sun blazes on the horizon like it wants to light the world on fire. The trees shift and whisper, settling in for the night. A herd of deer prance through the woods, far off in the distance. Everything appears normal, if you can call *anything* in this place normal.

As I stare, taking in the majestic view, a shape appears. Big and hunkered, it sprints forward. I press close to the tree and track the creature, but it's difficult. Whatever it is, it's fast. Muffled snaps of twigs sound beneath me. Before I know it, the tunnel's entrance is being torn apart, and all that's visible is an arc of flying dirt.

I've got to stop it, or else it'll break through, and no telling what it'll do to the others when it reaches the main tunnel.

The tree soundlessly lowers me to the ground. The air is thick with debris, and I have a hard time seeing exactly what I'm about to confront. One thing's for sure. It's big. The height of its rounded back reaches my shoulder. The snuffles and grunts coming from the creature are so low, they make the ground shake. Spying a discarded tree limb, I scoop it up and test its heaviness. If I can take the creature by surprise, I might be able to do some damage.

Optimism always breeds confidence.

Silently creeping forward, I get within a few feet when the digging stops. I freeze.

Red glowing eyes snap toward me. My mind falters. This thing can't be real. The low, rumble of growls warn me this is no illusion, but I can't stop staring into its green eyes, something everyone says not to do when faced with a predator. I'm pretty confident even the most experienced biologist would be hypnotized by the appearance of a two-headed, monstrous, wolf-like creature.

Except, instead of fur, it has quills.

Its hackles rise, flexing the quills into lethal darts. The heads lower. I stand like a statue, unable to move for fear it'll pounce, and I'll become a pincushion. My breathing has become so shallow, I'm lightheaded.

The heads move and tilt. The eyes are tiny, set deep within its heads, and I begin to suspect it can't see too well. The creature sniffs, and I've got a sinking feeling there's nothing wrong with its sense of smell. One nose comes within an inch of my leg and the other sniffs at my hand. It snorts, and jerks back. Air whistles between its jagged teeth as it sucks in a deep breath.

Time just ran out. From statue to sprinter, I use my power to rocket me toward a tree as quills zip past. Sharp pain races up my leg as one hits, and another lances my shoulder before I duck behind a tree. My legs give way and I crash to my knees. My hands dig into the bark for support. Numbness spreads from each quill point.

Poisoned quills. Figures.

My heartbeat accelerates, driving the poison though me. My vision grows spotty. I can't pass out. Not here on the ground in plain sight. Tree limbs bend and scoop me up, but they stop short of the high branches. My power begins to fade.

Without my full strength, the branches crack under my weight, and I tumble through the limbs. I hit the ground like a crash dummy, arms and legs splayed, face planted in an inch of earth. I'm dying. I'm positive I am. With the last of my strength, I draw the poison toward my stomach and spew it out again and again, until I'm shaking from the effort.

I roll onto my side. My head thuds to the ground, too heavy to hold up. A pile of moldy leaves cushions my cheek. I lay panting, watching the monster dig. Only it's stubby tail shows and soon that disappears. My vision is blurring. I grit my teeth and reach out my hand. I squeeze my fingers into a tight fist. The beast lets out a sharp yelp and whine as the ground closes in, crushing it.

I exhale. My arm drops to the ground. Sprawled like some kid's forgotten GI Joe action figure, I pass out. But not before a tiny light hovers above me, then darts away.

UNEQUAL

The taste of dried blood lingers on my lips, and I crack open my eyes to the nightmare I've fallen into. Darkness lies thick. The air is still, yet it weighs down my body in a way I can't explain. It reeks like dead things.

My hands are firmly tied behind my back. I work up a bead of spit and swallow, and then gag on the taste of old blood. As I heave, pain spikes through my body. Ribs tender. Head sore. Arms numb.

Rumbling sounds in the distance. Voices. One rises in volume. "Bring him out."

The door screams as it's opened. Bright specks of light blind me, lift me, and the next thing I know, I'm shoved to the ground—more dropped, really—by the *pux*, and land face down near a pair of highly polished boots.

A foot lashes out and catches me in my ribs. I groan. "*This is what the fuss is all about?*" a deep voice asks. "Am I to be threatened by *this*?"

Forced chuckles echo in the room. With my eyes closed, I call out for strength. I strain at my bonds. Nothing happens. Somehow they've taken my powers.

A hand grabs my hair and yanks my head up. I struggle to my knees, twist my body around, and find myself staring into the heated eyes of Navar. Granel and a few others hover near the door. They don't appear happy to be in this place and seem more than eager to leave.

Navar's nostrils flare, and his eyes narrow with ruthless intent. He wedges the hilt of his riding crop under my chin, constricting my air flow. "This half-breed isn't even worth my time. How could any of you think he'd threaten my position? He's unequal to me in every way. It's laughable."

Blood pounds in my veins. My head feels heavy. My lungs hurt. My ears ring. My throat sticks and struggles to pull in air. I try to pull away. No one seems to notice.

Granel steps forward. "He had two of our swords, my lord."

"A thief? I thought he'd be a man of worth, not some thieving weakling."

He lets go, and my head sags to my chest. I gasp in air. I hear him, but his words flow past, as if my brain can't catch them quickly enough. Why am I so weak?

"What do you want us to do with him?" someone asks.

"Kill him," comes Navar's emotionless reply.

The *pux* give a collective shout. By their chatter, it's clear they wanted me for their own, but Navar isn't in the mood to barter. Why should he? To him I'm no better than a bug—best squashed rather than kept alive for any other purpose. He sends the *pux* out, and everyone else is told to leave.

From his place in the doorway, Navar glances into a darkly shadowed corner. "Not too quickly, Sidon. We must make sure everyone understands the folly of challenging the law."

A bone deep grunt is followed by the tang of death. The shadows shift, revealing a huge shape unfolding, stepping forward.

The door thuds shut, and I'm alone with my executioner.

Odd. I don't seem to care. I manage to lean on the wall and rest my head against the cool stone. My willpower is gone. I only want to sleep. I fight the feeling and lazily watch Sidon lumber around the room. He's not one of the *firsts*. I don't know what he is. His face is broad, and his nose is a bulbous, tuber-shaped mass he constantly rubs into a chapped and red eyesore. His arms are thick and longer than his torso. On legs shorter than his arms, he moves ape-like about the chamber as he finishes his preparations. He's as filthy as a mole, his expression as dead as a corpse. He was made to live in this dank and smelly place.

"Why can't I move?"

He plunges a short, thin rod into a kettle sitting on a cushion of burning coals. I don't know what's in that kettle with its alien smell pluming into the air, but whatever it is, it sizzles and pops. Sidon pulls the rod out. It glistens with a shiny substance, and he grins, his mouth a gaping hole dotted with uneven, pointy teeth. "It's the iron around your wrists. It pulls all the power from your kind."

Behind me, my wrists burn within the iron shackles. When I try to use my power to wrestle free, the shackles glow eerily in the dim light. I pull and push at the shackles, pinching the skin around my wrists in my struggle to get free. When I glance up, Sidon is no longer hovering over the kettle.

He's beside me.

Squatting, he stares at me like a doctor would his patient. It's unnerving, thinking he's searching for just the right spot to start his torture.

When he's done with his inspection, he rips off my shirt sleeve. His thick fingers grab my arm and with a quick twist, he pulls me closer. "Now, this may hurt."

The rod slowly moves toward my arm. Already the heat bites at my skin, and when it touches, I jerk back and fall. The bones of my body no longer support me.

I try and hold them in, but in the end, my screams echo off the high, cold walls, like I'm sure all the others have before me. Sidon's annoyance grows. "Quiet," he hisses.

My feet kick spasmodically against the pain.

I don't see him stand and take his brand back to the bucket. I can only feel the heat of the fire rip at my skin. My cries decrease to short bursts as I gulp in air. The stench of burnt flesh permeates the chamber.

When my mind begins to think past the pain, I glance at what he's done to me. A silver brand mars my bicep. The design is simple, a circle with a wicked-looking nail splitting it in half, and three horizontal lines running asymmetrically through it. It's the same mark that marred the tree above the dead lamb, and it's as beautiful as it is horrible.

"Why?" I rasp. "If you're going to kill me, why brand me?"

"It's the mark of the tainted. Those who see it will know why you were killed."

Sidon turns away and begins laying an array of blades on a table. He's going to torture me, kill me, and *then* put my broken body on display?

The medieval slant to my impending death nearly brings me to hysterics. My mind races with all the *should-have-dones* and *wish-I'd-knowns* until I drown in regret and hopelessness. I'm beaten. I tried and I failed. That is the worst wound of all.

When Sidon is ready, he lifts me into his brawny arms and carries me to the table. He unshackles my wrists and then ties me to the table with three, thickly-made iron straps. The coldness burns and weakens me further. I can't even talk. My mind is trapped in a body that can't move, can't defend itself.

Kera. I think on her, on how lucky I've been to know her. When I'm gone, I won't be able to protect her, because when I'm gone, they *will* find out what she is. It's inevitable.

A worse thought tumbles into my head. Will Kera meet Sidon? My mind shudders at the possibility, and I push it away, burying it deep.

I close my eyes, unable to keep them open. The sound of Sidon sharpening the blade has a lulling effect. My time on earth is nearly over. I fantasize that I will be missed. Remembered.

The stropping suddenly stops. My heartbeat pounds in my ears. I'm not ready to die, but when have I ever been given a choice?

No Way Out

The laces on her corset were pulled so tightly, Kera feared she'd pass out. The women in attendance scurried around like nervous mice fearing the swat of a cat's paw. When Kera's ceremonial gown was fitted and hooked, the women stopped what they were doing and stared.

"A queen fit for a king."

"Lovely."

"You make us proud."

Gazing at herself in the mirror, not one word of appreciation for their efforts came to Kera's lips. She was decorated in the most extravagant manner, yet she took no pleasure in the beauty staring back at her.

Her maids soon left, and only her father stood watch. He stayed at the window, peering into the late evening sky, avoiding her as much as she was him, so it came as a shock when he spoke. "I have been thinking, Kera. There's a gift I wish to give you."

The only gift she wanted from him was her freedom. She didn't try to hide the sneer in her voice. "Is it to celebrate this grand occasion?"

"No. It's a gift I've never given you. It's one I gave your mother when she desperately needed it."

Her curiosity was piqued.

"It helped her save your life."

He turned and faced her, and the love she saw in his eyes took her breath away.

His voice grew hushed. "A parent will sacrifice anything to see his child safe."

Could she trust him? Kera wanted to, more than ever. "What is it?"

He motioned her closer. "You'll know once you have it, though it'll only last a short time. Don't hesitate to use it, Kera. I can't give it to you again until my powers revive. Do you understand what I'm saying?"

Was he offering her the gift of his power? Not a portion, but all of it?

He turned back to the setting sun, now more brilliant than the brightest fire. "Are you ready?"

"Yes," she said on a choked whisper.

He closed his eyes and allowed the bulk of his power to surge into her. She gasped at the intensity, reveling in the energy like she had Dylan's. When she opened her eyes, her father was on the floor, collapsed in a heap.

She bent and kissed his forehead. "Thank you, Father."

He weakly grabbed her wrist in an effort to keep her by him, his vow to Navar still strong even in his weakened state, but she easily pulled away. Gathering her skirts, she leapt onto the window sill and jumped to the ground. The fall would have seriously injured her before, but now it barely registered. She ran toward the woods, her speed twice that of normal.

She would find Dylan. They'd leave and never come back. Her father had given her freedom at his expense. She wouldn't waste this chance.

Just as she reached the woods, Faldon appeared. "What are you doing out here? Are you looking for me?" His gaze skimmed her finery. His hands grasped her shoulders and he frowned, no doubt feeling the surge of power that hummed beneath her skin. "Where's your father?"

"Is Dylan safe? Please, Faldon, tell me he's safe."

A tingling sensation grew where his hands rested, and just as quickly as her father's power appeared, it left. She felt exhausted. Drained.

Faldon inhaled deeply, then dropped his hands. "He's gone."

"Gone?" The word wouldn't stick. She couldn't have heard correctly. "What do you mean he's gone? Where?"

A distressed look crossed Faldon's face. "He had questions. I couldn't lie. He knows about Navar."

Kera took a wobbly step back. "But I don't love Navar. Did you not try and stop him?"

"Neither I nor Bodog could. He felt betrayed. Can you blame him? You said nothing of your betrothal."

"I wanted to tell him, but the time was never ripe."

"I hesitate to say, but in our search, we found one of Navar's hounds. There was blood on its quills. I don't wish to think harm came to Dylan, but he's the only one missing." Faldon easily turned her toward the keep and laid a comforting arm around her. "You don't look well. I'm sorry. Truly I am. Contemplating death is never easy. Whatever happened to Dylan, he deserved better."

"You think he's dead?" The thought turned her cold.

"All the evidence points that way." Faldon hugged her, and whispered roughly, "I know the sting of lost love. Hold it close."

Her shock quickly gave way to devastating sorrow.

After a moment, he pulled away. "But now you're free to give to your people what they truly need. A good queen. Can you accept your fate? To do anything less will risk a series of consequences that will plunge Teag into chaos."

Did Faldon really believe Dylan was dead? Killed by one of Navar's hounds? He must. He knew her heart and how deeply it would hurt to hear of Dylan's death. He wouldn't be so cruel.

The world closed in, pressing down on her lungs. Faldon steered her back to the manor. Any hope of freedom died, leaving her empty and alone. Why had she allowed herself to love Dylan? Now she faced the pain of eternal separation. "It would've been better to have never met."

Faldon patted her arm, his support the only thing keeping her walking.

When they came to the front of the manor, the yard overflowed with people. The time for the ceremony had arrived. Torches smoked, casting shadows on the ground, and Faldon urged Kera forward. No one seemed to notice her father's absence, nor did they think it strange that Faldon attended her. Everyone seemed lost in the moment.

Cheers went up when a woman presented Kera with a heavily jeweled cloak. At one time, she would've delighted in its richness. Now, she wanted nothing to do with it.

Faldon offered her his hand, and escorted her to the ceremonial mount, a large gryphon, its white and gold feathers gleaming in the torch light. Its talons clacked against the cobbles impatiently. All too soon, Kera was settled onto an elaborate saddle.

The journey that would change her life forever had begun.

The cleansing ceremony would see her on a path, once taken, she couldn't stray. What did she care what happened now? Without Dylan, nothing mattered.

Not Forgotten

I keep my eyes shut, preferring not to see my end coming. I can smell my own fear, even above the stench of the dungeons. My muscles clench, preparing for the touch of a blade. Seconds feel like minutes. What is Sidon waiting for? An invitation to torture me?

A sharp smack lands on my cheek. The unexpectedness of it makes my eyes fly open. Jason's standing beside the table, a wide grin on his face. "This is no time to fall asleep. We've got a torturer to tie up, a girl to save, an evil empire to destroy…"

Behind him, Leo and Bodog lay an unconscious Sidon on the ground. Leo hurries back to me. I'm alive, and humbled that anyone cared enough to find me. I throw a crooked smile their way, and fight to keep my eyes open. "Good to see you," I slur.

Leo takes a good look at me and frowns. "What's wrong with you?"

"He's strapped," Bodog says, glancing up from the rope he's using to tie up Sidon. "Iron poisons his kind."

Jason shoves Leo back. "Hang on, Superboy. We'll get you away from your kryptonite." As he manhandles the straps off me, his eyes light up. "I gotta tell you, hands down, this is the awesomest thing I've ever done. Did you see that thing that came after us? Two heads! I wish my phone had a camera, but my dad wouldn't get me one. Thinks I'm gonna strip, click, and send." He laughs. "Like a picture can do me justice."

With the straps off, Jason helps me sit up. Once freed, my arms slip to my sides. A bright red rash of blisters and swollen skin rings my wrists. I can barely move. I feel empty and loose and confused. "How did you guys get in here?"

Leo motions toward Bodog. "It was all him. Did you know there's a tunnel under this place?"

A soft, wheezy laugh escapes me. I should've known. Jason and Leo heft me between them, and I glance at Bodog. "Thank you."

With his large hands, Bodog easily pushes the heavy grate in the middle of the room to the side. His face isn't exactly smiling, but he looks smug, standing beside his escape tunnel. "Bodog make sure the King's court never imprisons him again."

Jason jumps into the hole, no sign of claustrophobia, and my other friends drop me in after him. When I fall, Jason breaks my landing, but my legs are still too weak to hold me upright, and I crumble to my knees in a pit of slushy, watery waste. The stink is terrible.

Leo lands beside me, and with help, I struggle to my feet. Above us, Bodog hangs from his fingertips along the rim and pulls the grate back in place. He lets go and splashes into the pit that stretches out into a narrowing tunnel. No one can fit through the far opening except for maybe a *pux*. There has to be another way out.

A head peeks out of another opening. Pop frowns. "You're making a racket." When he spies me, a shadow of a smile emerges. "I was beginning to wonder if they'd done you in."

I shoot a shocked glance at Leo. "He can talk?"

"Our odd new friend healed him. Apparently Pop was cursed by the *pux* years ago. And now he's making my life miserable because of it." The pitch of his voice grows higher. "Did you hear that, Leo? It's my footsteps. Did you hear that, Leo? I can hear myself breathe," he mimics. "Curses these days. They don't even last a lifetime."

Pop's smile stretches wider before he disappears.

Bodog rushes by and darts into the opening ahead of us. "Shhhh," he hisses. "Ears are everywhere in these parts."

I stare after him as he quickly disappears, startled by the eerie, pale light emanating from him.

Jason leans close and whispers, "If I were Pop, I wouldn't have eaten anything *he* touched, even if it gave me the power to fly. Nasty goop. The stuff made me want to throw up just looking at it."

"Yeah," I say automatically, more interested in Bodog, "but when did Bodog become a glowworm?"

Leo tucks his shoulder more firmly under my arm. "The mushrooms. He rubbed himself with them and then whamo! Grumpy glows. He wouldn't come anywhere near this place without his mushroom rubdown, and let me tell you, that was disturbing to watch. The sounds he made, his face…" Leo shuddered. "He really needs to do that in private."

They help me slip into a small crevice hidden in the darkened pit. I stumble over a natural step that keeps the majority of the water at bay, but not totally out of Bodog's escape tunnel. As we move forward, a feeling of dread splinters my nerves. I try to shake the sound of buzzing from my ears. It won't stop. Before we round the first bend, I glance back and see a pair of bright lights dart into the pit and hover near our tunnel opening.

"*Pux*," I manage to say.

Everyone spins around and stares at the twin dots of light.

"Get them," Bodog hisses at me.

I stretch out my hand and try and pull the power into me, but I'm still too weak. A dozen more lights suddenly buzz into view. Leo and Jason tense beside me. The last time they met with the *pux*, Leo barely escaped being enslaved.

Bodog pushes us forward, his craggy voice urging us on. We all sprint down the tunnel, Pop in the lead. Flashes of light shatter against the walls. It takes me a moment to realize the *pux* are flinging their dust and missing, only because Bodog is using his body to block their aim.

Leo and Jason's grips loosen as the tunnel twists and turns on itself. I push them ahead. "Go on. I'm fine," I assure them. I'm not nearly as wobbly as I was a few minutes ago. Neither guy needs more encouragement, and they charge past Pop. The buzz grows. We're running out of time. The *pux* are far more adept at maneuvering in the tunnel's tight space.

I search out my power again, feel it surging towards me, and when it floods my body, I gasp. With its strength infusing me, I turn and stand in the center of the tunnel. Arms held out, I call for the nearest tool I can see to defend us. Bodog stumbles to a stop, his back pocked with welts where the *pux* have used their magic on him. "Go on," I yell over the rising buzz.

A loud roar overtakes the buzzing, and a collective high-pitched scream sounds. Everyone stops and turns to see a huge wave of stinking water crash over the pux. It smashes them to the ground, dampening their light. They fight against the current as it sweeps them back toward the pit.

Whoops of joy rise from my friends. Pop laughs, overcome with relief. He sags against the wall and wipes the sweat from his eyes. Only Bodog refrains from celebrating and shakes his head. "They'll be back."

He's right. "Sorry to do this, but we don't have a choice."

Starting at the tips of my fingers, I press my hands together until my palms are firmly united. The walls rumble and slam together, stopping with a whoosh only inches from my feet.

Jason slaps my back as the dust I've stirred up with my trick swirls all around us. "It's good to see you're back to normal. Well, as normal as doing that sort of thing is. Can we get out of here now?"

Bodog scratches and knocks at the newly joined walls and grunts. "A fortnight's worth of work gone."

Knock and scratch. Knock and scratch.

"A vein of granite. Four weeks to dig it out again." He casts a displeased frown my way, and grumbles nonstop as he leads us back to his underground home beneath Faldon's house.

No *thank-you-for-saving-my-skin* from the cranky little mushroom guy.

I turn to follow, but Pop grabs my arm and stops me. "You okay?"

It's so odd to hear him speak. Even though I've known him only a short time, I've gotten used to his hand motions. As we trudge after the others, I nod. "Yeah. How much time did we lose?"

"Six hours. Bodog says you're lucky the quills didn't kill you."

If he only knew how close I'd come to dying. I don't want to think about it. My mind—finally clear of the poisonous dungeon— speeds onto what we'll need to do to get Kera back to my world. I can only hope she's at Faldon's, waiting for me.

"Maybe you should slow down," he continues. "Take a step back until your strength returns."

Pop's interest in my welfare makes me pause. Is he angling for a heart-to-heart about leaving this place before we find her?

That will *never* happen.

With my spine bullet straight, I glare down at him. "I'm fine, and I'm not going back until I get Kera. You can leave if you've changed your mind, but I won't go."

The wrinkles etched into Pop's leathery face are exaggerated by the faint light cast by the glow of the mushrooms lining the walls. "I won't lie and say I'm not scared. This is bigger than even I imagined. Someone is causing them to act out."

"Navar." Remembering the man's attitude only makes me more determined to succeed. "It's all him. Bodog says he's been itching to be king ever since the last one disappeared."

"They're leaderless? That explains a lot. They take on the attitude of their leader once they swear allegiance. They're splintering under the pressure. Taking sides."

"Let them. When Kera and I are gone—"

Pop shakes his head, his eyes full of pity. "This affects us all. They've declared war."

"On *me*," I remind him. "When I'm gone, they won't have a reason to bother anyone else."

He lifts a bushy eyebrow, his skepticism clearly written on his face. "You're pretty sure of yourself there."

"I'm the one with the tainted blood. I'm the rogue factor. They want *me*." I jerk my arm free. "Everything else is incidental."

"That's exactly what I'm afraid of." His face darkens; his eyes bore into mine. "I didn't come for you—I'm here for Leo. I won't let you sacrifice him because of your obsession with a girl. I know how you people get."

He acts like I'm some sort of biology project he's been studying. "I'm not like all the other ones, or haven't you noticed?"

His eyes rake me. "That's the problem. I *haven't* noticed a difference. Your kind is all about self. You may not mean to hurt others, but you always do."

The insult hits its mark. I grit my teeth, muting the angry words that want to come out. I *am* different. I'm not like the *firsts*.

But then the memory of my grandparents' burning house slices through me like a jagged blade, and my confidence falters.

The fear in Reggie's eyes when he accused me of trying to kill Grandpa, Faldon's shattered windows, how easily my mind wrote off my friends' lives because Kera is all that matters...

My weakness. My burning flaw.

My obsessive nature.

I'm *exactly* like the *firsts*.

Irresistible Pull

Twenty minutes later, we climb up from the bowels of the tunnel and into Faldon's house. Bodog drops the trap door, the sound a boom of warning in the eerie quiet. Pop, Leo, and Jason grip their rifles tightly, but the only sound comes from the tiny dragon dozing near the heat of the kitchen fire and a soft mewling from a fluffy, white cat whose head rises off its paws when we appear. There's an uneasy emptiness to the house, like it's unhappy to shelter me again.

I don't blame it.

"Where are they?" A wave of abandonment swells within me, and I quickly tamp it down. I expected Kera to be back by now. Turning toward Bodog, I ask, "You gave her the message I gave you, didn't you?"

His big ears wiggle. "Faldon took it."

"Faldon? Perfect." His says he's on her side, but he's clearly not on mine. "Something's not right here."

Bodog's large eyes sweep the area and rise toward the stairs. "Stay." He points to Pop and motions him to the window. "Watch."

While the two older men scout the area, the cat stands and trots directly toward Leo, the bell hanging around its neck a warning of its intent. It rubs against Leo's legs, purring and weaving between his feet. Basically, being a nuisance.

Jason pulls a distasteful face and cracks his knuckles. "Better you than me. I hate cats."

"Really? I kinda like 'em. Hey, Pop. She's a beauty, isn't she?"

"Shh." I wave them quiet. The fire colors the room with flickering light, slapping at the shadows and making them dance. The stillness of the night rakes along my nerves. If Kera hasn't made it back, at least Faldon should be here. It's what Bodog expects. So, where is the old man?

The cat's purr grows louder. Leo slips his rifle over his shoulder and picks it up, stroking its tummy and tickling it under its chin. The bell tinkles sharply in the quiet.

Pop frowns at his grandson. "Maybe you shouldn't — "

One moment Leo's holding a cat, the next he's cradling a naked girl with long, flowing, snow-white hair, and startling green eyes. Leo yelps and nearly drops her. She giggles and tucks her head under his chin, rubbing her cheek on his chest. Her pink choker with its tiny bell tinkles cheerfully with every move. Though Jason ogles her freely, Leo refuses to look at her. He spins this way and that, searching for a place to put her, but she hangs on even tighter, refusing to be put down.

Bodog rushes back into the room, and Leo whirls in his direction. Catgirl doesn't acknowledge the little man. She kicks her pale, bare legs playfully as they dangle over Leo's forearm and wraps her slender arms around his neck to better tease his hair.

Bodog pulls the girl from Leo's arms. "No playing, Lucinda. Where is Faldon?"

Lucinda pouts and cuddles into Leo's side, grinning up at him coyly. "Summoned. By Navar."

That can't be good. "Why?"

She doesn't even glance my way, but walks her fingers up

Leo's chest. He blushes, making it clear he'd rather be anywhere than under Catgirl's paws.

"It's your lucky day, Leo," Jason says with an amused smirk. "I think she likes you."

I don't have time for this. I grab her arm and turn her to face me. "Why did Navar want him?"

"Give an answer, true and honest," Bodog encourages her.

"I will if I want." She flicks her almond-shaped eyes over me and shrugs. "The ceremony has begun."

Bodog throws her a heated look. "Duplicitous devil. You let Faldon go?"

She lifts her chin high and glares down at Bodog. "I saw no need to interfere. What do I care about a silly ceremony?"

My voice grows firmer as my fingers tighten on her arm. "The wedding? It's begun?"

"Nay, the cleansing." She frowns and tries to pull away.

"Let her go," Bodog says carefully.

No way. I've got someone who knows where Kera is. "What's a cleansing? Where is she?"

A hint of anger flashes in the green eyes.

"Let her go," Bodog repeats, and this time the hint of warning in his voice is clear.

Her struggles stop. The dark pupils of her angled cat eyes enlarge, covering nearly the whole of her glassy, green irises. A strange energy tingles beneath my fingers, but I won't let go. Her long, white hair begins to crackle and fly about her like flashes of lightning. Slowly, she rises off the floor. Everyone else takes a step back, everyone except Bodog, who rushes forward and hooks onto my other arm.

"Release her," he demands.

Not likely. I tighten my hold, unafraid. I'm past worrying about me. "Catgirl seems to know more about what's going on than anyone else."

I shake Bodog off, but he's very insistent. Lucinda smiles that creepy smile all crazy chicks seem to possess. Bodog's large hands grab me about my waist and yank. I fall backward, and my fingers slip off her arm. When I hit the floor, Lucinda disappears.

"Whoa." Jason flinches, startled by her now-she's-here-now-she's-not routine. "Tell me that wasn't for real."

I turn on Bodog, my face flushed with anger. "What are you doing? Why'd you let her go? She knows what's going on. I could feel it."

Bodog's face is far paler than I've ever seen it. Fear emanates from his large eyes, and he whispers roughly, "Never hold a *lutine* captive. They will drag you instantly into the depths of the sea. Abandon you across the universe. Danger follows her. Never trust, ever." He nods toward Leo. "The one's they like, they love to death."

Leo looks ready to faint. "For the record, I don't like cats anymore."

Jason shifts his gun and pats Leo on the back. "But she was *hot*. Seriously. I could dig being loved by her." A strange expression crosses his face. "I wonder if she has a sandpaper tongue?"

Leo shrugs off his hand. "Shut up."

"Hey, it's a legit question. You know you were thinking it."

Bodog struggles to his feet.

I'm seething inside, swamped with hatred for myself and something worse. I can *feel* Kera's distress. It's killing me, and my best chance at knowing exactly where to find her just vanished. I get up and stare the little guy down, my chest heaving. "You'd better know where this ceremony is."

Why do I think I can intimidate him? He points his finger at me and snarls. "The time for anger has passed. Use your head." He stomps over to the hatch and opens it.

No way. He isn't doing what I think he's doing.

"Hey," I shout, as he descends toward his underground home. "Where're you going?"

The hatch bangs shut after him, cutting off any more questions. I close my eyes and battle the frustration that's rising within me. My ribs receive a sharp nudge. I open my eye to see Jason glancing at the trap door. His lips have grown firm and white along the edges. "You know, your new friend's a weird, little guy, but correct me if I'm wrong—we need him, don't we?"

"Boys." Pop waves us over to the window where he's standing and jabs his finger toward the east. "I think I know where the ceremony is."

Beyond the darkness of the cottages, a rising glow lightens the sky not more than a mile outside the village wall. That strange pull I felt the first time Kera touched me returns. "That's it. That's where she is."

"We can't go now." Pop faces us. "It's one thing to find her here. It's another thing to steal her from a ceremony. The word implies people. Lots of people. They're not going to let us waltz in there, glad hand everyone, and leave with her."

A loud bang sounds from behind us. We turn, my hands glowing, the guys' guns pointed and ready to fire. Bodog emerges from the hatch, hefting a large pickax over his right shoulder and a leather bag over his left. He lumbers over to the tables and spills the contents onto it—daggers, short swords, brass knuckles, and tiny, polished silver throwing balls. Curious, we congregate around the table. Bodog hands each of us a few medieval weapons.

Leo palms one of the balls. "Interesting collection. I can see this hurting but not much else. We are supposed to win, right?"

Our little friend picks up a similar ball and rotates it. A high-pitched hum sounds, and about ten seconds later, evil-looking pointy bits spring out. He gingerly rotates it back and the points disappear. He tosses it back to Leo. "Once it sticks, it explodes."

"Nice, in a sick kind of way," Leo says, "but I'm not exactly what you'd call athletic, I mean, I can throw, but—"

Bodog tosses him a mechanical sling and a bag filled with more silver balls.

"Sweet. Just point me toward Goliath."

I sift through the weapons, noticing they've been adapted with their own special kind of magic. The ax, Bodog tells us, will send out a shock wave that shakes the enemy to their knees when hit on the ground. I find another sword and a black bag holding a substance that, when spit on, turns to thick, lung-choking smoke.

Jason inspects each weapon, but in the end, doesn't choose one. "I'll stick with my gun."

"The *lutine* would have been nice," Bodog mutters. "Formidable in battle, but not reliable."

"Wait one minute." Pop glares at all of us. "What's going on here? This was supposed to be a quick grab and go. Dylan's girl isn't here, and for all we know, she never was. Now look at us. Are we seriously going into battle?"

We all stare at him, and my chest tightens. I've brought this onto them. It's my battle, not theirs. How can I explain the connection Kera and I have? I know she's in trouble, that something really bad is about to happen. I felt it in the tunnels, after we left the dungeons, but I ignored it, pinning it on the residual effects of my imprisonment, but it was more than that. Kera is being held against her will, and whether she knows it or not, she's calling out to me for help. I need to go. I don't have a choice.

But they do.

Indecision rages within me. Before I can begin to explain, Leo faces his grandfather. That smooth voice turns cold and his features harden. "Yeah. It's a war. You knew that before we came. You knew it could get bad. We all did."

Pop shakes his head. "Your father would kill me if he knew where we were. What we're about to do."

"Do you have a better idea?" Jason challenges.

"They want Dylan. I say, give them what they want and stop all of this now."

All eyes turn to me. I don't blame Pop for offering up my life so quickly. It's the most logical solution. I'm just surprised no one else thought of it first. "I-if you want to, I-I'm willing."

Disgust flares across Pop's face, and he waves his hand at me before looking away. "No. I don't know why I said that."

"Bodog does," the little guy says. "Your scars are showing."

"What does that mean?" I ask.

"He fought before. Lost. His heart is weary. His mind soft."

"That's not—" Pop begins and then stops. His face reddens, and he bows his head.

Leo steps closer to his grandfather. "You don't think we'll win. That we don't even have a chance. Why'd you come along?"

"To save you."

"From what?"

"Him," he says, pointing toward me.

Pop's assertion is so powerful, it vibrates the air, snatching all sound into its echo. When it stills, the quiet deepens until the fire snaps and a log cracks in two. The dragon stretches and spreads his diaphanous wings, beating them. *Whoop. Whoop. Whoop.* He settles back down.

"I get that the plan's changed," Jason finally says. "That something odd is going down, but this isn't going to stop. We've got to grab the girl and take out the bad guy, Chuck Norris style."

Pop sweeps his hand down his face and glares at Jason. "Do you hear yourself? This isn't an action movie you're in. Somebody's going to die. Hell, we could all die. *Dylan* nearly did."

Everyone stares at the brand that marks me as an undesirable, seared into my shoulder. I can't ask any more of them. Can't let my obsession destroy anyone else. "He's right. You all rescued me. I'll take it from here."

I snatch up my things and turn to go, but Leo stops me — physically grabs my arm — his body stiff with anger. "I'm not leaving you to do this alone. I don't care what Pop says."

His gaze slides to his grandfather. "You raised me to do the right thing, even if it means I might get hurt."

Pop's eyes grow misty, and he shakes his head, fighting the words his grandson is throwing at him.

Leo leans forward, the intensity on his face a scary thing. "You're right, Pop. This isn't a movie. It's reality, and I have to do what's right. I can't leave. Not after what they did back home."

"You want revenge? I've been down that road," he whispers back just as heatedly. "The rules here are different. They don't understand mercy."

"Good," Leo snaps, "'cause right now, neither do I."

Defeated, Pop shakes his head and walks away.

Latching onto the energy pouring off of Leo, Jason smiles wickedly. He grabs Leo's shoulders and gives them a hard shake. "I never knew you had it in you. That's the way to do it. Storm the castle and be damned the consequences. No guts, no glory. Fight to win, or don't fight at all." The clichés keep pouring out of him. He turns to me, his eyes glittering with excitement. "I'm with you to the end. We'll destroy them."

I've never experienced such fierce loyalty. It's humbling, but scary. "All I want is Kera. We can go after Navar later."

"Now or never," Bodog says. "Destroy him now, for when he takes the throne, he will be invincible."

That sounds ominous. "How invincible?"

"He will be infused with power above all others."

No wonder Navar is so desperate for his butt to warm that

throne.

Jason whistles. "Knowing all the crazy stuff Dylan can do, I'd say letting this Navar guy live isn't in our favor."

"And how are you going to kill him?" Pop's voice rises from his post in the shadows. "Unless you boys have been leading a double life, none of you have ever seen a man die, and you sure as hell haven't killed anyone."

I have.

Time's trickling through my fingers. I want all this to be over. "I'll do it."

"You can't rescue Kera *and* kill Navar." Leo puts his hands on top of his head and paces. "I saw this show about how war is similar to a game of chess. You need to see what your opponent is working with, where his men are, and then take them down one move at a time."

Jason nods his head enthusiastically. "That sounds good."

Bodog thumps the table. "Scout out the enemy. Find Kera and Navar."

Leo brightens. "Right. And then we come up with a plan."

They all stare at me, eager for my approval. Even I can see this is a complete crap shoot, but it's a bet I'm willing to take. "Let's do it."

We gather our weapons and head out. Pop rushes forward, grabs Leo, and holds him tight. "Don't go."

I stand outside the threshold, unsure if I should stay or leave. I'm not completely out of sight, though far enough away to suggest privacy.

Leo struggles out of Pop's desperate embrace. "I have to. I can't not help. I'm not like you."

Pop nods, his body sagging with inevitability. "Then I'll go."

"No." Leo backs away, his hand warding Pop off. "I'm sorry, Pop. You're a weak link. We can't take that risk."

Wounded, Pop's features crumple, digging the lines of age deeper. He steps back, shoulders as straight and as rigid as rebar in concrete. He clears his throat, his Adam's apple rising, then plummeting, once, twice. His eyes are hot, his voice scratchy. "Be safe. All of you."

Leo nods and backs away. "We'll be back. Keep out of sight." When he closes the door, he gives me a quick don't-press-me glance. "He's staying." Without any more explanation, he takes off after Jason and Bodog. I fall in behind him.

We quickly catch up to the others, and I let Bodog take the lead, my mind fogged with worry. The risk we're all about to take deepens my footsteps. I agree with Pop. The air is thick with the scent of impending death.

And if one of us dies, it'll be my fault.

HEARTACHE

Dylan was dead.

Kera tried to banish the thought, but it hammered into her, drowning her will, dulling her brain. She did whatever Faldon asked. No complaint. No joy.

Dead. Dead. Dead. She stared out over the crowd, a lifeless shell. No one seemed to notice. They thought she was honored, her demeanor somber because of the occasion.

She wanted to scream her pain. Curse at Dylan for leaving her. She bit her lips raw, tasting blood. Knowing regret.

She should have never found him.

The singing grew louder. The crowd's happy faces turned to her. Watched her. Yet the one she loved was dead, and no one could see how her soul was shriveling. Faldon had drilled into her the need to hide her emotions. She hadn't realized how well she'd learned the lesson until now.

The gryphon pranced beneath her, the only one cognizant of her sorrow. A commiserating whirl rumbled in its throat.

Kera clutched the pommel, feeling the roll and clip of the animal's gait, knowing each step brought her that much closer to everlasting misery.

WAITING IN THE DARK

Torches smoke and flare, breaking up the darkness in small pools of light that join to make a wider circle. The moon, an eerie blueish black, hangs low and lonely in the sky. Its dimness would normally be to our advantage, but not here. Not even the deepest shadows of night are dark enough to hide strangers from the *firsts*. If anyone turns around, we'll be seen.

We creep forward. Surely, they can hear us? Every time I shift, the leaves crunch under my hands and knees. I drop to my belly along with everyone else and wait. Nothing happens. The crowd congregating in the meadow outside the village only sways back and forth to the mournful chanting coming from a woman standing beside Kera. It's like the earth in this spot has fallen asleep. Even I feel the song slip under my skin and lull my mind.

I shake off the strange sensation and lock my eyes onto Kera. The light from the fire paints her simple, white gown a soft yellow. Her dark hair hangs loose down her back, anchored at the top by a crown of fresh flowers. She looks innocent and pure and…dead. I force myself not to rush forward and challenge them all.

The crowd shifts, and a large beast swivels its head in our direction, its eyes seeming to pierce through the underbrush. The head is that of an eagle, the body of an overgrown lion with wings. A gryphon—a mythological beast said to be able to disembowel a man with one snap of its beak.

Fantastic.

My breathing grows shallower until I'm nearly hyper-ventilating in my effort to remain still. Bodog grasps my forearm and casts me a hard look that says, "control yourself." I close my eyes and regulate my breathing. I need to refocus on what we're here to do.

Opening my eyes, I nod, the motion small, but firm. The beast stares for a few seconds longer, flexes its wings, and then turns its head away. I can feel Leo's sigh. I can smell Jason's awe. Whatever that thing is here to do, I hope it stays clear of us.

Bodog's touch keeps me grounded, and as soon as it's gone, my attention snaps back to Kera. I take note of how many people there are, and if anyone is armed. I crawl forward and dig my fingers into the earth, grasping at the power I've come to expect. I try to send a silent message to her, to tell her I'm here. It's like clawing through ice. Something cold and dark blocks my efforts. I try harder, concentrating on her face. No emotion flickers in her eyes. No recognition that she can even feel me.

I know that look.

She believes I've abandoned her.

The chant flows easily as the woman helps Kera step into a basin filled with shimmering powder. Taking up an ornate cup, she pours the powder over Kera's feet and ankles, casting up a cloud of gold. The woman walks in a circle, tossing the finely ground gold in higher and higher arches until the billowing cloud engulfs Kera. When the dust settles, every inch of her sparkles. Amid the growing hum, like the drone of bees calling the stragglers back to the hive, a single tear slips down Kera's cheek, cutting a pale track through the golden dust.

From a patch of shadow, a man approaches. Faldon. He cups the side of her face and whispers something before taking her hand.

The woman affixes a densely jeweled cloak around Kera's shoulders. Its heaviness engulfs her like a constrictor would its prey. The woman smiles at Kera as if what's happening is a good thing, an honor.

The crowd parts for Faldon, who escorts Kera to the gryphon. The hem of her cloak drags behind her like a warning of the unhappiness to come.

With care, Kera sits sideways on an elaborate saddle affixed between the creature's wings. Faldon squeezes Kera's hand before he lets go and leads her strange mount forward. As she passes through the crowd, people fall in behind her. A drum and lute sound, and everyone begins to sing. Soon the clearing is empty. Whatever strange spell they used to block my magic from reaching Kera lifts. The energy I sought earlier springs to life beneath my fingertips. I can feel Kera's heart breaking, smell the deep, molasses scent of her sorrow.

Jason sits, his gun cradled on his lap, and grunts. "What kind of ceremony is this? Human sacrifice?"

"They covered her in gold," Leo says on an awed whisper. "Like some virgin goddess."

I don't want to think about the symbolism behind the ceremony, but it buzzes along the edges of my brain anyway. I can't fail her. "Where're they going?" I ask Bodog.

"To the lake. She must be purified."

"Oh, man," Jason says, "that totally sounds like a human sacrifice I saw in a movie once."

"Shut up," Leo and I say.

My fist balls around a clump of dirt, and I fling it into the now-empty clearing, feeling the weight of defeat press down on me.

"How are we going to get her with all those people around? And a gryphon! How do you fight that? It's impossible."

A swift kick thumps my thigh. Bodog's face writhes between disgust and disappointment. Apparently, my sudden slump into self-doubt irritates him. "Not much time. We must beat them to the lake."

Does he mean what I think he means? "You've got a plan?"

He flashes me a rare smile. Good thing it's rare—that toothy, uneven crack along the lower half of his face isn't a pretty sight. But it's a welcome one. It pokes at my doubt, yanking me out of my self-pity with its snaggle-toothed jab. Without another word, he dashes into the trees.

Jason gives a soft whoop. "Cool! We've got a plan."

"Um, guys," Leo says, staring down the path Bodog took, "he's getting away."

I look to where Bodog went. "For a little guy, he sure is fast."

"Damn rabbit," Jason grumbles.

Time has a way of sneaking up on a person, or sometimes holding still. I hope for the latter. Navar and his men swarm the woods, clogging up the bulk of the paths. We barely make it to the lake undetected and ahead of the crowd when Bodog waves us quiet. We slow our steps and sneak to the edge of a huge lake. Its waters are smooth and deep, but on closer inspection, an unwelcome shiver slides under my skin. The lake pulses with energy. It has the power to destroy me, to take the one person I love above everyone else, and prepare her for another. For all its peaceful reflection, it holds the beginning to my end.

Our part of the lake sits farther down the shore than where Bodog says the procession will end, hidden by an outcrop of stiff reeds and tall brush. We have precious little time to get into position. Before we break apart, we do a quick weapons check. Leo gives me a thumbs up with one hand and holds his slingshot with the other. Bodog pats his ax. Jason inspects his gun, then nudges me. "I'm good. You?"

If no one messes with the lake or deadens its power, I'll be fine, but I don't like the glimmer skittering around in Jason's eyes. He's taken on a Rambo persona. I can see why he's the number one wrestler in the state of Oregon—he's got intimidation down to an art form. His hands grip the gun steadily enough, but there's a restlessness, like a gunslinger counting down to noon, that makes me pause.

"No shooting unless there's trouble," I remind everyone. "This is a sneak attack. Agreed?"

Leo and Bodog immediately nod. Only Jason continues to sight down his barrel.

"Jason?"

Tension makes the planes of his face stand out in harsh lines and deep hollows. He looks away. "Yeah, got it. Shoot when trouble shows."

I don't like the way he's twisting my words, but there isn't time to spare. As Jason ducks behind a tree and Leo and Bodog find cover nearby, I slip into the warm water of the lake, a hollow reed in hand. The plan is simple, but risky. My timing has to be perfect.

From my hiding place near shore, I see the glow of torchlight breaking through the tree line, then the procession. The crowd stops. Faldon helps Kera dismount, and they move onto a natural beachhead that juts into the water. The pebbles shift under their feet, and Kera's grip tightens on Faldon. He pats her hand and moves behind her. Unlatching the cloak, he pulls it from her shoulders and steps back.

I not only *see* her misery, our connection lets me *feel* it. I try to break through to her, but I can't. Despair has taken root, wrapping itself tightly around Kera. With each breath she takes, it strangles her inner light, weakening it. Isn't Faldon alarmed? Do none of them see what they're doing to her?

A hum rises from the crowd, and a flute spins a haunting tune that's far from comforting. Kera takes a step forward, her hands lifting her skirts in order to walk more easily. Even I can see them shake.

The lake laps against her toes. She slowly moves forward, water inching up her legs and rippling away from her body in ever-widening circles. When the water reaches her waist, I put the reed in my mouth and dive. I'm surprised when, after a moment of darkness, my eyes adjust, and I can see almost as clearly underwater as I can in the night. With long strokes, I plow forward. I see her shoulders dip, see her take a deep breath. When she submerges her whole body beneath the water, I grab her wrist, startling her eyes open. I quickly command the gold dust to gather into an outline of her body and float toward a large grouping of lily pads a few yards away. With the reed in her mouth, we swim in the opposite direction as fast as we can. In no time, we reach the thickly growing brush.

I help Kera out of the water amid the rumbles of apprehension slowly filtering through the crowd. The rumbles turn to alarm, and Faldon wades into the water, searching. Someone points to the golden outline near the lily pads and several of them jump in. The gryphon takes flight. Soon they'll know Kera's gone.

Leo begins to melt into the forest, his attention on Bodog's retreating form. "Come on," he rasps, his deep voice cracking with tension. "They won't be searching the lake for long."

Kera turns in my arms and kisses me, the scent of molasses quickly fading. "You're here, you're really here."

Holding her calms the raging obsession that brought me to her. "I told you I'd be back."

"They said you were dead."

I take her face between my hands. "They're idiots. I'll never leave you. Ever."

Jason pops out from behind a tree, his gun still trained on the *firsts*. "Gee, this is real sweet and all, but we gotta go."

He's right. I take Kera's hand and pull her after me. The weight of her fingers in mine calms my heart. She's mine. We're together. Nothing can stop us now.

We follow Bodog's lead down a faded path, our steps heavier on the debris than I like. Kera follows me closely, her whispered voice a constant in my ear. "It's not what I wanted. You understand, don't you?" Her words hang on a breath laced with fear. "I was given no choice in the matter. I told my father about us. Then you left, and Faldon said one of Navar's beasts had—"

Her voice cracks, and she grows silent.

"Why did you doubt me?" My hand stiffens within hers. "I told you I'd be back. You asked me to believe in you. I did. Why didn't you believe in me?"

Her breathing grows ragged. There's a feverish intensity to her gaze. A plea for understanding fills her voice. "Didn't you hear me? When you didn't return, Faldon told me you were dead."

"Faldon," I say on a sneer, remembering the ceremony and his hand in it. "I see where his loyalty lies."

"With me. He believes if I join Navar, I can help our people in some small way. You can't fault him for that."

"Yes, I can. He's using you. They all are."

Out of the corner of my eye, I see Bodog push through the overgrown path. "Time is precious."

Just then, a sound like a fire cracker rips through the night. My hand tightens on Kera's arm, and I instinctively hunch down, pulling her with me.

"What was that?" Kera asks.

My stomach twists and grows heavy with dread. I know exactly what that sound is.

And I know exactly who's to blame.

Jason had volunteered to bring up the rear. Because my attention was fully on Kera, I hadn't noticed how far back he lagged. I push Kera at Bodog. "Catch up to Leo and take them to the wall."

Leaving Kera struggling against Bodog's big hands and his insistent urgings to move, I run toward the sound of the gunfire. When I draw near, I see Jason pop up from behind a bush and fire at the men who've left the lakeside to search for Kera.

The bullet spins a man to the ground, and in the next instant, I'm staring down the hot end of Jason's rifle. He has fever eyes. He sees me, but not *me*. Before he can do anything, a tree branch snakes down and snags him around the waist.

I pull out my sword and slice at the tree limb, freeing him. He falls and lies there, sucking in air, fast and deep, his face etched with panic.

I thrust out my hand. "Come on." After I pull him to his feet, he grabs his gun, and we sprint down the path. Five of Navar's men spring out at us. Swords flash. Powers hum.

A shrill whistle pierces my ear and I see Bodog in the distance. He raises his ax. I've got only a brief second to swing myself and Jason into a tree before a loud bang rocks the forest, and the ground shakes with enough force to destroy an entire city. The ax delivers an electric shock that topples everyone else to the ground, where they lie, stunned. I look back to Bodog, but he's gone.

"Let's go," I yell at Jason. We drop to the ground and take off. All too soon, the forest rumbles to life, striking out at us. Once it's put in motion, committed to an order, I can't stop nature from doing its worst. Navar's men prove masters at manipulating their surroundings, forcing us to go on the defensive.

One. Two. Three. Jason and I bring Navar's thugs down with sword and gun. The remaining two pull back, surprised at our ability to defend ourselves.

One of them calls down a large bird. When it makes a sharp pass, I see a curved beak and wide wingspan. Instead of a feathered tail, a barbed whip snaps and cuts Jason along his cheek. On its retreat, the talons swipe at my head, and I dive out of the way.

Jason dabs at the blood dripping down his cheek, and glares at the half-bird, half-lizard. "What's with half-breeds and this place? If you're not good enough, neither is that thing."

He flips his gun into position and aims. The bird/lizard dodges in and out of the trees. Jason stands firmly in place and follows its course.

As he hunts his flying attacker, one of the remaining men appears, and face-plants me into the ground. He means to smother me. I slip beneath the earth, rise up behind him, and tap his shoulder. He turns.

"Surprise!" I say, then slam him against a tree and call down the branches. They coil around him, binding his torso, limbs, and head. They squeeze. Tighter. Tighter. Bones crack, then, only the hush of a life, gone. I don't look at what I've done. Instead, I scour the area for others. In the distance, I see plenty. They slide through the high branches and ride earthwaves toward us. Worse, the bird/lizard is back.

"Jason," I call.

"Done," he answers, a second before the gun fires. The creature drops from the sky, and in the next instant, one of the two closest men appears behind Jason. Before I can say anything, Jason rams the butt of his gun into the man's face, knocking him out with one blow.

From out of the forest, an arrow whistles past my head and lodges in a nearby tree.

I wrench the shaft out, spin it in my fingers, and heave it toward its maker. The wind catches it, and I guide the twirling shaft to its mark, felling the man. I grab Jason and build an earthwave beneath him.

"Stay low," I yell, and we take off, zipping in between trees and slipping beneath branches. My heart slams against my ribs like the deep beat of a heavy metal drummer. I can hear it in my ears and feel it pulse down to my soles.

Jason shoulders his rifle, whips his torso around, and shoots. I shout for him to duck. He barely misses being hit by a low branch.

A huge tree with massive, above-ground roots appears ahead. I jump over, but Jason is too slow and slams into the heavy root, flips head over heels, and lands on his back. I still my wave and rush back to him. He blinks up at me, the fire in his eyes doused with a healthy dose of pain. I take out a pinch of Bodog's black powder, spit on it, and toss the stuff in the air. It turns to a thick heavy smoke, obscuring our exact whereabouts.

I bend down. "You okay?"

"No," he rasps, his breath ripping in and out of his pale lips.

Although we're hidden at the moment by thick smoke and protected by a massive tree and its thick base of roots, it's only a matter of time before we're found. "You've got to get up. We can't stay here."

He nods and grunts and struggles to rise. I slip my arm around him. His weight sinks onto me like a drunken frat boy as he lurches to his feet.

"Good?" I ask, steadying him as best I can.

"Yeah." He throws me a muscle-bound grin. "Better. Got the wind—"

A sharp whoosh slices the air. Jason grunts and staggers forward, an arrow lodged in his back. He hangs on me, his eyes searching mine. His gaze slowly melts under the shock of being hit.

Another arrow cuts through the disintegrating smoke screen and spins toward us. My arm tightens around him. I try to move

Jason, but he's an immovable rock of thick muscle and dense bone. The arrowhead slams through my hand and into his back, pinning me to Jason in an odd embrace. Pain shoots up my arm and into my brain.

A surprised gurgle erupts from Jason's throat. He begins to slide to his knees, bringing me with him. The burn of his weight hanging from the arrow has me gasping, and I clumsily grope for the shaft. When I find it, we've sunk to the ground, and his skin has turned a waxy, pale hue. The blood seeping from the corner of his mouth glimmers deep crimson.

His gaze finds mine. "Oh, shi—"

The word is snatched from his throat. He shudders, his skin soaked in a cold sweat. I grab the shaft and with a quick twist, it snaps. I yank my injured hand along the shortened stick, freeing me from Jason. Blood gushes from my hand. Without my support, Jason falls sideways on the ground. Another arrow zings by and nicks my shoulder. I duck and pull Jason under the entwined tree roots. It won't be long until the *firsts* find the right angle to fire a storm of arrows at us.

I bend over Jason. His eyes are wide, his face a stunned mask of disbelief.

I ignore my injuries and grab his chin. "Don't quit. Not now."

He blinks. "I-I nearly made it," he whispers.

"Come *on*." My fingers dig so hard into his chin, I know I'm leaving bruises. "Get up."

Another arrow embeds in a nearby tree.

"Go," he says, pushing at my shoulder, his fingers soft and easy, his muscles lax. He's deflating before my eyes.

"I can't leave you."

"Yes, you can. You have to." His indrawn breath shakes his ribs like a caged gorilla. His lips draw down, thin, blue and urgent. "No point…in staying."

I won't abandon him. I call down a tree limb, but it struggles to rise. It's like the earth has already accepted Jason, and it's a tug-o-war I'm destined to lose. "Work with me, Jason."

That mischievous smile that usually warns of trouble flickers across his face. "Be safe." His ragged breath slips out on a soft rush. No sound of an inward breath follows.

"Do *not* give up," I cry. But even as I beg him, his eyes cloud, and the last hint of life drains from his cheeks.

"Jason." I shake him. He's unresponsive.

I should never have brought him here. He takes too many risks. Lives too close to the edge. I knew something bad would happen, but I chose to close my eyes to it, wanting my own happiness above anything. Willing to risk anything—anyone—to get it.

An arrow finds my hiding place and cuts its way into my shoulder, felling me to my side. All sound mutes. My vision narrows into pinholes of light. I stare over at Jason, at the peaceful look on his pale face. At the life I helped destroy. I don't feel like me anymore. I don't know who I am or what I've become. I touch his blood-encrusted hair, and my hand glows bright.

Live.

Live.

The glow eases, but he lies just as still, just as pale. My throat tightens on a need so desperate, I can barely breathe. I pull my hand away, hating myself for what I've done, for the damage that no amount of magic can fix. "I'm sorry."

An epiphany wells inside me, hard and cold and solemn. When I find Leo, I'll make him leave. I'll send him and his grandfather back. This is my fight. It doesn't matter that I didn't create it. I'm the one who has to clean it up, and I won't allow Leo to risk his life for me. I have precious few friends. I won't lose another one.

Sound abruptly screams back into existence and throbs against my ears. Arrows continue to make their progress toward me. I call on the tree and command its roots to surround Jason, to shelter him within its earthy legs. When I can no longer see him, I touch the nearest root. The grit of dirt slips through my fingers, and I balk at having to leave him in a faceless, nameless grave.

"I'll come back," I vow. "I won't leave you here."

I stagger to my feet, wincing at the pain of even the simplest movement. The arrow in my shoulder has lodged itself against a nerve ending, and every time I move, it tweaks my hand and chest as if Sidon still holds his branding iron to my skin. I grab the shaft and pull. My vision flashes, and I fight back a deep scream. When the arrow rips out, my throat is trashed, and my feet are unsteady. I sag against the tree. Nothing compares to this agony.

Yet through the pain, I hear something worse. The snuffle of a beast. The buzz of a swarm. I turn and see a multitude of *pux* gathering, and beneath them, a pack of double-headed wolves, their fur quills sharply pointed. On seeing me, their hackles rise. I dart to the right as a volley of quills whizz though my shadow and miss me.

Be safe, Jason had said. The probability of that isn't looking so good at the moment. My injuries have sapped most of my strength. Pulsing darkness and light distract my vision. Objects blur and focus at random, like I've walked into a funhouse full of distorted mirrors.

I've got to concentrate. My feet stumble over themselves and plow me into a nearby tree. The bark scratches into my palms, burning the rawness of my wound. My mind screams out for Kera. I'm scared I won't make it. That I won't get to see her one last time.

The *pux* descend on me, their hands brutal in their attack. Though I bat them away, I'm not fast enough, and cuts quickly checker my skin. I can't believe I'm losing this battle to a bunch of annoying gnats. It actually pisses me off in a way nothing else has. With the last of my energy, I call out for the power thrumming beneath my feet.

My body stiffens. My vision tints black, muting even the smallest amount of light. I no longer feel a part of this earth. Something big is clawing its way through me and is desperate to break free.

A wave of white hot energy pulses from my every pore, arching my body like a tightly-strung bow. My spirit clutches at my body, fighting the power that would strip them apart. A second later, my spirit slams back into me, and I double over, gasping for breath.

The light subsides. My vision clears. The forest is quiet. I'm weak, and I thrust out my hand toward a tree for support. Ash crumbles beneath my fingers. Everywhere I look, I see scorch marks and death—the tiny bodies of burnt *pux*, the sizzling quills of the hounds. A few of Navar's warriors, charred and smoking, sprawl face up within my circle of devastation.

My legs give way and I collapse to the ground, my eyes wide with horror.

Odder still, my pain is gone. I inspect my hand. There's a scar, but no open wound. My shoulder as well. Though my body is healed, I don't have inner peace. What has happened to me, that I can kill so easily? Why haven't any of the other *firsts* used such power against me?

As the last of the raw energy fades, I sense Kera's anxiety. Her fear climbs to a new level, one that urges me to my feet.

I've got to find her.

THE END IS NEAR

The desire to find Kera brings out another energy ribbon, this one a trail of her passing. It shoots down the path, and I push after it. Soon the burnt circle gives way to green foliage. Thin, low-lying branches slap at me as if condemning my power. I can't fix what's done. I can only be more aware, and use my power more wisely. I send up a silent vow, promising to keep my powers in check. The thought seems to soothe the forest, and I make my way easily through the overgrown path. I near the barrier and the ribbon fades. I stop and listen.

Pop, Leo and the girl from Faldon's house emerge from of the woods. Leo motions me over. "Navar and his men are close."

"What's she doing here?" I ask without looking at Catgirl.

"Her name's Lucinda. She brought help."

"What kind of help?"

"Does it matter?" The purr with which she says it irritates me.

I finally look at her, see the light armor she wears, and I'm not impressed. "Everyone says I shouldn't trust you."

"Then don't." One moment her hand is empty, the next she holds my sword. "But don't let your mistrust stop you from taking what's rightfully yours."

"We need back up," Leo says.

He's right. We don't have a choice. I grudgingly take my sword and strap it on.

Pop searches the woods behind me. "Where's Jason?"

I'm still having a hard time believing what happened. The words stick in my throat, halfway between disbelief and reality. An irrational thought—if I don't speak it aloud, maybe it won't be true—keeps me silent.

"He's dead," Lucinda says, her voice flat and brutal.

I cringe. I can't meet their gaze.

"Is he?" Leo asks when I remain silent.

I glance up, briefly meet his gaze, then look away. It's all I'm willing to do. Leo shifts uncomfortably, his height seeming to shrink as the news sinks in. Pop's condemning eyes heat my skin, but I've got my own question. "Where's Kera?"

It's now Pop's turn to look away.

"I'll show you." Leo starts pushing through the brush. "It's a miracle we even found Pop. We figured you and Jason would be along pretty quick, so Lucy, here, volunteered to help us get safely to the wall. We were almost there when Navar and his goons showed, and before we knew it, they'd caught Bodog and Kera."

"She was stupid to lag behind, mewling after her love." Lucinda catches Leo's arm and rubs her head against his shoulder. "I can't help the hopeless."

Leo pushes her firmly away. "Stay off. I mean it."

The air changes the closer we get to the wall. It doesn't take a genius to see why—people, clutching all kinds of weapons, from long sticks to knives to the occasional sword, stand scattered among the trees, staying hidden, but focusing on the commotion near the wall. "Who are they?"

Lucinda sniffs. "Your kind of people."

"They're the ones that nut-job fiancé of Kera's is hunting down and killing," Leo says. "Lucinda told them it was time to fight."

"Navar's time is up," she purrs.

Pop signals for us to stop, his hand firmly on his rifle. Voices, raised in anger, reach us. The smack of skin meeting skin and the cry of a woman chill me.

We ease closer, determined to regain an element of surprise in this fight. It won't be easy. A dozen or more soldiers stand in front of the wall. Four men, swords drawn, faces hard, surround Bodog. Granel and Faldon stand with an older man whose hands clench the lapels of his own greatcoat. I'm surprised the fabric doesn't rip. He takes a hesitant step toward Kera, who sags in Navar's grasp, crying.

"It's over, this little game of yours," Navar says with an unattractive sneer. "He's dead by now."

She strains away from him, looking in the direction of the blast that charred a portion of the forest. "I don't believe you."

"Why? Because he's *special?*" Disgust thickens Navar's voice, and he pulls her close, his fingers digging into her arm. "I can't believe you would pervert yourself by touching him."

She slaps him, and the clearing stills.

"He's bewitched you," he hisses, his fingers digging deeper. He gives her a shake. "I'm trying to save you."

"There's no need."

He turns and motions toward the man in the great coat. "Tell her, Hadrain," Navar jerks Kera's arm, forcing her to turn her shivering, wet body toward Hadrain. "Listen to your father."

Why would Kera's father stand by and let Navar abuse his daughter? I'm disgusted by his weakness. Do they really give up their free will when they make a promise, or is it easier not to get involved?

Hadrain, his hands still clasped to his lapels, approaches. Navar releases Kera and she rushes to him. He wraps her in his arms, presses his cheek to hers and whispers loud enough for me to hear. "Whatever you thought was real, it's not. He's gone, my child. He wasn't meant for this world."

"What about me?" she asks on a ragged whisper.

His face grows taut and his embrace more fierce. "Hush. You'll be queen. It's what the people want."

Faldon steps forward. "No one blames you. The boy is at fault. Whatever has happened, he's the one we blame."

Kera pulls out of her father's arms. "He's to blame for being born? He's innocent."

"His power was wild," Navar says. "He would've destroyed us all."

"You're wrong. He's not like that."

Navar grits his teeth. "Do not presume to tell me, woman. The charm his father used to ensnare the woman had great power. When it failed, it poisoned them both, sickened their minds, and made the boy unworthy of love."

He steps back, pleased with his assertion, but when he looks at Kera, her chin rises higher. "Then how is it that I love him?"

My heart swells, but fear closely follows.

Kera's father steps back as if hit. "No, Kera."

A loud, animalistic growl echoes through the trees, startling even the crickets into silence. All eyes turn to Navar.

His stance is aggressive, and his hand pulses on the hilt of his sword. He twists his body toward Faldon. "A queen who loves another. That's my prize?"

Faldon's features quickly soften. The once booming voice condenses into a simpering pool of appeasement. "It's her pure heart, my lord. She loves for she has known nothing but love. Rest assured, Kera is your equal in every way. She will make an excellent queen."

"My equal?" Navar whips his gaze around the assembled

firsts—though none meet his gaze, a few heads nod. A burst of angry power pulses from him, and he roars, "I have no equal!"

"Whoa," I say. "This isn't good."

"You lead." Leo says. "We'll follow."

I don't deserve him as my friend. "This is my fight now."

Leo's brows lower. "Don't go there."

"You need to go home, okay?" I look beyond him to Pop. He'd been right. This problem exists because of me, and only I can fix it. I won't let the *first* half of me win. "Go straight for the break in the wall. It shouldn't take much to push through. Don't wait for us. If I'm lucky, we'll be right behind you. Just make sure the both of you get out."

Pop nods.

Navar roams the clearing, his anger burning the ground beneath his feet. He pauses near Bodog. I can almost see the evil intent churning his thoughts. He moves straight to Faldon. "What do we do with those who stand in our way?"

Granel steps forward. "Kill them, my lord."

The ease with which he says it causes Faldon to flinch.

"You don't agree?" Navar's words rip into Faldon like a hawk's talons.

The sage hardly glances at Bodog, but there's fear in his eyes. "What the king desires, he's given."

Bodog whimpers. Kera takes a step forward, but her father grabs her arm. Heated whispers fly between them.

Navar straightens to his full height. "Good. There's no shame in death. And though I don't search to deliver the final blow, I won't shy from its calling. A king is only as strong as the loyalty of those he governs. I will have that loyalty, one way or the other."

From behind one of the trees near mine, a red-headed woman signals Lucinda. Catgirl turns to me. "Everyone's in place. If they see much more, they'll be frightened away."

It's now or never. I send Kera that thought as clearly as I can, hoping she can hear me.

Kera's stance suddenly grows alert. Almost immediately, she pinpoints my hiding place as if I'm standing, waving my hands in the air. She shoots a regretful glance in her father's direction, and slowly begins to back away. Her father reaches for her.

She shakes her head.

He looks to Navar, but Kera turns and runs before he can say anything.

"Now," I cry, and leap forward. When I draw my sword, it bursts into flame.

Chaos erupts. Lucinda and the others charge into the clearing, their shouts echoing through the forest. Bodog spins into his captors, taking their legs out from beneath them, felling them to the dirt. I dart toward Kera and take her hand. Her eyes light up, and I know she feels the same way I feel when we're together. Like I'm whole. Like I matter.

We closely dog Pop's and Leo's retreat to the wall. I swing my sword, fending off anyone who dares to come near. Before me, Pop has transformed into a ninja, taking down Navar's men one and two at a time. He's ferocious, kicking and slamming guys like a black belt fighter, popping off rounds from his rifle, and wielding it like a club when the need arises.

The air crackles with Lucinda's magic. Her hair and clothes whip around her in a frenzy of power as she lunges toward her prey. Men turn and run from her bizarre game of tag, knowing if they're caught, their lives are instantly forfeit.

The fighting intensifies. Leo slingshots the exploding balls, ripping through Navar's defenses. Even so, it's clear the cave people don't have the skills the full-blooded *firsts* have, and they're taking heavy losses.

Bodog snatches his ax from one of the men who'd captured

him—a dead man, now—and waves us forward. With a deep cry, he takes his weapon and slams it into the wall, busting open a hole as big as he is. Mist swirls out. Its fingers poke at my eyes and muffle my ears.

Kera and I pass Pop, who turns and fires his gun. A nearby man drops to his knees, wounded.

Leo's almost to the tear. He kneels, rotates the last of the metal balls Bodog gave him until the spikes pop free, slips it in the sling, and lets the ball fly. The ball explodes, but before he can get up, he's tackled by one of Navar's men.

Lucinda, all storm angry, suddenly appears. She grabs the soldier by the neck and whirls, grabbing another soldier whose coming to his friend's aide. In an instant, they're gone. I barely have time to register what happened before she reappears and yells at Leo to go. He doesn't hesitate and lunges forward, disappearing into the mist.

As soon as he's gone, the charge whipping through Lucinda vanishes, like a power switch suddenly turned off. She throws me her crazy chick smile that makes my skin crawl and saunters off, abandoning the battle without a second thought.

Without the *lutine*, very little holds Navar and his men back. We have to leave, and fast.

I step close to Kera and grab her shoulders. "Come on."

She resists my pressure to turn and go. Her attention is centered on the battle unfolding behind me. Horror glistens in her eyes. I call her name more than once, and it takes her a moment before she reacts.

"We're losing," she whispers. "My friends are dying. The rest are running away."

I know what she's thinking, and I can't believe it. The only thing I've wanted, ever dreamed of having, is slipping away from me. My fingers tighten, probably bruising her shoulders. I want to shake her, snap her back to reality. We never would've won. Navar had men and experience on his side. All we had for a brief second was a bunch of cave people and a crazy *lutine* who, once Leo was safe, abandoned us.

Blinking back her tears, she actually says the unthinkable. "I can't go."

"You can't stay. They'll kill you if you stay."

"But if I leave, how many more will die?" The battle fills her eyes, and she suddenly gasps. "No!"

I turn to see Navar, bow and arrow in hand. He lets an arrow fly, and it slams Pop to the ground. The next instant, a wounded *first* shoves his sword into Pop's chest before collapsing onto him. Pop's head lolls. His body sags. His eyes stare at me, sightless, his mouth agape in a quiet warning.

Anger burns my throat. Navar has already notched another arrow on his bowstring, and is aiming it right at me. His fingers let the string go. It quivers, snapping the arrow forward, its path straight and true.

I have no time to think. No time to move.

The arrow hits my chest, rocking me backward. Kera screams, and a second and third arrow hit my torso before Kera slams into me.

We fall back.

The mist cradles my suddenly unresponsive limbs. A bright light engulfs me, as I float on a cloud, not feeling, not seeing, not knowing, not caring. When my body hits the ground on the other side, I don't feel the impact, only the release, like floating in water.

Buoyant.

Free.

Safe, but not Sound

I climb to my feet and see Grandma running toward us. How she found this place, I don't know. I'm glad to be back. Thrilled Leo is safe. I hover over Kera, see the arrow protruding from her shoulder, and go to touch her. She scoots over to the body lying beside her and cries out, a sob so deep and so filled with anguish, I've got to look.

It's me.

My sword, its fire gone, rolls out of my fingers.

I'm still. Breathless.

Dead.

Biting her lip, Kera yanks the arrow from her shoulder. Her face drains of color, leaving her looking more like the ghost I thought she was when I first saw her. I expect her to pass out, but she only sways and blinks rapidly before tossing the arrow away. When she hovers over my body, the deep silkiness of her hair falls on my neck. Her pale, shaking fingers touch my hair, my cheek, my mouth.

Leo grips his head. He stares, his eyes wide with horror. "Do something!" he shouts at no one.

Grandma staggers forward, her face aging ten years in one

moment. Kera's fingers slip to my neck and feel for a pulse. Her body sags, and her too-bright eyes lift to find Leo. In an instant, Leo collapses to his knees.

Grandma kneels on the other side of me, and I watch her gently touch the silver brand Sidon gave me. "Oh, Dylan."

Her voice trembles with the ache of loss. Pain saturates her eyes, tightens the flesh along her cheekbones, sharpens her jaw. Yet, she ignores her own suffering, and with the compassion I've never known from anyone but her, she reaches out to Kera, not knowing who she is or why she's huddled so miserably over my body.

Suddenly the wall rips open. Mist snakes out, and from within its feathery fingers, Navar steps forward. He stands, proud and regal, a man who has won a desperate fight.

Leo shoots to his feet, and his hands curl into fists. Grandma straightens, her demeanor one of dignified calm. Only Kera ignores the newcomers, as one by one, they pour into our world. The last man to enter holds Pop's body.

My anger is so great, I rush at Navar—and run right through him. I'm powerless to protect those I love. I look back at the defenseless group, and a fear I've never felt for myself slices through my soul.

Leo takes a step forward, his breath catching when he sees the bloody mark of a sword along his grandfather's body. His gaze, full of rage, lands on Navar.

The heat of Leo's hate should have scorched Navar's clothing. Navar only seems amused. He nods, and the man holding Pop's body obeys the silent command, placing the body near mine. Turning, Navar waves Kera's father and Faldon forward.

I don't like this. I stand at Kera's side, desperation making my voice waver. "You're not thinking clearly," I say to her father and mentor. "You've misplaced your loyalty. You know it. Deep down you feel it. If you take her back, he'll kill her."

My plea is snatched away before it can reach their ears. Fear of Navar's growing power and their inability to retract their fidelity once it's spoken has them trapped. Kera's father stoops, his hands cup her head, and he whispers, "Come away, my love. You are so pale."

She shakes off her father's touch and spears Faldon with a look of disgust. "Did you see this outcome?"

"I saw misery. Death. But I didn't know whose." His voice drops to a ragged whisper. "I feared it was yours."

Kera motions to the large spot of blood soaking her dress near her shoulder. "The only harm I've received has come from the one who claims to love me."

"I would never hurt you," Navar says, clearly offended. "You acted foolishly, stepping in front of him."

Her gaze dips back to my body. Tenderness, fragile and worn, warms her face. "I would do it again to see him live."

I kneel at Kera's side and finger her hair. Though it flutters briefly, I feel nothing. Only emptiness. If my heart were still beating, it would stop from sorrow. I've finally found love, but at what price to her?

The concern Navar showed moments ago vanishes. The vein in his temple throbs.

"Why are you here?" Grandma asks, not an ounce of fear visible, despite Navar and his men.

I'm astonished. Proud.

"How dare you come here. You beat my husband within an inch of his life, but that wasn't enough. You had to kill my grandson. Why? Where is the honor in that? The nobility your kind claims?"

An uncomfortable silence filters through Navar's men. Feeling their devotion waver, a deep frown hardens Navar's features. "It's perfect justice. He reached too far. His very existence was a blight on the earth."

"You're the only blight I see." In the silence that meets her words, she says, "May God curse you, and those who've helped you."

As soon as the words are out, the men point their swords at her. Fear flashes on their faces before they can shutter their emotions. Navar's own sword swoops toward Grandma, hovering only inches from her throat, but she doesn't move, suffering the burn of its power so close to her skin. She only stares at him, condemning his actions.

"Be careful what you say."

Grandma lifts her chin. "I always weigh my words."

Navar's frown turns thunderous. The muscle near the corner of his eye jumps, and he stabs his finger at Kera's father. "Take hold of your daughter." He then turns to Faldon. "You know what I expect from you."

Then the man who would be king pivots on his heel and disappears back into his world.

As Navar's men follow, Kera's father wrestles her away from my lifeless body.

"No!" Her howl of misery, deep and fearful, claws free of her chest.

"I'm here," I say, but my words fall like stones in snow.

When her father finally drags her to the wall, I follow. I can do no less. In death, just as in life, my spirit is attached to hers.

When he passes his friend, he says in a solemn tone, "Be merciful, Faldon."

Kera focuses on the seer. "Please, don't do it."

"Hush," her father scolds.

Before he carries her into the retreating mist, Kera's face warns of the coming horror and she screams, "Run!"

FEVERCHILLS

Kera fought her father until the pain of her injury sapped her strength. She hung in his arms, a rag doll dressed in ripped and bloody cloth. "How could you?" she asked over and over again.

Her father kissed her forehead and sighed. "I do only what I believe is best for you. Nothing else matters but your safety."

"You believe the lies Navar has spun."

"He can't lie."

"He spills his view of the truth, twisting it until it doesn't resemble reality. What is that if not a lie?"

Lips pinched, her father continued his walk in silence. The procession wound through the town, and people began to filter out of their homes to stare. He held her closer and said, "What's done is done. Rest, now."

Navar and his men strutted ahead of them. Kera could hear Granel calling out Navar's bravery in rescuing his bride-to-be from one of the tainted. Cheers rose. Did no one see him for what he really was?

Once home, she was put to bed. Her maid clucked and moaned and made a nuisance of herself when Kera only wished to be left alone. Her wounds were dressed, her bloody clothes burned, and the candles doused. She pushed back into her pillows and closed her eyes until the last of her watchers slipped out.

They waited for Faldon to return. He was their healer. Did they know he was a murderer as well? Did they even think it murder, killing a human? When she was found out, would they feel sorrow when she was put down and nailed on the beam in the town square?

It didn't take long for the fever to set in. The spikes in heat were terrible, but the chills were beyond miserable. A hush of whispers wondered at the cause. Kera knew. Navar loved his poison. He'd tipped his arrows. That he hadn't offered a cure only showed his lack of care for her.

If she lived past this night, she would be his wife.

And when he found out what she really was, his anger would be unstoppable.

ⅿⓞ𝖱𝖭𝖨𝖭𝖦 𝖡𝖱𝖤𝖠𝖪𝖲 𝖱𝖤𝖣

I stop as the echo of Kera's warning pulses through the woods. The next moment, a flash of light ignites a tree. Again and again, light flashes, and then the boom of it hitting resounds. Fire snakes from tree to tree like an out-of-control virus, following Leo's darting form.

It's no wonder Faldon has a dragon for a pet. Apparently, like the dragon, the sage can harness the element of fire, bend it, shape it, and throw it at will. Wherever he points, the earth flares with heat, scorching, and marring. All too soon, the woods are on fire. I rush to Grandma, who's thrown herself over my body, protecting it. Though I know it's useless, I shout, "Get up! Move!"

She hunkers down lower, gasping against the rising heat and thickening smoke.

My attention returns to Faldon. Frustration lacerates my mind. There is nothing I can do physically to stop him. My spirit has no effect here. I need form. Something solid. Tangible. It's that need which drives me to slip into the earth and rise anew, baptized with dirt that clings to my spirit in the shape of my body. I hold out my arms, marveling at what I've done. I may be dead, but I'm not completely useless.

The sight of me interrupts Faldon's pursuit—long enough, I hope, for Leo to get Grandma out of here. "I wondered," Faldon says. "Your power was so great. I thought there might be a residual effect. It shouldn't last long."

The first shot of fire slams through me, digging out a hole the size of a dinner plate. I call on the dirt to rise, and cover the expanse like a waterfall flowing up a cliff, and with it vines and pebbles and all sorts of debris weave around and along my limbs, filling out the gaps and bulking up the monster I've become.

Faldon's face twitches, as if the sight of me is more humorous than scary. "Impressive, for a garden gnome. You have the determination of your father. I sensed it the first time I saw you. It pleased me as much as it scared me." His face froze as if the memory hurt. "I should have sent you away as soon as you showed up. Misery is all you've wrought. It's time our worlds were separated for good. I don't wish to hurt anyone, but I have no choice. You know I don't."

He may have known my father, but he doesn't know me. I'm not the one killing innocent people. I'm not the one taking orders from a lunatic.

There's no question in my mind. He's weak. They all are.

Somehow, either from the look on my dirt-encrusted face or a telepathy I'm not aware of, he knows what I think of him. With a sneer, he shoots one, two, three shots in quick succession, and my imperfect cover blasts apart, showering the area in stinging dirt.

My plan works, sort of. Leo pulls Grandma to her feet and urges her forward, but together, they're now an easier target.

Without knowing if it's even possible, I run and thrust my spirit into Leo's body. With a shudder rippling from the base of his skull to the tip of his tailbone, I'm accepted. The feel of skin and bones is shocking. Though I haven't been a spirit long, I've missed the sensation. Pushing Grandma forward, I command her to go, to run.

Then I wheel around and face Faldon.

Surprise at Leo's boldness registers on his face. "Do you know who I am? What I am? You're no match for me."

"No," Leo's deep voice rolls as I speak. Power surges into Leo's body and lights him up, a living demonstration of the burning man. "But Dylan is."

Faldon gapes and stumbles back. I call down a flame-engulfed tree, bending it so it slams the ground. Sparks fly into the air, and then it whips straight again. The smoke between us slithers skyward. The earth-shaking event leaves Faldon speechless.

"I'm a pretty cool residual effect, huh?" Another tree slams to the ground, this time closer to Faldon, and it jolts him out of his stupor. He heaves several balls of flame in my direction. Saving Leo's skin from third degree burns isn't going to be easy. I dart to my right and slide baseball style behind a thickly trunked tree. Flames slam into it, creating a shower of tiny sparks that ignite the underbrush. Leo begins to cough.

"Growing weak, Dylan?" Faldon taunts. "Your host can't survive much longer."

He's right. Leo's body wasn't made for this.

I sift through my limited options and come to the startling conclusion that I've used them all up. I have nowhere to go that Faldon can't follow. Nowhere to hide where he can't find me, and Leo is in eminent danger of dying from smoke inhalation.

Faldon suddenly appears in front of me. I expected to see victory lighting his eyes, but a real sadness clings to the edges. "I take no pleasure in killing. I really am sorry. If there were any other way..."

Regret colors his words, but it doesn't change a thing. He's bound himself to Navar, and Navar wants Leo and Grandma dead. No witnesses. No loose ends living on this side of the wall. I've seen the weakness that mars their world, the flawed obedience that chokes out what's right. How it can devastate a man who can see into the future, but who still can't change the outcome.

"I'm not bound by your flaw," I say, "and I'm not sorry about that."

A limb whips down and hurls Faldon into the air. He crashes against a tree, breaking through the burning skin of bark. The wood splits. Faldon's face pales. He struggles against the tree that is pulling him in. I pant heavily until his cries for mercy are deadened by the bark slowly covering the wound of Faldon's making.

Leo's body gags. I hold tight, knowing I've one more thing to do before I leave this world. I lift up Leo's hands. They glow amid the haze of smoke, and it takes a few minutes until the first drop of rain falls. I urge it on, calling for a heavy downpour. The forest sizzles. Fires die. Everywhere except one lone tree. I want it to burn: it's the only way to release Faldon from his word and keep Leo and Grandma safe.

Filled with ash, the raindrops plop heavily onto the forest floor, collecting into muddy, vile-smelling rivulets. In the distance, someone's calling Leo's name. Grandma has sent a search party. I wrench my spirit out of Leo, and he scoots away, his eyes wide and disbelieving.

"Bro, don't you ever do that again. Seriously. I nearly peed my pants."

Poor Leo. I can only imagine how much he regrets ever saying hi to me. "Sorry," I say. "I didn't know what else to do."

He rubs at the goose bumps running up his arms. "I feel it. You had to do the rescue thing. I'm grateful, but that doesn't mean I've got to like it."

Wait a second. "C-can you hear me?"

"Yeah." Leo raises his head and looks around. "Can't see you, but I can hear you."

I pull the dirt onto my spirit again, showing him that I'm standing right in front of him.

"That is so weird." He pokes a finger through my earthy skin, and pulls it away, heavy with mud.

There's another yell from the rescuers. "I need to finish this," I say. "You've got to go, too. It's still not safe. Not yet."

"I know. Listen," he blinks away the rain falling into his eyes, "if you see Pop—you know, his ghost—tell him...tell him thanks, and that I love him."

I nod. Leo's family is close. I can't express how badly I feel for causing Pop's death. So much has gone wrong. I've got to find a way to make it right.

I let the dirty muck fall from my spirit. I'm halfway to the wall when Leo yells, "When you're done, go toward the light. I mean, if you want to. There's no rush. I'm cool with you being a ghost."

I smile. I'm going to miss that guy. Without a word, I slip through the wall and enter Teag.

THE PRICE OF LOVE

War, even the tiny clash we were in, isn't a pretty sight. Men and women clean up the mess of bodies littering the ground. The "kinds" are separated. The *firsts* laid out respectfully, the "tainted" tossed in a pile. I stop counting the *firsts* pile at twenty-eight. Pop did some major damage. No wonder Navar singled him out. I glance around for his ghost. For all I know, he's done what Leo's advised me to do, and walked into the light.

I don't see a beckoning light. Is that a bad sign?

I move through the forest, seeing everything through a misty lens, like a gray cloud separates me from everything else. I hadn't noticed it before, because the forest in my world is dense and dark. Here, the light penetrates, as if the leaves are only a veil and the branches more tissue that solid wood.

As a spirit, I'm not sure what I can do, or if the same rules apply here as they do in my world. I'm hoping they don't. Faldon's surprise at my continued existence makes me think they do, though. I'm glad I was able to surprise him with a few tricks.

Whatever the result, there's no denying I'm being drawn to Kera. While alive, I craved the comfort she offered, the feeling of belonging. Now, I suspect my need is more honorable. The obsessive yearnings I constantly fought when I was alive have been replaced with an altruistic desire—I need to make sure she's all right.

What if she isn't? I refuse to think of that possibility. Her father would never harm her, but Navar? I can't stop the doubts. Just like Bodog has warned me, Navar's heart is encased in cold, hard granite. He's the epitome of a *first*—self-serving, and obsessed with attaining his own desires.

Just like I'd been.

I enter a familiar clearing and see a lump lying under the drooping boughs of an old oak tree. Bodog. He's bleeding. I draw near, seeing he almost made it to the tunnel before he fell. His eyelids crack open and a tear slides down his cheek. "All for naught? Was it all for naught?"

"What can I do?" I say aloud.

Bodog taps my knee. "Stop Navar. Take his power."

At my shocked look, Bodog smiles. "Surprised Bodog can see you? Touch you? You move in a different space. To Bodog, you are as alive as you ever were. Bodog's kind sees everything, good and bad." A hiss of pain rattles through his teeth. "Bodog failed you. Tried hard not to. Still did."

I can't look at him. "I failed *you*, Bodog. Faldon's dead. I killed him."

"His heart broke long before his body." He lifts himself on an elbow. "Bodog wants to go home now."

I call on the powers hiding deep within the earth and open the tunnel, widening it. Bodog smiles and scoots toward it. "How long will my powers last?" I ask, thinking about what Faldon had implied, that I would weaken until I was nothing more than a misty memory.

In true form, Bodog says, "Need is a power all its own. Take Navar's powers. Only then can Teag find peace." With that, he slithers into his tunnel and out of sight, but not before demanding that I return the tunnel entrance to its original size.

I'm supposed to destroy Navar? "But I'm dead," I say to the empty forest.

My death doesn't seem to affect Bodog's faith in me. I can't let it destroy my own. To save Kera, I'll do whatever it takes. I'll go to hell and pound on the devil himself if I need to.

I follow my instincts, and like a homing pigeon, I find myself staring up at the manor. Its main doors are thrown wide in a welcome that is in contrast to my prior treatment. The place is swarming with people.

I enter the main hall. Worry is etched into every face. Concern hums through every voice. Kera is loved. Her people adore her. I'm not surprised. I move to the back stairs and climb. The burden of movement no longer hampers me. I float, even though I move my legs like I still need them. I wonder if time will cure me of the habit.

I move along an upper hall and stop at a thick, oak door, delicately carved with an image of a unicorn and a girl. My body slips past the heavy barrier. The ability to walk through walls is shocking, but definitely convenient. Once inside, I find Kera being attended by a woman as Kera's father stands nearby.

"She'll be fine?" he demands. "No problems healing?"

"Once the cure takes effect, and if she limits her movements until her muscle can repair itself."

Kera's father begins to pace. "Where's Faldon? He should be here by now. He could heal her in no time."

I'm drawn to Kera's side, to the heat of her life and the ache of her soul. "I'm here," I whisper, studying her face, wishing I could hold her. Comfort her. "I'll never leave you."

For a moment, her face softens and her eyes grow misty. Does she know I'm here? Can she feel my presence?

"I'm fine," Kera says, though I can see she isn't. Her skin is too pale, blending with the white undergarment she wears, and her violet eyes no longer sparkle. "I'm tired."

Without even a cursory knock, the door opens, and Navar strides in, followed by Granel. The lieutenant darts ahead of Navar and waves toward Kera. "See, my lord. What did I tell you? She's fine. The ceremony can resume this evening."

Kera's father blinks, his cheeks redden with his tightly controlled anger. "She's wounded!"

"The pain doesn't seem to affect her overly much," Navar says.

If only I could manifest in some way, I'd gladly kill him, but I need to be smart about this. I'm pretty sure I've only got one more chance to make him pay for all he's done.

Kera's father steps in front of her, blocking Navar's view. "An arrow has pierced her shoulder. Your *poison*-laced arrow."

Navar takes a threatening step forward, his voice a rumble of violence. "Do not test me further, Hadrain. We all make sacrifices. A little discomfort isn't much compared to the sacrifice Faldon made. I expect her to cleanse herself and rise a woman worthy to marry the future king."

"You go too far."

"And I tire of your interference."

The two glare at each other like pitbulls before a fight.

Kera slowly rises, her legs unsteady beneath her. Her father turns and murmurs for her to stay in bed, but she shakes her head and clutches his arm. She faces Navar, her breathing deep, tattered. A flicker of defiance hides behind her deference. "I swear, I'll do as you wish."

I stare at her in disbelief. "No, Kera."

Within her eyes, a twinge of sorrow uncurls before she can hide it, and I begin to wonder. "Kera. Can you hear me?"

She doesn't respond, only stares at Navar. He takes her fingers and kisses the back of her hand, gazing at her with greedy eyes. "Clearly, you see what your father's forgotten. This is a great alliance, one that must be formed quickly, if the throne is to be mine. Ours."

He releases her hand, his smile triumphant. When he turns to the woman standing with a wad of bandages and tells her to see to the preparations, Kera slyly wipes the residue of his kiss on her skirts.

I lean close. If I were alive. I would smell the scent of summer that lingers on Kera's skin. My lips move against her ear. "What game are you playing?"

She turns her head away, her hair cascading over her ear and across her suddenly flushed cheek. I have my answer, though not directly. She can hear me.

Navar considers Hadrain. "She has until nightfall to regain her strength." He flicks his wrist at a nearby basket. "Granel brought you the sage's medicine basket. Surely you can scrounge up something to ease her pain. We needn't wait for Faldon's return to see her comfortable."

If they did, they'd be waiting an eternity.

Hadrain helps her back in bed, and Navar eyes her possessively. "Rest. Tonight we begin anew."

"A new *nightmare*," I say, watching Kera's father bow and the woman curtsey. When Navar and Granel leave, the three breathe a sigh of relief.

"Is there anything for her pain?" Hadrain asks.

The woman rummages through the basket. "I'm not as familiar as Faldon with the art of potions, but this," she pulls out a brown bottle, "I've seen him give this, a strong painkiller. Mixed in water, it works in minutes."

Her father puts a few droplets in a glass of water.

"I'm fine," Kera says, but she doesn't fight when he lifts her head for her to drink. She makes a face. "Bitter."

The woman presses the bottle into Hadrain's hands. "She'll need more in a few hours."

Kera's father places the bottle on the bedside table and walks the woman to the door. I bend and read the hand-written label. Opium. It's nothing like taking a few Advil. People go crazy on the stuff.

When her dad comes back, Kera catches his hand, her eyes big and imploring. "What sacrifice has Faldon made?"

"That was long ago."

"I need something to take my mind away from the pain."

He sits on the bed and adjusts her hand in his. "Faldon had a son. He was bright and ambitious, and a good friend of mine. His name was Baun. You know him as the Lost King."

"But he's evil, isn't he?"

A sad smile crosses her father's face. "Sometimes I wonder. Greif can destroy honorable intensions. I believe forgiveness can heal all wounds. He was never afforded that mercy."

"Do you know where he is?"

"I'm one of the few who do. I was his guard. I went with him everywhere. Over time, he became obsessed with power. Obsessed with knowing everything about the world. We were young. And we crossed a line. We entered the human realm.

"At that time, only a few were allowed the privilege. Being king, he thought it ridiculous that he'd never seen what others had. We traveled throughout the human realm, performing miracles, or so the humans believed. We had fun...and then I fell in love with your mother. She became pregnant." He smiles at her lovingly.

"Unfortunately, Baun was not amused. He didn't like my devotion wandering. I had become more of a possession than an equal. He insisted we go home, and that I leave your mother behind.

"I was, and ever am, a servant to the throne. But on the day we were to go back to our land, Baun met a girl. She was wild and beautiful, and he fell in love."

"Why are we such foolish creatures when it comes to love?" Kera asks.

Her father shrugs. "Foolish, but lucky. There is no doubt. No regret."

"No," she whispers. "No regret."

"Baun sent me back, refusing to leave his new love. I was angry. Then I did a thing I never would've thought possible. Before I returned to Teag, I found you and your mother and brought you with me. Faldon's wife took you both in.

"Life was good, but our king's continued absence caused frictions to rise. Within months, humans became our enemy. A terrible war threatened to break out. Faldon's wife died protecting you and your mother. During that time, I was dispatched to bring Baun back. It was hoped he would calm the rising storm."

"He didn't want to leave," Kera says.

"No, he didn't, but he did. He wasn't a complete fool. He loved his people, had taken an oath to protect them, and that oath called him back. His strong leadership calmed tempers. The threat of war abated."

"But I know there was a war."

"Yes. When tempers cooled, he went back to bring his love home, but she was gone. His heart broke. His spirit shattered, and he turned bitter. Insane, even. After that, nothing would please him. It was he who called for the extermination of all humans in Teag. That was when your mother died, and I pretended to find you in a nearby village. Many fought the order. Most didn't. So crazed had Baun become that he entered the human realm and went on a rampage. It was clear to everyone he was out of control. Our king was no longer able to rule. Faldon and I were sent to find him." His eyes grew dark. "To kill him, if he couldn't be reasoned with."

Her father grew quiet. "It was a fate no father should endure, but Faldon agreed. The things Baun had done, the pain he'd caused, made his life forfeit. We both understood that, but in the end, neither Faldon nor I could do it. We ended up offering Baun to the *pux*, but only if they kept him chained. And that's where he is to this day."

"Faldon knew Dylan was Baun's son."

"From what I saw, they favor each other."

"How could he stand there and do nothing to help his own grandson?"

"I can only imagine he saw the same character flaw in Dylan that he had in his son. I know the boy frightened him."

Kera shakes her head, and then stares directly at me, her eyes heavy. "Dylan's nothing like his father."

I lay down beside her, and she tilts her head to face me. "I love him."

Her father rubs her arm and says in a tight voice, "I'm sorry for your loss." He then stands and snuffs all but one candle.

Tears prickle her eyelashes. "The pain is still there," she says, staring at my ghostly image. I lay my hand gently on her cheek. She closes her eyes.

Her father hesitates near the open door. His voice trembles with sadness. "As it will be, forever." He then leaves, closing the door behind him.

She forces her eyes open. "I see you, now. I've been watching you for a while. Your spirit is beautiful."

"Not as beautiful as you are."

Her eyes flutter closed. "How can I live?"

"You will. For me."

She sleeps.

I guard her, knowing she's fragile, feeling her heart break, and racking my brain for a way for her to escape what's coming.

I'm the son of the Lost King. If anyone can find the fine line between insanity and genius, it's me.

DYING TO SEE

Kera's in pain. Throughout the day, the skin around her shoulder swells and turns an ugly red. Though I still don't understand why she can hear me, I find out how she's seeing me. The opium. Somehow it helps blur the line between the living and the dead. I know exactly when the effects are wearing thin. Her face clouds with panic and she begins to toss and turn, mewling like a kitten. She quickly takes the glass, pours water, and puts a few drops into it. Lying back, she waits and in a few minutes, she's relaxed and is following my every move with her eyes. Soon after, she falls asleep.

Between those fits of sleep, she talks. I can't shut her up. She tells me how she has no real power of her own, and how her father has shared his to keep her safe. "I'm a fake, Dylan. More human than even you. I've survived only because of my father. I owe him everything."

I'm across the room, trying my best to move a chair like ghosts do in the movies. I'm not having much luck. "Fathers should be there for their kids."

"You know who your father is." Her voice carries a hint of feverish excitement.

"Yeah. A crazy king imprisoned by the *pux*. I'm a lucky guy."

Her forehead puckers. "Would you rather not know?"

"No. I'm glad you asked." And I am. The odds of my dad being a classy guy were never in my favor. It would have gone against everything else in my life. Crazy mom. Crazy dad. Miserable, dead son. That's what you call destiny.

A maid comes in and checks on Kera's shoulder. The woman clucks her tongue at the warmth of Kera's skin. "I wish Faldon were here."

"He's dead," I say. "I killed him."

"You did?" Kera asks.

There's no remorse in me. "He was going to kill my grandma and Leo."

"Oh." Kera turns to the maid. "Faldon's dead," she says so brightly that the girl blinks.

"How do you know?"

Kera smiles and glances at me. "I just know."

The maid looks in my direction, though she can't see me. Her eyes hold a hint of worry. She looks back at Kera and pats her hand. "I'll be right back."

The poor girl nearly runs from the room.

"What else do you know that I don't?" Kera asks.

I tell her everything. About the fight. About inhabiting Leo. About Bodog. I tell her about all the men I've killed and the darkness that's hiding in a corner of my soul. I want to scrub it away, but I don't know how. "I'll most likely go to hell if I follow the light."

"Don't." She's suddenly agitated. Her face flushes an alarming, burnt pink.

I stop pacing. "Don't what? Talk about hell? Don't you believe in it?"

She grows so intense, it's hard to keep eye contact. "Don't follow the light," she pleads. "You can't leave me. Please."

I draw close and give her my best smile. At least I hope it is. I can't see myself in a mirror, so who knows what I look like? Hopefully, not all bloody and pale. "I'll be here for as long as you need me. I promise."

"You can break your promise. You're like me. Neither of us is a pure blood."

A gasp sounds from across the room, and I turn to see the woman who bandaged Kera's shoulder standing in the doorway. The younger maid hovers near the woman's shoulder. "It's like I told you," she whispers. "Feverish and talking to herself."

The woman nods and shoos the girl out. A tiny speck of fear gathers in the pit of my stomach. They had to have heard Kera. But did they believe her? The woman doesn't act any differently. Her smile is warm. Her hands gentle.

After changing the bandage, the woman pours Kera a glass of water and adds the medicine.

"I'll be back in an hour or two to check on you. Drink plenty of water."

Kera nods, and the woman leaves.

The sun slides lower in the sky, and the preparations begin in earnest. Women come and go, and Kera falls into a pensive state. The dress is laid out, and her hair combed until it shines. Kera's father comes when the woman is checking on her shoulder. Red streaks shoot out from the wound's center, and everyone whispers their concern. Hadrain isn't pleased.

"What does he not understand? You're not fit to walk." He turns and holds up his hands. "Stop! No more."

He hustles everyone from the room, all but the woman tending Kera's shoulder. He presses a kiss to his daughter's forehead and murmurs, "I'll make him listen." His determination holds a promise as he leaves.

"It won't work," the woman says, while she rebinds Kera's

shoulder wound. "Navar is determined."

Kera winces at the bandage's pressure. "My options are dwindling."

I can't let her live in a fantasy anymore. "You've only had one option. You have to marry Navar."

"I only said I would marry him to buy us time."

Kera's despondent voice garners a flicker of interest from the woman. Nothing more.

"We can't pretend," I say. "Your people need you. I-I think marrying Navar is the right thing to do."

"No," Kera says louder.

The woman stands and checks on the water jug. "Have you been drinking the plain water I brought you?"

Eyes glassy from the drug, Kera nods. "Yes."

The woman hesitates, and then pours Kera a glass. While she waits for her to drink, a butterfly floats into the room from the open window. It makes a tight turn and floats back out. The woman smiles. "It's a lovely evening. Have you noticed? The stars will light our way."

Kera hands the glass back, and then the woman leaves.

Ten minutes pass. I try talking to Kera, but she won't talk back. I stare down at her. "Can you still hear me? See me?"

Is my power fading like Faldon said it would?

Kera reaches for my hand, but I'm as solid as vapor. Sadness shadows her eyes. She slides out of bed. Woozy, she stands still for a second.

"What're you doing?"

She won't answer. She's ignoring me on purpose.

"Kera?"

She carefully walks to the window and leans out to stare at the sky. If I could hold my breath, I would. She could tumble out if she's not careful, and I tell her so. The only response I get is a loopy smile and a slurred, "Lovely."

"What is?" The sky's clear, though darkening.

She pushes away from the window and heads for the door.

"Where are you going?"

"Butterflies are beautiful."

What's wrong with her? "Yeah. Now go back to bed."

"I'm not thirsty."

"I bet you aren't." Her stomach must be sloshing with all the water she's had.

She opens the bedroom door and walks out. I expect a guard or at least someone to be nearby in case Kera calls out. No one. The hall is oddly empty. She shuffles down the stairs, clinging to the railing as she goes. I'm scared she'll fall, and there's nothing I can do to catch her.

A side door leads outside, and she opens it, wincing at the pain in her shoulder. Something isn't right. I've carefully monitored her drug intake, so that can't be it. Something else is happening, but I don't know what.

"Kera, what are you doing?"

"Finding peace." She walks on her tiptoes, sneaking away.

"Go back inside."

She spreads out her arms, twirls and falls to her knees, marring the perfect white nightgown. "Stain," she says, and rubs at it, making it worse. I encourage her to stand.

The woman who's been caring for her emerges from the manor and helps Kera to her feet. I'm thankful someone is paying attention around here.

"What a horrible mess. It needs washing. Come with me."

Instead of going inside, the woman leads her down a path and into the woods. A cold chill sweeps over my spirit. "Kera, ask her where she's taking you."

By now, Kera's feet drag furrows into the ground, her progress becomes as slow as the coming night. The only conversation I can draw out of her has to do with pretty, twinkling stars and delicate, blue butterflies. Her eyes are heavy, and her shoulders droop. As the woman drags Kera through the forest, I suddenly realize where we're going. The lake.

When Kera's legs wobble, the woman's grip becomes firm. "Not much further. Keep walking. We'll rinse it in the lake, take the stain right out, then you can stargaze all night and play with the butterflies."

That caring voice makes me cringe. Why couldn't I see the danger standing beside Kera? Even now, Kera's every step is nurtured. Who would guess the evil hiding behind the woman's loving praise? She has acting skills. No doubt about it.

The lake appears through the forest in cool tones of blue, shading to black. On the shore stands a man. He doesn't need to turn around for me to know him. Navar.

The woman releases Kera, but Kera's too drugged to stand and collapses. I stoop and yell at her to get up. She only smiles and reaches out a hand to touch me. "Beautiful."

Navar whirls around, his face icy with disgust when he spots Kera. "Did anyone see you?"

"No, my lord." The woman backs away. "I've done what you asked, but no more. It's your pride that wants her dead, not mine. She's a sweet girl. I beg of you. Don't do this."

"By the maid's own report, she's of mixed blood, a taint to our kind. You were there. You heard. It's a far gentler thing I do now than let her die in the manner that our law demands."

"As king, you can change that law."

Hearing that, hope stirs within me.

Confusion crosses his face. "Why?"

At his careless word, the woman looks ready to throw up, and seeing it, Navar waves her off. "Go. You've done enough."

Backing away, she puts a hand to her mouth and mumbles, "I've done too much. I'll never forgive myself." Sickly pale, the woman turns and runs.

Unaffected by the woman's distress, Navar walks forward, his strides big and strong. I rush at him, ready to dive into his skin and make him carry Kera back to the castle, but I slip through his body like steam through air. My frustration climbs when I realize his powers prevent me from entering him.

Asleep, Kera mutters incoherently as she's lifted into his arms. She's completely defenseless.

My soul cries out for help when Navar enters the water. "Why?" I shout at the heavens. "Stop him!"

My call for help ripples over the lake, but for all I can see, it's gone unanswered.

A school of fish draws near, but as Navar wades into the lake, he sends them away. Soon the water is up to his waist. I yell at Kera to wake up. She sighs, lost in her dreams.

Water laps at Navar's chest. I cuss at him as he slowly pulls his arms from beneath her. She floats for a moment. He cocks his head and looks at the dark waves of her hair fanning out in the water, her pale, perfect skin, and beautiful, sleeping face. His hand sweeps along her hairline and down past her chin. "It's a shame. You really are a pretty thing."

And then his hand settles on her chest, and he pushes.

Stealing What's Mine

Kera plunges under the water.

My mind explodes with rage. There's only one way I can get her out of Navar's hands and into safety. I slam my spirit into Kera.

Her lethargy attacks me, but I fight it off and force her eyes open. I grab Navar by his shirt and climb out of the water, gasping for air when I break the surface.

I get right into his face and snarl, "Don't *ever* touch Kera again."

He's caught off guard, but not for long. The air hums as he gathers his power. I'm tired of playing by this realm's warped rules. Pulling back, I slam a fist into his face, rocking him back on his heels.

He ducks and splashes backward, but I find his face two more times. He flounders in the water. His splashes sting my eyes, and for a second, I'm blinded. When I wipe the droplets away, I see him clawing at his waist for his weapon. A familiar glint of metal draws my eye, and I lurch forward, snatching Kera's dagger from him.

He pulls his sword free and arcs it down, but I hold the dagger up and stop its descent. Kera's weapon hums against the longer blade, deflecting any magic Navar instilled in it.

Navar curses and backs away. The dagger pulses like it's breathing. From the shore I hear Bodog shout, "Dip it into the water."

I don't know where the little man came from, or how long he's been there, but I don't need to be told twice. Once the tip meets the water, an electric wave shoots toward Navar. He dives to the side and disappears underwater.

I stalk him, wading forward, careful Kera's feet don't slip on the slick rocks. The lake's surface stills, smooth as glass. No bubbles or telltale signs of movement. I spin around, holding the dagger out in front of me, but it's like Navar has disappeared.

"Do you see him?" I shout, hearing Kera's voice instead of my own.

Just when I think Navar's somehow managed to escape, Bodog hops up and down, pointing to my right. I see a spot beneath the water begin to glow. I call on my power, feel it flood into Kera's body. When Navar pops up, I'm ready for him. Stones he's collected from the lake bed burst from the water. Ten feet in the air, they abruptly reverse direction. When they hit me, they'll feel like a stoning from God.

I crouch, then thrust out my hands, pushing the stones back up and toward Navar. He volley's them back my way, and I use a surge of energy to explode the rocks into dust.

Navar's rage grows to a level I recognize. It's the same emotion I felt in the forest before I burned everything around me. I don't know if Kera's body can take a direct hit—I doubt it, but there's no time to move. I hope to God the only option I've got won't kill her.

Navar throws out his power, rippling the air in bright angry waves. It slams into Kera like a semi skidding on a slick road. The life within her flickers for a moment, and I fear the worst. I will her to hold on, to move her lungs. One breath. Two. Kera's spirit revives, and together, we absorb the power, pulling on it until our spirits stretch and threaten to explode.

Panic enters Navar's eyes. He tries to stop the waves, but they disappear and pulse within Kera, filling our spirits.

Navar tries to tap into his power again, but it fizzles into nothing. Shock colors his face. He glares at me and his mouth contorts into a sneer. "You think you've won, but I'll regain my powers. All I need to do is kill you."

With purposeful strides, he wades forward. I crack the lake bottom in an effort to slow him down while I urge Kera backward, but her legs get entangled in her skirts. Before I know it, Navar's hand encircles her throat, and he squeezes. Her fingers wrap around his wrist as he lifts her higher, dangling her body above him.

I call out for anything that lies in the depths of the lake, hoping there's something more useful within its murky depths than those tiny fish Navar sent away.

With no way to escape, air pressure builds in Kera's lungs. Her vision blurs. I kick her feet, churning the water between them. Light pulses behind her eyes, and I feel her going.

I hold on, sending spikes of hot power under Kera's skin to burn his fingers. He grimaces and lets go. Kera sinks beneath the water, and when she surfaces, sputtering for air, I hear Navar yell. The look of surprise on his face warns me something isn't right. He's unexpectedly jerked under the water. A swirl of red rises to the surface, and I stumble back.

"*Priserps*!" Bodog screams. "Get out! Hurry, before they attack Kera!"

The head of a serpent appears. Massive jaws open, revealing row upon row of jagged, sharp teeth. *This* is what answered my call? I take a stab at its head and miss. It plunges back into the water, its body twisting and writhing around Navar.

Bodog jumps along the shore, arms waving, voice cracking, as he screams, "Save Kera!"

Navar struggles to the surface, blood seeping from wounds on his face, neck, and arms. He swings his sword, but all he hits is water. A long cord whips out of the water and coils around his neck, pulling him under as more serpents latch onto him.

As tempting as it is to let the serpents have him, if they continue their feeding frenzy, Navar's body will never be found. Teag will have another Lost King on their hands. Someone like Granel could use his legend to inspire a twisted loyalty that would only strengthen Navar's evil plans.

I can't let that happen.

I lunge foreword, slashing at the *priserps*. They hiss and snap, but they back off. I don't think it'll last. With Navar's arm around my shoulder, I help him wade toward shore. Sure enough, before we're totally out of the water, a *priserp* charges. It skims into the shallows after us, its teeth grinding close, but not close enough.

When we make it out of the water, I drop to my knees. Navar falls to the ground and rolls onto his back. He blinks up at me, his face expressionless.

A firestorm of emotions roll through me, and I can't quiet my bitterness as I glare at him. "Now you're just like every human you've ever killed. Powerless."

I move away, feeling the need to separate Kera from him. Her body quivers through a cough.

Bodog stomps around, his voice is frantic. "Why save him? You were to save Kera!"

I don't have much time. I need to make sure she's safe, but the drug is weakening her. I'm not sure I've made the right choice. When my spirit leaves her, she'll be vulnerable once again.

I struggle toward Bodog. "Get rope. Tie him up."

"And?"

"And..." I have no idea.

Kera's vision darkens, but I force back the blackout. Bodog's mournful howls draw my attention. He's fallen to his knees and is rocking back and forth, pointing toward where Navar has escaped. "Mark my words," Bodog says. "Trouble will come."

Navar staggers toward the forest. I don't know where he's going, but I know Bodog is right. Navar is the kind of person who doesn't like to lose.

Clinging to whatever thread is keeping me in Kera's body, I close my eyes and tap into my and Navar's combined power. The call pulses from within me, a desperate plea. Whatever is in the forest, I demand it stop Navar.

It's too much. Kera's knees give way. Her body crumples onto the shore, and without warning, my spirit slips from her.

"Dylan," she says in a thin voice, before her eyes close. She's alive, but barely.

Navar has made it to the trees, but he stops abruptly. It's then I hear a strange flutter and clacking noise. Bodog darts erratically along the shore before grabbing Kera's hand and dragging her toward what I can now see is a tunnel opening at the edge of the trees.

"Millispits," he whispers fearfully.

I don't know what they are, but by the look on Bodog's face, I know they're not good. I seriously have the worst luck.

Navar steps back and holds up his hands, searching for power that's no longer there. A split second of horror flashes on his face before he's covered in tiny, gooey, lizard-like creatures with broken wings. They fling themselves from the trees and onto Navar, their curled, scorpion tails stabbing. They cover him from head to toe, a mass so thick, I can't see the man behind the swarm.

Navar's screams are swallowed by the trees. I can't watch, but I can't look away. He staggers, his body tilts, and then he falls.

An eerie quiet descends over the forest. One by one, the dead millispits fall away, leaving their pulsing tails attached to Navar.

Bodog stills and shakes his head. "It's done."

I would never wish such an end on anyone, but with his death, I can only hope his hold on Teag will fade. People who had vowed to follow him are now free.

I go to Kera. Her knuckles are swollen, and she's far too pale. I bend close and whisper, "He'll never hurt you again."

Bodog clucks his tongue, mutters about my ill treatment of her, and covers her with his dirty scrap of a cloak. I'm jealous that he's able to help her when I can't, and I begin barking orders. In the middle of a command, a bright light shines down on me. Confused, I glance at Bodog. "What's happening?"

His big eyes blink, and his mouth forms a circle of surprise. A jolt of pain rips thorough me, and I suddenly know what's happening. I reach out to Bodog. "I'm not ready."

He knows all about the dead. He'll know how to keep me here. Instead of helping me, he cringes away, and against my will, I'm yanked into the blinding light, screaming, "No! Not yet!"

Beyond Death

Heaven isn't as grand as they've led everyone to believe. It's all plain white walls and ugly linoleum floors and nasty antiseptic smells. I cough. Pain that should be saved for the deepest level of hell lances through my body.

I crack open my eyes and Kera's face slides into view. She's dressed in a white, frilly shirt and blue jeans. "He's awake."

Grandma bends over the bed rail and clasps my hand. "Dylan! I thought you'd never wake up. How do you feel?"

"Like a dozen monkeys used me as a jungle gym," I croak.

"Praise the Lord. Can I get you some water? Another pillow? George!" she shouts toward the door. "Dylan's talking!"

"Does he still have a brain?" Grandpa asks in his sandpaper voice. He's got a black eye, a week's worth of beard growing, and he's leaning on a cane, but I'd lay bets on him being fighting ready.

Grandma lets go of my hand and gives him an exasperated look. "Of course, he has a brain."

"You never know. I signed so many papers, one could have been for a brain donation."

As Grandma argues about the improbability of brain donation, I nudge Kera's hand. "What's going on?"

She slides the bed rail down and rests her hip near mine. A dark wave of hair flutters forward and tickles along her jaw. Pushing it away, she flashes me a radiant smile. "You're not dead."

I shift—for future reference, that's *not* a good idea—and suck in a quick breath. It feels like my liver has been put through a shredder. Obviously, I'm not dead. No one who's dead can be in this much pain. My jaw clenches, and I manage to grit out, "Why not?"

That sounds… strange. It's not like I want to be dead. I'm beginning to fear I dreamed it all: the wall, Bodog, Navar, the war.

Kera's existence is problematic. If I dreamed all the other stuff, shouldn't she be a dream, too? She was before.

Her eyes twinkle down at me like twin amethysts. "Your grandmother saved you."

The arguing stops and Grandma leans over and tucks the blanket to my chin. "Now, don't start giving me credit for what the doctors did. They hooked you up to all sorts of machines and got your body going. Your brain was another matter. You've been in a coma."

"She gave you CPR until help arrived." Grandpa reaches around Grandma and folds the blanket lower. "We just got him back. Smothering him isn't the best idea."

Grandma blushes and tucks the top edge of the blanket even lower. "You lost a lot of blood." Her tucks turn into pats, and then she turns away. The sound of light sniffles reaches my ears.

It's now or never to find out if I'm crazy. "How?"

Kera and my grandparents exchange worried looks. "Don't you remember?" Kera asks.

"Just tell me." I brace myself to hear the worst.

Kera's voice lowers and she leans close. "Navar shot you three times. I jumped in front of you and took the forth arrow."

"It wasn't a dream?"

"No." Grandpa draws closer, until all three are huddled over my bed. "Those doctors think some crazy cult went on a drug-induced killing spree, and that's exactly how I'm spinning it."

The doctor comes in, along with a nurse. Everyone else leaves, so they can give my body a thorough once over. They poke and prod me in places I didn't know existed, but after the pain med is delivered, the nurse calls in Kera, who's waiting outside the room.

"He'll get a little goofy and probably fall asleep for a while."

Kera nods, and the nurse leaves.

Step by small step, Kera approaches. Shyness colors her face. "The doctor is talking to your grandparents."

I don't say anything. I'm not sure what to say.

She returns to her spot on my bed and slips her fingers into my hand, her touch a warm reminder of how much I love her. "You saved me," she whispers.

All I want is to sink into Kera's eyes, but there are certain things I can't forget. "But not Jason. Or Pop."

Kera slowly shakes her head. "I'm sorry."

"What did you tell his dad?"

"He thinks Jason ran away. Your grandpa says he's done it before. Until we can retrieve the body, it's best to let his dad think that."

I don't like it, but there isn't much I can do about it until I'm better. "I was afraid you'd die."

"How could I, after you went to so much trouble to save me?" She leans forward and rests her head on my chest. "I wanted to die after you disappeared at the lake. I wanted to take the rest of the drug and fall asleep forever."

"Why didn't you?"

"I kept seeing your face, and then I had a dream." She turns her head and looks straight into my eyes. "You were asleep, deeply asleep, but alive."

I run my hand down her bare arm. She's even prettier in modern clothes. "And you're here, dressed like this, because…?"

Grandpa and Grandma return and hear my question. Grandpa stands at the end of my bed, while Grandma takes up her station near my head and says, "Kera showed up yesterday. Leo told us what happened, and when we heard it all, I knew exactly what to do. We put all the sculptures from the shed back along the barrier. I should never have let your grandfather talk me into taking them down in the first place."

"They're ugly," he grumbles in his defense.

Her back snaps straight and she grumbles, "They're protection, and they stay."

He grunts. "I'm not arguing, woman. Not *now*."

Grandma's hand slips over mine and she takes Kera's hand in her other one. A warm smile brightens her face. "Kera will stay with us. We won't let them take her. Or you."

I have to ask even though I'm afraid of the answer. "Do they know she's here?"

The skin around Grandma's lips whitens. "They do."

"Don't worry, son," Grandpa says. "They won't catch us sleeping again."

I turn to Kera. "Do you think they'll try to take you back?"

"Navar's dead, but many who followed him are still of the same mind. Half-bloods like us won't be tolerated."

"Enough of this ugly talk. Dylan needs his rest." Grandma rounds the bed and slides her arm around Kera. "I'm hungry. How about we let Dylan take his nap while we go out for a quick bite?"

She doesn't give Kera a choice, guiding her through the door and into the hall. Something about the look on Kera's face tells me she won't be gone long.

Grandpa stands at the end of my bed like a soldier on guard duty, but I know how much he likes to eat. "You can go, too. I'm starting to feel the drug." It's not a lie. I can barely keep my eyes open.

He nods, takes a step toward the door and stops. His gaze captures mine. "If I believe all Kera has told me, this isn't over, Dylan."

"I know."

"I'll help you as best as I can, but I'm afraid you're going to have to take the fight to them."

"I've already tried. You know what happened. It was a disaster."

"Preparation. Precaution. Precision. Those are the tools that win battles. We'll figure something out."

I'm having a hard time following him, but I nod, and that seems to appease him. For emphasis, he gives the mattress a quick slap and says, "Good," then leaves.

I sure could have used him earlier.

The drug warms my body until my insides feel gooey. I smile, blink, and when my eyes open, I see Kera standing in the doorway. She really is the most beautiful girl I've ever seen.

She enters and closes the door. "Your grandmother is a very persistent woman. I convinced her I was too tired to eat, and that I'd be happiest sitting next to you."

"That'd make me happy."

Kera moves straight for my bed. Without saying a word, she sits and eases the blanket off my chest, exposing my injuries. With the gentlest touch, she places her hand over the first cut. Her skin begins to glow, encouraging my wound to heal.

"You can heal?"

"Shh," she says, and slips her free hand into mine. "Sleep. It will all be over soon."

I sigh and relax and let the drug overtake me.

The dream I'm dumped into is unexpected. I find myself lying in a meadow, but this place is brown and dried, as if all the life has been burned away. I sit up and search for a familiar landmark. Nothing. Dried sticks pass for trees, and within those trees, a sharp movement catches my eye.

I pop to my feet, my bare toes digging into the dusty ground. "Who's there?"

A man steps forward. He glares at me, and my skin crawls. A harsh wind ruffles his smoke-colored hair, and tugs at his tattered clothes. He carries himself with a regal air, demanding my attention, yet it's his eyes that hold me still. They glitter bright blue. With a flick of his hand, a swarm of *pux* appear, hovering about him, sighing into his ears.

His gaze rakes my form and a harsh smile touches his lips. "I hear you've been looking for me."

I don't know what the *pux* have been telling this guy, but it's all lies. "I don't know you."

The *pux* disperse and dart around the clearing, buzzing so close that I have to duck to avoid getting hit.

Their antics amuse the man. "You don't know me yet, but you will. It's unavoidable now."

There's a threat to his tone that puts me on edge. "Where am I? Did you bring me here?"

His laugh is rich and full. "You don't know what you've done, do you? No matter. Soon, everything will become clear."

He releases a high-pitched call and the *pux* gather around him once again. As he steps back into the decimated forest, they flutter after him.

I pull out of the dream and open my eyes to find Kera staring down at me. "Where were you?"

She squeezes my hand. "Here. I'll always be right here." She bends and places a soft kiss on my lips.

I sigh and my dream fades, replaced by the light of love shining from Kera's eyes.

My dream girl is real.

I don't have to be alone anymore.

Acknowledgments

I was told, all good authors acknowledge those who have helped them achieve their dream of publication. (Okay I was threatened by one of my critique partners, who will remain nameless, but she's an accountant and she can seriously mess up my finances if I don't do this right.)

To my family: I'm blessed. Blessed to have a loving, overly affectionate family who spoils me rotten by letting me do something so impractical like believe I can actually write a book and get it published and people will buy it. To Roberto: Thank you for working hard so I can live my dream. Have I mentioned you're crazy, but totally adorable? Thank you, sweetie for everything. To Brenna, Lauren, Mara, Rachel and Emma: You, my beautiful, amazing girls are equally insane. Thank you for always making time to play make-believe with me, which I know is sometimes totally weird, but I'm still thankful. Oh yeah, stop telling your friends you are motherless and that the woman talking to herself while she's folding laundry is the "help." (yeah, like we can afford a maid.)

To my critique partners (Tammy Baumann, Louise "the accountant" Bergin, and Robin Perini): I seriously have the awesomest critique partners ever! Really. You're my bestest buddies in the whole wide world. You contain the monster that is me by slapping my hand and telling me, "No more adjectives. Bad author." (I love adjectives.) You cannot hide from the massive squeeze I'm going to give each of you. I love it that we're loud, we're argumentative and we're a force to be reckoned with. I will NOT trade any of you for anyone else, and to those who want to steal you away…you are mine. Only mine. Muahahahaha!

To my agent (Laurie McLean): I'm amazed you never got tired of pitching my ideas to editors. You are one fearless woman, and I'm very grateful you offered me representation. You were my first fan, 'cause seriously, my family doesn't count and my critique partners have to like me or I'll hit them, so without threat of violence, or starvation and piles of unwashed laundry, you actually liked my stories enough to push them at the right people. Thank you, thank you, thank you, thank you!!

To my publisher (Liz Pelletier): You know, sometimes it takes fresh eyes to see the possibility of what can be. I don't know what you saw in *The Marked Son,* but I'm so very thankful you saw whatever it was that you saw. (yep, that sentence is eloquence in motion.) Your faith in me is humbling and slightly scary, but I'm always up for a challenge.

To my editor (Heather Howland): You have been one of my biggest fans and have pushed me to reach into my story and pull out something special. It was painful and eye-opening and…oh my gosh! You're gonna make me do it two more times aren't you?! Crap! (grin) S'okay. You made *The Marked Son* a better story, and for that, I'll always love ya.

To my publicist (Danielle Barclay): You are a publicist extraordinaire. You've worked tirelessly to get a buzz going about my book, and you've held my hand through the maze of self-promotion, (which I hate with a passion of a thousand burning suns), but like you said, it's got to be done. (Umm, excuse me, but why do I have to do it?)

Honestly, the whole Entangled Publishing team is so amazing, I keep pinching myself wondering when I'm going to wake up, and praying I never do.

To my parents: Thanks for understanding that I couldn't play when you came out to visit until I got my edits done. And thanks for having my back when I refused to come out of the playhouse at kindergarten. I didn't need no stinkin' friends in that playhouse with me. I had all the friends I needed in my head. You understood that. Even though I'm grown, I'm that same five-year-old girl. I'm pretty sure you still get that.

To my kickboxing boys (Logan Sims, Mitch Herig and Reece Killebrew): Thank you for keeping my body from curling permanently into a fetal position. You are experts at kicking my hinny (giggle, snort. I said hinny), and I love you guys for it.

To my friends: Thank you for keeping me sane. (These are real friends, not the ones in my head. I swear. I have real friends.)

To God: Thank you for the imagination overload. You are constantly in my thoughts when I write.

And last but not least, to my neighbors: Thank you for not calling the cops on me and my family. I know we're loud and out-of-control, but we don't mean you any harm. Really.